MY ENEMY, MY LOVE

"I don't know why I should want you, but I do." His voice grew low and husky. "I want you all night long . . . every morning . . . every time I look at you."

Shimmering heat rose inside her. Edeva tried to remember her hatred. He moved closer, trapping her. His arms reached around to imprison her and his mouth met hers.

The kiss was long, slow, searching. When he drew back, she could hardly stand.

He stared at her. "I think there is a woman inside you, beneath all the snarling rage and fire."

Edeva swallowed. The way he looked at her . . . it made her feel weak, helpless. He leaned down and kissed her again. She gave a low moan and her arms came up around his neck.

His body felt warm and solid against hers, his mouth like liquid fire. She tasted, reveled . . . and surrendered.

<u>BOOK YOUR PLACE ON OUR WEBSITE AND MAKE THE READING CONNECTION!</u>

We've created a customized website just for our very special readers, where you can get the inside scoop on everything that's going on with Zebra, Pinnacle and Kensington books.

When you come online, you'll have the exciting opportunity to:

- View covers of upcoming books
- Read sample chapters
- Learn about our future publishing schedule (listed by publication month *and author*)
- Find out when your favorite authors will be visiting a city near you
- Search for and order backlist books from our online catalog
- Check out author bios and background information
- Send e-mail to your favorite authors
- Meet the Kensington staff online
- Join us in weekly chats with authors, readers and other guests
- Get writing guidelines
- AND MUCH MORE!

**Visit our website at
http://www.zebrabooks.com**

THE SAXON'S DAUGHTER

TARA O'DELL

Zebra Books
Kensington Publishing Corp.
http://www.zebrabooks.com

ZEBRA BOOKS are published by

Kensington Publishing Corp.
850 Third Avenue
New York, NY 10022

Copyright © 1998 by Mary Gillgannon

First Printing: November, 1998
10 9 8 7 6 5 4 3 2 1

Printed in the United States of America

To my father, Robert Marquardt,
who raised me to have the faith and courage
to pursue my dreams.

ONE

England, A.D. 1067

"Hang them!" Jobert de Brevrienne barked out the words, glaring at the group of Saxon prisoners.

Beside him, Alan Fornay, his second-in-command, rubbed his chin thoughtfully. "All of them?"

Jobert scanned the bedraggled gathering. They looked young for warriors. One prisoner in the back did not even need to shave yet.

But as Jobert's gaze met the Saxon's defiant blue eyes, his vague sympathy faded. Wolf cubs grew up to wolves. He would not leave any alive to fight another day. "All of them," he said.

Jobert jerked around and began to walk away, wondering if Alan questioned his method of dealing with the rebels. King William would have cut off an arm or leg each rather than hanging them. His treatment of prisoners at Alençon had earned him the appellation "the Crippler."

Jobert set his jaw. Hanging was better. Less brutal than leaving men alive but ruined. And there was not the need to cauterize the stumps, a messy business and time-consuming. They had enough to do.

The manor must be secured and the food supply guarded, the livestock gathered up before the Saxons could steal it. Some of his men were already seeing to that. He heard the low of cattle as they struggled to enclose the beasts in paddocks near the pastureland down near the river.

A woman's scream in the distance reminded him that he had sent a group of soldiers to search the village. He hoped they had the sense not to harass or injure the remaining villeins too badly. They would need workers when planting time came next spring. If all the able-bodied workers were dead or had fled to the forest, they would be hard-pressed to get a crop in.

Jobert pushed the worry from his mind and turned his attention to the wooden palisade built on a rise above the valley. With hills to the east and the river to the south and west, the place had a fair defensive position. If he deepened the ditch at the bottom of the hill and replaced the timber defenses with a stone curtain wall, they would be able to withstand all but a long siege.

He followed the upward sloping trackway a distance, then turned to gaze across the valley. Fat, white sheep dotted the dun-colored hillsides, while farther down, the golden stubble of harvested barley and cornfields and still-green haymeadows banded the silver river. On either side of the valley, the autumn foliage of oak and beech blazed like molten metal.

A bountiful land, abundant in forage for livestock and game, with a river full of trout, lampreys and eels. Jobert felt almost dizzy with his good fortune. England was all King William had promised. To a landless knight, it seemed paradise.

He began walking toward the palisade again, squinting against the afternoon sun. Above the timber walls, he could see the thatched roof of a large two-story hall and several other buildings.

Oxbury, the place was called in Saxon. It had belonged to a man named Leowine, who supported Harold, the Saxon eorle who unlawfully claimed the kingship of England. Now Leowine was dead and all his property forfeit to the new king.

Jobert wondered briefly if Leowine had any choice in

whom he supported. If Harold was his overlord, how could he have done other than fight for him?

He shook off the vaguely troubling thought as he neared the manor.

The timber walls were heavily weathered and the ditch around the fort half filled in with rubble. Despite the turmoil of the past year, Oxbury seemed untouched, utterly peaceful.

One of the men he had sent ahead greeted him as he crossed the ditch. "All's quiet, milord. Either the place has been abandoned or everyone inside is hiding."

Jobert nodded at the man's words even as he drew his sword and gestured that the knight should do the same. He would not forget the ambush attempt in the woods. Although one of his men had seen the archers in the trees and sounded a warning, the scheme had cost them a good warhorse who foundered in a mantrap set by the Saxons. Jobert had no intention of underestimating his enemies again.

Calling over the half-dozen other knights he had sent to secure the fortress, Jobert gestured that they were going in.

He used his sword to pull open the unlocked gate. It swung aside with a creaking sound, and they advanced cautiously into the courtyard.

Chickens pecked in the dirt. A sow and her half grown piglets rooted around one of the buildings. Otherwise everything was quiet.

Jobert took a deep breath. It did not seem possible that conquest would be so easy.

"Over here." One of the knights pointed toward a timber structure. Jobert indicated that his men should search it.

As the door of the storage building swung wide, two dozen women and a few children huddled together blinked solemnly in the sunlight shafting in on their faces. One of the children whimpered, but otherwise there was no sound.

"What do we do with them?" a soldier named Hamo asked.

Jobert's gaze took in the Saxons' utter dread. He pushed back his helm and addressed the gathering. "My name is Jobert Brevrienne. I claim this land in the name of William of Normandy. You will serve me now."

They stared at him as if they did not understand his words, which in all likelihood they did not. Although the Saxon king Edward the Confessor had brought many Normans into the country during his reign, their influence had not extended beyond the royal court at London. Everywhere else, none but the Saxon tongue was spoken.

"Search the rest of the place," Jobert ordered. "I would know how many remain."

They found an old man cowering in one of the stalls of the stables, while an inspection of the other storage buildings yielded mountains of gleaming grain and several older boys who were probably grooms. In the kitchen lean-to, they found skullery wenches hiding under the tables and behind the storage shelves. Jobert was on his way to search the manor house proper when someone hailed him.

He turned. "What now?"

Alan, who he had left in charge of the hanging, hurried across the courtyard. "There's a problem with the prisoners. One of them is a woman."

Jobert thought back to the ragged group they had dragged out of the woods. Barefoot, filthy wretches dressed in long, loose tunics. He'd observed no females among them.

"What are we going to do with her?" Alan asked. "You can't hang a woman, even a Saxon one."

"Give her to me." Hamo drew up beside them, brown eyes gleaming. "What better way to subjugate a Saxon bitch than to fill her full of good Norman seed?"

"I don't need my men fighting over a woman," Jobert said.

"If we mistook her for a man this long, how many others will want her?" Hamo retorted.

Jobert sheathed his sword. He supposed he must have a look at their unexpected prisoner. God knew, he did not want to. His thoughts were all on his new property.

They left the fortress and made their way back down the hill. Jobert told Alan the results of their search. "Nothing but women, children and men too old or too young to do battle. The force we met in the woods must have been what is left of the old thegn's fighting men."

"Then we are fortunate. The rebels will all be swinging from the trees by evening."

Jobert shook his head. "The leaders of the ambush escaped." He pointed toward the gold-cloaked woods. "I wager even now that they watch us, waiting for their chance."

"They are fools if they do not surrender."

"Fools?" Jobert's russet-colored brows rose. "Because they do not let us hang them? Do not forget that in their minds, we are the usurpers."

"They are outlaws," Alan argued. "When they chose to support Harold in his unlawful pursuit of the kingship, they forfeited their rights."

Jobert considered his earlier reflection that the Saxons had had little choice in whom they followed. In the conflicts of kings and great lords, it was easy to be caught on the wrong side.

When they arrived at the edge of the woods, two of the prisoners had already been hung and cut down. They lay under one of the trees, their limbs growing rigid, their skin gray beneath their fair hair.

The rest of the outlaws remained shackled together, looking miserable. Except one who sat with head up, back straight. Defiant. Jobert realized it must be the woman.

He had attributed the lack of a beard to the prisoner's youth. Even now, dirt so obscured her features that it was hard to tell if she were ugly or fair.

He gave the order for one of his men to bring her to her feet, then moved closer to get a better look.

She was near as tall as many of his men, and from what he could observe beneath the loose tunic, broad-shoul-

dered and brawny as well. Her blue eyes were filled with
unwavering hatred. She put the rest of the prisoners to
shame with her bold fury.

He wondered what to do with this fierce, half-savage
Saxon wildcat. If he let his men have at her, she'd probably
maim someone.

He jerked his gaze to meet Alan's. "There must be a
cellar or *souterrain* back at the manor. Put her there."

Alan and another man went to take hold of the prisoner.
As soon as they severed the rope which bound her to the
others, she began to struggle. Jobert, watching, saw that it
took both his men to subdue her. After a few blows from
the bitch's flailing elbows, Alan lost his temper and
grabbed the thick braid which had been hidden beneath
the tunic. Using it for leverage, he managed to get behind
her and thrust her forward, her head jerked back.

She passed Jobert, her eyes like blue daggers, raking
him with fury.

The Norman soldiers huddled around the hearth, eating salted meat and tough bread from their saddle kits,
washing their food down with water. They had yet to find
the manor's supply of ale, and there was little wine left.
Despite the plenty all around them, no one had been able
to communicate with the frightened Saxons enough to get
hot food made, nor had they time to roast the sow they'd
killed.

Jobert put down his bread and dug his fingers beneath
his padded gambeson, searching for an elusive itch. A
bath. What he would not give for a real bath. He'd given
his men leave to bathe in the river and many of them had
done so before they supped. He'd not had time himself.

There was a large wooden bathing tub in the upper
chamber. He'd seen it when they opened the room and
been assaulted with stale, stuffy air.

The lavishness of the furnishings had surprised him. A
big carved bed, elaborately embroidered wall-hangings, a

tall wooden coffer, and several bound chests he'd not had a chance to look inside. The Saxon lord's family had obviously fled as soon as they heard of the Normans' approach, and taken little with them. No doubt they hoped that their ambush would turn the invaders away, and they would be able to return to their home.

He wondered if any of the rebels they had captured had been of the Saxon thegn's family. The people all looked alike to him, with their golden hair and broad, sun-burned faces. Once they were said to be famed warriors, but at Hastings, the Saxons' weaponry and armor could not match that of Lord William's men, and they had no cavalry. They were a subject people now, useful only as farmers and servants.

He thought suddenly of the woman. She did not have the compliant nature necessary for a serf, but he could not kill her outright, either. He did not know where his men had put her. Mayhaps he could forget to ask.

A sudden screech disturbed his thoughts. It was one of the women they'd found in the lean-to. Two knights, stripped to their hose and gambesons, chased her around the hall. The woman's pale hair had come unbound, flying around her shoulders. Her thin face was flushed, her eyes desperate.

Jobert frowned at the men but said nothing. A certain amount of brutality was inevitable. If the woman were clever, she would submit to the knight she preferred, then convince him to protect her.

They needed to find a way to communicate with the remaining Saxons. If only one of them could be found who knew a little Norman French. Otherwise, it would be the devil's own work to make them understand what was wanted of them.

One of the knights finally caught the woman. In his grip, she quieted, although she still looked like a bird caught in a snare. To Jobert's relief, her captor did not immediately thrust her down and mount her, but led her away to a private corner of the hall, speaking soothing words.

Adam of Aubrey was the knight's name. Jobert recalled him as a man who had a way with women. All to the good if he could use persuasion to convince the Saxon wench to cook for them. They were all hungry for something besides soldiers' rations.

Jobert closed his eyes. Fresh food. A bath. The big bed. The luxuries so close at hand tormented him. But he had yet to inspect the guard he'd set on the manor. They dare not become too comfortable. If his assessment were true, the nearby forest teemed with plotting Saxons.

He opened his eyes and rose. As he turned toward the door, a young knight named Rob came striding in and plunked a bucket of apples on the trestle table. They gleamed red and gold in the torchlight. "A new crop," he said, grinning.

"Where did you find them?"

"In the cellar where I put the woman." Rob spread his arms wide. "There's bushels more. And cabbages and onions. We'll eat well this winter."

The reminder of the woman made Jobert's stomach clench. "Did you leave her bound?" he asked.

Rob nodded. "She fought so hard, we dare not untie her. We did not put her in with the food, but in another chamber. Like an oubliette it is, dank, dark. But secure. She'll not escape."

Had he wanted her to escape? Jobert surprised himself with the thought.

The men reached greedily for the apples, and he took one for himself. It was crisp and tart, delicious.

He made the rounds of the palisade. The guards were alert, albeit high-spirited. Like him, they knew the exhilaration of possession. It meant something to them to follow a lord who held such rich property.

Satisfied that the manor was secure, Jobert returned to the hall and climbed the stairs to the upper chamber. He would have to forego a bath this night. They'd made no cooking fires, and it would take forever to heat water on the main hearth. Besides, he was too tired.

The events of the day rushed through his mind as he lay down on the broad, comfortable bed covered with a blue silk coverlet. He recalled the near-ambush in the forest, where they'd captured the Saxons. Many of them had escaped, including, he suspected, the leaders of the attack. Surprising that they'd abandoned the woman. What was she, some warrior's leman? Nay, too feisty for a camp follower. The memory of her blazing blue eyes reminded him of her current predicament. Bound and abandoned in a dark hole.

A shudder swept his body as he thought of how helpless she must feel.

He forced his thoughts along a different pathway, thinking of all they must accomplish before winter. The surplus livestock must be slaughtered and the meat preserved. They must have fodder for the animals. Firewood. Thank the saints that the harvest was in, mountains of golden grain filling the storehouses. Apples, cabbages, dried peas, and other vegetables. They would not starve.

But were there any spices to be had in the storehouses? And what of salt? They would need sacks of it to preserve the meat.

He had only a vague idea how all of this was to be done. The life of a fighting man had not prepared him to be chatelaine of a household. Mayhaps one of the knights had some idea. And the Saxon women. Somehow they must find a way to communicate with them.

Utter blackness. Vermin crept through the filthy straw, crawling over him. His limbs cramped, his wrists and ankles felt raw from the weight of the shackles. He would die here, rotting into the slime covering the stone floor.

He could not breathe, and his heart thundered in his chest. He opened his mouth to scream. A scream no one would hear . . .

Sweat streamed down his body as he jerked upright. In seconds, Jobert recognized where he was and the clawing dread subsided.

He let out his breath. The nightmare had not troubled him for years. It must be the woman's circumstances which aroused these memories. Try as he might, he could not block out the thought of her.

He reminded himself that she was the enemy. She'd taken part in the attack, would willingly have killed him or any other Norman if she could. Foolish to pity her.

But a woman . . . For all that she acted the warrior, the Saxon must be petrified, down in the darkness with unseen creatures scuttling across her flesh. It seemed cruel to imprison her so. She was guilty of no more than trying to defend her home.

Jobert climbed out of the bed. He'd slept naked, to avoid transferring any more dirt to the fine, clean bed linens than necessary. He pulled on his worn hose and mud-caked boots, then glanced toward his sword, visible in a shaft of moonlight shining through the unshuttered window.

No reason to take it. He meant only to find the cellar and drag the woman out of it. Put her in the stables or some storeroom for the night, decide what to do with her on the morrow.

He crept down the stairs to the hall. Soldiers snored everywhere, sleeping on the benches. He moved past them, irritated that they did not wake and relieved that there would be no witnesses to his folly. At the door, he took a pitch torch from the bracket on the wall.

Outside, moonlight glazed the hall and the other buildings silver. Jobert moved stealthily to the back of the hall. Beyond the jakes was an old storage building, the foundation of stone. It was beneath this structure that the food-stores lay.

He found the wooden door and, taking a deep breath, lifted it. In the moonlight he could see steps leading down into the ground. Sweat broke out on his skin as he eased himself into the opening. He had never been able to shake his fear of small, confined spaces.

A sour, rotting smell rose from the damp stonework,

churning his already agitated stomach. At the bottom, the odor was overwhelmed by the earthy scents of foodstores. The passageway branched to the left and right. Jobert took the right-hand way.

Entering a chamber, he lifted the torch to see mounds of apples and baskets of leeks and cabbages lining the walls. After a brief but satisfying look at the manor's produce, Jobert turned and went back the other way.

The passageway grew narrower and lower, and he had to stoop to enter the chamber at the end of it. The tightness in his chest increased. He pushed away images of the entrance being closed off behind him, of being trapped.

Despite the torch, he didn't see the woman at first. He almost tripped over her as he moved into the room.

Her head hung forward, and for a moment he thought she might be dead. Then he lowered the torch to shine on her face and saw her flinch. Her eyes opened, and she stared at him. No hint of fear softened her steady, hate-filled gaze.

He didn't want to touch her; it was like reaching out for an adder.

There was no other way. Propping the torch in a niche in the wall, he cautiously groped for her shoulder. He grasped her upper arm and attempted to pull her to her feet.

She tried to rise, but lost her balance and fell into him. A heavy, solid weight. He grunted as he braced his body and dragged her upward with both hands. Her face came to his chin. Jesu, she was tall. He overtopped most women by a head or more.

She swayed again, her legs obviously stiffened by hours of immobility. When she fell again, he was ready for her weight, but not for the sharpness of her teeth against his chest as she tried to bite him. With a furious reflex, he swung his hand and hit her on the side of the head. She crumpled. Resisting the urge to desert her to her miserable fate, he grabbed a handful of her tunic.

After catching his breath, he roughly hauled her up,

and with significant effort and much cursing, managed to get her limp form over his shoulder. He glanced helplessly at the flickering torch, then left it.

His muscles screamed in protest as he maneuvered through the narrow corridor back to the stairs. Blind determination carried him up the slippery steps. He paused outside the storage building, considering what to do with his prisoner.

He could dump her on the ground and hope she roused and escaped. A foolish whim. He was the commander of an invading army, not a court gallant. Chivalry was a luxury he could ill afford.

Besides, this fierce Saxon was nothing like the dainty, helpless women of the troubadours' tales. She was a prisoner of war and potentially dangerous.

He began to walk, staggering slightly. As he passed the stables, he considered leaving the woman there, then discarded the notion. His men would wonder at the change in her circumstances.

He glanced up at the watchtower above the gate of the palisade. There was no sign that the guard had heard his struggle. Their attention must be focused outside the fort. Either that, or they were sleeping on duty. The thought fueled his determination to deal warily with the woman.

He readjusted his burden and headed toward the manor house. Somehow he got the door open and wiggled through, bumping the woman's buttocks soundly against the doorframe. When she moaned, he knew a twinge of satisfaction.

The rasping noise of his breathing sounded loud as he lurched his way past the sleepers in the hall. He paused, rigid, when one knight raised his head. "Who goes?" the man mumbled.

"Brevrienne."

The man grunted, then lay back down. Jobert exhaled a sigh. He had no idea what he was doing. He certainly didn't want to explain his madness.

The trip up the stairs was hellish. The woman seemed

to weigh as much as a horse. His shoulder ached furiously. The sweat poured off him, mingling with the reek he'd already accumulated.

In the upper chamber, he stumbled across the room and dumped the woman urgently onto bed. Relief flooded him. His absurd venture was finished.

Except, he had no idea what he meant to do with the unholy, vicious wench he'd rescued. He glanced at her unmoving shape, recalling the many weeks since he'd had a woman in his bed. For all her war-like ways, the Saxon was a female like any other. Her body could satisfy . . . all he had to do was ruck up that filthy tunic . . .

He grimaced at his own thoughts. From what he'd seen of her, the Saxon would probably try to bite him again.

Besides, the experience was bound to disappoint. Every whore and camp follower he'd bedded these past few years only made him yearn all the more for a certain petite, dark-eyed demoiselle who smelled of flowers and aromatic oils.

Jesu, he truly must be tired, mooning over a woman like a green squire. Damaris was probably wed by now. Even if she wasn't, she could never be his. It was hopeless infatuation, and one he'd meant to leave behind in Normandy.

Sighing, Jobert took off his boots, and leaning over the bed, rolled the woman to the other side. He climbed in and stretched out. Almost immediately, he fell asleep.

TWO

Edeva shifted on the bed, trying to ease her misery. Every part of her body hurt, and the stabbing pain in her shoulders from having her hands bound behind her back brought tears to her eyes. Her brothers had warned her that the Normans would treat her cruelly if she were captured. But even if they tortured her, she would not capitulate to the wretched Norman swine. Never!

The man next to her on the bed turned over, and his weight made the supporting ropes sag and the bed slope downward. Although she tried to remain still, Edeva rolled against him until her breasts were squashed against his arm. Impotent fury enveloped her, and she tried to decide if she could reach to bite his bare shoulder.

She would be a fool to do that. He would only hit her again, and with her hands still bound, she had no means of defense.

She stared bitterly at the side of his body, wondering why he had brought her here, dragging her out of her prison in the middle of the night. She assumed he meant to rape her. What else could he want?

But his actions toward her had been brutal, not lustful. Had he found her too unappealing to bed? Her brothers often teased her that she was a "handful of a woman," and told her no man could desire such a virago. Their taunts hurt, but now she realized good might come of her unfeminine demeanor. If the Norman left her alone, she'd have an opportunity to carry out her plan. To cut his throat as soon as she got her hands on a weapon!

She shifted again, trying not to moan. How wretched it was to be tied up and helpless. She had not minded being in the root cellar so much except for that, the ignominy of being trussed like a Martinmas pig.

She supposed she should be grateful she had not been hanged. It had been dreadful to watch. Only the Normans would mete out such a shameful death to their enemies, rather than allowing them the chance to die in combat and spare their honor.

Norman filth! She wanted to spit in the face of the man next to her.

But that would not be wise. If she sought to live long enough to gain revenge, she must be clever. She might even have to submit if the Norman decided to ravish her.

She did not know how she would endure it, to allow him to put his hands on her, to mount her. She'd want to retch in his disgusting face or claw his eyes out.

She had no choice. Her captor was a big man, all lean muscle and powerful arms and legs. He could kill her without even trying.

Spawn of the devil! Whore's bastard!

As if he sensed her hatred, the Norman shifted in his sleep, mumbling something. Edeva squirmed away. It took all her strength to edge her body out of the trough made by his heavy weight.

Panting, she managed to put some distance between herself and the enemy. She could see him clearly in the early morning light coming in the overhead window. Gone was the ugly helmet with the nose guard he had worn when she first saw him. He had no beard and his hair was reddish, the color of a fox's pelt in summer. Unlike his companions, who wore theirs cropped short and shaved at the neck, his red-gold tresses reached nearly to his shoulders. It gave him a savage look, as if he were a warrior from one of the old legends.

Yet he was undeniably young, only a few years over a

score. In sleep, his face did not seem as grim and blood-thirsty, and his features could almost be considered pleasing. Thick auburn lashes, a fine molded nose—not like the beaks she had seen on some of the Normans. Only his slightly wide mouth betrayed his base, cruel nature.

Her gaze edged downward. Broad swordsman's shoulders. An expanse of muscular chest, the goldeny skin shaded with hair of a paler red than that on his head. She could see where the line of reddish fuzz trailed down into his dirty hose.

The sight made her wrinkle her nose in disgust. He had not bathed in some time. Not that she was so fragrant herself. A week they had been in the woods, awaiting the Normans. Eating uncooked food so that no fire had to be built. Sleeping in piles of dried leaves. Living nearly like animals.

Worsening her dishevelment, before the attack she had deliberately smeared herself with mud in an attempt to disguise her fair skin.

Her plan had almost succeeded. No one had noticed she was female when she was first captured, and they had come close to hanging her with the rest of their prisoners. Then, some instinct alerted one of the Normans. He suddenly grabbed her and peered at her more closely. She saw the shock on his face as he realized she was woman. He smiled suddenly, then felt for her breasts.

Too startled at first to do anything, she finally mustered her outrage and spat in his face. He had laughed as if she had made a fine jest. For a moment, she considered enticing the man, then reason returned. She had no skill in womanly seduction, and she would not submit willingly to an enemy.

At the thought, Edeva directed another hate-filled glance at the man lying next to her. If this man wanted her maidenhead, he would have to take it at swordpoint!

She squirmed again. Her hands seemed to be going numb, and she wondered how she would be able to fight even after he untied her. Sighing, she closed her eyes. She might as well try to rest; she would need her strength.

* * *

Jobert came awake, remembering that he lay on a bed in a Saxon manor, not on a bench in some noisy hall. No wonder he had slept so late. The sun was well up. His men would think him a sluggard.

He sat up on the side of the bed. As he shifted his weight, he felt something roll toward him. The woman. The memory of his journey to the cellar came back to haunt him. His act of madness.

He turned to look at her. She lay very still, her eyes closed. For a moment, he wondered if he had killed her with his blow, then he decided she slept.

Daylight improved her looks. Some of the dirt had rubbed off, and he could discern the femininity of her features. Or, mayhaps it was that for once she was not glaring at him as if she wished to stick a knife in his belly.

She had full lips, not like a man at all. And under the dirt, her hair was likely as gold and gleaming as others of her race. But it was her body which stirred his morning-heavy loins. She lay on her side, with the shapeless tunic wadded beneath her, and he could make out the unmistakable outlines of her full, rounded bosom.

He reached out a hand to touch her, then halted. Jesu, what was he thinking of? He had no desire to lie with a treacherous Saxon.

The woman's eyes opened. They grew wide, then turned dark with revulsion.

At her venomous look, Jobert's lust vanished. He'd sooner bed a whore with the pox than this nasty-tempered wench!

They glared at each other for a moment, then a knock sounded at the door. Jobert got up to answer it.

"Are you well?" Rob asked, entering. "I've never known you to sleep so late. The men need to know—God's holy teeth," he swore as he saw the woman. "What does she here?"

"She's my prisoner."

Rob's eyes swept the Saxon. "You left her bound?"

"I could not have slept otherwise. I fear she would have taken my sword and tried to cut my balls off."

Rob raised his brows. "Why is she here? Last I knew, you had her thrown into a hole in the ground, presumably to rot."

"I changed my mind," was Jobert's tight-lipped reply.

He crossed the room and pulled on his soiled chainse. "God's bones, I need to have a bath and my clothes washed." He shrugged toward the coffer shoved into the corner. "Look in there, Rob, and see if there are any clothes which might fit me."

"You?" Rob said dubiously, going to open the coffer. "I doubt it much. Some of the Saxons are fair-sized, but I see no giants." He fumbled through a stack of clothing and pulled out a heavily embroidered woman's overgown. "Jesu, but they have fine things here. I've not seen such skilled needlework since we left Rouen." He held up the crimson garment. "The Duchess Matilda's own ladies could not match this."

"Queen Matilda now. Queen of England." Jobert walked over and pulled the overgown from Rob's hands and examined it. He could not help wondering how it would look on Damaris, the deep color against her dark hair. Not that he would ever see her again.

"We're not here to admire women's gowns." Jobert thrust the garment away and gestured toward the nearest storage chest. "Look in there."

Both men began to paw through piles of clothing. Much of it was women's, but they also found creamy linen underclothes and embroidered men's tunics made of lavish materials. Rob held up one especially fine overtunic of green sarcanet embroidered with gold scrollwork and ornate designs. "What of this? It looks almost large enough."

Jobert made a disgusted sound. "I am to butcher cattle and fight rebels in that? I think not. I will save it for when Lord William comes to visit."

"King William," Rob corrected him.

A moment later, Jobert threw down the pile of clothing. "What ails these Saxons? I've found naught a man can wear, except to a banquet. Have they no chausses, no simple wool garments? I thought these lands were renowned for their woolen cloth?"

"You should have purchased clothing in London," Rob reproved. "You know you must always have things made to fit."

Jobert gave the growing pile of garments a resentful kick. *Should have.* Instead, he'd spent what little coin he had on a fine mail shirt and a carved ivory and onyx brooch for Damaris. The jewelry was still tucked away in his saddle pack. He'd known even as he bought it that he'd never dare give it to her.

His father had sent him some coin soon after, but it had been too late to purchase clothing, if he had thought of it. His mind was all on claiming the manor which William had given him.

His buoyant mood returned. No longer was he a landless younger son. He was a real lord now. All this—the land, the manor hall, yea, even the clothing tumbled on the floor—was his.

With that thought, he bent to pick up the discarded garments and clumsily stuffed them back in the coffer. "Put those away," he ordered Rob. "I'll think of something else. Mayhap one of the men we killed has something which will serve."

"You'd wear a dead man's clothing?"

"I'd take his armor and his weapons—why should I not make use of what else I need?"

"What of the woman?" Rob asked.

The two men stared toward the bed.

"She might be useful," Jobert said.

"How? You can't ransom a Saxon."

"She could be used to entrap the rebels."

"If they did not try to rescue the others, why should they come for her?"

"If she was the woman of one of the rebels, he might seek her back. Anyway, for now she is my prisoner."

Rob looked dubious. "If you keep her bound, who will help her to the chamber pot and feed her? We can scarce spare anyone for the task."

Jobert clenched his jaw. Rob was right. He'd been a lackwit to rescue the woman. He should have had her hanged with the men, despite Alan's protests.

"I'll be down anon," he said, dismissing Rob. "Tell the men who aren't on guard or sleeping to gather in the yard."

Rob left. Jobert put on his sword belt, then looked again at the woman. Her expression hadn't changed. Defiance oozed from every part of her prone body. Yet, she was undoubtedly in pain, and probably unholy uncomfortable as well. She had not passed water this morn, and even if she had not drunk since yesterday, she must feel the need. He would not treat a prisoner so inhumanely, especially a woman.

Drawing his dagger, he approached the bed. Her eyes widened, affording him a hint of satisfaction. Why not let her think he meant to kill her? That might shatter her maddening insolence.

He brought his knife to her neck, a hairsbreadth away from the smooth skin.

The contempt in her cornflower blue eyes never wavered. Only the way she parted her lips, the faint pulse in her throat, gave away her fear. Jobert felt a stirring of respect. She was brave—he'd give her that.

He hesitated another moment, thinking that if she meant to fool her enemies into believing she was a man, she should have used more dirt. In the full light of day, her sex was obvious. Never had he seen a male with such long eyelashes.

He gripped her tunic and pulled her to her knees, then reached around to cut her bonds. He saw her intake of breath as he stepped away. She bit her lips as if forcing back a groan, and he felt an uncomfortable sympathy. For a few seconds, as the blood came rushing back into her arms and her shoulder joints unfroze, she would be in agony. The numbness might last for several hours.

He should have freed her the night before. If she proved unmanageable, he could have tied her to the bed.

Now there was a provocative image—the Saxon woman bound to the bedposts, her arms and legs splayed wide.

Nay, he would not allow his thoughts to roam along such pathways. She was a prisoner, and he would treat her as he would any other captive. It was a matter of honor that a knight held for ransom must be dealt with respectfully.

But she was no knight, and, as Rob had pointed out, there was no hope of ransoming her. Using her to entrap the other rebels was equally improbable. She was useless as a prisoner.

So, why did he keep her? Because he did not know what else to do was the answer that came to him. Having spared her life twice, he would look even more of a fool if he killed her now.

And why take a life when he did not have to? Especially that of a woman. She did not match his usual taste in bed-partners, but she undoubtedly had some crude appeal. The longer he looked at her, the more she aroused his lust.

He imagined the warrior wench's body beneath his, bucking and straining . . .

Then what would he do with her, having satisfied himself? She would not be easy to tame, to mold into a trustworthy, useful servant. He might have to beat her, to pound some servility into her thick Saxon skull.

The thought displeased him. He did not have time to undertake such a project.

Impatiently, he turned away from the bed. He would let her alone, give her some time to consider how fortunate she was that he was generous to women.

He moved to the door and left the room. Outside, he shoved his short sword in to the doorjamb to lock her in, then went down the stairs.

* * *

As soon as the Norman left, Edeva climbed gingerly off the bed and moved her aching body toward the storage chests in the corner. She began to refold and smooth the garments the Normans had carelessly thrown down. Tears filled her eyes. Pigs! They did not appreciate what they despoiled.

Nay, that was not true. She had heard their admiring words. They knew the workmanship was fine. They had compared her embroidery skills to that of Norman noblewomen.

The memory did little to ease her fury. The garments in the chest belonged to her! *She* was mistress of Oxbury!

The lap in her throat tightened. Her father had been killed at Stambridge, her eldest brother at Hastings. Her mother was dead two years of a fever. All that was left were her, Beornwold, Godric and Alnoth.

She was a prisoner, and her brothers were forced to hide in the woods like wolfsheads, while the Norman pig slept in her parents' bed and pawed through their possessions as if he had a right to them.

Anger and grief almost overcame her, but she shook them off and moved to a smaller chest behind the others. She opened the chest and lifted up the yellowed linen. Underneath, three exquisitely crafted weapons rested on an old scrap of dyed leather. Jewels glinted from the handle of a dagger sized to fit a woman's hand. A short sword with a pommel of braided gold and a smaller, plainer knife lay beside it.

Edeva lifted the dagger, her breath quickening. The Norman had aided her in one way. When she saw him going through her parents' things, she had remembered the weapons stored away. Here was the means to fulfill her vow.

She removed the dagger and the smaller knife, then smoothed back the linen and closed the chest. The short sword would be too difficult to hide. She would have to manage with the smaller weapons.

Her hands trembled as she searched the room, seeking

a place close at hand, yet hidden so she could take her enemy by surprise.

She finally decided to hide the smaller dagger in a crack in the wall behind one of the tapestries, the larger one in the bed itself.

When the weapons were secured, she lay down on the bed, her plan solidifying in her mind. She would wait meekly on the bed, and when the Norman tried to climb on top of her, stab him in the throat. It would probably not kill him, but the quick loss of blood would weaken him and the damage to his throat prevent his calling out for aid as she finished him off.

A brutal end, but the Norman deserved it. He and his kind had killed her countrymen and unlawfully seized control of English lands. God would forgive her for murdering him.

But the rest of the Normans would not. As soon as they learned their leader was dead, they would seize her and exact revenge. There was little hope she could escape, although she could try. If she hid after she killed him, she might flee later.

Nay, they would know it was she; they would hunt her down. A tremor traveled down Edeva's spine. Was she brave enough to endure torture and defilement?

And what of her people? In their quest for vengeance, the Normans might well lay waste to the manor, burn the village, slaughter everything in their path. She had heard the tales of what they had done to the countryside around London after the battle at Hastings; it was said the region would not recover for a generation.

How could she bring such a fate upon the villagers and servants who had served her father and her father's father?

She sat up wearily. If only there were someone to advise her. But her brothers were off in the woods, consumed with their own schemes for revenge. And even if they were here, she doubted they would take her plan seriously. Always they mocked her.

Except Alnoth. He had a kind heart. Edeva's insides

twisted as she thought of her younger brother. She must do something to help him.

Tormented, Edeva went to the window and looked out at her enemies. Her earlier plan returned to her, goading her to take action. Despite the risks, she must be bold. She must kill the Norman.

THREE

"Do you think any of the men know how to operate a mill?"

Jobert turned and stared at Rob. The knight gestured across the yard toward the kitchen lean-to. "You told me to set the women to baking, but there's no flour. Bushels of wheat, but none ground. I took some down to the village, but there's no one to run the mill."

"Damn them! If they've killed the miller . . ." Jobert started toward the gate. "How could they be such lackwits! I told them to spare any men who had useful skills."

"Nay, the miller's not dead." Rob hurried to fall in step behind him. "Merely stubborn. Refuses to work. From what I can make out, one of our men raped his wife, and now he does not care if he lives or dies. I held my sword to his gullet, and he did not flinch. But if we kill him, we're no better off."

"Torture," Jobert muttered. "We'll torture him until he agrees to serve us."

Wretched, stubborn Saxons, Jobert thought as he took Rob and another man and walked down to the village. They seemed determined to thwart their new masters at every turn. He could not understand such foolishness. They were serfs, villeins at best. Why should it matter that they now served a Norman rather than a Saxon lord?

It should be the easiest of tasks to control such people. They'd seen him hang the rebels. Did they care so little for their own necks that they continued to challenge his will?

The village was quiet when they arrived, eerily so. No dogs barking; no children crying. Wispy trails of smoke wafted up from the smokeholes of only a few daub and wattle huts. It appeared half of the inhabitants had vanished.

Jobert swore softly, wishing he'd thought to set a guard on the place. But the Saxons would come back eventually. They were not so stupid that they would freeze in the woods this winter rather than serve him.

That did not help now. He needed capable hands to butcher the excess livestock and preserve the meat. To prepare food for his men. To make ale and churn butter. To gather honey and fish the river.

If he set his men to such tasks, they would grumble and swear, and eventually drift away to try their fortunes elsewhere. There was plenty of opportunity in England for fighting men. He could keep his troops only if he offered them an incentive to stay. If he could not offer them conquest and plunder, he must at least fill their bellies and allow them their leisure when they were not on guard duty.

The miller's house was a neat timber structure a distance from the mill on the river. The three men paused outside it. Jobert drew his sword and stooped to enter.

He blinked in the dim light and made out a man of middle years seated by the fire. He regarded Jobert with a steady, wary gaze. A soft, scuffling sound came from the sleeping loft above the main room. "The wife," Rob mouthed.

Jobert glanced up at the loft. "Was she injured?"

"Nay. But she is a comely thing, young enough to be the man's daughter." Rob shrugged. "Mayhaps the miller fears that she will come to prefer brawny, virile Normans to him."

Jobert looked back at the miller. Easiest to threaten him by telling him what they would do if he refused to grind the corn. But he had not the words to make the man understand. In exasperation, he asked Rob, "Have we found no one among the Saxons who speaks our language?"

"None, milord. At least that will admit it. I think some understand more than they let on."

Jobert nodded. Sneaky, perfidious bastards. He wished he could string up the whole lot of them and start over with good, solid yeomen from Normandy. Seeing the mulish set of the miller's grizzled jaw inflamed him to action. "Seize him!" he ordered Rob and Niles.

The two each grabbed an arm and began to drag the miller across the room. Jobert bent down to go out the low doorway and then set off toward the river. When he reached the millhouse, he glanced back to see his men bringing the Saxon; the man looked pale, but his expression was stubborn.

Jobert jerked his head to indicate that they should take the prisoner into the millhouse, then went in after.

The building was closed and hot, stifling with the oversweet scent of rotting grain. Jobert felt a renewed sense of aggravation at having to deal with petty insubordinations.

The lower room was filled with shelves piled with empty grain sacks and woven sieves. Measuring pots and scoops hung from the walls. "Take him upstairs," Jobert said.

They all climbed the ladder to the upper story. Jobert told Rob to turn the pulley which opened the sluice gates. The sound of water pouring in to the millpond could be heard. Jobert gestured to the mechanism which turned the shaft which rotated the huge millstone. "Take him over there and bind his hands to the wallover."

Rob's eyes widened. "What do you mean to do?"

"Once the water wheel begins to turn, the wallover will rotate and the force of it will tear his hands from his body. I'm hoping he sees the wisdom of resuming his duties before that."

The two men led the miller over to the wallover. He gaped in confusion as they placed his hands in the wheel of the mechanism, then began to babble as he realized what they meant to do. He struggled as they tried to bind him. Rob and Niles hung on gamely.

"Now, we'll see how stubborn he is," Jobert said.

Outside, the water wheel began to turn. The miller's eyes widened in terror. He turned to Jobert beseechingly.

Jobert approached him. "Do you obey?" he asked, thinking that the miller must guess the gist of his words.

The cogwheels connected to the wallover began to creak; the miller nodded frantically.

"Release him," Jobert said, "then bring the grain and see if he does not near kill himself to grind it."

Jobert turned, satisfied, and began to climb down the ladder.

He left the millhouse and went down to the millpond. Willow and alder grew near the water, and the fallen leaves shone bronze in the blue water. Jobert inhaled deeply, breathing the earthy smell of wet vegetation.

He walked along the bank and eyed the deep pools among the rocks. There would be trout and pike there. He should set the village children to fishing, and the women to weaving weirs. Salted and dried fish would make a welcome change this winter, and they would need plenty for Lenten.

He could do none of those things unless he found some way to communicate with the Saxons besides brutal shows of force such as the one he had just used.

On the way back, he saw Rob and Niles coming out of the millhouse. "Should we stay and see that he does the work?" Rob asked.

Jobert shook his head.

"He could poison the grain," Niles suggested. "He hates us even more now—he will want vengeance."

For a moment, Jobert considered. The miller might not fear death, but he obviously dreaded torture. He must know he was defeated. "Leave him," he said. "I do not think he will trouble us further."

They walked back through the village. Jobert regarded the silent huts with narrowed eyes. With luck, word of his treatment of the miller would convince the other Saxons that resistance was futile. And he must find someone who spoke their tongue, someone they would listen to.

The rest of the day continued in the same frustrating fashion. A half-dozen knights complained to him of the demeaning nature of their tasks. Why could he not order someone else to gather firewood and find forage for the horses? Must they be the ones to haul sacks of grain between the storage sheds and the mill? What had they done to deserve the ignominious task of feeding the livestock?

The only ones who did not complain were the men with the duty of supervising the women in the kitchen lean-to. When Jobert went to inspect their progress, he found out why.

He actually had no thought to go there, until he heard the giggling. The feminine sound, so out of place among the coarse male shouts echoing through the rest of the manor, drew him to investigate.

The kitchen was smoky and hot, but instead of the enticing odor of food cooking, it was filled with the sharp reek of something burning. No wonder, when he saw what the kitchen wenches were up to. There were a half-dozen of them, stripped utterly naked. Two of them were splayed across the wide tables used to prepare food. A bare-chested knight licked some sort of liquid off the nipples of one, while the other was fondled by a different man. The two of Jobert's men not occupied in such titillating fashion stood watching, a naked wench on each arm.

A shriek from the woman being licked masked the sound of his entrance, and Jobert stood unobserved for long seconds. Then one of the men standing turned to the skinny, barely developed wench on his right and said, "You're next."

She gave a squeal, broke away from the man's grasp, and headed for the door, running smack into Jobert. She drew in her breath with the terrified squeak of a cornered rabbit, and all eyes turned to look.

Silence settled on the kitchen. Jobert could hear the

sound of fat sizzling in the ovens, and the dull drip of the
liquid the woman had been anointed with—from the sour
smell, it must surely be ale—running off the table into the
dirt below.

"Milord . . ." one of the men mumbled.

"I see you have found a means of persuading the Saxons
to cooperate," Jobert said. "I presume the evening meal
will be a veritable feast." His gaze moved over the men.
"If it is not, I will have the lot of you staked out on the
tables, and it won't be giggling maids who dine upon your
privates, but men eating scorching hot food off your balls
with their knives!"

Dead quiet met his words. No one moved.

Jobert turned and left the lean-to. He began to walk
across the yard. Despite his harsh words, he did not think
completely ill of his men's behavior. They had managed
to control the skullery maids, and he had hopes that there
would be decent food at last.

He glanced up at the upper story of the manor hall.
The image of naked breasts and female thighs reminded
him of the woman prisoner.

He could deal with her as his men had the kitchen
wenches, but he did not think it would work. The women
he had observed were willing to do anything to secure
their captors' good will. The Saxon she-cat was another
sort of creature altogether.

He looked again to the narrow upper window. What had
possessed him to rescue her?

The thought was interrupted by a shout from the gate.
Jobert turned to see Alan hurrying toward him. "Milord,
come quickly! The Saxons are stealing the cattle!"

Jobert swore furiously and began to run.

Something was happening. Edeva stared out the window at
the deserted manor yard. Some time ago, she'd heard
shouting and the noisy chaos of men arming themselves.
Now all was quiet.

Frustration seethed through her. If her brothers attacked, she should be there to help. While she might not be able to take on an armed man in combat, she was a fair shot with a bow. Hidden among the trees, she could have killed or disabled some of the enemy and contributed to the English cause.

Instead, she was locked away, forgotten. The Norman leader had sent no one with food for her, nor had he come himself.

Edeva gritted her teeth. She hated this helplessness. If only she were a man. She would not have to endure the humiliation of being a prisoner; she would be either dead or fighting alongside her brothers!

The familiar resentment welled up inside her. Why had God cursed her? She was as brave and strong as many men, but because of her feminine form, she was not allowed to do the things they did. She'd grown up among boys: fishing, hunting, shooting a bow, fighting. Of those her age, none of them could best her. Then, wretchedly, at fourteen winters, her body betrayed her. Her breasts grew—and grew. Even when she bound them as tight as she could bear, they still jiggled when she walked and filled out her clothes in embarrassing fashion.

The rest of her life changed as well. Most of the boys would no longer wrestle or fight with her, and the ones that would often tried to kiss her when they got her down.

Her indulgent father suddenly demanded that she stay inside with the women. Instead of roaming the woods with her brothers, she was forced to spend her days sewing, weaving and helping with all the tedious tasks involved in running a manor.

Although her soul chafed at the unfairness of life, she had tried to do her duty. She had learned to make soap and tallow candles, to supervise the butchering and preserving of meat, to tan leather and clean wool. Taught at a very young age to spin and weave, her skills now advanced to sewing garments and doing fine embroidery.

And her efforts were not grudging. She put the same

toil into her feminine tasks as she had in keeping up with her brothers. She meant to make her father proud.

But her father had not lived long enough to wear the beautiful green tunic with bands of carefully worked gold embroidery along the neck and sleeves, and now she feared the Norman would take the garment for his own.

Edeva glanced at the chest where the tunic was packed away, wondering if she should destroy the garment before the Norman pig returned. She could not bear to see her enemy wear her handiwork.

Bitterness suffused her as she turned back to the window. She would not give up. Her brothers might yet succeed in routing the Normans from Oxbury. If they could draw the enemy into the woods and attack . . .

Nay, she thought glumly, they had tried that and it had not worked. With fewer men, her brothers had even less of a chance to defeat the Normans. Having seen them up close, observed their numbers, the superiority of their weapons and armor, Edeva knew that the Normans could only be overthrown by treachery.

If only her brothers realized that. She felt a stab of aggravation at the thought they might even now be attempting another doomed ambush. If only she could help them . . . if only . . .

Her attention shifted as she heard voices in the yard below. She held her breath, praying it would be the exultant shouts of her countrymen.

The hated sound of Norman French drifted up, destroying her hopes. Edeva sighed, then strained her ears to make out words.

It pleased her to know that she understood the invaders' tongue, while they treated her as if she were deaf, speaking freely before her. It gave her an advantage, an advantage she intended to use as long as possible. Although she had resented it at the time, she now felt gratitude that the woman brought from Flanders to teach her embroidery had insisted on speaking the language of the French court.

Edeva pursed her lips as the voices drew closer. The Normans were not pleased. Apparently, much of the cattle herd had been scattered and lost in the woods. The Norman commander was livid; she could hear him shouting at his men.

Edeva smiled, blessing her brothers for their shrewdness. While it might be impossible to defeat the Normans in open battle, their lives could be made miserable, especially with winter coming on. If their circumstances grew too hellish, the enemy might abandon Oxbury and move to a place where there were easier pickings.

She would do her part, Edeva decided. If she could kill their commander, the rest of the Normans might be too dispirited to remain at Oxbury. She looked around the bedchamber and thought of the weapons she'd hidden. She would bide her time; then, when the Norman was not expecting it, she would strike.

FOUR

"What happened?" Will's blue eyes grew wide with dismay as he surveyed his lord's mud-caked clothes.

"I fell." Jobert forced his voice to civility. The lad was not to blame. It was the miserable Saxons who provoked him.

The squire hurried to help him out of his filthy chainse. "At least you were not wearing your mail," the youth observed as he peeled the garment away from his master's soaked skin.

"If we'd been fully armed, we could have pursued them into the woods. As it was, we had to content ourselves with retrieving the cattle along the river bottom."

"How many lost?"

"Near thirty head." Jobert's mouth tightened. Half the herd scattered. What should have been food for his table would go to feed the rebels instead, and he would have to redouble the guard on the remaining livestock until butchering time, taking men away from other tasks.

"Even so, the Saxons will starve this winter." Alan came into the stable behind Jobert and began removing his own muddy clothes. "They can't defeat us. We have only to wait. There'll come a time when they will crawl to the manor gate begging us to take them in."

"I would have them crawl," Jobert growled. "I would have them slither in the mud as we have done."

Alan gave a bark of laughter. "You did look the sight,

sliding in the muck after that one cow. I thought I'd split
my side when you went down."

"Jesu, must you always make merry at my expense?"
Jobert glared at him. "If I did not chase the cattle, none
of the men would, either. I don't fancy eating naught but
bread this winter!"

"No one disputes you," Alan answered. "Art too grim,
Jobert. You cannot see the humor in anything."

"Mayhaps if I were clean, with my belly full of good,
warm food and wine, I'd not be so short-tempered."

"Have a bath then. Since there is no other mistress here,
the wench we captured can bathe you."

Jobert raised his brows.

"Why not?" Alan asked. "She must make herself useful
like the rest of them."

The thud of footsteps on the stairs brought Edeva to
her feet. Although she'd had hours to prepare for this
moment, her chest was tight, her palms sweaty.

The door handle rattled. Suddenly, the Norman was in
the room with her. Edeva backed toward the bed as fear
gnawed at her resolve.

The Norman scarce looked at her. Instead, he directed
a youth and two soldiers to drag out the bathing tub in
the corner of the room while other men carried in steaming buckets of water.

Edeva gaped at the scene. The bare-chested Norman
was filthy, much worse than before. Still, she had not expected him to bathe.

The Norman began to peel down his hose. Edeva looked
away, wondering what she should do. The men were so
preoccupied with their leader, they might not notice if she
slipped away.

She moved as unobtrusively as possible toward the doorway. Her bare feet scarcely touched the woven mats on the
floor, while her heart seemed lodged in her throat as she
contemplated the prospect of freedom.

She'd made it to near the bed when the Norman's angry voice rang out. "Stop, wench. I mean to have you wash me."

Edeva went rigid at his words, then took another step. She would not let them guess she knew their language. At her second step, his hand grasped her braid, his voice was low and dangerous, "Stop, I said."

The hair prickled on the back of her neck, and the horrendous thought came to her that he might rape her while the others watched, or force her to service them all. Better to have hanged than endure such a fate. She recalled the weapons she had hidden. If necessary, she would turn a dagger upon herself and cheat the Norman of his pleasure.

His hand moved up her braid, and when he pulled on it, Edeva was forced to turn and face him. Unhelmed, disheveled, he stared at her with his grayish green eyes. She started to meet his gaze with angry defiance, then reconsidered. It better served her plan to appease him. Once he let down his guard, she would get her chance.

At the change in her mood, the green in his eyes deepened and his mouth curved. Without releasing his hold on her hair, he said softly, "Ah, she'll do."

Waving the men out, he pulled her over to the bathing tub.

When the latch dropped, Edeva jumped. She took a deep breath, waiting for his next move. He released her, then sat down on a stool to remove his boots.

She shot a glance toward the tapestry where the knife was hidden. Nay, 'twas too soon. Better to let him get in the tub first.

Nervously, she clutched the dirty tunic she wore. She'd thought of changing but there was nothing stored in the room appropriate for what she meant to do. It seemed wasteful to ruin fine linen or silk garments by committing murder in them.

Not murder. She would squander no guilt on the Norman swine. His kind had killed her brother, and he himself ordered the deaths of men she had known all her life. She could still see their anguished, contorted faces as they strangled.

Justice drove her. She would make the foul Norman pay for what he had done.

"Come closer, wench. I would have you soap my back."

Edeva jerked her attention back to her enemy. He had climbed in the tub and sat facing her, a slight smile on his face.

"Closer," he coaxed. "I won't bite you . . . at least not very hard." His grin widened. "So you are shy. I would not have thought it."

Edeva's resolve to appear agreeable abruptly vanished. She wanted to plunge his head in the tub, to see that mocking grin disappear beneath the water . . .

At her hesitation, his smile faded. "You try my patience, Saxon. Fetch the soap ere I lose my temper." He pointed to where the wooden bowl sat on the table, then gestured that she should bring it.

She didn't move. As wise as it might be to pretend agreeableness, she could not manage it.

He stood up and water streamed off his body. Despite herself, Edeva could not help looking at his groin. The sight of his upthrust, engorged shaft riveted her. His hair was red there, too, blazingly so. She could not tear her gaze away.

He got out of the tub and grabbed her arm, pulling her toward him. She shrieked and tried to jerk away. He put his wet arms around her, gripping her tightly. "Listen to me, wench. I saved your life. The least you can do is bathe me."

Edeva swallowed thickly, smelling him. Horse, mud and pungent male.

He thrust her away and pointed again to the soap on the table, then got back in the tub and waited.

Unsteadily, she moved to get the soap. Clutching the bowl, she approached the tub.

Her hands shook as she rubbed some soap on his back,

and she wondered how she would keep them steady long enough to strike a killing blow. A sense of unreality crept over her. Her enemy was naked and weaponless. All she had to do was fetch the dagger and thrust it home.

She pushed aside his long hair to wash his shoulders. His flesh beneath her fingers felt firm and smooth, reminding her of the strength, the maleness of his body.

Carelessly, she soaped him, trying not to think about what she was doing—and meant to do. She dare not imagine how his body would look lying stiff and cold in death, how his fair skin would run with blood . . .

"Your touch is gentle," he said, startling her. "Not like a warrior, but a maid. Mayhaps I mistook other things about you." He reached upward to grab one of her hands. "Art not so fierce now, Saxon."

She pulled desperately from his grasp and backed away from the tub. He turned to look at her, his gaze speculative, vaguely amused. "Water." He pointed to the buckets of clean water. "Rinse me."

Edeva took a deep breath, her thoughts in tatters. What should she do? She could not retrieve the knife while he watched.

She got the water and poured the bucket over his head. He sputtered and rubbed his hands through his hair. "Jesu, I'm filthy. Wash my hair, wench." He turned again and gestured to his head, indicating that she should soap his hair.

Woodenly, she grabbed another handful of soap.

His hair was thick. It took a long while to lather it. As she did so, he leaned back in the tub, his eyes closed.

Edeva's heart began to pound. *Now! Now, with his hair wet and full of soap!*

She glanced at the buckets of water only a few paces from the tapestry where the knife was hidden. He would think she went to get clean water, but instead, she would retrieve the dagger. Then she would plunge the weapon into his back.

She took a deep breath and began to walk toward the

tapestry. Twice, she glanced around. He still faced away from her, head back, relaxed.

She found the knife and quickly thrust it into the back of the piece of rope binding her tunic at the waist, then grabbed a bucket of water and approached the bathing tub.

She looked at the Norman's broad, muscular shoulders, glistening with moisture. A tremor of fear shook her. Her puny dagger would do little damage to such a powerfully built man. She would have to keep to her first notion to stick the dagger in his throat, but that would be much more difficult.

"Hurry, wench," the Norman broke her thoughts with a muffled voice, "rinse me now."

Edeva moved toward him. She dumped the water over his head and watched it sluice down his body. With shaking hands, she dropped the bucket and reached for the dagger.

"Another," the Norman called, spluttering. "I've got soap in my eyes!"

Strike while your enemy is blinded, Edeva's mind screamed, but her body refused to obey. Never had she killed a man, nor even struck with an unblunted weapon. The bloodthirsty nature of what she meant to do unnerved her.

Replacing the dagger in her girdle, she went to fetch the other bucket, then poured it over him.

The Norman rubbed the water from his face. Then he lay back in the tub and sighed. "Jesu, but it feels good to be clean."

Edeva stepped away, stunned by her failure. She had missed her chance; she might never again have the opportunity to kill the Norman. She took a shaky breath, overcome with self-loathing.

"Bring me a cloth. I would dry myself."

His command reignited her hatred. He would have her wait upon him like a slave!

When she stayed where she was, the Norman turned as much as the small tub would allow. "There, wench," he motioned to a cloth laying on the floor, "bring it to me that I might dry, ere the dirt sticks on me again."

Edeva's shoulders stiffened. She might not have the courage to kill him, but she would not wait upon him, either!

The Norman pushed his wet hair back from his face and regarded her intently. With a splash, he stood. Water streamed off his impressive physique. "I ask you again— fetch that cloth for me." He pointed.

Edeva maintained her mutinous expression. Having shown her cravenness once this day, she would not give in to it again.

He crossed to her in three great strides, dripping water all the way, then grabbed her. "What ails you, Saxon? Sometimes it pleases you to serve me, other times you are the most bedeviling creature in creation." He shook her gently. "Don't you see that you have no choice? Don't you see—"

The dagger clattered to the floor, dislodged by his jostling. Edeva froze. She heard his intake of breath. When she dared to glance at him, his green eyes were like shards of ice. "Damn scheming slut. You meant to kill me, didn't you?"

His breath hissed over her face, and terror swept through her. Using all her strength, she pulled from his grasp and backed toward the door.

He followed her, slowly, patiently. She realized she could not escape. Changing tactics, she lunged past him, trying desperately to reach the dagger lying on the floor.

He caught a handful of her tunic as she swept by. Edeva struggled, but she could not budge his brutal grip. When she reached up to claw at his face, he shook her until her brain seemed to rattle against her skull.

When her awareness returned, he was gazing down on her with a thoughtful expression. "Cease your struggling," he said, "you cannot escape."

Edeva fought to catch her breath. No matter what he

said, she would not give up. He was a lying, wicked Norman; never would she submit to him!

Exasperation seethed through Jobert as he regarded the wild-eyed woman in his grasp. Never had he had so much trouble with a captive. Mayhaps he should beat her senseless and be done with it.

But even that might not stop the woman from scheming to kill him as soon as his back was turned. A chill went through him as he thought how he had lain back in the tub, eyes closed, neck exposed. Why had she let her chance slip away? Could it be that her womanly nature had overruled her murderous intent?

It would be reassuring to think so, but he was not such a fool as to depend on her soft heart. He must break her will. Defeat her, subjugate her, make it mercilessly clear that she was helpless against him.

Even now, she glowered at him. He wondered how she still stood after the jarring he'd given her. Her hands were balled into fists, her stance rigid, as if she waited to strike.

He admired her courage; if Harold Godwinson had had an army full of men like her, the Saxons would never have—

"Jesu!" Jobert cried out as the woman kneed him in the groin. It was a glancing blow, but still, it stung. He leaned over, catching his breath. When the pain faded, he saw the woman standing a few feet away, dagger in hand.

Rage swam in his brain. The bitch had tried to maim him! He would make her pay!

He crashed into her, and the dagger spun harmlessly across the room. There was a "whoosh" of air from her lungs as he landed on her flailing body, and he did not hesitate this time, but ruthlessly hauled her up, carried her over to the tub and dumped her into the soapy water.

She landed with a splash. He grabbed one of the buckets of water and poured it over her. She sputtered and tried to rise. He heaved another bucket over her, then leaned down and seized her braid.

He dunked her under. Once, twice, three times. He

heard her garbled scream and prepared to douse her again. The sight of her newly clean face stopped him. As the dripping water revealed creamy skin and unmistakably feminine features, Jobert reconsidered his plan to drown her.

He had been taught to honor and protect females, and for all her size and fierceness, the Saxon was a maid. The sight of the wet tunic clinging to her breasts further softened his intent.

Suddenly, he had no desire to kill her. In fact, his desires tended in a much different direction. When he saw the flicker of fear in her eyes, he knew he'd been a fool. Why murder the wench when he had a much more effective— and pleasurable—means of restraining her?

Half-smiling to himself, he moved around the tub so he stood behind her. Although near-drowned, she twisted her neck to keep him in view. He reached out and grasped her long braid, holding her still.

He unfastened the thong which tied the end of her braid, then began to unravel it. When he had loosened the plait, he ran his callused fingers through the thick, wet mass, smoothing the tangles. Flecks of dirt caught in his fingers, and he released her hair and leaned down to grasp a handful of soap from the bowl.

Roughly, inexpertly, he soaped her hair, then retrieved the last bucket of clean water. He watched her face as he approached. Gone was the look of savage defiance; she looked cowed, fearful.

Trying to hide his exultation, he poured the bucket over her head, carefully this time. When he could see that her hair required a more thorough rinsing, he filled the bucket from the tub and rinsed her again.

He grasped her arm and made her stand, then gave her a final dousing.

The bucket clattered to the floor as Jobert stared at his captive. Her long, loose hair, wet though it was, reminded him even more that she was a woman. The tunic clung to her like a second skin, outlining her breasts and the cleft between her thighs. With a swift movement he pulled the garment over her head and dropped it to the floor.

He stared. Her breasts and belly were like fresh cream, her nipples budding roses. And the pale thatch of hair at the juncture of her thighs—sweet heaven, but she made him hard!

Desire thundered through his veins and his mouth went dry. He reached out and pulled her body next to his, then ran his fingers over her smooth shoulders and slim but strong arms. He placed his hands on her narrow maiden's waist, moving upward over the flare of ribs, then finally allowing his fingers to close over the full, soft weight of her breasts. Heat ignited his blood.

Silky skin, liquid flesh . . . He leaned down to kiss her— and saw the naked dread on her features.

He drew back. Never had he had a woman unwilling, and he did not think it would be pleasant to bed a terrified wench. A soft, wet woman's sheath was what he craved, not ramming his way into dry, unyielding flesh. Although rape might serve his purposes, it would not satisfy his lust.

Yea, but he was not thwarted. He knew the secrets of wooing a woman.

Picking her up, he moved toward the bed. On the way he was reminded that she was no dainty flower, but a strong, long-limbed wench. He grunted as he heaved her onto the silk coverlet, then crawled up after her. She froze as he kissed her, and her body felt taut against his. Undeterred, he moved his mouth down to her breasts and began to lave and suck her nipples. He felt her shudder beneath him but guessed it was not a response of acquiescence.

He slid his hand down her belly to her woman's mound and began to stroke. The hair there was pale and golden, fascinating him. With slow, persistent pressure he forced her thighs apart. She inhaled sharply. He fondled her silky, feminine folds and looked at her face.

Her pink mouth caught his attention. Moving upward, he lowered his head to kiss her again.

Something glittered in the late afternoon sun filtering

through the window. Jobert jerked backward. Damn bitch! Even after he tried to pleasure her, she brandished a dagger against him!

He grabbed for the weapon. The dagger caught him in the palm of the hand. He swore, then, on his second attempt, managed to grasp the woman's wrist and twist it until she dropped the weapon.

Blood flowed down his arm and dripped on the blue coverlet. Jobert released his grip on the woman and drew back his throbbing, bloody fist to strike.

Edeva felt her breath catch in her throat. Now, surely, he would kill her.

FIVE

The Norman's mouth worked. His strange, mossy-colored eyes seemed to pin her to the bed. In the silence, Edeva could hear the faint sound of blood dripping on the coverlet.

She closed her eyes, waiting for the blow which would crack her skull and knock her into oblivion.

It did not come.

The ropes of the bed creaked. When she dared to look, he was standing across the room, sucking on his injured hand.

A painful awareness of the fragility of life filled her mind as she shakily exhaled. Her vow of vengeance seemed foolish now. She had risked her life, and for no good purpose.

She was not ready to die. She wanted to live, to bring children into the world, to feel the soft earth under her feet and the sunshine upon her skin. *Was it too late?*

She watched him tear one of the drying cloths and use it to make a bandage for his hand. He moved back toward the bed. As he bore down on her, she felt like a defenseless coney being stalked by a gleaming-eyed wolf.

With his good hand, he swiped at his wet hair to push it out of his face. Such tawny hair he had. Edeva had never seen the like. None of her countrymen had tresses like maple leaves in autumn. His coloring made his chiseled features seem even more savage, his greenish eyes more arresting.

His manner was oddly calm, as if the storm of his fury had passed. Edeva decided that this side of him, the cool, calculating commander, terrified her even more than the furious warrior had.

His gaze held hers for long seconds, then he bent to retrieve the dagger which had fallen to the floor. With easy grace, he crossed the room to pick up the other abandoned weapon. He took both daggers and went to the window and tossed them out. After another look at her, he went to the storage chests and began to rifle through them.

A sense of reprieve swept through Edeva, so strong it was almost painful. He was not going to kill her.

She sat up slowly, afraid to draw his attention, but he took no note of her. He was busy searching through the chest. Edeva strained to see if it was the one containing the short sword. If he did not find it, she might try to kill him later. *If she could.*

He made a satisfied sound and held up a plain linen tunic. Edeva recognized it as one of her father's cast-off garments, torn at the neck and already much mended. Her mother had obviously kept it for the purpose of using the fabric for rags.

The Norman shrugged into the tunic. Pushing up the too-short sleeves, he looked down at himself. The garment hung to the tops of his thighs, barely covering his groin.

He abandoned the clutter of chests and padded over to pick up his hose. As Edeva gaped, he dunked them into the dirty bathwater and whished them around, then squeezed them out.

He carried them to the window near the bed. Taking no note of her, he reached up and hung the faded, dingy hose out the window to dry, securing them on a hook on the shutter.

When he stretched to adjust the shutter, the tunic rode up and revealed his buttocks. The sight made Edeva feel strange. Although she had certainly seen naked men before, the Norman's lanky, powerful build unsettled her.

She forced herself to look away as he moved from the bed. Then, telling herself that she must not be so weak and foolish, she returned her gaze to her enemy.

He went to the bathing area and retrieved a small, strangely-shaped piece of cloth. Edeva watched, fascinated, as the Norman lifted up the tunic and fastened the codpiece over his privates.

The sight caused an odd tingling between Edeva's legs, and she suddenly recalled the image of his swollen, upthrust shaft.

The Norman sat down on a stool and began to strike his mud-caked boots together to clean them. Clumps of dirt scattered across the bare wood floor. Edeva's interest turned to irritation. Who did he suppose would clean up after him? Was he a lord, and used to having others do his bidding? Or was he merely a swinish lout who cared not if he wallowed in filth?

When he had removed most of the dirt, the Norman put on the boots and fastened the laces around his ankles, then retrieved his sword belt and girded it around his hips. He made an odd sight, with the too-short, too-small tunic exposing his wrists and thighs and the makeshift bandage on his sword hand. She stared at him, wondering if he could possibly mean to leave the room like that.

He crossed to the door, and after calling out to whoever guarded it on the other side, went out.

His men filled the benches of the hall, and from the intent looks on their faces and savory smells wafting to his nose, Jobert guessed they were eating well at last.

He crossed the spacious room, relieved that most eyes would be focused on the food. He felt half-dressed, which he was. With luck, his hose would dry quickly and he would be able to put them on again. The chainse would serve, despite the rip and the shortness. The fine linen felt smooth and soft against his skin, reminding him of women, sweet-smelling, dainty women, plying their needles with nimble, white fingers. So very unlike the she-cat upstairs.

He joined Rob, Alan and Hamo at one of the tables. His squire, Will, immediately appeared to fill his cup with ale, and a woman came up with a platter of roasted pork. Another carried a basket of bread. Although they were now demurely dressed with their heads covered, Jobert recognized the women from the scene in the kitchen lean-to. The memory reminded him of the Saxon upstairs—as did his throbbing hand as he reached for the bread.

Rob glanced his way and immediately noticed the bandage. "Jesu, what happened?"

Jobert grimaced and did not answer.

Alan turned to look. "What's this? Did the woman do that to you?"

Jobert speared a piece of meat with his eating knife. "I did not cut myself shaving."

Both Alan and Rob stared at him. Hamo said, "How came she by a weapon?"

"Fool that I am, I left her up there with an arsenal at her fingertips. I wrested two daggers from her—there are undoubtedly more."

Alan whistled. "These Saxons breed unnatural women."

"The rest of them seem docile enough," Hamo said. " 'Tis only the unwomanly giantess who fights."

"Who is she, do you think?" Rob asked. "Surely not the lady of the manor. Look at this place. " He gestured toward the gleaming white-washed walls and rich tapestries, the herb-scented rushes on the floor. "The chatelaine of this holding was obviously a woman of refined and elegant tastes, a lady after the manner of Queen Matilda herself."

Jobert took another bite of pork. He had puzzled on the matter himself. Where had the warrior-witch come from? And what was her connection to the rebels?

"When you've finished eating, you should have Odo look at your hand to make certain it does not fester," Rob said.

"At least she did not bite you." Hamo gave a chortle. "She might have poisoned you like an adder."

Jobert stopped chewing as he remembered how the bitch had tried to take a chunk out of him when he rescued her from the *souterrain*. What had he been thinking of, to free such a vicious creature?

"I say you should stake her out in the yard and have everyone have a turn at her," Hamo said. " 'Twould slake the men's lust and also help subdue her unnatural, heathen temper."

Jobert frowned; Hamo's suggestion displeased him.

Alan shook his head. "Not I. I would not want to tumble such a fierce female, even if she be bound. There are other women who better fit my notion of comeliness."

"Yea, there are prettier women here by far. I especially favor their fair coloring." Hamo cast a speculative glance toward the woman who served bread. She looked down shyly, but did not move away. "You may have your hellcat, Jobert. I will make do with one of the tamer, gentler ones."

For some absurd reason, Jobert disliked their disparagement of the prisoner. "You have not seen her clean," he said. "She is as comely as any of them, merely larger." A vision of the Saxon's bountiful breasts flashed into his mind, instantly arousing him.

"You have been pining too long for your Norman sweetheart if that savage upstairs heats your blood," Alan said. "God's face! She attacked you with a knife! What sort of maid knows how to wield a weapon, and dares to do so?"

Jobert tensed. He sorely wished that Alan did not know about Damaris.

But mayhaps the knight was right. Going so long without a woman had begun to affect his judgment regarding the opposite sex. His rod sprang to life at the mere sight of a naked female, even one intent on murdering him.

"What did you do to her after you took the knife away?" Hamo asked.

Jobert felt a twinge of uneasiness. If a male prisoner had attacked him, he would have killed the man on the spot. But the woman—he had not even thought to refasten her bonds.

"What could I do?" he said. "As Alan pointed out before, I cannot execute a woman."

"Why not have her flogged as punishment?" Hamo suggested. "You could do it outside the palisade, in full sight of anyone watching from the forest. It might even drive the rebels to show themselves."

Jobert pushed away the sickening image which rose to his mind. "I will deal with her in my own way," he said.

Edeva paused in brushing her hair when she heard the door rattle. What did the Norman intend to do to her this time?

She looked around the room. The short sword still lay in the leather wrapping in the chest. She had considered hiding it somewhere, but, in the end, she had decided to leave it where it was. It seemed she did not have the courage to kill the Norman.

The door creaked open. Edeva went back to brushing her hair, concentrating on a particularly nasty tangle in the back. Footsteps sounded, and she discerned her tormentor's distinctive tread.

He stopped near the bed. From beneath her veil of hair, she glimpsed the toes of his battered boots. The Norman might command a formidable army, but he dressed like a beggar.

She repressed her vague stirrings of sympathy. A beast like him deserved no better than rags!

"I have brought you food." He held out a wooden platter filled with meat, bread and onions.

Delicious odors wafted to Edeva's nose. Her stomach growled and her mouth watered. It had been a long time since she'd had a proper meal.

She longed to reach out and shove the platter in his face, but some part of her would not allow it. The food would spill, and she could not bear the thought of it lying ruined on the floor.

He edged the platter closer. Edeva gritted her teeth. She was not *that* spineless!

"Mmmmm, it is delicious. See?" He took a bite and loudly smacked his lips.

Her hand curled around the handle of the hairbrush and clenched until her nails dug deep into her palm. She wanted to strike him with the brush, to turn his self-satisfied grin into a grimace of pain.

He held a piece of meat under her nose. Her nostrils quivered. She stared at the scars and calluses on his long fingers, the rough, broken nails. Anything to keep from looking at the succulent temptation he offered.

Her stomach growled audibly.

"I will tame you," he said. "I will."

Edeva closed her eyes. Only two days since she had eaten. People had endured much longer than that and not starved. 'Twas merely a matter of will.

Her eyes flashed open and she struck out. Although he maintained his grip on the platter, it turned sideways and spilled half its bounty. Spatters of grease flecked the woven mats on the floor. Pieces of onion and pork scattered far and wide.

For the first time since he had entered the room, she met his gaze. His green eyes were thoughtful, calm.

Why should he not be content? He'd already eaten. Stuffed himself on the bounty of *her* lands!

She balled her hands into fists and glared at him.

"Ah, my little she-cat, you are a stubborn one," Jobert said, then thought—*and beautiful.*

Waves of silken gold swirled down past her waist and her skin glowed pink and creamy, making him wonder if he had stumbled into the wrong room by mistake. This creature, with her dewy skin and glossy tresses, could not be the filthy harridan he had rescued from the root cellar.

But he recognized the steely expression in her cornflower blue eyes, the stubborn set of her chin. Never had he met a woman of such will, such obstinacy. Had he really thought she would grow docile at the promise of a meal?

He could probably starve her for days, and she would not relent.

There must be some other means of breaking her will. Hamo's suggestion of flogging flashed briefly into his mind. Jobert rejected it even more quickly than he had the first time. He wanted to make the woman obey him, not utterly ruin her.

What then? What was the means of frightening this aggravating wench into accepting her proper place? She was only a woman, after all. No one would think poorly of her for capitulating. Women were raised to submit, to be complacent and meek.

Another glance at her haughty mien reminded him exactly how "meekly" she had behaved so far.

But woman she was. There could be no mistaking her femininity. Full, pink lips meant for kissing. Fine, arched brows. Slender neck. The unmistakable softness of her body beneath the loose gown.

She had changed clothes, discarding the shapeless peasant's tunic for a woman's garment. It was worn and patched, as his shirt was. He wondered if she had retrieved it from the same collection of rags.

He wondered even more why she had not put on some of the finer clothing. Every woman he had ever known preferred silks and samites to plain wool.

But the simple garment suited her. Obviously, she needed no adornment to make *his* blood boil.

Jobert took a deep breath and set down the platter on a table near the bed. Let her continue to smell it, to suffer.

He took a wineskin from his belt and took a hefty swallow. She watched him, eyes defiant. She still gripped the wooden hairbrush, and Jobert kept a wary eye on it.

He held the wineskin out to her, letting her smell the rich scent. It was the last of the wine they had brought from Normandy. He had been saving it for the right circumstance. Torturing a prisoner seemed an appropriate use for the Bastard's best Bordeaux.

Her delicate nostrils flared. She might have a will of

iron, but her body would betray her eventually. The flesh always weakened.

Flesh. Jobert's body responded to the thought, and not as a gaoler's should. Merely being in the same room with this woman seemed to make him hard. His fingers ached to stroke her alabaster skin, to see if her freshly-washed hair felt as soft as it looked. To sample those petulant lips with his own, wine-heated mouth.

She seemed to sense that his mood had changed. Her attention focused on his face, rather than the wineskin. Did she guess that his thoughts had turned from torture to seduction?

Thoughtfully, he recorked the wineskin and set it on the table with the food. How stubborn and sure of herself she was when he tempted her with food. But when he raked her with lascivious looks, she grew uneasy.

Why had he forgotten the powerful weapon he had discovered earlier? She feared his lust. His caresses had provoked her last attack.

The knowledge intrigued Jobert, but also made him uncomfortable. Desire was a double-edged sword. He might intimidate her into submission with the threat of rape, but he also gave her power over him. In the cause of such a devious mind, her woman's wiles could be very dangerous indeed.

He reached out slowly. When she drew back, he lunged and wrested the hairbrush from her. He threw it across the room.

Her body tensed in warrior fashion. She looked as if she meant to scratch his eyes out if he tried to touch her.

Which was exactly what he meant to do. This time he would be ready for her tricks. He would make certain she was weaponless, helpless.

He approached her deliberately. The tension in her body increased; the wariness in her eyes grew. When his knees were touching hers, he pounced.

She tumbled backward on the bed, the breath going out of her as he hit her with his weight. She squirmed and tried to free her hands. He held her fast, his body pinning hers. He sought out her wrists and grasped them tightly, then awkwardly rolled, propelling them both further onto the bed.

They lay there, face-to-face, panting. He did not give her time to catch her breath before his mouth found hers. She pressed her lips closed and jerked her head away, fighting the kiss. He shifted his weight to his elbows and knees and considered that the wisest course would be to find some rope and tie her to the bed. But, to do that, he would have to release her, then wrestle her down all over again. It seemed a great deal of trouble, especially when he almost had her subdued.

Instead, he straddled her lower body with his thighs, then brought his right hand over to his left and grasped both of her wrists with the fingers of his uninjured hand.

Now she was at his mercy. Her arms pinned, her legs secured, her furious mouth powerless.

It had been harder than he thought. She still strained against him, every muscle taut, her eyes wild and desperate. Her desperation made him recall his purpose. He meant to remind her that she was a woman, and vulnerable in a way a man could never be.

His breathing quickened as he regarded her provocative sprawl beneath him, her face flushed, hair wild, her breasts heaving from exertion. 'Twould be a lesson he would enjoy teaching.

He used his free hand to smooth her flaxen hair away from her face, then trailed his knuckles across her cheek. The expression in her eyes told him that she feared his tender caresses more than brutality. He met her gaze, then he lowered his mouth to the thin fabric of the garment she wore, where he could discern the peak of her nipple. He sucked it into his mouth, fabric and all.

She gasped. He sucked harder. She thrashed, her body twisting wildly. He used his free hand to try to pull up her gown, which was wedged beneath her body. He gave a jerk;

the threadbare fabric tore. She screamed at him, cursing in Saxon.

Panting heavily, he found her bare thigh and moved his hand upward. She clenched her legs together, but he found her cleft and stroked her, gradually easing one of his fingers between her thighs to press the hidden nub there.

She gave a low moan, then cried out in clear Norman French, "Mother of God, please stop!"

Jobert froze. "What did you say?" he whispered.

For long seconds, they stared at each other. At last, he said, "I will stop, but only if you tell me how came you to learn my language."

She hesitated, her features in torment. Her voice was a rough moan. "I'm only a serving girl. I was brought here from . . . from Rouen . . . to serve the lord's wife. I . . . I am skilled in embroidery . . . the mistress wanted me to teach her . . . 'tis a special kind of needle art, called *ora-frais*."

He did not move his hand away. "I have been to Rouen, more than once. The maids there do not speak as you do."

"My family . . . they . . . they were from Flanders."

"Yea, and I have been to Flanders as well."

Edeva held her breath, praying silently. If only the Norman would believe her!

His green eyes were narrow with suspicion. "You understood everything?" he asked. "All my orders? My threats?"

Edeva nodded. She must keep to her story at all costs. If he found out who she really was, he might use her to entrap her brothers.

The Norman shook his head. "I've never known a servant as bold as you. Indeed, I've never known a *woman* as bold as you."

Edeva squirmed, still feeling the bedeviling pressure against her intimate parts. "You said you would stop if I told you how I knew your language. Now you must honor your part of the bargain!"

"I do not bargain with liars." His russet-colored brows rose. "Nor do I bargain with prisoners."

Desperation surged through Edeva. She had given away her secret and it availed her not. He meant to rape her anyway!

She squirmed harder, which only gave him better access to the pulsing flesh between her thighs.

He watched her, a slight smile turning up his mouth; then, abruptly, he moved his hand away. "It is good to know what you most fear, wench. Let us come to an agreement. I will not ravish you—that is, unless you defy me." He grinned wolfishly, gazing down at her body. "If you dare to fight me, to refuse food, to defy my orders, I will tie you to the bed and have done with it." His smile widened with lascivious threat. "It has been a long time since I had a woman. I fear it would take me many nights ere I was satisfied."

His words chilled her. But 'twas hope he offered. Hope that she could save her maidenhead.

"What say you?" He looked down at her again, licking his lips in a way that horrified her. She remembered exactly how those lips had felt suckling her breast. "Do we have a *bargain?*" he asked.

Mutely, Edeva nodded.

He released her, then stood up and retrieved the platter from the table. "Now, you will eat. You will drink the fine wine I offer. Then, since you *say* you are a seamstress by trade, you will sew me some clothes."

SIX

Edeva jabbed the needle furiously into the thick wool.

Overgrown oaf! It had taken nearly all the remaining els of wool in her mother's chest to cut out pieces large enough to fit the Norman's lanky body, and she had no means of replenishing their supply. The lazy serving girls who should have been weaving the bales of wool in the storage shed were instead cavorting shamelessly with the lustful soldiers.

She turned the huge tunic sideways and examined her handiwork. Did the foolish Normans think that a holding like Oxbury ran itself? That servants and workmen fulfilled their duties without direction? Already, Edeva could name a dozen vital tasks which had been neglected.

All the Normans cared about was their stomachs! If the women saw fit to cook for them, they were satisfied. Meanwhile, the weaving, candlemaking, soapmaking and cleaning remained undone.

She could only imagine how the hall must look. The rushes filthy with refuse and the noxious pests it attracted. The trestle tables coated with grease and spilled food. The whitewashed walls black with smoke. And the whole place reeking of stale ale and *men!*

Edeva gritted her teeth. Her home, defiled and ruined by Normans, and she could do nothing. She remained locked away, sewing for the leader of her enemies!

Putting the tunic aside, she went to the window. Some

of the soldiers were out in the yard, practicing with blunted swords. A group of kitchen wenches watched from the sidelines. Edeva wanted to scream at them, to demand that the women get to work.

She could not. 'Twas not the task of a seamstress to give orders, and she must stick to the story she had given the Norman leader. If he knew she was Leowine's daughter, and the proper mistress of Oxbury, he might take advantage of that fact and use her to lure her brothers into a trap.

But she worried that the Norman had already guessed who she was. Had his attitude not changed completely as soon as he knew she spoke his language? One moment, he was ravishing her; the next, he bargained with her, promising not to touch her if she did his will.

So far, he had honored their agreement. He kept his distance when he brought his ruined tunic so she could measure it for size. He had slept elsewhere the last few nights and had another man bring her food and drink, a sweet-faced soldier a head shorter than the monster Norman. This knight was more than respectful; in fact, he appeared to regard her with dread.

Edeva began to pace. Despite her improved circumstances, she felt restless and uneasy. Part of it was her frustration at watching the Norman's appalling mismanagement of the manor and her worry over her brothers. But part of it was something else—a vague disappointment that the Norman could forget her so easily.

Would he leave her locked away forever, endlessly sewing garments for him and the other men?

She had never understood why he rescued her from the storage cellar. And why not rape her then, when she was bound and helpless, rather than grappling with her later? Most of all, she could not imagine why he did not beat her, or worse, when she attacked him. There was an element of restraint to his actions which baffled her.

Mayhaps he was being cautious. In truth, he was a clever, devious bastard. It had not taken him long at all to guess that nothing horrified her as much as the feel of his hands on her.

She closed her eyes, swallowing hard. 'Twas unthinkable that her enemy could beguile her traitorous body. Why, he had made her wet . . . he had made her want . . .

She tried to force the distressing sensations away, but they seemed imprinted on her flesh.

Edeva took a deep breath. She must stop thinking about the way he had touched her. Instead, she should turn her mind to escaping. His vigilance over her grew lax. Gone was the guard from the stairs; now all that stood between her and freedom was a dagger jammed into the door, securing it.

She went to the heavy oak door and pushed. The heavy iron weapon barring it seemed to move a fraction. She tried again, throwing all her weight behind the effort.

She drew back for another attempt. The sound of a sudden commotion in the yard stopped her. The Norman had returned.

She could hear his loud voice berating the soldiers, and when she went to the window, she saw him, dressed in his new hose and old tunic, pacing up and down the yard, gestulating angrily. He, too, had noticed the idleness of the women and other servants. He was yelling at the men to find something for the "damned Saxons" to do. He rattled off a dozen tasks which needed attention.

Edeva considered all the things he forgot in his tirade. The Norman was concerned with the livestock and the defense of the manor, but he had no comprehension of the many other things which desperately needed attention before winter.

And she would not tell him. Let him discover that there were no tallow candles or oil for the lamps to light the hall during long winter evenings. Let them live on bread and cabbage because the Norman had not seen fit to see to their other foodstores. Let them all go barefoot next season when there was no cured leather to make new shoes.

A twinge of guilt went through her. The villagers and their families would suffer most. They depended upon the manor workshops for the goods they could not raise or make themselves. If she allowed the Norman to make an utter muddle of things—to set the skilled workmen to menial tasks, permit the weaving women to act like slothful whores until their bellies swelled with half-Norman brats, endured his men behaving like brainless squires—'twas her people who would pay the price.

Edeva sighed and went back to her sewing. She would like to think that her brothers would reclaim the manor before any of those disasters befell them, but she no longer had much hope. Oxbury could not be taken unless some of the Normans left the area. Only against a smaller garrison could the Saxon rebels succeed. And it did not look as if the Normans were going anywhere.

"Jesu, Jobert, you are in foul temper this day," Alan said as they went into the hall. "You've done naught but yell from the moment you rose from your sleeping place."

Jobert grunted and took a seat on one of the benches. Something stuck to his hose and he stood up, bellowing, "This place is a pigsty! Don't any of the women know how to clean?" He reached down and swiped at the bench, grimacing at the gob of honey encrusted there. "Christ's bones! My new clothes!"

Alan snapped his fingers and a puffy-faced woman left the group of other servants standing in the corner. He gestured toward the filthy bench. She took an already soiled rag and rubbed at the spot.

"As if that will help," Jobert said sarcastically. "How long has it been since they did any laundry? Their own clothes look disgusting, and I doubt there is a clean piece of linen in the place."

Alan shrugged. " 'Tis Hamo's responsibility to order the women."

"Well, see that he does it!" Jobert grumbled, then said,

"Nay, I will talk to him myself. He obviously does not understand what is expected of him. He sees his duty as a license to bed every wench he takes a fancy to!"

"I gave him your orders. In fairness, I do not think he knows what the women are supposed to do. He has no experience in managing a household. Nor do any of us."

Jobert heard the resentment in Alan's voice and felt an answering aggravation. 'Twas not all the men's fault. They had never been charged with these sorts of tasks before. In an army train there were washer women and cooks, and every castle had a whole crew of servants working under a skilled steward.

"Mayhaps I should have Rob take over supervising the women," he said. "He has a gentler manner and would be less likely to encourage them in drunkenness and fornication."

"Mayhaps." Alan shrugged again and took a swallow of the warm ale another woman brought them. He made a face. "I would not drink it." He pushed Jobert's cup away from him. " 'Twill make your belly ail."

"God's blood!" Jobert pounded his fist on the table. "Where is the brewer? I'll have him flogged for trying to poison us!"

"I sent him out to herd cattle."

"You what?"

Normally unflappable, Alan flinched at Jobert's livid expression. "We're short of men to care for the livestock, and he's a brawny, lively sort. I thought he could manage both. But he must have drawn off the ale too soon."

Jobert shook his head. His dream of possessing a prosperous demesne was being thwarted by a group of incompetent nitwits! Worse yet, he could not be rid of them because they were his own soldiers.

"What this place needs is a chatelaine," Alan said. "A woman's touch. 'Tis a pity none of the old thegn's womenfolk remain."

Jobert looked at the stairs leading to the upper story.

Alan followed his gaze, then shook his head. "You cannot mean the hellcat. What would one such as her know about managing a household?"

"She sews as well as any woman I've known. Never have I had such a comfortable, well-fitted pair of hose." Jobert touched the soft wool covering his legs, still in awe of the fineness of the garment.

"But you said she was a seamstress from Flanders."

Jobert snorted. "She is no seamstress."

Slowly, Jobert climbed the stairs. He was uneasy with what he was about to do, but he had no choice. Alan spoke the truth. Oxbury needed a chatelaine, a competent, strong-willed woman who could set things right.

He was not certain what countless, important tasks the Saxons were leaving undone every day. But he knew there were many. If they were not to starve this winter, they must begin the butchering soon, and he had not found the salt necessary to preserve the meat. In a Norman household, it would be kept in a hidden cache and the chatelaine of the keep would have the key.

The chatelaine. He could think of only one person who might possibly fill that role.

The Saxon woman was almost certainly a member of Leowine's family. His daughter, or a younger sister. Only a woman born to privilege and wealth would act as she did, daring to defy and fight her conquerors. No servant or seamstress would even think of it.

He had avoided facing the obvious because he did not want to get more entangled with the wench. She made him nervous, not only because she was shrewd and devious, but because he desired her. He could not get the image of her tempting body out of his mind. Her bountiful breasts, smooth creamy skin—that remarkable golden thatch between her thighs.

Jesu, he had to stop thinking about it! About how she was his helpless prisoner. About how he could do anything he wanted to her. If he did not force the tantalizing ideas from his mind, he would completely forget the bargain he had made and ravish her like a wild beast!

He'd avoided her the past few days. Slept on a bench in the hall like the other men and had Rob attend to her needs. But if he asked her to be his chatelaine, to help him in running the manor, he would no longer be able to keep his distance. He would have to speak with her regularly, to look at her. And all the while, he would be painfully aware of what exquisite treasures her clothes concealed.

Jobert paused before the bedchamber door and took a deep breath. He had no choice. If he did not want to watch his dreams sink beneath the mire of his own and his men's incompetence, he had to ask the woman for aid.

He jerked the dagger out of the doorjamb and went in. Crossing to where the woman sat sewing by the window, he planted his feet. "I need your help."

The Norman's words stunned Edeva. This man, this ruthless warlord who did whatever he willed, was asking her for aid?

"I know that you are a noblewoman, that you understand the running of a household. I would have you take charge of this place, ere it falls down around our heads."

"How . . ." Edeva's throat was so dry, she could hardly speak. "What makes you think I am a noblewoman?"

The Norman's face grew calculating. "You would not have dared to fight me as you have if you did not feel a claim to this place."

"I am merely a seamstress from Flanders." She twisted her hands in the tunic fabric, trying to appear frightened.

He moved within a pace of her, staring her down with his green eyes. "Nay, you are not."

She struggled to maintain her demure pose. "Are you dissatisfied with my needlework? Do you find it lacking somehow?"

He moved a few inches closer. "Your work is excellent, but I doubt that sewing represents the extent of your skills. I believe you can do much more."

She raised her chin. "And why should I? Why should I lift a finger to aid a Norman swine like you?"

He smiled, slowly, chillingly, and reached out to touch her cheek. "As I recall, I have already discovered an effective means of coercion."

Edeva tried not to draw back. If she did not cooperate, he obviously meant to forget their agreement. "You said if I obeyed you and sewed you new clothes, you would not molest me!"

His fingers moved to smooth a strand of hair away from her face. "I wish your cooperation in other endeavors."

He stared at her long and hard, until Edeva's heart fluttered in her chest like a helpless bird. Then he drew his hand away and pointed out the window. " 'Tis your home. I would not think you would wish to see it ruined. But 'twill be, if someone does not see to the ordering of it."

He looked back at her. "The women will listen to you. They will not pretend to mishear your orders or try to distract you with feminine wiles. You understand what their tasks should be. And those of the workmen and other servants. I believe that you can make this manor run smoothly."

Edeva took a deep breath. A part of her longed to do exactly what he asked. Another part believed she should defy him at any cost. "How do you know I have any authority remaining? All think that you have . . . that you have made me your leman. Why should they listen to me now that you have shamed me?"

" 'Tis your natural stubbornness and authority which will give your commands weight. My men are afraid of you. I do not think that any servant or workman would dare challenge that viper's tongue of yours. If they did, you could always draw a knife or take aim at *their* privates."

Edeva felt herself flush, recalling her violent behavior toward the Norman. No wonder he did not accept her pretense of being a meek servant.

"And what is my share in the bargain?" she asked.

"Your share?" He cocked his head. "You will have control of your own household and a claim in Oxbury's prosperity."

"And freedom from your attentions?"

He studied her coolly. "For the moment."

Edeva sucked in her breath in anger. Twas not enough! She bargained with the devil himself, and still he gave her no assurances!

But what else could she do? Besides, the longer she held him off, the greater chance that her brothers would think of some plan to retake Oxbury and free her from this nightmare.

"How will you make certain I do not escape?" she asked.

"One of my men will guard you."

"And at night? Will you continue to lock me in?"

His green eyes glittered. "At night I will sleep beside you and guard you myself."

Edeva walked out in the yard, taking deep breaths. Though odors of dung and garbage tainted the fresh autumn air, she refused to let it ruin her mood. At last, she was free of that stuffy, stultifying chamber. For a few moments, she meant to enjoy the sheer pleasure of being outside.

She longed to climb the gatetower and look out at the valley, to drink in the colors of the turning forest and the sparkle of the river. But she feared that the man guarding her would complain to his commander that she sought to escape.

She turned to look at her gaoler, boldly facing him down. It was the same young solder who had brought her food and drink. He flushed under her gaze, but did not look away. Mayhaps he had learned that she did not really bite. Certainly, he took his duty seriously, trailing her like a devoted puppy. She worried a little what he would do when she needed to use the jakes.

"What's your name?" she asked him in Norman French. He looked startled.

"Your name," she repeated. "If you are to spend your every waking moment with me, I would know what to call you."

" 'Tis Rob," he said. "Rob of Lascalles."

"I am Edeva."

"Edeva," he repeated. "Where did you learn our language? None of the others understand us."

"My father brought a woman from Flanders to teach me sewing. She spoke the Norman tongue and considered it much superior to Saxon. She would speak naught else with me, so I was forced to learn your speech."

"That is good. Now you can help us deal with the other Saxons."

Edeva's ire immediately rose. "I have agreed to see that Oxbury continues as a prosperous, efficient manor, but I will aid you Normans in naught else. You are still my enemies!"

The young soldier stiffened, and Edeva felt a stir of satisfaction. She would not be unkind to him, but she would not allow him to grow easy, either.

A moment later, Edeva considered the foolishness of her prideful words. Why did she inflame his suspicions? 'Twould it not be wiser to lull him into complacency?

"Where are the kitchen wenches?" she asked him. "The weaving women?"

He shrugged. "I know not. Some of them might still be abed. The men . . ." His face flushed.

"Have them all brought out to me," Edeva ordered. "Tell them to make themselves presentable. Their mistress commands them."

Rob glanced at her, then toward the manor outbuildings. She could see he was torn. Would he do her bidding even if it meant allowing her out of his sight?

"I will remain here," she said. "I give you my word."

It took some time, but eventually, all the women straggled out into the yard. A few had managed to braid their hair, but the majority looked disheveled and filthy. Some—

the younger, prettier ones—had dark circles under their eyes and a strained look to their faces.

Observing their listless expressions, some of Edeva's irritation faded. 'Twas clear they had been well-used by the men. By now most of them had discovered that being a servant in her household was less demanding than whoring for Normans. She would not chastise them. How could they do otherwise than they had?

"Many things have been neglected these past days," she said. "Neither you nor I have been free to pursue our duties. But that will change now. Our first task will be to restore the hall to its former tidiness. When we have finished with that, I will assign you other work. There is much to do before winter," she warned, "and we are sore behind."

"But what about . . . them?" A slight, curly-haired girl spoke, her voice barely above a whisper. Several women glanced nervously around the yard.

"The Normans will molest you no longer."

"How can this be?" one of the women asked. "How will you make them leave us alone?"

"The leader of the Normans has given me complete authority over the running of the manor. If any of his men bother you, come to me and I will take the matter up with him."

"See how cozy she is with the red-haired giant?" Golde, a cat-eyed wench who worked in the weaving shed, stepped forward and planted her hands on her curvaceous hips. "He's made her his doxy. Why should we listen to *her*?"

Edeva tensed. She had warned the Norman that this would happen. "I am not his whore," she said coldly. "And I am still your mistress. If you do not obey me, I will have you flogged."

Golde smirked, but moved back, as if accepting Edeva's authority.

The group was silent for a time; then the curly-haired girl spoke again. "I, for one, am happy that Lady Edeva commands us. I am tired of the crude Normans and their disgusting, lustful habits. They scarce give me any peace . . . and I worry . . . what will happen to me if I get with a babe!" she ended in a wail.

Two other women put their arms around the girl, who began to weep. Soon the whole mass of women had seemingly dissolved into tears. For a time, Edeva allowed them to cry and complain and comfort each other. Then she said, " 'Tis enough. We have work to do. You can curse the Normans while we clean."

Jobert gazed in satisfaction around the hall. Only one day had passed, and already things appeared much improved. The sweet scent of rosemary and lavender rose from the fresh rushes, and he could run his hand along the trestle table and feel smooth wood, not encrusted grime.

Even the food seemed better—the pottage more skillfully seasoned, the bread crustier. The brewer had not had time to make another batch of ale, but Jobert knew Edeva had spoken to Alan and made it clear that certain servants were not to be taken from their specialized duties. Alan had complained to him, grumbling that the Saxon bitch left them with no sturdy laborers. Jobert had pointed out that now that the men weren't constantly rutting with serving wenches, they had time to do more themselves.

Things were much improved, indeed. And he had the Saxon woman to thank for it.

He glanced to where she stood at the side of hall. With her fair hair covered and her simple gown, she looked demure and womanly, like some minor lord's wife.

But she was no biddable, dutiful matron, and well he knew it. At any moment, those clear blue eyes could flash with cold fire, those full lips shout oaths to burn his ears.

Nor was she as plain and ordinary as she sought to appear. He recalled the voluptuousness of her body, the ivory perfection of the skin. His shaft rose at the memory.

And he was to share a bedchamber with her this night.

What madness had made him tell her *that?* Though sharing her bed might intimidate her and keep her fearful, it was going to be pure hell for him. He was not certain he could resist the lure of her beauty, no matter that he had given her his word.

For a moment, he let his mind linger on the idea of parting her white thighs and thrusting deep. Of feeling her dewy, pink sheath closing tight around him.

Shifting uncomfortably on the bench, he forced the enticing image from his mind. He dared not lose the only leverage he had over the Saxon. If he could not threaten her with rape, how would he ever control her? He would be a poor commander indeed if he indulged his body's hunger and lost a strategic advantage over his opponent. Bedding her must wait.

As he watched, a young woman came up and spoke to Edeva. The girl's face was pale, her cheeks tear-streaked. Edeva consoled her for a moment, then grasped her sleeve and gave her a little shake. The girl sniffled, then went off.

Edeva continued to stand and observe the comings and goings of the hall. Jobert had the sudden thought that she must be tired. He motioned to one of the squires. "Have the woman come and sit with me."

She looked startled when the squire spoke to her. Her gaze found Jobert, and she shot him a hostile look. He met her expression with amusement. Their eyes locked and held.

Jobert let his glance move down her body. Her face went rigid as she guessed his thoughts. She walked stiffly toward him.

He gestured to the bench beside him. "Sit down, Lady Edeva."

"I am no lady to you," she said through clenched teeth, although she did his bidding.

He pointed toward the bowl of pottage a squire had brought. "Eat. You have worked hard today, and I am well pleased."

"I do not do any of it to please you!"

"But you have." He touched the wool of his new tunic. "Your needlework is the finest I have seen. And your skill at ordering servants—verily I proclaim you a worker of miracles for the changes you have wrought in this place in one short day."

A muscle jumped in her cheek, and she clutched her eating knife with a vigor which suggested what she wished to do with it.

"I'll say no more," he said. "I would not have you claim a bellyache because I disturbed you while you ate."

She made a disgusted sound, then began to take careful bites of the stew.

SEVEN

Edeva could feel his eyes on her as she ate. It made it difficult for her to swallow.

Putting down her eating knife, she took a sip from the cup in front of her. She made a face. "What is this?"

"The last of the wine from our traveling rations."

" 'Tis wretched stuff."

He regarded her with a wry expression. "Better than the ale we had last even. None of the men would drink it. The brewer tapped it too soon. Now, we must wait for another batch."

"Water would be better."

He nodded. "I'll have some fetched for the ewer in the bedchamber."

The word "bedchamber" made the rest of Edeva's appetite depart. Any moment the Norman could suggest that they go upstairs. *Would he sleep with his clothes off? Insist that she remove hers?*

Heated images swirled in her brain.

She forced herself back to the present. There were important things they needed to discuss. "I have promised the women that your men will leave them alone," she told him. "Otherwise, they will not have the time nor energy to do their duties."

He nodded. "I agree with you, although 'twill not be easy to make them give up their pleasure. They have grown used to rutting wherever they please."

"Well, they will have to learn to curb their lust!" Edeva said hotly. "To run smoothly, the manor requires not only the efforts of the servants who live within the palisade, but the sokemen and their families in the village. We cannot do the butchering, nor process the wool, nor do many other important tasks if the villagers are afraid to enter the palisade. I am used to having several of the sokemen's daughters spin and weave for me all winter, but they will not come this year unless I can assure their parents that they will not be ravished by your men!"

The Norman grunted. "I am aware that I need the aid of the villagers. Without them to fish the river, to gather nuts from the wood and to tend the beehives, we will be doomed to a monotonous diet this winter. And by next spring, they must be ready to plow and sow the fields or we'll all starve." His voice rose in frustration. "I know these things, but I am not sure of the means to gain their cooperation. How can I convince them I do not mean them ill?"

"You will not convince them until it is the truth! As long as your men feel free to rape any woman who crosses their path, why should my people trust any Norman?"

"Have any of the men bothered you?" the Norman asked, his voice sharp.

"Of course not. As you have said, they are all afraid of me."

"Mayhaps that is the means of it then. You must teach the other women to be as fierce as you are."

He was teasing her. Edeva felt certain of it. She cleared her throat. "Promise me that you will speak to them. That you will give them strict orders to leave my women alone."

"Agreed," he said. " 'Tis time they settled down and behaved as proper soldiers rather than worthless louts."

Edeva ate in silence for a time. She could still feel the Norman watching her, and the tension in her belly did not abate. With every bite she took, the time grew nearer when they would go upstairs to bed. She both dreaded that moment and felt a vague sense of expectation.

When the last bits of meat on her trencher were gone, the Norman reached over and threw the gravy-soaked bread to the floor. It was immediately consumed by one of the dogs which were let into the hall at mealtime to keep the rushes free of refuse.

Edeva took a final swallow of the sour wine, then met the gaze of the man beside her. "Ready, my lady?" he said. "I'll escort you upstairs."

There was courtesy in the way he helped her up from the bench and took her arm as they crossed the hall. At the stairs, he gestured that she could go ahead while he carried the cresset torch.

They entered the room, and the Norman put the torch in a bracket on the wall and went to close the shutters. Edeva remained by the door, uneasy not only with what this man might do, but also with her own feelings. A few days before, she and the Norman had been bitter enemies; now they shared a meal and spoke congenially. She wished she could go back to hating him and plotting his death. But she feared she could not.

Of course, that did not mean that they were not adversaries. She only cooperated with him for the sake of Oxbury and its people, to keep things running smoothly until her brothers could regain control. Eventually, they would find the means to oust the Normans and reclaim what was theirs.

Restless, Edeva went to the table and dipped her hands in the washbasin and rinsed her face, then dried herself on a cloth. When she looked around, the Norman was undressing. She turned back to face the wall, dreading to see him naked. She could still recall how he had looked the first time—and the peculiar way it made her feel.

With suddenly clumsy fingers she fussed with her braids. When she could no longer pretend to busy herself with redoing her coiffure, she sat down on a stool and began to remove her shoes and stockings. She could not go to bed in her gunna, but the idea of wearing only her shift made her mouth dry.

And what would he wear? His undertunic? His hose? *Or nothing?*

"Edeva, will you quench the light when you come to bed?"

She could not delay forever. If he touched her, she would remind him of their bargain. Surely he would not be so foolish as to risk losing her aid by violating their agreement.

Taking a deep breath, she pulled the gunna over her head and hung it on a hook. She put out the torch and walked to the bed. The Norman lay on the outer side; she would have to climb over him.

She closed her eyes and planted a knee on the bed, then carefully rolled herself over the Norman's bulk. 'Twas a struggle to get under the covers, but at last she was abed. She sighed heavily.

A second later, the Norman gave a faint snore. At the sound, her mood went from anxious to irritated. She wanted to strangle him for making her endure such turmoil, such awkwardness—especially when he was going to fall asleep as if she were not even there!

Edeva stared up at the darkness. She had agreed to do his bidding if he left her alone. Obviously, 'twas no hardship for him. He apparently found her so unattractive that he could sleep beside her and not be even a tiny bit tempted!

The embers of her hatred flared to life. He was a crude, stupid pig, and she should have let him ruin Oxbury rather than help him!

She gritted her teeth, wondering if she would ever sleep.

She woke later, in the darkest, deepest part of the night. For a few moments, she wondered what had aroused her. Then she heard it—a faint noise coming from the stairwell.

She strained her ears. Who would climb the stairs this time of night, and so stealthily? Her heart began to pound.

The noise seemed to stop outside the door; she took a deep breath and turned toward the man beside her. With only the merest hint of light creeping through the cracks in the shutters, she could make out no more than the shape of him. But she could hear his slow, even breathing.

She froze in place as she heard the quiet footsteps near the door. The Norman had not seen fit to lock them in. Why would he? He had a whole army below to guard him. She would lie here and wait and see who the intruder was.

Nay, she would not!

With elaborate care, she climbed over the Norman. As her feet touched the floor, the door creaked. Edeva backed toward the wall. The door opened slowly and someone came into the room, but she could not see who it was. She reassured herself that she could not be seen, either.

Long, painful seconds passed. She sought to press herself further back against the wall. Her foot bumped into something, making a noise.

Strong hands grabbed her. At the moment she thought to scream, a sweaty hand clapped over her mouth. "Edeva, it's me," a familiar voice whispered in Saxon.

She nearly fainted with relief. Then she realized all the other dangers facing them, and a new wave of panic overwhelmed her.

The hand covering her mouth moved away. She took a deep breath and whispered, "What are you doing, Godric? Are you mad? The Norman sleeps there, in that bed. If he wakes and calls an alarm, you have no chance."

"Do you want me to kill him?"

"What would that accomplish?" she whispered back. "His army holds Oxbury. They are not like to leave even if he dies."

Her brother grunted.

The Norman sighed in his sleep and rolled over. Edeva pulled on Godric's arm. "Let us go in the stairwell," she whispered.

They crept out the bedchamber door, closing it gently behind them. Halfway down the stairs, Godric halted.

"How fare Beornwold and Alnoth?" Edeva asked.

"Tired of eating squirrel and rabbit and sleeping on the ground."

"Have you thought of a plan? Is that what you have come to tell me?"

"I came to see how the place was guarded. And how you fared. It seems you have been treated well enough." There was a sneer in his voice which raised Edeva's ire.

" 'Tis not what you think. I have not cooperated with the Normans any more than necessary. I could not let the place go to ruin while I waited for you to think of a way to take back our home. I had to see to the servants and the preparations for the winter!"

"And warm the Norman bastard's bed. For certes, you must do that!"

"He *makes* me sleep at his side!"

Her brother's voice turned thoughtful. "That you are his leman may aid us. You'll be able to learn his plans ahead of time."

"I am not his leman!" Edeva said hotly.

"Truly? He has not bedded you?"

"Nay."

" 'Tis odd," Godric said. "But mayhaps he fears that if he beds you, he will have to take you to wife. I've heard that the Conqueror is most particular of his men's conduct toward women."

"Then why do the other Normans fornicate like rabbits?" Edeva demanded.

"I suppose the standards are higher for the men William grants land to."

Edeva pondered this information. Learning that the Norman might have declined to bed her because he did not want to be forced to marry her did not make her feel any better.

"A pity he has no liking for you," Godric said. " 'Twould help us a good deal if you were his leman."

"Jesu, a moment ago you were scorning me for sharing his bed!"

"Well, you cannot blame me for being a little resentful of your circumstances. You sleep here, warm and dry, and eat hot food every day, while the rest of us suffer in the woods."

"Do you have any sort of plan at all?"

Godric sighed. "Beornwold stalks around our camp in a fury, but he has no more idea of how to dislodge these devils than I do. I was hoping you had thought of something."

Edeva shook her head. "There are too many of them and too few Saxon warriors. You cannot defeat them unless a part of their force leaves the valley."

"Or their leader is killed. That would demoralize them, throw them into disorder."

"Or cause them to burn the manor and kill all of us!"

" 'Twas merely a thought," Godric said. "Surely you would have no complaint if we murdered the bastard." He turned toward the door at the top of the stairs. " 'Twould be easy to do. I could cut his throat in his sleep."

"Nay!"

"You puzzle me, Edeva. The Norman has obviously shown no interest in making you his woman, and yet you argue for his life."

"I am being practical! If you kill him in his bed, who do you think will be punished? His men will assume that I did the deed. They will show me no mercy, nor any to the rest of the people of Oxbury."

"You could flee with me."

"Nay, I would not leave others behind to suffer."

"You were always difficult, little sister. Argumentative and stubborn. No wonder the Norman does not favor you. Your unfeminine nature likely repels him."

Edeva took a sharp breath, feeling Godric's words cut into her. He was a fool, but nevertheless, what he said stung.

"Well," Godric said as he started down the stairs, "I can see we'll get no good of you. We'll have to depend on Golde for aid."

"Golde!"

"Keep your voice down, wench. Golde is the one who smuggled me in. At least *she* remembers where her loyalties lie," Godric said as he disappeared into the blackness.

Edeva clenched her hands into fists. Damn Godric! And damn the Norman! Between the two of them, they were driving her mad.

She crept back up the stairs. The sound of the Norman's heavy, even breathing fueled her fury as she climbed back into bed. She had saved his life this night. And for what? So he could use her to run his household.

Why was she helping a man who found her so unfeminine, so repellent, that he did not want to bed her?

Bitterness suddenly gave way to tears.

She had not cried when word came of the Normans' victory at Hastings. Nor when the enemy was first sighted in the valley. Not even when she watched her countrymen die at the end of a rope and believed she would be next.

But now the tears came, and she wished dearly for another woman to talk to. A sister. Or her mother, dead for two years.

There was no one but her, and she must be strong. The people of Oxbury depended upon her. Her brothers would never think of them, concerned as they were with their own misfortunes. Three-score lives hung in the balance. Children and women. Hard-working, loyal sokemen.

All of them, looking to her. Edeva—Leowine's daughter.

He was dreaming. He knew that because he had never been to this place before, at least not with Damaris. They were in no gentle, peaceful garden like the one behind her father's house, but a forest, wild and bright with golden leaves.

Damaris was there, talking to him, her dark eyes shining, her delicate lips moving as she spoke in her soft voice. He knew not what she said, only that she was near. He reached out for her, seeking a kiss.

Her lips felt plump and ripe beneath his, her body warm and alive. He drew back to look at her.

No brown eyes met his, but cornflower blue. Lips, not the garnet red he remembered, but rosy pink. And fair hair . . .

The Saxon. 'Twas not Damaris he held but the Saxon woman.

He stared in surprise even as the dream dissolved.

He woke slowly, adjusting to the darkness, the unfamiliar surroundings. A dream. That was all it was, the only way he would ever see Damaris again.

But the Saxon lay beside him, snuggled close, as if she sought out his warmth. He could still remember the sweetness of her lips from the dream, and his shaft rose, hard and wanting.

He reached out for her, then stopped, realizing that he could not find his release in the flaxen down between her thighs. There was a bargain between them, and he would not go back on his word, even with a Saxon.

Torment. His men thought he had bedded her a dozen times by now. In the meantime, he burned. Burned like he had for no woman except Damaris.

Nay, that was not true. He did not burn for Damaris. He loved her, adored her, worshipped her. Over the years, she had become almost a dream to him. A fantasy.

The Saxon was real. Agonizingly, excruciatingly real. He could smell the scent of her. Warm and fresh, like new-mown hay. An earthy odor, unlike the perfumed oils that Damaris favored.

He stifled a groan and sat up. Not yet dawn, but it seemed unlikely that he would sleep again.

Getting out of bed, he fumbled around in the darkness. He found his clothes, his boots and sword belt. As he pulled his tunic over his head, the softness of the garment reminded him of who had sewn it for him.

'Twas too difficult, sharing a bedchamber with a woman he could not have. Mayhaps he should go back to locking the Saxon in and sleeping elsewhere.

But then his men would think he tired of her. Some of them might even dare to approach her, believing that she was no longer under his protection.

A wave of rage went through him as he imagined another man putting his hands on the Saxon. Nay, he could not endure that! If anyone was to have her, it would be him!

She was his prize, the symbol of his victory over her people. As her conqueror he should have the right to bed her. Every night if he wished. *Several times a night.*

Instead, because of his foolish agreement, he was forced to live like a monk.

He swore again as he started down the stairs, then slowed as he felt a draft. Someone had left a door or shutter open somewhere.

He ventured into the main part of the hall where his men slept soundly, stretched out on the benches. There was no sign of anything amiss, but he felt edgy. In the night, before he dreamed of Damaris, he'd had the familiar nightmare about being in the oubliette. This time, there had been voices whispering outside his prison. The dream had gradually turned into the other, but the memory of those voices stayed with him. One of them had belonged to the woman, the Saxon.

The yard was empty and dark as he made his way to the jakes. A dog barked from the area near the stables, but otherwise, everything was quiet. He relieved himself and walked back to the hall.

As he approached, he spied an unshuttered window at the rear of the building. The sight made him uneasy. He walked toward the gate to see if the guards had noticed anything amiss. Climbing the gatehouse ladder, he walked out on the wall. When no one hailed him, his heart leapt into his throat.

The guards had been killed! It was an ambush! He hurried down the ladder, ready to call an alert . . . and nearly tripped over a man sprawled in the shadows. The man sat up, groaning.

"Blessed Jesu, what happened?" Jobert demanded.

"Milord?" Osbert croaked.

" 'Yea, 'tis Brevrienne. Now, tell me what happened!"

Osbert didn't answer. A sickly sweet scent wafted to Jobert's nostrils. Not wine, but strong drink of another kind.

Fury built inside him. He wanted to grab the guard by the throat and dash his brains out against the palisade wall. Instead, he said, "Where's the other sentry? Is he drunk as well?"

"Milord . . ." Osbert spoke in a slurred voice. "We did not mean to drink so much. It went to my head so quickly, I can scarce believe it."

"Do you think you were poisoned, that the drink had something in it?"

"Poison? Nay, Golde would not do that to us. 'Tis merely . . ." He groaned. "I've never had this stuff before. The Saxons brew it out of honey. I had heard that it was strong, but I did not think 'twould do this to me."

"Who's Golde?"

"One of the weavers," the man groaned. "The comely one."

"I should have you flogged!" Jobert snapped.

Osbert said nothing.

Jobert stood over him, disgusted. If he had these men whipped as punishment, then he would have to worry about their welts healing. While they mended, he would lose the services of two of his soldiers. It seemed a waste. There must be other means of teaching them a lesson.

He glanced around the yard, lit now by the beginning glow of dawn. "The stables need mucking out," he said. "I was going to have some of the Saxons do it, but you and your companion may have the job instead."

"Clean the stables? Today?" Osbert asked weakly. Jobert could imagine his distress. Raking out months of dung and soiled straw was an unpleasant task in the best of circumstances. With a raging hangover, 'twould be hell itself.

"Get to it, man. I'll wake your fellow tosspot and tell him the good news."

The guard rose shakily, then hurried off. Jobert found the other man snoring nearby, propped up against the palisade wall. A swift kick in the ribs and some well-chosen words had him on his feet in seconds, although Jobert wondered how long he'd manage to stay upright.

After the guard left, Jobert found the empty skin lying on the ground. He picked it up and sniffed it.

Mead. He'd heard of it, though never sampled it himself. 'Twas said to be several times as potent as the same amount of wine. He wondered why the woman Golde had seen fit to share a skin of it this particular night. Would the weaver be about her work yet, or was she also sleeping off an aching head?

After searching the weaving shed, empty except for spools of wool, several looms, and dye vats, Jobert returned to the hall and approached the screened-off area where the unmarried women slept. Several of them were already up, braiding each other's hair. They froze at the sight of him. "Golde?" he asked.

They all shook their heads.

He left the women, wondering where to search next. Mayhaps he should wait until Edeva rose and discuss the situation with her.

He went outside and followed the wall of the palisade to where it abutted the manor workshops. As he turned back toward the gate, he saw a figure hurrying toward the weaving shed.

He gave chase, and in a few long strides, grasped the fabric of a cloak and whirled the figure around.

Wide-set hazel eyes regarded at him. A swirl of tawny hair spilled over the drab cloak.

One of the comely ones, Osbert had said.

"Golde?" Jobert demanded.

The woman smiled.

He shook her. "Where did you get the mead? What have you been doing with the guards?"

She still smiled at him placidly, obviously unafraid. Either she was innocent, or she did not anticipate that he would punish her.

Jobert loosened his hold on the woman's cloak. His inability to speak Saxon was proving to be a real trial. He could not properly question the woman.

She licked her well-shaped lips suggestively, and Jobert felt his muscles tighten. For a moment, he considered accepting her invitation, then drew back in disgust. She'd probably pleasured both the guards already. Even as sex-starved as he was, he had no desire to sample such well-used wares.

From a distance, Edeva saw the Norman and Golde standing close. He bent near, as if whispering an endearment, then walked off.

Edeva drew back behind the hall. She did not want him to catch her spying on him and his lover.

EIGHT

Edeva left the weaving shed and started across the yard. As she rounded the corner of the hall, she saw the Norman. He had apparently just come in the gate, for his boots were muddy and his hair disheveled and windblown.

She watched him stride toward the storehouses, and her eyes narrowed as she remembered that she had sent Golde to fetch some woad for making blue dye. If the two met along one of the pathways between the storage buildings, she could well imagine what would happen. They would end up rutting like animals in some secluded spot. For the past few days, the Norman left the bed early, and Edeva was convinced that his first business of the morning was a tryst with Golde.

She continued across the yard. 'Twas none of her affair. If the Norman sought to ease his lust with that conniving slut, 'twas his own stupidity. *She* would not tell him that Golde was a spy for her brothers. Let him find it out on his own.

She neared the hall, then suddenly reversed direction. Golde was *her* servant. If Brevrienne wanted to dally with the wenches, let him find one who had her work finished!

Edeva headed back toward the storage buildings. As she strode purposefully past the grainary, she met the Norman coming out of the smokehouse—alone. He met her gaze, smiling. For a moment, she was tongue-tied, then she mumbled something about getting herbs for dyeing. She started on her way, but the Norman grabbed her arm.

"You are exactly who I wished to see. I have come from the cattle pen where the men are culling the herd. 'Tis past time we began the butchering. I need your aid, Lady Edeva. I need to know where the salt is kept."

His green eyes entreated her. "You know that we must preserve meat before winter. If we do not, all of Oxbury will go hungry."

His hand still gripped her arm and Edeva could feel the strength of his fingers through her tunic. A shiver passed through her. Even when he touched her thus, her body responded.

She had put off this moment as long as she could. If they were to have sufficient foodstores for the long winter months, she would have to tell him. Sighing, she said, " 'Tis under the floor in the chapel."

"Show me."

He continued to hold her arm as they walked across the yard together. The air felt cold and damp, and the Norman paused briefly to look up at the sky. "A storm is brewing," he said. "I can smell it."

Edeva thought of her brothers and the others in the forest. They would be miserable when the autumn rains began. While she remained safe and warm, sharing Leowine's bedchamber with the enemy.

The Norman held the chapel door open for her. She hesitated.

"What's wrong?"

She shook her head and went in.

A rush of cold air followed them, stirring the dust on the floor. The Norman pulled the door closed, then took the one candle burning by the entrance and went to light the others set in holders at either side of the nave.

As the small chamber leapt into light, an ache started in Edeva's throat. The chapel had been her mother's dream. She had wanted a "real" church, and Leowine had indulged her. The ornately-painted screen behind the altar, the carved wooden arches of the ceiling, the trefoil windows set high in the whitewashed walls, their exotic shapes gleaming with precious rose-colored glass—every detail lovingly rendered, as if fashioned for a fine cathedral.

Once there had been a priest as well. Father Saxfrid, sent by the bishopry at Winchester. He had died shortly before the Battle of Hastings, and there had been too many other things to do to see to a replacement.

Since then, the place remained unused. Edeva sometimes came here to pray, but she had not done so in months. Her grief made her too bitter and angry for petitions to heaven.

The Norman stepped back, surveying the high-ceilinged space. His expression was admiring, almost reverent. Edeva felt a stir of pride which helped assuage her pain. Her mother had created a worthy legacy.

"You said it was in the chapel," the Norman said. "Show me where."

She wanted desperately to refuse, but could not. 'Twas not right to force her people to go without meat this winter.

She pointed to an area where the paving stones made a pattern, with a large square stone in the center. "There, in front of the rail." Her hand shook.

The Norman went to the spot. He took out his dagger and began to pry up the flat middle stone. Edeva watched, her distress increasing. She should not have told him of her father's hiding place. She should have come here alone at night and dug it up herself. Why had she not thought of that?

She shook her head, wondering what was wrong with her. Why did she keep doing things to help the Norman?

He swore loudly. She saw that he had worked the stone partway out and it had squashed his fingers. "Help me," he said.

Taking a deep breath, she knelt beside him. Together they eased the stone out of the way. He motioned that she should pull out the wooden box beneath.

She tried but could not budge it. Grunting, he pulled the paving stone all the way out, then reached in and took the other side of the box. They heaved it onto the floor.

In the space underneath the box, surrounded by straw, were several barrels. The Norman pried open the top of one with his dagger and grunted in satisfaction. The salt. Then he turned his attention to the wooden box.

He used his dagger to wrest off the lid. Inside were several cloth bags. He began to pull them out and open them. He tossed the first one aside, and Edeva saw a curl of parchment poking out the end. She guessed it contained charters and grants from the long line of Saxon kings her family had served. All worthless now, good only for scraping and reusing the vellum, if it were not too old and brittle.

The next bag made a clinking sound when he shook it. He smiled, then put it aside.

He hefted the final bag, and the look of expectation on his face deepened. He opened the bag and stared at the contents, then carefully dumped them on the floor. The wealth of Leowine's lineage winked and twinkled in the candlelight—rings, necklaces, bejeweled daggers, belt buckles and brooches fashioned of gold and precious gems.

A sick feeling went through Edeva. Her father must have hidden away his treasure horde before he left for Hastings. Now it belonged to the Normans, their enemies.

Traitor, a voice in her head accused. *Better you all starve this winter than to lead him to this!*

She glanced up and saw the Norman looking at her, his features softened by an expression of awe and gratitude. She wanted to spit at him. "I did not know it was there," she said in a voice full of venom. "If I had, you could not have forced me to tell you of it even if you tortured me to death."

"Always the hellcat," he said softly.

She stood, wanting to weep. She had betrayed her family, her heritage. And all for a man who thought her an uncouth, savage . . . hellcat.

Whirling around, she stalked out of the chapel. When she reached the yard, she began to run. She dashed into the hall. People turned to stare at her. Edeva sucked in her breath and headed toward the stairs.

She reached the bedchamber and slammed the door behind her. Briefly, she thought of trying to lock it. But why bother? The Norman would be busy gloating over his good fortune for hours.

She threw herself onto the bed and pressed her hand to her mouth, forbidding herself to cry.

If her brothers saw her now, they would be appalled. They thought she was strong. A hellion and a virago, they called her.

But she was not strong. 'Twas so hard to always be thinking of everyone else, to forever remember to hide her own breaking heart.

Oh, how she missed her father. He had seemed as formidable and enduring as the hills themselves. But he was gone, and she must carry on and do the best she could on her own. It seemed like such a heavy burden, and there was no one to share it with. Even if her brothers reclaimed Oxbury, she knew they would not aid her in the running of the manor. They were concerned only for their own comforts, their own prestige and power. 'Twould be up to her to see that Oxbury and its people thrived.

She sat up slowly. At least she had a purpose, something to work toward. She could see that the manor prospered, *despite* the Normans.

There was a sound on the stairway. Edeva jumped to her feet and looked around for something to bar the door with.

Too late. The door opened. Edeva hurried toward the storage chests in the corner, hoping the dimness of the chamber would hide her turmoil.

"Edeva?" The Norman stepped into the room. Edeva knelt down and opened one of the chests, pretending to look for something inside. "Lady Edeva, I would speak with you."

She continued to ignore him, pulling out pieces of cloth and examining them. He approached her and tried to take her arm. She jerked away.

"Jesu, woman, I am trying to be civil!"

He stood there a moment, and she could sense his growing anger. Good. Let him understand that she was not willing to do his bidding unless it served *her* purpose.

"We are back to this, then—your fighting me, snarling like a wildcat?" He heaved a sigh. "I do not want it to be like this, Edeva. I have tried to show you courtesy, to treat you with deference. I had hoped to win your cooperation and respect in return."

"Respect?" Edeva straightened. "How can I respect you, you greedy, lustful pig!"

"How can you call me lustful? I have honored our agreement. I have not touched you!"

Edeva went rigid. She longed to tell him that his lover was a Saxon spy. But then she would have to tell him how she knew of Golde's perfidy.

His eyes suddenly glowed with anger. "I can see my forbearance, my attempts at honor, are wasted on a shrewish bitch like you! 'Tis clear that I should never have rescued you, but left you down in that foul cellar to rot!"

He turned and started to leave. In the gloom, he tripped on the stool in his pathway. He swore violently, then picked up the stool and threw it into the wall.

"Stop!" she screamed. " 'Tis not yours to break. None of this is yours! All the things in this room—the furniture, the chests, the clothes, the jewels you found in the chapel—they belong to me! I am the heiress of Oxbury, and I will command this place as I see fit!"

He approached her once more and his voice was deadly calm. "You are wrong, lady. King William gave Oxbury to me. It is mine now. All of it." He reached out and grabbed her sleeve. "Even you. Although why I would want such a quarrelsome, viper-tongued creature, I know not."

As he glared at her, Edeva felt her fury fade. She did not want him to despise her. As ridiculous as it was, she still sought his regard.

His anger also seemed to ease. His fingers relaxed on her arm, then stroked. "I don't know why I should want you, but I do." His voice grew low and husky. "I want you all night long . . . every morning . . . every time I look at you."

Shimmering heat rose inside her. Edeva tried to remember her hatred. He moved closer, trapping her. His arms reached around to imprison her and his mouth met hers.

The kiss was long, slow, searching. Edeva felt her legs turn the consistency of gruel, her head swim. When he drew back, she could barely stand.

He stared at her, the pupils of his eyes huge and black. "I think there is a woman inside you, beneath all the snarling rage and fire."

Edeva swallowed. The way he looked at her . . . it made her feel weak, helpless.

He leaned down and kissed her again, his tongue probing, inflaming. She gave a low moan and her arms came up around his neck.

His body felt warm and solid against hers, his mouth like liquid fire. She tasted, reveled . . . and surrendered. When he took her hand and led her toward the bed, she did not try to resist. Her will was gone. Utterly vanished.

He began to undress her. He pulled the loose gunna over her head, then knelt down to take off her shoes. She did nothing. He reached under her shift to find her garters and roll down her stockings. Edeva stood, trembling, nerveless.

He grasped the hem of the linen shift and eased it upward. As he pulled it over her head, Edeva's gaze met his. His face was soft, intent. Not the fierce mien of a warrior but the misty countenance of a lover.

"Edeva, my beautiful Edeva."

His admiring words melted her last vestiges of resistance. As if in a dream, she watched him lower his head to mouth her nipple. She sighed and closed her eyes. He caught her as she swayed. Throbbing need radiated out from her nipples, swirling and whirling inside her.

He drew her nipple deeply into his mouth, and Edeva cried out from the sudden, urgent restlessness afflicting her. She longed for something, some wild, unnamed thing.

When he released her, she wanted to weep for the loss. But then she saw that he was undressing and her breath came faster. She could not forget the first time she saw him naked. How proud and invincible he appeared. How intriguing. She remembered staring at his groin, and the way it made her feel. Aching and weak inside.

She wished it were brighter in the room, so she could

more clearly see his triumphant masculine beauty. Those wide, well-muscled shoulders, strong arms and chest, the lean, flat line of his belly. The warm sheen of his skin and the vivid body hair accenting his underarms and chest.

His tunic lay in a heap on the floor, and he bent down to unfasten his boots and crossgarters. He stripped off his hose, then approached. Edeva stared at him, marveling, as always, at his size. Most men made her feel overtall and unfeminine, but with the Norman she knew what it was like to imagine herself as a dainty thing.

'Twas threatening to be near a man so big and strong. Also intoxicating.

His eyes raked over her, admiring her as she had him. "I've never had a maid before, but I will be gentle with you, Edeva. I promise."

His words made her impatient. She did not want him to be careful and restrained. She wanted the passionate fire which he had aroused before.

Her whole body felt hot, her nipples tight, rigid points. The sensations surging through her were near unbearable. Overcome, she parted her lips and regarded him through slitted eyes.

A look of surprise came over him, then his nostrils flared. "God help us, woman. I am not made of stone. If you look at me like that, I am like to pounce on you like a beast."

Very deliberately, Edeva looked at his groin.

He made a low noise, a sound of hunger barely mastered. Then he pushed her onto the bed and climbed up beside her, his eyes like pools of desire. "You know not what you ask for," he said.

He bent over her, his hands suddenly rough as he pushed her thighs apart. Edeva gasped as he touched the part of her which yearned and pulsed the most. She closed her eyes as he stoked the fire there, his fingers parting and fondling her. Helplessly, she moaned. It seemed the more he caressed her, the more she wanted. Her hips shifted restively.

She tried not to think how wanton she must appear. How wet and eager.

His provoking fingers changed position, and when she opened her eyes, his face was near hers. He leaned closer and teased her lips with his tongue even as he used his hand to tantalize her lower regions. Then his lips slanted hard across hers and his tongue invaded her mouth as he slipped a finger deep into her silky wetness.

The shocking sensation of him penetrating her body both soothed her and drove her to madness. Her hips pushed violently against him, seeking some perfect magic position which would fulfill her.

His thumb found the top of her cleft and supplied the miracle she sought. Waves of heated pleasure drenched her. She writhed and twisted, falling into dazzling sensation.

She was barely aware of his fingers leaving her and then pressure, impossible pressure as he fitted his shaft against her opening. He thrust deep, and Edeva gave a cry of surprise and pain.

"I'm sorry," he whispered.

She stared up at the ceiling, wondering if anything could have prepared her for the feel of his big shaft deep inside her.

He lay quiet, letting her catch her breath, then he began to move. A rhythm she fought against, wincing at each thrust, then gradually giving way. Her body stretched, adjusted. The discomfort turned to a nagging pang, then spiraled into a familiar longing. Each time he moved inside her, she felt a twinge of pleasure. The twinges grew to something more. A great, heaving energy.

He raised himself above her, neck arched and straining. His eyes were closed and his hair poured over his shoulders like blood. She reached up to stroke his chest and urge him on. Then she clutched his upper arms and closed her eyes, finding her own release.

He collapsed onto her, sweating and panting. "Sweet heaven," he whispered. She caressed his back, feeling a remarkable sense of fulfillment.

After a moment, he rolled away. He lay panting a moment, then leaned on his hip and regarded her, his eyes a pale, shining green. "What a wench you are, Edeva. I vow there is fire in your veins. And you have burned me to a cinder."

She basked in his admiring gaze a moment, then slowly grew uncomfortable as the languorous heat of her passion ebbed away and the implications of what she had done struck her.

God help her, she had lain with her enemy. Passionately. Wantonly.

A kind of numb horror replaced her feeling of contentment. She started to get out of bed. He caught her wrist. "Rest now," he said.

She pulled away. "I must see to the evening meal . . . I must . . . there are many things I must do."

When she stood up, she felt the wetness of his seed between her thighs. Dread afflicted her as she realized that he might have planted a babe in her womb.

She hurried to get her clothes, desperate to get away from him. Away from the shameful thing she had done.

He sat up on the bed. "Let me help you wash."

"Nay! I'll wash later, after I have seen to things below."

She jerked on her gunna, not bothering with her shift or stockings, then jammed her feet in her shoes and fled the room.

Jobert stared after the woman, frowning. What had come over Edeva, that she ran from the bedchamber as if demons were in pursuit? Did she really regret what they had done that much?

Well, she'd had no doubts earlier. Never had he bedded a woman so responsive, so eager. Indeed, he had not even realized a woman could be like that, had not imagined they might be made that way. The females he encountered previously had been of two kinds, either bored and businesslike harlots, eager to have him finish so they could collect their payment, or pure, untouchable virgins like Damaris.

Edeva was different. Her desire seemed as strong as his, her release as uncontrollable. 'Twas a revelation that a woman's craving for lovemaking could be as intense as a man's.

But Edeva's boldness was mixed with a confusing sort of

innocence. She had been a virgin, touchingly new to the wonders of sex, and he had hurt her with his lack of control. He had not meant to, 'twas simply that he was so aroused by her uninhibited release that he could not hold back in seeking his own.

He winced as he remembered her cry of pain. He'd promised to be gentle, but she'd taken him so by surprise. From her thrilling acquiescence when he first kissed her to the ease with which she allowed him to undress her—he'd been so keenly, wonderingly aware that she *wanted* him.

Or her body had. Her mind and heart might be another matter. Mayhaps that was why she could not wait to get away from him. Though she desired him, she still saw him as her enemy.

Jobert rose from the bed, discomfited by his thoughts. He had not meant to get so involved with this woman. He'd rescued her out of pity, then later realized that her help was essential if he meant to fulfill his plans for Oxbury. But things between them seemed to grow more complicated by the day. Now he had bedded her and discovered exactly what he feared—that he felt things for Edeva that he'd sworn never to allow himself to feel again.

Casting an uneasy glance at the bed, Jobert began to dress.

NINE

Two red-and-white oxen stamped and paced in the corner of the yard, bellowing anxiously. A short distance away, a newly butchered animal hung from a scaffolding, its blood draining into a huge pot, while axes thudded as workmen chopped brushwood to stoke the cooking fires. Near the kitchen shed, women armed with cleavers and knives cut up the meat, while other servants pursued the unpleasant task of cleaning the animals' entrails to make casings for sausages.

Edeva moved through the noisy, chaotic atmosphere, giving directions. She had already overseen the mixing of spices to season the sausages and tasted the salty brine which would be used to preserve most of the meat. Now she must make certain the bones were kept to boil down for soup stock, the hides carefully stripped and the sinews saved for bow strings. Nothing would go to waste if she could help it.

She'd been able to persuade several of the villagers to come to the palisade and help with the butchering. Although they were obviously uncomfortable around the Normans, at least they no longer cowered in terror at the sight of them. Two of the sokemen had even agreed to allow their daughters to stay at the manor house and help Edeva with the weaving and sewing during the winter months.

She scanned the yard for the two young women now,

remembering her promise to their parents to keep them safe. Eadelm would be no trouble. She was stocky and plain, with a cheerful moonface and lank brown hair. Edeva did not think the knights would bother her. But Wulfget—as she caught sight of the girl, dutifully mixing the sausage spices, Edeva sighed. Wulfget was a rare beauty, with a delicate, almost fragile build, huge blue eyes, and hair paler than cornsilk. Edeva had already caught several of the knights staring at the maiden, then talking among themselves in low voices.

Mayhaps she should send Wulfget back to her family and ask for another village girl to train. But that did not seem fair. Wulfget's beauty was no fault of hers. Edeva would simply have to keep a close eye on her—and make certain Brevrienne controlled his men.

The Norman was busy at the butchering pen, holding the animals' heads while another man cut their throats. 'Twas exhausting, messy work. His face gleamed with sweat, and his ancient hose and ripped chainse were stained nearly as red as his hair.

Despite his dishevelment, Edeva could not glance his way without a shiver of longing coursing down her body. She could not forget what they'd done in the bedchamber two days past, nor how it had felt.

Since then, she had gone out of her way to avoid him. She slept downstairs with the other women and spoke to him only when necessary. Which was actually quite often. Planning for the butchering required that they converse at length on several occasions. It had been torture, but she had managed to get through it with her dignity intact. She simply reminded herself that he was her enemy, and she cooperated with him only for the sake of her people.

Fortunately, he had said nothing regarding that fateful afternoon. His manner continued to be courteous and respectful, giving no hint of the intimacy they had shared. She blessed him for his discretion, but also wondered what it meant. Had their lovemaking meant nothing more to him than a release of sexual tension?

Of course that's all it was, for her as well. They had both acted like animals, but it changed naught of the circumstances between them. They were still foes. Nothing could alter that.

"Milady, do we have any more casks?" Beorflaed's voice awoke Edeva from her musings. She gaped at the cook, realizing the crucial thing she had forgotten. "The meat won't be ready for several days," Beorflaed added, "but I thought we should plan for how much we will salt."

"Mother of God," Edeva cried. She turned and ran toward the storage buildings.

Panting, she finally reached the small stone structure which was used as the buttery. She peered into the low-ceilinged chamber, then found a stick and propped the door open so the light from the outdoors shone in.

The air of the buttery was ripe with the sour smell of the rounds of curing cheese piled on shelves around the chamber. Edeva brushed past flitches of bacon hanging from the ceiling and carefully stepped around large jars of honey. Behind the spare butter churn and a broken vat, she found a dozen wooden casks. "Not enough," she whispered. The sinking feeling inside her deepened.

She hastened back to the buttery entrance, slammed the door closed, then began to search the other buildings.

When she was climbing out of the root cellar she saw the Norman's tall form looming at the top of the stairs.

"What's wrong?" he asked. "I saw you running off, but no one knew where you'd gone."

She shook her head, still breathless from her exertions. "We don't have enough barrels." She felt near tears to think that after all her careful planning she had overlooked something so important. "I've found two dozen in all. Already, we've enough meat soaking in brine to fill those, and there are more cattle to butcher."

Her words triggered a sudden thought, and she took off running again. She called over her shoulder to the Norman, "Hurry, we must stop them before they kill the last few animals."

"Why?" He ran along beside her, his long stride matching two steps of hers.

"Because the meat will be wasted," she gasped. "We don't have enough barrels to store it in."

"Can't the workmen make more?"

Edeva shook her head in exasperation, "The wood slats must be cured before they are fitted together. 'Twould be several weeks before the casks were ready. In the meantime, much of the meat will rot."

They reached the yard. The absence of lowing animals told Edeva that they were too late. She came to a halt, sighing heavily. She had imagined she was being so efficient, remembering every detail of the butchering process.

" 'Tis not the end of the world," the Norman said. "We could always kill more of the pigs and cure their meat in the smokehouse. Bacon will fill our bellies as well as beef."

"But the waste." The Norman's patient understanding distressed her all the more. *How could she have been so stupid?*

"We'll not let the meat go uneaten," the Norman said. "We'll have a feast and dine like kings. Invite all the villagers, anyone who wishes to come."

She stared at him.

He shrugged. "I've been seeking a means to let your countrymen know that I am not cruel or unjust, that if they will work for me, I'll treat them fairly. A feast would be the perfect means."

"I . . ." She did not know what to say. Never had she imagined the Norman would do something like this. 'Twas beyond generous. Even her father had only held a feast at Yule.

"I'll go tell the men to leave the last two animals whole for roasting." He strode off, back into the commotion. Edeva gaped after him.

The Norman was a constant surprise. The manor was already better off for his stewardship. Her brothers would never have concerned themselves with something so mundane and messy as butchering, yet the Norman dove into the task, unafraid to dirty his hands or to sully his dignity working side by side with servants.

She glanced at him now, watching him use his formidable body and exceptional strength to help drag a whole carcass across the yard. The muscles in his arms bunched and rippled, his broad shoulders strained beneath the sweat-soaked chainse, and his long hair swirled around his face like a vivid banner.

Her turmoil deepened. The Norman was always doing things which met with her approval, even admiration. How could she despise him when he showed himself to be reasonable and fair? How could she hate him when he did so many things to win her regard?

Of course, she did not hate him. That was the problem. She was fast learning to like the Norman, or even, dare she think it, falling in love with him.

She was a traitor to her people. Only a weak, malleable woman would allow her loyalty to be suborned so easily. She must remember her duty.

She stoked the old hatred as the Norman approached. He smiled at her, his teeth very white in his blood-stained countenance. "Do not fret," he said. "I have marked the animals we will roast for the feast. When this is finished, we will all celebrate, Saxon and Norman." He reached out and touched her face, wiping at some streak of dirt on her cheek. His green eyes glowed with lazy warmth.

Edeva froze as heated memories whirled through her brain. The Norman saw her distress and withdrew his hand. "I think they need you for the sausage-making. Why don't you go see to it."

She nodded jerkily and left him.

Edeva walked along the pathway which ran behind the scattering of daub and wattle dwellings. From here she could see the gardens and backsheds of the villagers. The gardens were now bare, dark squares, covered with refuse from the middens to enrich the soil for next year's planting. Here and there a goat was tethered to a stick or a few chickens pecked in the dirt, but most of the other live-stocks had been slaughtered. The villagers knew there was often not enough corn to keep both beasts and people through the winter.

As she started toward the forest, she saw a yellow striped cat moving among the tall, dry grasses which edged the common pasture. It ignored Edeva as she passed by, and she wished it well in its pursuit of mice and other vermin. They could do with more cats in the palisade, she decided, to protect their store of grain. She would have to ask around the village to see if any of them knew of any re-cently born kittens. If she transferred the cats to the manor while young, they would probably make their homes there.

But that task would have to wait for another day. She'd already been gone from the palisade long enough. When the Norman had asked her to personally extend his invi-tation to the villagers to come for the feast, she'd jumped at the chance to walk out in the fresh air and smell the crisp scents of autumn. To her surprise, he had not asked the young soldier, Rob, to accompany her, but allowed her to walk down to the village alone.

Her news about the feast had been greeted with wari-ness. Many of the villagers were concerned that they might not be allowed to leave once they had entered the palisade. Did she trust the Norman? they asked her.

Edeva had reassured them, telling them that she had seen the Norman do nothing deceitful or unjust since the hangings. She even mentioned Brevrienne's remark that he wanted them to know he would treat them fairly if they did their duty.

The villagers had nodded and whispered among them-selves. Then one of the men had asked her if she was going to wed with the Norman.

The question had caught her completely off-guard. Her face grew flushed and hot, and she had mumbled some-thing about having no say in the matter.

That had angered them. Before she knew it, the villagers

were debating whether they should go to the Norman's feast if he would not do the proper thing and wed with their lady.

Exasperated, Edeva had finally told them that nothing was decided yet, and that if they were wise they would show good faith by coming to the feast. They would eat well, she told them. The Norman was roasting not one, but two oxen for the meal. The promise of fresh, rich food distracted the villagers. By the time she left the common, there was no more talk of her wedding the Norman.

But the whole incident had aggravated her already frazzled nerves—which was why she decided to take a walk before returning to the palisade.

She moved briskly now down the pathway toward the river, trying to quell her unsettled thoughts. God in heaven, she was having enough trouble recalling that the Norman was her enemy without the villagers suggesting that she wed with him! Did they truly expect her to share the bed of a man who had seized her home and killed her countrymen? To forget her brothers, living like outlaws in the woods?

Of course, there was the fact that she had already given the Norman her maidenhead. *Willingly. Eagerly.*

Her face grew hot. There was no excuse for what she had done. Raw lust and jealousy over Golde had driven her into the Norman's arms. And there was no way to take back what she had done.

In truth, the villagers were probably right. She should wed with the Norman. If he would have her.

Which was questionable. He thought her a hellcat, a virago, and now probably, a slut. What man would want to wed a woman like that?

Edeva was so deep in thought, she did not see the man standing among the trees until he stepped forward and called her name.

"Beornwold!"

"Aye, little sister," his voice was harsh with mockery,

"I'm surprised you recognize me. It seems you have spent the last few weeks making every effort to forget your kin."

Edeva said nothing. Although she had not forgotten her brothers, she had failed them in other ways.

Beornwold moved closer. "The time draws near when you can aid us. I have come from the village, which is all abuzz with the news that the Norman bastard means to hold a feast. 'Tis clever of him to try to win their loyalty through their bellies, but I mean to turn his plan *our* way."

Beornwold smiled, but it was a bitter expression and did little to soften the grim lines marring his handsome face. "The Norman says he welcomes all Saxons to his table. 'Twould be easy for a group of warriors to enter the palisade, pretending to be sokemen."

Edeva's blood ran cold as she saw the direction of Beornwold's thoughts. "Your plan is too risky," she said. "The Normans still outnumber you greatly. And your weapons are inferior, your armor nothing compared to theirs."

Beornwold moved even nearer. "But we have an advantage, Edeva. We have you. With your aid, we have a chance."

"What . . ." Edeva asked breathlessly, "what do you want me to do?"

"Cause a distraction to keep all the Normans occupied in the hall. Once the doorway is blocked, 'twill be easy to pick them off."

Edeva was horrified. "There will be women and children inside! How can you think of involving them in a *battle!*"

Beornwold's blue eyes grew hard. " 'Tis a war, Edeva. We will try to spare those of our own, but if a few perish, it cannot be helped. This is our only chance. The only way we can regain Oxbury."

"Nay," Edeva whispered. "I will not help you. I will not be part of this."

Beornwold's lip curled. "I told Godric we had already lost you to the Norman. Tell me," he said, his voice thick with contempt, "does he pleasure you well? Do you scream with passion as he mounts you?"

Edeva reached out and slapped her brother, then sucked in her breath in shock at what she had done.

To her surprise, Beornwold did not retaliate, but merely shook his head and turned away.

As he disappeared into the forest, Edeva's vision blurred with tears. Her brothers wanted her to betray the Norman, to bring about his death. She could not do it. Every fiber of her being screamed that it was wrong. But how could she prevent it? How could she keep her brothers' plan from coming to pass?

She could tell the Norman, warn him of what was to happen. He might decide the feast was too risky and call it off. 'Twould be the best thing. The villagers would be disappointed; the meat would rot. But that was better than the bloodshed which would take place if she said nothing.

Edeva took a deep breath and began walking. Back through the forest, where the beech trees shone smooth and bare and ochre-colored leaves clung to the broad boughs of the oaks. Where the ground beneath her feet crunched with fallen leaves and nuts.

She passed the hedgerow, bare now also, except for the gleaming red berries on the hawthorn branches. Past the mill, from where she could see the river, foaming white as it swirled around the rocks.

She walked up the trackway and through the open gate. As she looked around for the Norman, a woman's voice called her name.

Edeva whirled and met Golde's mocking gaze. "Milady, you have returned at last," the woman said. "What kept you? The Norman remarked to me that you had been gone much longer than necessary to convey his message."

"Indeed," Edeva said faintly. "Where is Brevrienne?"

Golde cocked a brow. "I imagine he is still setting his clothes to rights. 'Twas a *most* satisfying afternoon."

Edeva's hands clenched into fists. She wanted to hit Golde in the nose and ruin her provocative allure. Only the thought that the Norman might think her actions crude and unfeminine helped her restrain her rage.

She turned away, intending to leave Golde and her taunts behind. But she could not help listening as the wench called out in a husky voice, "*Afterwards,* I had the most entertaining conversation with Jobert. He told me all about the Norman woman he intends to wed. Her name is Damaris. Damaris de Valois. Her father is vastly wealthy, but that is not the main appeal. It seems our Norman lord prefers his women dainty and elegant. A pity, poor Edeva, that you are so . . . large and awkward."

Edeva whirled, no longer able to control her fury. But Golde had run off, laughing.

Edeva kicked the ground furiously. Jobert. The Norman's name was Jobert. She had known him three sennights, had shared his bed, and not learned his given name.

She wanted to kill him. To singlehandedly bring about his death. But she could do better than that. She could ruin all hope of his reigning as lord of Oxbury.

She would have to think of a way to get the women and children out of the hall before the attack came. That was not an insurmountable problem. The servants and workmen posed more difficulty. She could not completely prevent their being caught in the conflict between the Normans and her brothers.

But, as Beornwold had reminded her, this was war, and men inevitably died. Once her brothers and their warriors entered the hall, the sokemen would be able to choose which side they wished to support. She would not rob freemen of the chance to decide their destiny.

As she had decided hers. The Norman might be a just and generous lord, but he was still a usurper. He did not belong here, had no right to Oxbury. She must help her brothers rid her home of the cursed Normans.

"I don't like this," Alan said. He and Jobert stood on the ramparts above the gate and watched the Saxons file in.

"I know your thoughts well," Jobert answered, "but it is too late to rescind my invitation. I have said we will feast, and so we shall."

"No doubt half of the scheming devils have knives hidden in their belts or daggers in their boots."

"Then they will have to surrender their weapons." Jobert nodded toward the guards who were searching each person as they came in through the gate. A plump, older woman stood in the entryway. As the soldier motioned for her to lift her skirts, she made an outraged noise like a hissing goose.

Jobert looked away. The Saxons could not think him such a fool as to allow them to enter armed.

"You cannot take their eating knives," Alan reminded him. "And iron utensils might be used to cut throats as well as meat."

"Have you so little faith in our men? Do you really believe that we could be overpowered by a group of peasants brandishing puny blades?"

"Nevertheless, I do not like this," Alan grumbled. "Look to the woman, Jobert. Why is she so edgy and restless? When you asked her when the food would be ready, she snapped at you as if you were an impertinent page."

"You know how women are, always fretting over little things. 'Tis no doubt the only feast she has ever hosted, and she seeks to make everything perfect."

Alan snorted. "Your lust for the wench makes you blind. Can you not see how she keeps looking around? I've caught her glancing toward the gate every time she is in the yard. 'Tis as if she expects something to happen."

"Mayhaps she wishes to see how many of her countrymen have come."

"Nay, I wager she wishes to see if the rebels from the forest have readied their attack. Mark my words, disaster is brewing. You'll soon come to find that your magnanimous gesture is wasted on these conniving Saxons." Alan made a disgusted sound and left the tower.

As if to demonstrate the truth of his words, Edeva came

into the yard and immediately looked toward the gate. The expression on her face could only be described as anxious. Jobert stroked his jaw and considered his captain's warning.

After a moment, he climbed down and approached her. "I never realized so many people dwelled in the valley," he told her.

"Yea, and I am surprised they are so eager to come," she answered, her voice tinged with bitterness. "I would think they might fear you would lure them here for a lavish meal and then slaughter them."

"Why would I do that? Without them, I have not the men to tend the fields come spring. They are my people now. I'd be a fool to destroy my own property."

"Property!" she spat. "That is all we are to you!"

Jobert looked at her, startled by her vehemence. He'd thought that Edeva had begun to develop some fondness for him, some acceptance of her lot. Mayhaps Alan was right, and she only pretended compliance. She might still hate him and plot his death behind his back.

A chill moved down his spine as he looked toward the gate. A stooped older man came hobbling into the palisade, supported on either side by two children. Jobert suddenly imagined the man's twisted limbs straightening, the stick he leaned upon transformed into a sword. *A sword aimed at his heart.*

He shook off the image. His men were no fools. They would not fail to search every Saxon, even if they be old or infirm. The rebels might enter the manor, but they would have no weapons to fight with.

Unless they knew of a secret cache inside. He recalled how Edeva had procured two daggers while locked in the bedchamber. There might be other weapon stores. She could lead the rebels to them, even as she had led him to the treasure in the chapel.

"Edeva," he said, "you've done enough to prepare for the feast. You must join me at the high table in the hall."

She frowned at him. "But who will see to the serving of the meal?"

"The kitchen women can manage the rest." He took her arm firmly and began to propel her toward the manor house. "Go now and dress yourself for the meal. I saw many fine garments in the coffer upstairs. Choose one and put it on. And wear a veil or coif over your hair. I would have you look the part of a lady this day."

Edeva hurried downstairs in an amber-hued gunna decorated with gold embroidery. A hammered gold belt of her mother's girded her waist and a circlet set with topaz stones secured the filmy veil over her hair. She felt elegant and queenly, but, as she reminded herself, she had no time for vanity. The fate of Oxbury would be decided today.

She had gone over her dilemma a hundred times, trying to decide a course of action. As soon as her jealous anger had passed, she'd realized that she did not truly want to see the Norman killed, his magnificent body ruined, his proud nature humbled. Vengeance was not a good reason to support her brothers' plan.

But, having made that discovery, her predicament grew even more difficult. She'd waited too long to warn the Norman of the rebels' scheme. He would not cancel the feast now, even if he knew there might be treachery afoot. Instead, if she alerted him to the danger, he would set a trap for her brothers and *they* would die.

Either way, there would be suffering, and she would be responsible.

Her only option was to prevent the confrontation from taking place. As soon as she saw one of her brothers, she must convince him that the Norman knew of their plans and that it would be too dangerous to carry them out.

But she'd lost precious time dressing, and she feared most of the rebels were already inside the palisade, hiding until the attack came.

As soon as she reached the hall, Edeva pushed past the

crowded rows of trestle tables, fast filling up with villagers, and out the door.

Thankfully, the Norman was not in sight as she made a beeline for the gate.

She nodded to Osbert and Payne, the two guards searching the villagers as they entered. "I'm looking for the miller," she told them. "I have something to discuss with his wife. Have you seen either of them?"

Osbert gestured toward the hall. "I think they have already gone inside."

Edeva nodded, deflated. She had not thought the miller would come, and had planned to linger by the gate on the pretense of waiting for him. Now she had no excuse to stay and keep watch for her brothers.

She walked off slowly, trying to think of a new scheme. A faint whistle made her turn, and she saw some one of her father's house ceorls gesturing to her from the shadows near the palisade.

She looked around furtively, then approached the warrior. He held himself bent over, as if he were an older man, and dirt had been smeared on his face to help hide his youthful features.

"What do you here, Edeva?" Ernwin asked. "Do you mean to aid us, or betray us?"

Edeva shook her head. "Neither. I want you to tell Beornwold that he must give up his plan. The Norman knows something is afoot, and he is prepared. 'Twould be suicide to attack."

Ernwin smiled grimly. "Our plans have changed. Beornwold said you would betray us, so he thought of another scheme."

Hot anger swept through Edeva. "I did not betray you. I sought to prevent your deaths! 'Tis too risky to attack the Normans, even from inside the fortress. There are too many of them, and they are too well-armed!"

"But we are cleverer," Ernwin sneered. "We will prevail—despite you."

The man turned and hobbled away, giving a passable

imitation of a decrepit old man. Edeva watched him leave, her stomach churning. There would be bloodshed, and there was naught she could do to prevent it. If she warned the Norman what was to take place, he would search the palisade for the rebels and kill them.

She walked slowly back toward the hall, feeling nearly ill with anxiety and dread. As she reached the doorway, she felt a hand on her arm. Turning, she met the Norman's enigmatic green gaze.

"There you are, Lady Edeva. Come sit beside me at the lord's table. The feast is about to begin."

TEN

A dozen eyes focused upon her as Edeva walked into the hall, and she heard the scraping of benches as the Saxons rose to their feet. Tears filled her eyes as she realized they honored her as the lady of Oxbury. She straightened, remembering her mother. Alegefru always moved with a flowing grace. A sense of poise and calm surrounded her, touching everyone who saw her. *If only she could measure up.*

The miller's wife bobbed a curtsy as Edeva passed. Edeva inclined her head and tried to smile back.

She reached the lord's table. The memory of her mother and father sitting there increased her turmoil.

The Norman helped her sit down in one of the high-backed, ornately carved chairs, then took his place beside her.

Edeva darted a glance his way. She could not guess his mood, and the awful thought came to her that he might have seen her talking to Ernwin. *When the rebels showed themselves, would he think she had been part of their plot?*

She cast an uneasy glance at the man seated on her right. Alan of Fornay. Unlike her gentle watchdog, Rob, this Norman knight felt no warmth toward her. In fact, she suspected he hated her.

Certainly he did not trust her. When the attack came, he would be the first to blame her for helping the rebels.

"Lady Edeva, you look exquisite."

Edeva froze at Brevrienne's compliment, then took a

nervous swallow from the ornate goblet in front of her. It was filled with ale rather than wine. She looked questioningly toward the Norman.

He shrugged. "I believe we should learn to drink what your people do. Although my men will grumble, for certes."

She glanced out into the hall. Tension seemed to crackle in the air like lightning before a thunderstorm. The Saxons sat at the tables, looking wary and uneasy. The Normans stood around the edges of the room, more like guards than revelers at a banquet.

She took a deep breath. With no wine, the Normans would not get drunk nor let down their vigilance. Her brothers' plan would be less likely to succeed.

Was that what she wanted, to see her brothers and countrymen lying dead in the mud?

Of course not, and yet, and yet . . . She did not want the Norman to die, either.

Would he ever believe that, she wondered. Or, had he already marked her as a traitor? If the Saxon assault failed, what would become of her? If he believed she had betrayed him, surely the Norman would kill her.

She shivered. Immediately, she felt the Norman's hand on her shoulder. "Art cold, Edeva?"

She shook her head.

His hand smoothed her hair against her back. " 'Tis pleased I am that you wore you hair down. Your golden tresses bewitch me."

Edeva struggled not to draw away. She'd worn her hair unbraided because she'd not had time to arrange it otherwise. So intent was she on getting down into the yard and warning the rebels, she'd given little thought to her appearance.

But her unbound hair was a lie. It proclaimed her virgin status, which she was no longer.

She was a Jezebel, a Delilah. A traitorous harlot who slept with a man, then brought about his ruin.

To distract herself from her depressing thoughts, she

glanced out at the crowd. The Saxons' tension seemed to be easing. Mayhaps they were pleased by the deference the Norman had shown her. *After all, they wanted her to wed with him!*

The Norman's squire brought a platter of steaming beef and put a thick slice on the trencher in front of Edeva, then ladled glistening rich broth over it. She stared at the food, wondering how she would ever force a mouthful down.

The rest of the hall was also being served. More beef, carried on an enormous board it took two men to carry. Baskets of bread. Pots of vegetable pottage for every table.

Edeva watched the stunned, eager looks on the faces of the villagers. Their stomachs rejoiced at the sight of the bounty before them. For this alone, they would willingly serve the Norman.

The arrival of the food seemed to break the spell which bound the hall. The knights abandoned their posts around the room and sat down at the tables. The Saxons began to talk among themselves. A baby cried. Someone made a jest and others laughed. The mood lightened.

The Norman leader rose. The sound of his chair grating against the dais echoed loudly in Edeva's ear. "A toast," he said, raising his goblet.

The hall fell silent, staring at the man who towered over them, like a giant from one of the ancient stories, a huge, long-limbed Goliath with gleaming hair and a fierce green gaze. "A toast," he said, "to peace and prosperity for Oxbury."

His men grabbed cups and raised them. Slowly, the Saxons did likewise.

Edeva felt the Norman's strength and power reaching out and compelling her people to obey. There was something about this man. 'Twas hard not to look at him and do his will.

"To Oxbury," he said, then surprised them all by speaking in halting Saxon, "peace and prosperity for her people."

A faint gasp swept the room. The Saxons turned and whispered among themselves, amazed that their conqueror had seen fit to learn some of their language. Several of them looked to Edeva, and she recalled the times the Norman had asked her to give him Saxon words for Norman ones. She had complied, thinking his questions rose from his frustration at not being able to communicate directly with the servants and workmen. That he remembered the phrases she gave him astounded her.

He spoke again, raising his goblet in her direction. "To Lady Edeva."

The people in the hall again held up their cups, and the thought shafted through her like an arrow. *He seeks to be generous. And I have repaid him with treachery.*

Jobert speared a piece of fat-laced meat with his eating knife, then flicked it into the open, slobbering mouth of the brindle hound waiting patiently beneath his chair. Even as he performed the movement, his gaze drifted toward the woman beside him.

Like a queen she was, magnificent in a deep golden gown which set off her hair. Every detail of her appearance affected him. The creamy smoothness of her skin made his own flesh ache. The plump softness of her mouth caused his lips to tingle with wanting. The voluptuous curve of her breasts beneath the elegant gown made his whole body thrum with longing. He was uncomfortably, wretchedly aroused.

He looked away, taking a deep breath. Hard to imagine that he had once mistaken her for a man. His wits must have been addled, his vision distorted by his anger over the ambush in the forest. She was the enemy then, so his mind had made her into a man.

But she looked like no warrior now. Every inch of her exuded femininity and womanliness. She was beyond beautiful. Enticing, erotic, a dream come true.

Which made him more wary of her than ever. Was Alan right, did she use her beauty to lure him to his doom?

He tossed a treat to another dog crouched nearby, then resumed watching his tablemate. She kept her face trained upon the trencher in front of her. Did she seek to behave as she thought a demure and proper lady should, or was she hiding something?

Alan's warning words echoed again in his mind, and Jobert turned his gaze to the crowded hall. He saw a people intent on gorging themselves, eating enough beef, bread, cabbage and peas to see them through the long, lean winter. But 'twas a smaller number than he expected. Where were the rest of the Saxons he'd seen entering the palisade?

Uneasy, he inspected his men, making certain they were not succumbing to revelry and drunkenness.

The lack of wine had aided him. Although the Saxons, from children to the aged, drank ale freely from rough pottery beakers, most of his men appeared remarkably sober. They did not favor the bitter taste of the Saxon beverage.

Jobert allowed himself to relax a notch. He should be celebrating. Here he was, lord in his own hall, with a beautiful lady beside him . . .

He jerked upright as there was a commotion in the back of the room. His hand flew to his sword.

Standing, he saw two men facing off. Around them, voices rose in a babble of Saxon and French.

Jobert left the dais and pushed his way through the crowd to the source of the dispute. One of the Saxons, his eating knife flashing, yelled belligerently at a knight named Jocelyn. The Norman had not drawn his sword, but his hand rested on the pommel and his face was twisted into an contemptuous smirk.

"What goes on here?" Jobert demanded.

The room immediately went silent, but no one answered. He glared at his men. "Will no one speak?"

"Milord," Giles stepped forward, "it appears that Sir

Jocelyn said something the miller took exception to. Although how he knew what was said remains a mystery."

Jobert jerked the Saxon around and beheld the man who had defied him during the first days at Oxbury. "So," he said, "mayhaps the miller understands Norman French after all."

From beside Jobert, Alan spoke. "I warned you that he was a crafty devil."

Jobert set his jaw. He would have to punish the man. 'Twould spoil the spirit of the feast, but it could not be helped.

Feeling half-guilty about what he intended to do, he looked toward the dais. Edeva's place was empty.

He glanced around the hall but failed to locate her. A sudden uneasiness went through him. Before he could ask if anyone had seen Lady Edeva, a knight burst into the hall, yelling, "Fire! The kitchen is on fire!"

"The kitchen!" Edeva whispered furiously. "How could you torch the kitchen?"

"Shut up, Edeva," Beornwold hissed back. "We needed a distraction. Kitchens can be rebuilt, so what does it matter?"

They stood in the shadows of the granary within sight of the blazing building. Around them gathered the Saxon forces, two dozen ragged, determined men armed with staves, rusted knives and short swords they had dug up from an old cache of Leowine's.

Looking at them, Edeva felt like weeping with despair. There was no hope they could defeat the well-equipped Normans. None at all. Even with the distraction of the fire.

Which fueled her anger all the more. 'Twould not be easy to replace the kitchen, the pots and spits, the big stone oven and cutting boards, the utensils and serving ware. All of it, destroyed for naught.

"You might as well all go back to the forest," she said. "There is no way you can win."

"Don't listen to her." Beornwold stepped in front of Edeva. "For all we know, a Norman bastard already grows in her belly. And what does she know of warfare? She cannot tell us we are beaten. I say we are not beaten until we try!" His arm swung up in a triumphant gesture.

Edeva tried to push her way in front of Beornwold and talk reason to her countrymen. Strong hands gripped her from behind and a familiar voice coaxed in her ear, "Edeva, we need you. Go now and find the Norman leader. Once he's dead, I doubt his men will fight so furiously. All you have to do is bring him to us."

She turned to face Godric. "Where's Alnoth?" she asked. "Is he well?"

"We did not bring him. In fact, several of the younger men stayed away. I thought it would be better so. In case we do not succeed."

Edeva closed her eyes. If she failed to convince them of the futility of her plan, Saxon blood would run red on the ground of the manor yard. Somehow she must prevent that. "I'll do what you ask," she told Godric.

"Good girl," he whispered.

The yard was a vision of tumult and disorder. The fire had spread to one of the outbuildings, and knights and servants ran here and there, carrying buckets of water from the well and the cisterns. They worked furiously, trying to keep the blaze from spreading further. The vivid glow of the flames eerily illuminated the faces around Edeva. She searched them, seeking the Norman. From what she knew of him, he should be in the thick of things, shouting, cajoling, urging the others on.

She approached the remains of the kitchen shed. The supporting timbers glowed orange against the evening sky, but the rest of the building had collapsed to ashes. Nearby, exhausted servants and soldiers caught their breath. Edeva spied Beorflaed the cook and grasped her arm. "Thank God you were not caught in the blaze!"

Beorflaed shook her head sorrowfully. Her face was smudged with soot, her blue eyes haunted in the dusky mask. "I was fortunate. Edwina and Wulfget did not fare so well."

"Wulfget!" Edeva gasped.

Beorflaed nodded. "Poor thing, she breathed too much smoke and collapsed. And Edwina was burned trying to retrieve the big cooking pot. The Norman and one of his men carried them both into the hall."

"I must go to them," Edeva said.

Inside the hall, frightened villagers lined the long room, their faces stark with dread. The miller's wife clutched at Edeva's sleeve as she passed. "What will happen to us?"

"Nothing," Edeva answered. "The fire is under control. As soon as the danger is passed, you will all go home."

"You're certain?" The woman's eyes were pleading. "You don't fear they will lock us inside here and burn the hall down?"

"Of course not."

Edeva tried to push past her. This time it was the miller himself who halted Edeva's progress. "The soldiers won't let me leave the hall. I fear the worst!"

"This is foolish. Why do you think something is going to happen to you?"

The man's eyes shone defiantly. "Did you not see when I drew my knife upon one of them?"

"Aye," Edeva answered. "Why did you do something so witless?"

The miller thrust his jaw out. "In truth, I do not regret it. I could not endure what he said about Azelina. The man is a pig! First he rapes my wife, then he taunts me with crude remarks!"

Edeva sighed. She did not want to be drawn into this. She had enough difficulties. "You will likely be punished for causing a disturbance during the feast," she told him, "but I doubt it will be anything worse than a quick flogging." She made her voice stern. " 'Twas unwise of you to threaten one of the knights. You are fortunate he did not draw his sword and kill you."

The miller remained mutinous. Edeva looked from the

outraged man to his sweetly pretty spouse. "The Normans hold the power of life and death over all of us," she said. "Do not forget that."

She moved away. The miller's harsh whisper made her stop in her tracks. "What of the rebels?" he hissed. "Are they not going to come and save us?"

Edeva whirled, then glanced around the hall. There was no sign of any knights within listening distance, but her heart still pounded in her chest. She glared at the miller. "I know nothing of any rebels, nor of their plans."

She went to where the kitchen women were gathered. They moved aside as she approached, and she saw stout Edwina lying on one of the benches, her singed forearm cradled against her chest.

The woman struggled to sit up. "I put some lard on it," she told Edeva, "but ooh, it hurts yet."

"Lie down and rest," Edeva said. "I will fetch some healing salve after I examine Wulfget."

Edeva's body went tight with worry at the sight of Wulfget. The young woman's face was ashen, her breathing weak and shallow. Edeva bent over her and felt the thready, faint pulse at her neck.

Guilt tightened around Edeva's neck like a noose. She was responsible for Wulfget, had promised the young woman's parents that she would be safe. If she had warned the Norman about her brothers' plan, she might have prevented this.

She looked toward the doorway. Soon the men waiting behind the granary would realize that she did not mean to bring their quarry to them, and they would attack. She must find a way to stop them.

"Rest now," she said hurriedly to Edwina. "I'll be back anon."

She left the hall and found the Norman leader outside, surrounded by a dozen knights.

"How fare the wounded women?" he asked.

"I fear that one of them is quite ill from the smoke."

He nodded.

From the shadows nearby, the man Fornay spoke, "And where have you been, Lady Edeva? Why are you not fighting the fire? 'Tis your home which is threatened."

"I was seeing to the injured."

"You were not around when we rescued them. Even stranger, you were not in the hall when the alarm was sounded for the fire." He looked to Brevrienne. "Jobert commented on it, did you not?"

The Norman's gaze pierced Edeva, and her throat went dry. Now was the time to tell him about the rebels. But she could not. He and his men would kill her brothers and the rest of them.

"I must leave the fortress," she said. "The miller's wife told me of some herbs she has which make a soothing salve for burns. Besides Edwina, there will likely be others who suffer burns this night."

"Are there no simples and salves in the bedchamber upstairs?" the Norman asked.

"Not like this. The miller's wife told me about this special preparation only a moment ago."

The Norman frowned at her. "You mean to leave the palisade? Now?"

"Oh, she is clever," Fornay sneered. "She leaves the fortress and then the rebels attack. No doubt it is some sort of signal."

"You cannot go alone," the Norman said. " 'Tis not safe."

"I don't mean to go alone," Edeva answered. "I want you to accompany me."

"This is richer yet." Fornay gave a mirthless laugh. "Now she plots to lead you into an ambush."

"I'll take Rob and Hamo," the Norman said. "We'll be fully armed. I don't think a handful of Saxons can defeat us."

"What if there are more than you expect? Nay, my lord! You cannot risk this!"

"Nothing would please me more than to draw the cowards from their forest den where they skulk. They are like a burr in my flesh. I know they wait and watch for their time. I would fight them now and have done!"

Edeva took a deep breath. 'Twas a risky thing she did. By convincing the Norman leader to leave the fortress, she might deter her brothers from attacking. It appeared that they desired his death most of all.

On the other hand, her brothers might see this as their best chance of taking the fortress. If the Brevrienne returned to find the palisade in the hands of the enemy, he would never forgive her.

"I would not wait, my lord," she said. "Edwina is in grievous pain, and I would bring her some relief. Detain me no longer, I beg you."

"We go," he said.

ELEVEN

The night was cold and clear, the black velvet sky adorned with glittering stars, like an unharvested field rampant with poppies and cornflowers. Jobert breathed deep of the crystalline air outside the palisade, eager for a breath not tainted by the noxious reek of smoke.

A shame about the kitchen shed. He'd enjoyed the first truly fine meal he'd had in months. Now the source of that delicious repast stood a blackened ruin.

Not for a moment did he believe it was a chance fire, set by a spark from oven or spit. 'Twas clearly part of a larger plan to distract him and his men.

Yet, the Saxons had not attacked. *Why?*

He could not fathom the enemy's motives. If the blaze were set to draw them out of the hall and into the unprotected yard, then it made no sense that the enemy took no advantage of the situation.

Unless they had another plan—mayhaps for the woman to lure him and his men out of the palisade and then strike.

Jobert's caution increased, as did his wariness toward Edeva. He'd believed her resigned to having Normans control her home. Now he feared that she plotted and schemed like the most hardened of soldiers. *How far would she go to dislodge him from Oxbury?*

The thought made his stomach clench. He and his men might be walking into a trap. Even full armor would not protect them from a large force of attacking Saxons. Ten men or less they could fend off. More than that, they were doomed.

Why did he go? Why follow the woman to what might be his death? Was it because he wanted so desperately to be wrong? To find that she cared for him?

Only the most green-gilled squire would risk his life on a woman's soft heart. And this was not some tender maiden, but a fiery, determined Saxon. What little softness Edeva had shown him had been drawn out of her as a barber pulls an aching tooth. Why could he not accept the truth—that she hated him and wanted him dead!

He glanced ahead, taking in her proud silhouette. She still wore that splendid dress. Though it might be smoke-scented and soiled, and its golden glow hidden under her mantle, that did not diminish his memory of how she looked in it. Like royalty. A provocative, alluring princess. An enchanting beauty who made his cock grow hard and his head spin.

He moved closer to her, thinking that if he survived this night, he would not be put off any longer by her skittish behavior. She had let him bed her once, and he would see that she did so again. He had been too long the courteous, patient knight. 'Twas time he forced her to accept what was between them.

His men's footsteps sounded heavily behind, and Jobert suddenly regretted taking an escort. There were things he needed to settle with the woman, and he wanted to do it without three pairs of eyes looking on.

He paused on the pathway. They were near the village. If they were going to be attacked, 'twould be soon. "Go on ahead," he told his men. "Search the area and make certain no one lies in wait for us."

"But milord," Rob exclaimed, "what of you and the lady?"

"She and I have something to discuss."

Edeva felt the breath leave her body as the knights disappeared into the shadows. This was the moment she had dreaded. *The Norman meant to confront her with her deception.*

He moved closer. His hand came up and rested on her neck. With his other arm he drew her against him. She could feel the heat of his body, the strength. He leaned down so his breath wafted gently against her cheek. "Where are the rebels?" he whispered. "Do they watch us now? Will you betray me with a kiss?"

His lips lightly brushed hers. Edeva's nipples immediately tightened and her loins grew hot.

He released her and stepped away, watching her.

She felt his gaze upon her like blades thrown through the dark, and her body responded with sharp quivers of longing. In the midst of the horror of this night, her desire for this man would not abate; it hummed through her flesh, an ache only he could soothe.

She longed to forget all else—her brothers, the other Normans, the servants and villagers. Banish everything from her mind except the red-haired knight. Succumb to the thrilling hunger he aroused. Surrender to the dangerous passion she saw in his eyes.

"Jobert," she whispered, savoring the foreign, mysterious sound of his name. "I do not betray you."

He released his breath in a sigh, then drew her close and bent his head to kiss her. His lips felt luxuriously warm, his chest so strong and comforting. She wrapped her arms around his neck and leaned into him. One of his thighs pressed between her legs, rubbing against her heated groin. Edeva moaned.

"Damn my wretched mail," he muttered between rough kisses. "I wish that we were alone, and I could take you into one of these cottages, find a bed and make you mine."

Edeva mumbled some breathless assent.

He fumbled under her mantle, searching for openings in her clothes.

"Brevrienne? Ah . . . excuse me, sir, but we've searched the village, and all is quiet."

Jobert swore, then released her. "Thank you, Rob," he

said in a tight voice. He took her hand. "Shall we go now and find that damnable herb you need so badly?"

They walked quickly to the miller's house. One of the knights opened the door for Edeva while another held the torch, lighting her way.

She looked around the main room of the dwelling and wondered where the miller's wife kept her simples. Or, if she had any. Such a timorous creature as Azelina might well wring her hands and run to her mother to treat the slightest ailment.

The torchlight drew Edeva's gaze upward to the loft. Most women kept their simples and herbs either with their foodstores or near their beds. Since she knew Azelina to be a poor cook, that left the other option.

She began to climb the ladder. The wooden rungs creaked. Behind her, she heard the groan of a heavier step as the Norman followed her.

"Can you see?" he asked as she reached the top.

"Yea, well enough."

There was a straw pallet well padded with blankets and cushions. Next to it stood a large chest. Crouching over to avoid hitting her head on the sloping eaves, Edeva went to the chest and opened it.

Only the barest traces of torchlight reached this far, so she had to examine the contents by feel. Clothes. A leather bag which appeared to contain jewelry. Another bag, soft to the touch, containing tiny seeds.

She opened it and inhaled. A familiar but indefinable fragrance tickled her nostrils. She could not discern what it was, especially without looking at the color of the seeds. But no one could deny that it was a herb of some kind.

"I have found it," she said.

She turned and saw Jobert, his head and broad shoulders rising above the top of the ladder. "Come down now," he said. "Unless you wish to try the miller's bed for comfort."

"You'll hit your head if you try to come up," she answered. The heated promise in his voice made her breathless.

He made a sound of frustration, then backed down the ladder.

They walked back to the manor. No one spoke. The tension which hovered over them earlier remained, but in a different form. Edeva's whole body throbbed with unfilled longing.

At the gate, they were met by Fornay and the other guards. "Nothing happened?" he asked, sounding incredulous.

"Nay. She retrieved her herbs as she said she would."

"They must have been scared off for some reason. I cannot believe—"

"Forget it, Alan," the Norman said. "Let the rest of the Saxons leave. The danger has passed, and they will want to return to their homes."

"Should we not search them?"

"You think they rob us?"

"Of course. The thieving wretches will try to take all that is not nailed down or guarded!"

"So they steal a loaf of bread or a chicken. We have food to spare."

"I speak of weapons and valuables."

Jobert turned toward Edeva. "Then they rob from their mistress. What say you?" he asked, looking directly at her. "Do we search your people as they leave?"

She shook her head. "Nay. I do not think they will take overmuch. They have seen your generosity—they will trust you not to let them starve with winter."

"And the weapons?" he asked. "Do you think they steal arms from us?"

"Surely they can see you will look to their defense better than they could themselves."

"Jesu, you cannot take her word for it!" Fornay complained.

"We have no proof that she has done anything deceitful," Jobert said.

"She left the hall before the alarm was even sounded, and she has no good explanation for where she went."

Edeva went rigid, wondering if Fornay would ruin everything. To her relief, Jobert answered, "She does not have to make excuses every time she leaves my side."

"But milord . . ."

"No more," Jobert said. The tone of his voice brooked no argument.

"I must go to the hall," Edeva said. "The herbs require some preparation."

"While you are there, tell the villagers that they are free to leave the palisade."

"What of the miller?" Fornay demanded.

Jobert rubbed his jaw. "I suppose I should punish him. Not for his quarrel with Jocelyn, but for lying to me." He put his hand on Edeva's arm. "What do you recommend, lady? If I show him mercy, do you think he will cease his struggle against my will?"

"If you keep your soldiers from his wife, I think he would gladly do whatever you ask."

He nodded and released her. " 'Twill not be easy. Jocelyn appears to have a genuine fondness for the wench. But the miller's services are valuable to Oxbury. I will ask Jocelyn to turn his attentions elsewhere."

Edeva excused herself and hurried off. Before going to the hall, she took a quick detour to the granary. To her relief, she found no trace of her brothers or their men. They must have dispersed when they discovered that she did not mean to bring them Jobert. Her plan had succeeded.

She headed back toward the hall. As she passed the still-smoldering kitchen shed, she heard a low whistle. Her heart sank as she glimpsed Godric in the nearby shadows.

"What do you here?" she whispered as she ducked beside him. "Where are the rest of them?"

"Gone," he said bitterly. "The fools could not agree on a course of action, so we missed our chance. Why did you fail us, Edeva? 'Twould have been so easy to defeat them once we had their leader. Does he really please you so much that you favor him over your own blood kin?"

"He's done right by Oxbury. Mayhaps if you went to him and said you would be willing to serve him . . ."

"Never! I'll serve no Norman swine! I'd rather die!"

Edeva shook her head, thinking that Godric's angry words might well come to pass.

"Edeva."

She jerked around and saw Jobert standing a few feet away. "Is everything all right?" he asked. "You said that you were going to the hall to prepare the salve."

"I am . . . but I . . . stopped to speak to someone . . ." Edeva glanced behind her and saw that Godric had vanished.

"Who was he?" Jobert asked.

"One of the herdsmen. He does not live in the village."

Jobert drew nearer. "The man seems brawny and strong. We could use men like that when we begin work on the curtain wall next spring."

"I don't know if he would be willing to serve you," Edeva said breathlessly. "I think he would rather live in poverty in the forest than work for a Norman."

"A pity. Men like him will find that there is no place for them in William's England."

Jobert's voice was calm and matter-of-fact. Edeva could not tell if he believed her explanation or not.

"Come to the hall. You have medicine to make."

They went to the manor hall, and Edeva stopped briefly to check on the injured women. Edwina was sitting up, eating heartily, and Edeva spared no more concern for her. But Wulfget had worsened. Her face was paler, her breathing more erratic. "Did you bring her something?" Beorflaed asked.

"Aye, but I must prepare it first. Fetch me some water and put it to boil over the fire. I will go upstairs and find some other things to mix in the brew."

She hurried up the stairs. Thankfully, her mother had taught her something of herbal lore, and she knew how to steep thyme leaves to soothe a cough. And mayhaps there was some poppy juice left, to ease Wulfget's pain. She would have to be careful of the dosage. Wulfget's lungs were badly damaged. If she lay too still, she would be more like to succumb to a fever and die from that.

Edeva used the taper she had taken from the hall to light the lamp in the bedchamber, then went to the storage chests where her mother kept her supplies. Finding the thyme, she wrapped a portion in a cloth to carry downstairs, then remembered the herb she'd brought from the miller's house.

She opened the small sack and spilled a little of the contents in her hand, examining it by firelight. 'Twas difficult to discern one kind of seed from another, but the color and scent of these aroused a memory.

Caraway seeds, she decided. A remedy for griping bowels as well as impotence. She recalled a peddler trying to sell the herb to her mother, jesting with her.

Suddenly Edeva knew the reason for the miller's foolish actions. He dreaded losing his fair, young wife to a more virile man. He had even sought out an aphrodisiac to aid him.

Edeva stared at the caraway, trying to decide what to do with it. No need to dose the Norman, for certes! The very thought was ridiculous. As if he was not as potent as a prize stallion already! But she could not bring herself to discard the seeds. Besides its medicinal uses, caraway was said to be good seasoning for breads and pastries.

Crossing to one of the chests, she stashed the bag inside. If the Norman checked to see that she had made use of the medicine they had gone to so much trouble to procure, she would tell him that it did not take much to make the salve.

Edeva went downstairs and brewed a tea for Wulfget over the fire. She added a bit of poppy juice and swirled it around before offering the drink to the invalid.

Wulfget drank haltingly, gasping between swallows.

Then her eyes closed and she fell back, still breathing in uneven rasps.

Edeva watched her a moment, frowning. The thought that the young woman might die brought her guilt rushing back. She'd promised to look after Wulfget. But how was she to guess that the danger would come not from the Norman knights, but her own kinsmen?

Anger quickly replaced Edeva's worry. Her brothers had never considered that innocent people, *Saxons,* might die in the fire!

"How fares she?"

Edeva looked up to see the Norman standing near. "I do not like the sound of her breathing. If she contracts a fever, there will be little I can do."

"The villagers have left. I was surprised at their numbers. I do not recall so many joining us in the hall."

Edeva said nothing. Though relieved that her brothers and the other men had gone peacefully, she was unsettled by the thought that the Norman had guessed their scheme.

"You look tired, Lady Edeva," he said. "Mayhaps you should retire."

She looked at him, wondering if he meant to join her. Edeva forced her dry mouth to form the words, "Do you come?"

Something flickered in his eyes, then he said, "Mayhaps later. I have things to attend to."

He lay in the silence of the night, wide awake. The bench beneath him seemed unbearably hard. He thought of the comfortable bed in the chamber upstairs. As lord, he had every right to sleep there—as well as avail himself of the other pleasures Oxbury offered.

'Twas ridiculous to deny himself. The woman was clearly willing, even eager, to bed him. If it turned out she was a deceitful, scheming bitch, he would still have had his pleasure of her.

Why shouldn't he climb the stairs and crawl into the

soft, warm bed? Relieve his burning lust between Edeva's silken thighs?

The thought made a shiver of yearning vibrate through him.

Which was why he did not do it. Because he wanted her far too badly. He could not be sure that in the act of joining their bodies, he did not lose what little objectivity and reason he had left.

Alan argued that she was a traitor. Jobert's instincts told him that she was not. But those instincts might be hopelessly skewed by his feelings for the woman. If he bedded her, knew the wonder of her compliant, passionate response, he would be even more lost.

He wanted to trust her, ached to trust her. But to do so would be madness. His grip upon Oxbury remained tenuous. Tonight, they had come within a hairsbreadth of attack.

He knew it, felt it in his very bones. The rebels had been inside the palisade. He had seen Edeva talking to one of them. A tall, well-made Saxon. Her lover?

Jealousy heated his blood.

Nay, Edeva had been a virgin when he took her. If she'd had a fondness for one of her father's warriors, she'd not acted upon it.

Jobert recalled the brief scene in his mind. Although he had not understood their words, he believed that Edeva and the Saxon had been arguing. There was tension in their bodies, an edge to their lowered voices. Could it be that Edeva had persuaded the rebels not to attack? That she had been trying to help him?

His heart favored this explanation. His weak, blind, foolish heart.

But how could he trust that part of himself? His devotion to Damaris had nearly cost him his life, had caused him years of disquiet and unhappiness. 'Twas dangerous to care for a woman.

And all the more dangerous if the object of a man's affections were not an unattainable Norman maiden, but a passionate, fiery hellcat whose people were his deadly enemies!

Edeva was no meek creature to be forced into accepting the will of her conqueror. She would do what she believed right, and damn the consequences. If only he had convinced her that supporting him was the wisest course. She obviously cared deeply for Oxbury and its people. If he could make her understand that he had Oxbury's best interests in mind, she might decide to uphold his authority.

But that was what he had been trying to do, and still he was not sure of her. He could not forget that she had ties to some of the rebels—brothers, uncles, cousins. There was always the worry that those bonds of kinship were stronger than her concern for Oxbury.

Jobert shifted on the bench as his tired muscles protested. He could not endure this self-denial and doubt much longer. He must find a way to determine Edeva's loyalties or he would lose his mind.

He turned over a final time, then forced himself to close his eyes and seek a few hours of sleep before dawn.

TWELVE

Edeva awoke to the sound of banging and crashing. The realization that they were tearing down the remains of the kitchen shed spurred her to get out of bed and dress.

'Twas barely dawn. Only the faintest light seeped through the crack between the shutters. The Norman was up and ordering his men very early, especially considering all the activity of the night before. Mayhaps he had not slept at all. Certainly, he had not joined her in the bed-chamber.

Why not, after his tantalizing words? Did he think her a traitor, and was loath to be near her because of it? If only he had not seen her talking to Godric. She sensed that discovering her in the company of a Saxon had made Brevrienne suspicious.

But was that all it was? Doubts suddenly crowded her mind. 'Twas foolish to assume the Norman cared for her, or even desired her. His passionate words might have been a means of getting her to let down her guard so she would reveal her involvement with the rebels. Once he was satisfied she did not plot against him, there had been no reason for him to follow through on his whispered promises.

A stab of anguish went through her. The Norman might have no interest in bedding her at all. He'd used the threat of rape to manipulate her in the beginning, but since then, he'd made no advances except when he wanted something of her—her aid in running the manor, her help in winning the support of the people of Oxbury, and finally, last night, her promise not to betray him to the rebels.

The wretched truth stared Edeva in the face. Golde had said that Brevrienne meant to wed some elegant Norman woman. If he had a betrothed to take his name and bear his children, and Golde to ease his lust, he really had no use for Edeva—except to manage his household and smooth his way with the servants and villagers.

Edeva's stomach felt queasy as she began to comb the tangles out of her hair. Her brothers had called her an "overtall, unfeminine wench," and said that no man would want her, except for her rich dowry. Now her dowry was gone. The Norman already possessed her lands; he did not need the bride who went with them.

She fought her growing anger and despair. The Norman had bedded her once, and to her mind at least, it seemed he had enjoyed it. He had said fond words to her on several occasions, and sometimes the look in his eyes seemed genuinely admiring. Mayhaps he did care for her—a little.

'Twas not enough!

The vehemence of the thought startled Edeva. *How had she come to hunger so terribly for her enemy's regard?*

She jerked the comb through her hair a final time, then rapidly began to plait it. 'Twas witless to worry about these things; she had much more serious problems to occupy her. There was Wulfget to tend . . . rebuilding the kitchen shed . . . getting the manor back to normal . . .

She forced her mind to concentrate on the multitude of duties awaiting her. With a twist of a worn ribbon, she fastened the braid, then left the bedchamber.

As soon as Edeva entered the hall, Beorflaed approached her, looking grim. Wulfget had worsened. Beorflaed feared she now had a fever.

The young woman's forehead did feel warm to the touch, and Edeva advised Beorflaed to steep some willow bark and give the infusion to the injured woman. She would see about having the healer come if Wulfget did not improve.

Edeva left the hall, wondering if she should fetch the healer, Helwenna. It would require another journey to the village, and Edeva was not certain how the Norman would react to the idea. He might wonder why she did not mention the healer the night before, but instead insisted on getting the herb from the miller's house. In truth, Edeva simply had not thought of the ruse of fetching Helwenna. In her desperation to get the Norman out of the palisade, she had seized upon the first excuse which came to her.

Edeva crossed the yard to where the knights and workmen were demolishing the black skeleton of the kitchen. She gained their attention, then warned them not to drag everything away as refuse, but to search for things which might be salvaged and reused. Pottery, stone and metal objects did not burn and could be cleaned up and refurbished. She especially admonished them to be on the watch for the hearthstone, the walls of the bread oven, even bits of wooden utensils which might not have been ruined.

As usual, she had to repeat her instructions in both Saxon and Norman French so both groups of workers could understand her. As the men nodded and expressed their consent, Edeva wondered where Brevrienne was. The restoration of the kitchen was crucial to the well-being of the manor. Why wasn't he supervising the job more closely?

"I tell you, the fire was set deliberately, and some of the Saxons must know who did it," Alan said. "Mayhaps they would tell us if the right sort of pressure were applied."

"You mean torture?"

Alan shrugged. "Or even the threat of it. Most servants and peasants are weak-willed, full of fear and anxiety. 'Tis only a matter of intimidating them, and I believe they would give up the rebels."

Jobert fingered the pommel of his sword and stared at the rows of mail shirts and helmets hung on pegs on the stable wall. He had agreed to join Alan here to talk privately about the events of the night before.

"What good would it do if you did get them to speak?" he asked. "If they told us the name of the man or men who set the fire, we would still have to find them. And you know my feelings about scrambling around in the woods searching for the rebels' camp. 'Twould be pure foolishness."

"How can you be so certain that it was one of the rebels? One of the workmen or the villagers could have set the fire."

"Because I believe the rebels were inside the palisade yesterday."

"One or two, mayhaps," Alan said doubtfully, "but I cannot imagine . . ."

"Not one or two. The whole lot of them."

"But how?"

"Can you discern the difference between a village sokeman and one of the old thegn's warriors?" Jobert shook his head. "They were here. I noted a large discrepancy between the number of Saxons who came in the gate and those who joined us in the hall. The enemy was within our very walls. *They* set the fire."

"But why didn't they attack?" Alan demanded.

Jobert stroked his whisker-roughened jaw. "I don't know. I pondered the matter for most of the night, but could come upon no explanation except that Edeva convinced them to leave peaceably."

"Edeva?" Alan snorted. "Why would she miss a chance to rid her home of us hated Normans?"

"She cares for the welfare of her people, and she must realize that an armed conflict inside the palisade would be disastrous."

"She cares for her people, yea, but she also cares for the cause of the rebels. The Saxon wench obviously has ties to some of them. I vow she will not forget her kin!"

Jobert sighed, acknowledging the truth of Alan's words. Despite the angry exchange between Edeva and the Saxon warrior, they clearly knew each other well.

Alan's voice softened. " 'Tis clear you care for her, which is exactly why I question your judgment. Remember, this is not some shy, gentle-hearted maiden like Damaris. When we first encountered her, Lady Edeva appeared as fierce and formidable as any warrior. There is no reason to think her nature has changed."

"Mayhaps you are right. When I see her dressed in feminine garments . . ."—or spectacularly naked, a voice in Jobert's head added—"I forget how ruthless and determined she can be."

Alan nodded. "I tell you, I am wary of Saxon women. Though some of them are fair to look upon, I would not marry one, unless the king himself ordered it. After I make my fortune here, my intention is to return to Lisieux and find a proper Norman wife."

He had also tried not to entangle himself with a Saxon woman, Jobert thought, but it had not worked. In the beginning, he'd seen Edeva as a means to an end, a way to secure his newly-acquired manor and see that it prospered. But things had changed in the past few weeks. His passion for Edeva had grown, her place in his thoughts expanded until he could barely remember what Damaris had meant to him.

"Have you ever bedded a virgin?" he asked Alan.

Alan shook his head. "Nay, that sort of woman can seldom be had except by marriage, and until now, I've not dared hope to wed."

Jobert stared off into the distance, remembering the incredible experience of making love with Edeva. Was it because she was a maiden that it had seemed so wonderful, so utterly unforgettable?

An alert sounded at the gate, breaking his reverie. Both men reached for their swords, then hurried into the yard.

Edeva was in the buttery, trying to figure out what they were going to eat until the bread oven could be rebuilt, when she heard the commotion. She made her way past the precious foodstores and went out, locking the door behind her with the key at her belt.

Anxious thoughts whirled through her mind, mostly concerning her brothers mounting an attack against the palisade in broad daylight. But her worries did not prepare her for the sight of a dozen Normans in full armor riding through the gate.

She shrank back against the sheltering wall of the manor house and watched as Brevrienne went to meet them. He wore no armor, only the tunic and hose she had made him, but he appeared formidable, taller than all the rest of the men, his long hair blowing wildly around his face.

He spoke with the visitors as they dismounted and squires took their horses.

Edeva left her hiding place and hurried to the manor house. In the breathless moments before the visitors entered, she tried to compose herself. Should she greet them as though she were the lady of the household? And how would Brevrienne behave? How would he introduce her?

She waited in the shadows as the knights entered. Brevrienne gestured that the men should seat themselves, then he barked to the women spinning wool by the fire, "Bring us wine." The Saxon women regarded him with frightened eyes but made no move to obey.

Edeva stepped forward and the Norman saw her. "Ah, Lady Edeva," he said. "See that refreshments are brought for our guests."

Edeva tried to get his attention, finally moving to his side. "Milord," she said. When he looked at her, she bent low to speak in his ear. "I thought the wine was gone."

"There is another cask in the stables. I had my squire hide it in a recess in the wall behind where the armor is kept. Find Will and have him drag it out for you."

"What of food? We have no oven and naught but a few loaves of bread left from yesterday."

"Bring what bread there is, and the remainders of the beef. 'Twill have to do."

Edeva left him, feeling irritated. He treated her as if she

were one of the servants. But then, was it not the lot of women to serve men? She was doing no more than what her mother had done when they had guests.

"That's the Saxon thegn's daughter?" Iovin of Masey asked as Edeva left the hall.

Jobert nodded. "Without her aid, I could not have accomplished so much in the few weeks since we arrived. She is very capable, and she speaks Norman French quite well."

"Have you thought of wedding with her?"

The idea startled Jobert. Had he not vowed that if he could not have Damaris, he would take no other wife?

"After all, William advised his earls to secure their lands by proper, legal methods as he wants no quibble with the Church about the righteousness of his conquest," Iovin pointed out. "It seems to me that wedding the old thegn's daughter would be the ideal means of securing the property—Oxbury, I believe it is called in Saxon?"

Jobert nodded slowly.

The Norman knight saw his befuddled expression and grinned. "I know an uncultured Saxon may not be what you'd hoped for in a wife, but consider it a means to an end. Once you have gained your fortune, you can return to Normandy and take a proper lady to wife. The Bastard need never know of it!" Iovin threw back his head and laughed.

"Lady Edeva is not uncultured," Jobert said tightly. "Indeed, her skills in running a household rival those of any woman I've known. Her needlework is extraordinary, her ability to calculate the amount of food—"

"Hear, hear," Iovin interrupted, still laughing. "I meant no offense, Brevrienne. Obviously, you find no fault with the wench. If you're that fond of her, I would not delay in asking William for her hand. You must have his permission before you wed her. Although he advised his captains to secure their new estates by any legal means, he is wary of men who show too great a relish for seizing power. He fears the troubles his family has had in Normandy may follow him here to England. He wants his barons to be strong, but not overly independent."

Jobert stared unseeingly at the table in front of him. If he wed Edeva, he might better be able to control her. From what he knew of her, she was not the sort to betray her husband, even if she had married the man less than willingly.

Besides, if he wed her, he would have the right to bed her *anytime he wanted*.

"How would you suggest that I go about petitioning the king?" Jobert asked.

"I have a man among my force who is headed for Winchester. He could carry a message for you. From there, couriers carry reports to Normandy nearly every fortnight."

"Unfortunately, I have no scribe, and although I cipher well enough, my letters are scarcely legible. Do you also have a cleric among you who could pen a message for me?"

"Your prayers are answered, Brevrienne. It seems the bishopry at Winchester has sent a man named Father Reibald to serve at Oxbury." Iovin gestured to a cowled figure near the doorway. "His first duty could be to write your message to the king."

"I did not request a priest be sent."

"Nevertheless, there he is. Mayhaps William ordered the bishopries to send holy men to every manor claimed in the king's name."

Jobert regarded the priest uneasily. When he had caught the cleric's eye, he gestured that the man should join them.

"Lord Brevrienne." The priest bowed his tonsured head politely as he approached. "I have been sent to Oxbury to succor the spiritual needs of its people." He reached for the purse slung across his rounded shoulders and withdrew a rolled parchment. "I have a letter from Bishop Walchelin."

Jobert waved the parchment away. "Your word is

enough, Father Reibald. 'Tis only that I am surprised to learn that the Bishop concerns himself with a small demesne such as Oxbury."

The priest smiled, although the expression did not warm his wintry gray eyes. "Bishop Walchelin is an amazing man. Like the Lord himself, he takes it upon himself to attend even the smallest sparrow."

Jobert's unsettled feeling grew. Could he trust this man to write a message to William? He truly had no choice. It could be weeks before he had another opportunity. He could not spare a man to act as courier, and at any rate, it would not be safe for a lone rider to make such a journey.

Two squires entered the hall, rolling the last precious cask between them. They tapped it and cups were filled all around. Jobert toasted the visitors and waited for the servants to bring the food. There was no sign of Edeva. He began to wonder if she would ever return.

"Tell me," Jobert said, intending to distract the visitors from his poor hospitality, "what brings you to Oxbury? Are you passing through on the way to the coast?"

"Nay, 'tis you I seek, Brevrienne. I have come on behalf of the king. In Gloucestershire some of the rebel Saxons have joined forces with the Welsh and have begun to harry Ralph of Berkeley's lands. William would have you send forces to aid Berkeley in ridding his property of these noxious vermin."

"But I have my own troubles here," Jobert protested. "Last night, the kitchen shed was set afire, and I'm certain it was the doing of the dispossessed Saxons. If I send a force of my men to aid Berkeley, I leave my own holdings at risk."

Iovin made a harsh sound. "The king counts Gloucestershire as a strategic buffer with the north, while he sees this area as already won. 'Tis not merely you whom he calls upon for support and men, but all of the Wiltshire lords."

"But if I send men to serve him, I diminish the security of my own property."

Iovin nodded. "If you came yourself, you could get away

with bringing fewer knights. More than numbers, the king values experience fighting the Saxons, and you have that, Brevrienne."

Jobert considered the other soldier's words. Would a larger force left in charge of Oxbury fare better than himself and fewer men? Was it sheer numbers which kept the Saxons from attacking, or fear of him?

And then there was Edeva. His leaving might encourage her to show her true nature. If she were a part of a rebellion against his authority, he would know that she still intended to drive him from her home, despite her cooperation in other matters. Before he wed her, he should know for certain if she plotted against him or not.

"Berkeley expects a band of Brevrienne knights to meet him in Gloucestershire in three days," Iovin said. "I suggest you make arrangements."

At that moment, Edeva entered the hall, followed by servants bearing platters of cold meat and baskets of bread and round white cheeses. It was not the food which drew Jobert's attention, but Edeva. She had changed from her sensible work kirtle into a gown of soft blue wool. While not as striking as the one she had worn to the feast, the garment brought out the vivid color of her eyes, the milky perfection of her skin and the gilded luster of her golden braids.

Jobert stared at her, thinking he would have the priest pen the message to William that very day. It hardly mattered whether she was a spy or no—he wanted this woman.

"You keep a well-ordered household, Lady Edeva. The inhabitants of Oxbury must find favor in the eyes of the Lord to have such a competent mistress."

Edeva murmured her thanks to the priest, wondering if he were sincere. His narrow face and keen gray eyes struck her as crafty and sly, his whole manner slightly condescending. No wonder Brevrienne had asked her to show the priest to the chapel and his quarters. The Norman likely did not feel any more at ease with the cleric than she did.

She glanced over at the priest as they walked across the yard and saw that he was picking his teeth with one of his grimy fingers. Inwardly, she shuddered. Although she knew some holy men disdained bathing as a worldly affectation, Father Reinbald's slovenly appearance still disgusted her.

" 'Twas a fine meal," the priest said. "You are fortunate that more of your foodstores weren't lost when the kitchen burned. I suppose kitchen fires are common, although I have heard talk among the men that this one was set deliberately."

Edeva felt a shiver of warning, but she said calmly, "Who told you that, Father?"

"One of the knights spoke of a plot among the servants. They planned that the fire would distract the Normans while other Saxons attacked from outside the manor."

Edeva met the priest's opaque gaze. "Well," she said, "their plan did not succeed, did it?"

They reached the chapel. The door creaked as Edeva opened it. She set the smoking lamp in a bracket by the entrance and took a rushlight and went to light the candles along the nave.

" 'Tis finer than I would have guessed." Father Reibald walked toward the altar. "It must have cost a small fortune to build this."

"My father built it for my mother as a gift."

The priest turned to face her. His long face appeared somehow sinister in the flickering candlelight. "You must despise the Normans for taking all of this from you."

Edeva froze. Had the Norman asked the priest to spy on her?

The cleric moved nearer. "Has Brevrienne forced you to share his bed?" He tsked sadly when she did not answer. "Men like Brevrienne have no subtlety. A pity King William did not give Oxbury to someone deserving of it, instead of a common knight."

This remark surprised Edeva so much, she could not help asking, "A common knight? What do you mean?"

The priest tsked again. "Jobert Brevrienne is a nobody, a younger son who cannot claim even an acre of land in Normandy. If not for King William's absurd generosity toward the knights who fought at Hastings, Brevrienne would be no more than a paid soldier to this day."

"He seems well educated and honorable," Edeva said. The priest's criticisms of Brevrienne set her on edge. "His manners are quite pleasing."

The priest scowled at her. "Don't be a fool. I can see that you are from a family of wealth and nobility. Don't waste yourself on a man like Brevrienne."

The priest's words startled Edeva. She was on the verge of asking him what he thought she should do about her circumstances when there was a creaking sound.

They both turned and saw Brevrienne standing in the doorway, his tall frame filling the entrance.

Edeva's cheeks felt hot. Despite the fact that the priest was the one who spoke disloyally, she was unsettled by the Norman's sudden appearance. *Would he think she plotted with the priest?*

"Have you shown Father Reinbald where he will sleep?" Brevrienne asked.

"Nay, I did not have a chance yet," Edeva answered.

"I will do it," Brevrienne said. "Bleorflaed is looking for you."

Edeva hurried toward the door. As the entryway was narrow, Brevrienne had to move aside so she could get by. Their arms brushed as Edeva passed him.

A familiar aching warmth rose in her loins, and she was halfway to the manor hall before she could gain control over her nerves once again.

"A beauty, isn't she?" Father Reibald said as Edeva left.

Jobert nodded. His flesh still hummed with the thrill of having been so near to her.

"For a Saxon, that is," the priest added. "A handsome people, but treacherous and cunning. I vow the king will have his hands full subduing them."

Jobert regarded the priest warily. Had Edeva said something to the cleric to make him suspect her of deceit?

Father Reibald cleared his throat. "From what I gather, Brevrienne, you have been a most generous conqueror, yet the Saxons still plot your overthrow. Does that not anger you?"

"In what way do you think they plot against me?"

"All of Oxbury knows that the kitchen fire was set deliberately. Most commanders would be determined to wipe out all trace of resistance. They would not let such a thing go unpunished."

Jobert poked the toe of his boot into the pool of hot wax collecting beneath one of the candles by the rail. "How am I to know for certes who is to blame? Do you think I should make all the Saxons suffer for the actions of a few?"

"Some would say 'tis your duty to impose your will upon these lands, no matter how distasteful you find the responsibility. King William is not known for his lenience, and he might not understand your squeamishness in carrying out his laws."

Jobert struggled to keep his temper under control. The priest seemed to be deliberately baiting him, although why, he did not know. He kept his voice smooth as he asked, "And have you seen William recently then, Father? Is that why you imagine yourself so intimately acquainted with his wishes?"

The priest shifted, like a hawk whose feathers have been ruffled. "I have not had the honor of being in King William's presence since the coronation. I merely repeat what I have heard upon the lips of so many of his trusted commanders. They all speak of the dishonor and perfidy of the English."

"I have not found the Saxons to be particularly untrustworthy," Jobert said. "There is a pocket of rebels in the woods who would do anything to rout me from Oxbury, but the rest of the people—I am confident they will eventually come to accept me as their lord."

The priest shrugged. "You must do as you see fit, Brevrienne. Although I pray your faith in the English is not misplaced. As I understand it, you and a party of your men are being called up to do battle against Saxons in the north. I hope nothing disastrous befalls the manor in your absence."

Jobert's jaw clenched. The priest's warning echoed his own worries. What a wretched time for the king to call him into service. Only a few more weeks, and he would be much more confident of his hold upon Oxbury, as well as where things stood between him and Edeva. Which reminded him . . .

"I have a task for you already, Father," he said. "I want you to write out a missive to the king. I am petitioning him for the right to wed Lady Edeva. I would have my hold upon Oxbury strengthened by the holy bonds of matrimony."

"Tomorrow I leave Oxbury with a force of soldiers to join another lord in fighting Saxon rebels on his lands."

Jobert watched Edeva carefully as he made his announcement. They were alone in the bedchamber. He had asked her to meet him there as it afforded the only real privacy in the manor.

Something flickered in her eyes. Surprise? Satisfaction? "How long will you be gone?"

"I owe the king service for a month, longer if the need is dire."

She nodded. "Who will you leave in charge here?"

"Sir Alan."

This time there was no mistaking her expression of displeasure. Either she disliked Alan or she guessed he would prove a formidable opponent if the rebels decided to attack.

She raised her eyes to his. "How many men go with you?"

A shaft of disappointment went through Jobert. Her question could only mean she sought to assess how well the manor would be guarded in his absence. "I take only ten men, and leave a garrison here of forty knights."

She nodded again, her manner stiff and formal. Hard to imagine they had once indulged in passionate, uninhibited lovemaking.

Unthinkingly, he looked toward the bed. When he glanced back at her, he saw her cheeks had flushed. She, too, remembered.

He cleared his throat. "You have done well in overseeing the servants and workmen. I hope you will continue in my absence."

"Of course, my lord." Her voice sounded strained, almost melancholy. Was it possible that she would miss him? Mayhaps that afternoon meant something to her after all. For certes, he could not forget it. His mouth went dry merely at the memory, and his shaft grew hard.

He looked again at the bed, considering. Four long sennights he would endure a grim soldier's existence, sleeping on the hard ground with naught but a bedroll for comfort. Why should he not avail himself of this woman's bounteous pleasures before he left?

His breathing quickened at the thought of her spread out beneath him, all spun-gold hair and skin of rose and cream. And all that glory awaited him a mere arm's length away.

Edeva repressed a sigh. He was leaving. She'd once longed for this day, but now that it was here, she felt a sense of loss rather than triumph. The thought of being left alone with Fornay's cold, knowing glances and Father Reibald's sly innuendos made her feel sick inside.

And then there were her brothers. They would take Brevrienne's departure as a clear signal to attack the manor. Could he not see that he was throwing her to the mercy of the wolves who circled Oxbury?

She wanted to argue that he could not go, but she knew he would not heed her. Mayhaps this was a test, a trap devised to discover where her loyalties lay. If the Norman returned to find Oxbury lost, she had no doubt that he would seek vengeance.

But at this moment, vengeance seemed the last thing on his mind. The green of his eyes had deepened, becoming the shade of foliage in the depths of the forest. His nostrils flared, like a hungry man scenting a banquet.

Waves of longing echoed inside her. If he reached for her, she would not resist.

A knock sounded at the door. "Brevrienne, my lord, Sir Iovin requests your presence below."

The Norman grimaced in acknowledgment. Edeva felt the mood shatter.

Brevrienne left. As he opened the door, she caught a glimpse of Fornay on the stairs. A slight smile lit his dark, handsome features.

Edeva started toward the storage chests. A stool lay in her pathway; she gave it a kick. Damn Fornay, if it were not for him, she might have had another chance!

But the stupid knight had interfered, deliberately. If ever she had an opportunity to repay him, she would do so.

She jerked off her gunna, then took her comb and began to violently unsnarl her hair.

THIRTEEN

"Milady, I would have a word with you." Golde spoke softly as she leaned close to fill Edeva's cup with ale at the evening meal.

Edeva stiffened with irritation. She could not bear the thought that Brevrienne had bedded this smug-faced servant woman. That he had left the day before without even returning to the bedchamber to say goodbye made her mood even more foul. "Speak, then," she answered harshly.

A slight smile played over Golde's face. "I do not think this is the place to give you a message from Beornwold."

Edeva's annoyance turned instantly to anxiety. "Where?" she asked the servant.

"Follow me while I get more pottage," Golde suggested.

Edeva got up slowly and went to the main hearth, which was being used as a cooking fire until the kitchen could be repaired. Golde leaned over and stirred the kettle of dried beans and peas simmering over the fire. "Beornwold says he must speak with you. Find some excuse to go to the village. He will meet you there."

"Does Beornwold not know I am watched?" Edeva hissed.

"He knows of your situation. But he believes you are clever enough to dupe the Normans. Are you, Edeva?" Golde's amber eyes glinted. "Mayhaps you need some advice on dealing with men. I vow I could arrange the matter easily, if I were in your place."

Edeva's fingers twitched to slap the woman's arrogant face, but she restrained herself. This was not the time nor place to display her jealousy.

"Tell Beornwold that I will try to meet him, but he must give me some time to arrange it."

"Do not delay long. You know how impatient your brother is. He said to tell you that if you ignore this summons, I am to go to Sir Alan and reveal that you have been working with the rebels all along." Golde cocked her head toward Fornay, who sat at the far end of the high table. "I imagine *that* Norman would be delighted to believe the worst of you."

Edeva's blood was boiling. Bad enough that she must endure Golde's gloating; she would not tolerate the slut threatening her! She forced a confident smile to her lips. "You overestimate your power, wench. Fornay may command the garrison, but he would not be so stupid as to take action until his leader returns."

"Think you that he would not have you flogged for fear of Brevrienne's wrath? Poor Edeva, what a miserable judge of men you are." Golde spoke in a low, almost purring voice. "This Norman hates you. He would love to see you endure some painful, humiliating punishment."

A shiver passed down Edeva's spine as she realized the truth in Golde's words. Unlike Brevrienne, whose actions were tempered by feeling for her, Fornay would not restrain his fury if she were revealed as a spy. She doubted he would risk having her put to death, but he might do as Golde said and have her whipped. The thought of it horrified Edeva, not so much for dread of the pain, but the disgrace. How would she ever hold up her head among her people if they saw her so brutally humbled?

Golde moved away, her expression smug. Edeva watched her go to Fornay and fill his bowl with soup. Golde leaned close so that one of her honey-colored braids fell against the Norman's shoulder. Fornay looked up and gave Golde a look that was condemning but also lustful.

An idea came to Edeva. Like any man, Fornay was prey to weaknesses of the flesh. If she could find some woman capable of enticing him, she would have a weapon to balance his mistrust of her.

But the dark-visaged Norman seemed immune to the fairer sex. Edeva had never seen him dally with the serving women, nor did he respond to the few, like Golde, who openly tried to seduce him.

A pity. She needed some sort of leverage over Brevrienne's captain.

Edeva glanced again at Golde, now using her charms on poor, tongue-tied Osbert. Though she dreaded doing so, Edeva realized she had no choice but to obey her brother's summons. She could not risk Golde carrying tales to Fornay.

In truth, she had a real reason to go to the village. Wulfget had not improved, and it was time to see if the healer had any advice on how to help the injured woman.

She crossed to where Fornay sat. "Sir Alan," she said, trying to train her voice to submissiveness, "do you recall the young woman who was injured in the fire? Not the one who was burned, but the other, who breathed in the smoke?"

Fornay nodded, his face wary.

"She grows worse, and I know not what to do for her. I would like to take her to the healer in the village."

"Why cannot the healer come here?"

"Old Helwenna suffers from a disease that twists her joints and made them ache. She cannot walk without great pain."

"So, you contrive that we should take the wounded woman there?"

Edeva nodded. "You may accompany us yourself if you fear trickery."

Fornay's dark eyes pierced her. Edeva endured his gaze, confident he could find no deception in her face.

Wulfget's need was real. He would realize that when he saw the young woman.

Wulfget lay on a pallet piled with blankets. She tried to raise her head as Edeva and Fornay approached.

"Nay, do not bestir yourself," Edeva said. "We've come to help you."

Wulfget's huge iris blue eyes rested on Fornay, then she looked at Edeva, her expression full of fear. "The Norman," she whispered, "what does he here?"

"He means to help you. He's going to escort us into the village to see the healer."

Edeva's words did not seem to ease Wulfget. Her already milk-white skin grew paler still. Her stunning eyes widened.

Edeva shot a quick glance at Fornay. "She fears you," she told him. "She sees you as one of the monsters who have hurt so many of her people."

"I would never hurt such a delicate flower," he said, his expression troubled. "Tell her that."

Edeva gave the Norman a sharp look. *Delicate flower?* Mayhaps Fornay liked his women fragile and needy.

She turned her attention back to the wounded woman. "Wulfget, you know you can trust me. I would not have brought the Norman here if I thought he meant you harm. You must not fear him."

The young woman gazed at Fornay a moment, then lay back with a sigh.

"I will carry her," Fornay said. " 'Tis clear she cannot walk."

"Nay, she has not the strength for that. But we could arrange a litter."

Fornay shook his head. "I will carry her. She will be more comfortable that way."

He leaned over the bed and prepared to pick up Wulfget. Edeva tensed, wondering if the young woman would anger him by pulling away.

She need not have worried. Wulfget lay passive and still

as the knight lifted her. As he straightened, she reached a slender arm around his neck and pressed her face to his chest.

"She scarce weighs anything," Fornay said. "Her bones are like those of a bird."

"She has not eaten well since the injury," Edeva said as they left the hall. "And she was never very robust."

"Are you certain she is a Saxon? I've seen no other women here who look like her."

"She may have Danish blood," Edeva allowed. "But she has lived at Oxbury all her life, and her parents look the same as any of the villeins."

"Is she a virgin?"

Fornay's question startled Edeva, then she grew angry. "Wulfget was raised as a modest, virtuous girl," she snapped. "Unless one of your men has raped her, she is a maiden still."

"One such as her could not endure a crude defloering and keep her wits intact," Fornay mused. "I believe she remains untouched."

At the gate, Edeva said, "Are you not going to take an escort?"

Fornay adjusted his delicate burden. "Do you think it necessary? Are your countrymen going to attack us?"

Edeva gritted her teeth. This man was impossible! "I know naught of their plans, but it seems a reasonable precaution. Brevrienne always took a guard when he left the palisade."

"And how do I know that you do not seek to lure a greater number of Normans outside where we will make easy targets?"

"Jesu, do you think me so heartless as to involve *her* in an ambush?" Edeva asked bitterly, gesturing toward Wulfget. "Even the best shot among our archers would be hard put to hit you without risking her life as well."

"I think the rebels care little for the life of one small Saxon maid," he retorted. "I believe they might well consider her a worthy sacrifice if they met their goal of killing me. Did they think of her welfare when they set the fire?"

Edeva felt a weight settle on her shoulders at his words. Wulfget had already been injured because of her brothers' ruthlessness. They might indeed think her life inconsequential in the scheme of their plans. "Take an escort or no," she told the knight. "I merely give you the benefit of my advice."

Fornay stared at her, as if trying to read her thoughts. Finally, he said, "Very well, we take an escort. Payne!" he called up to the guardhouse. "Find another man to watch the gate. You and Warmund will come with us to the village."

Helwenna's healing skills had made the healer an object of awe and trepidation to the rest of village, and for that reason, she lived some distance beyond the main group of dwellings. Edeva watched the Norman knight's eyes narrow in distaste at the sight of the shabby hut.

"Helwenna has no one to care for her, and her health is too poor for her to do many things," she said. "Do not judge her harshly. She is Wulfget's best hope for recovery."

The knight glanced at the woman in his arms and tenderly shifted her weight.

Edeva bent down and led the way into the hovel. The smell almost made her gag. Gradually, her eyes adjusted to the noxious haze and she was able to see the healer, propped up on a pallet in the corner. She was a huge woman, plump as a stoat. Tufts of thinning hair stuck up from her large, round head, and her dark eyes missed nothing.

"Helwenna," Edeva said. " 'Tis Edeva, Leowine's daughter. I've brought someone who needs your aid."

The woman sat up awkwardly. "My, you've grown into a pretty one," she said. In the murk, Edeva caught the gleam of Helwenna's crafty gaze. "What will you pay me? Have you any gold? Helwenna likes gold. Lots and lots of gold." The healer dissolved into cackling laughter.

"She's mad," Fornay whispered from behind Edeva.

"Nay, she has her wits as much as you or I. Have you any coin with you?" she added urgently. "I forgot she would insist on payment."

"She wants money? I carry none. Certainly she must do healing for barter. These villagers could not afford her services otherwise."

"She accepts food and firewood from them, but she knows I can pay more." Edeva gave a sigh of aggravation. "I should have thought of this. I have nothing with me . . . wait . . . the clasp of my belt." She undid the woven girdle and removed the silver clasp, then retied the belt. Bending down, she handed the clasp to the healer.

The woman turned it over in her gnarled hand, then bit it. Giving a satisfied grunt, she said, "Bring the hurt one here."

"She wishes you to bring Wulfget closer so she may examine her," Edeva translated. "Lay her down on the pallet next to the healer."

Reluctantly, Fornay did as she bid him.

"Don't leave me!" Wulfget gave a piteous cry.

"I don't like this," the knight said. "She's obviously frightened."

"Then, stay with her."

He knelt down beside the pallet.

"You," Helwenna pointed to Edeva. "Leave us now."

Edeva gave the healer a startled look, then realized that Helwenna, like the rest of the villagers, must know of the plan for her to meet Beornwold.

She went outside and looked around for the Norman escort. When she did not see them, she grew uneasy.

Moving stealthily behind the healer's hut, Edeva entered the underbrush, then paused and listened. Her heart thudded loudly in her chest. Had their escort already been captured or killed?

"So nice of you to come, little sister."

She whirled to see Beornwold's grim countenance. "Where are the Normans?" she demanded.

"Foolish bastards, our archers could have easily picked them off ere they even reached the village."

"What have you done?" Edeva asked in panic.

Beornwold narrowed his eyes, then said, "Nay, we did not kill them. I had some of the village women invite them into one of the huts. Lustful swine. They value their randy loins more than their lives."

Edeva breathed a sigh of relief, and Beornwold's lips curled. "Do you love all Normans so much then? Not merely the one whose bed you share? Or do you service *all* of them?"

Hot anger surged through Edeva. She reached out to slap his face. He caught her hand before she could land the blow. "Little vixen," he hissed. "I told Alnoth and Godric that we could no longer trust you."

Edeva pulled away, shaken. Once again, she had tried to attack her own kin.

"At the very least, you can provide us with some information. We saw ten Normans leave the palisade. How many are left?"

"Forty, not counting squires and servants."

He nodded. "And how long does the red-haired whoreson and the others stay away?"

"He said they would be gone four sennights."

"That long?" Beornwold looked thoughtful.

"What are you planning?"

"Would you not like to know?" he jeered. "You'd probably betray us as you did last time."

"I did not betray you!"

Beornwold grabbed her arm. "Godric told you to bring the Norman commander to us. Instead, you warned him to leave the palisade."

"But I did not tell him of your plans. I did not!"

"It does not matter." He gave her a shake. "Clearly you have chosen a Norman over your own kin."

"Stop, you're hurting me!" She tried to pull away.

Beornwold drew her close and whispered in her ear, "Does he have you dress yourself up in fine gowns and act as mistress of his household? Does he allow you your comforts—even as we freeze and go hungry in the woods?"

Edeva shook her head, tears stinging her eyes. "I will not betray you," she whispered, "but I cannot help you, either. Even with the Norman commander gone, there are not enough of you to take Oxbury. Your cause is hopeless."

"What do you suggest we do? Resign ourselves to being serfs and slaves to the Normans, as you have?"

Edeva longed to answer 'aye,' to argue that the rebels must surrender sooner or later. If it were Godric or Alnoth she spoke to, she might have dared it, but she deemed it too risky with Beornwold. If he struck her, she would have to explain the bruise to Fornay.

"Jesu, that's exactly what you wish." Beornwold's eyes shone with disgust. "I thought you had more spirit than that, little sister. You joined us once as a warrior—now you grovel at the Normans' feet."

" 'Tis not my own welfare I think of, but that of our people! If you attack the palisade, they are the ones who will suffer. The kitchen fire injured two women—how many more will come to grief if this struggle continues?"

"There is always suffering in war. They are merely peasants anyway. Their lives are of no account."

"If the fire had caught hold, the entire palisade might have burned!"

Beornwold shrugged. "If Oxbury burns, then we rebuild."

"With what?" she asked furiously. "How many servants and sokemen will stay to serve you? Even if you defeat these men, William of Normandy will send more. Your life will be naught but endless strife all your days!"

"At least I will die like a man, rather than a Norman lackey!"

Edeva sighed. 'Twas hopeless. Beornwold could not see the futility of the rebels' cause. She prayed that Alnoth and Godric were not so stubborn. If only she could speak to them, reason with them.

And there were other Saxons who might be swayed by

her arguments. Beornwold, by himself, could do little. If she won the others over, their lives might be saved.

"I must go back," she told her brother flatly.

He gave her a cold smile. "Aye, go back to your Norman lover's bed. Don't bother to feel any guilt about betraying your own blood, for I no longer claim you as my sister!"

Beornwold vanished into the woods. Edeva watched him, grief choking her throat. Better that he should have struck her. His words were like a dagger in her heart.

"Edeva! Where are you?"

She hurried around the side of the house. Fornay stood there, his eyes coldly suspicious. "Where are the other men?"

"I don't know. Mayhaps they went into one of the houses."

"If you have set a trap for us . . ."

"I don't know where the others are, truly. I have been looking for them."

"Go in and see to Wulfget."

Edeva went inside the healer's hut. The young woman seemed to have gotten over her fear of Helwenna, for the healer now leaned over her, listening to Wulfget's chest.

Helwenna straightened and made a clucking noise.

"What do you think?" Edeva asked.

"Her lungs are badly damaged. When she takes a breath, the air only goes partway down."

"What can we do to heal her?"

"She is young. Sometimes the body repairs itself. But she must eat well. Meat and vegetables, milk and eggs."

"Medicine?"

"Comfrey helps wounds heal. It might aid her. If she gets a fever, then give her willow bark. But if she fevers, there is likely no hope anyway." The healer sat back and regarded Wulfget. "More than anything, she must not give up. She must fight."

Edeva detected a note of doubt in the healer's voice. She obviously worried whether Wulfget had the strength of will for the upcoming battle.

Fornay pushed his way into the hut. "We leave now."
He glanced at Wulfget, then the healer. "What did she
say?" he addressed Edeva. "Will Wulfget recover?"

"She must eat good food and in plentiful quantities."

Fornay nodded.

" 'Tis not as simple as you think. So far, Wulfget has
refused all but a little broth."

"She will eat," the Norman knight announced. "If necessary, I will feed her myself."

The healer looked at Fornay, then at Wulfget. She gave
a cackling laugh. "It seems she has someone else to fight
for her."

Edeva also observed the intent look on Fornay's face.
She had hoped to find a maid who might tempt the knight,
but now she was worried. What would happen if the Norman seduced Wulfget, then abandoned the young woman?

Fornay lifted Wulfget and they went outside. Their escort waited nearby. "Where did you find them?" Edeva
asked.

"Whoring with the village women."

"You see?" she told Fornay. " 'Twas not my doing."

"We have not yet reached the safety of the palisade. We
might yet be ambushed."

Edeva's heart seemed lodged in her throat on the way
back to the fort. At any moment, she expected an arrow
to come whizzing through the air and strike one of the
knights in the back, or a band of axe-wielding warriors to
rush out of the woods. If the rebels killed a few Normans
whenever they left the palisade, they might gradually whit-
tle down the enemy force and demoralize them.

The rebels must have thought of that approach, but
something stayed their hand this day. Did some of them
argue to hold off attacking for fear of Edeva and Wulfget's
lives?

She could well imagine Godric and Alnoth insisting that
the risk was too great.

She could also imagine Beornwold arguing the other
way, reminding his brothers that she had chosen to side

with the Normans, that she was a traitor and a slut and
deserved to die.

A sob rose in Edeva's chest as she remembered Beornwold's cruel words. If her father were alive, would he think
the same of her? And was there not a bit of truth in it?
Did she accept the Normans because she truly thought it
best for her people, or had her loyalty been suborned by
the Norman leader's beguiling lovemaking? Was she, like
she'd heard it said of men, thinking with her loins rather
than her head?

"You seem distraught, Lady Edeva." Fornay spoke beside her, his voice low so as not to wake the woman sleeping
in his arms. "Did the healer say something which distressed you?"

Edeva shook her head.

"But you are troubled," he insisted. "Could it be that
things did not go as planned? Were the Saxons supposed
to attack and then didn't?"

"Must you always think the worst of me? In everything
I do or say, you find some malevolent meaning. Have I not
acted in good faith so far? 'Twas I who suggested we take
an escort. Mayhaps that is why the attack you expected did
not come."

Fornay shook his head. "I cannot trust you. Guilt is writ
upon your features, and always you act uneasy, unsettled."

"Mayhaps my guilt comes from the fact that I have for-
saken the cause of my people!" Edeva was angry now, and
she did not hold back. "Mayhaps I despise myself for giving
in to my enemies!"

" 'Tis a possibility, but not a likely one."

"And what about Wulfget?" Edeva demanded. "Do you
think that she is trying to trick you, that she uses her sickness to win your favor so she can betray you later?"

"Wulfget is different. She thinks and acts the way a
woman should."

"Which is?"

"Women should concern themselves with their house-
holds and children, not the doings of men."

Edeva gritted her teeth. Fornay was as irritating as her brothers—nay, worse. They had allowed her to dress as a warrior and watch with them in the forest. This mule-headed knight would never have endured that!

"So, you think I am not a proper woman," Edeva fumed. "My skill in managing a household puts food in your belly, sees that your clothing is washed and mended and the hall where you sleep remains warm and comfortable. Yet you mislike me because I am not an empty-headed fool who allows men to make all the decisions in my life!"

"I never said I did not admire your competence as chatelaine. 'Tis the rest of it which disturbs me. *Norman* noble-women do not dress as men nor brandish weapons." Fornay raised his brows. "If I had been the commander rather than Brevrienne, I would have done things differently. I would never have allowed you the power you have."

"But you are *not* lord," she reminded him.

"Brevrienne entrusted me to look after his property while he was gone, and I will do whatever is necessary to make certain Oxbury remains in his hands. *Whatever is necessary.*"

His warning was clear, and infuriating. Until Brevrienne returned, she would have to endure this man's disapproval and suspicion. If the rebels attacked, he would blame her.

Edeva glanced over at her antagonist and caught him bestowing a fond look on the woman in his arms. A pang went through her. Had Brevrienne ever looked at her like that? Mayhaps women like her did not inspire affection. Lust might be all any man was able to feel for her.

An ache started in her throat. Apparently, she should have greeted Brevrienne at the gates of the manor in her best gown and thrown herself at his feet. But how could she have known that their conqueror would be a just, decent lord? How could she have risked her people's future by surrendering before she knew the intentions of the enemy?

"I suppose Norman women are much like her." Edeva jerked her head toward Wulfget.

"In some ways. But few of them have her delicate coloring."

"But they probably act like her," Edeva persisted. "Dainty and helpless."

"Oh, they can be lively, too, full of jesting and fun. And many of them play music and sing."

"Do you have a special lady, Sir Alan?" Edeva asked coldly.

"A landless knight cannot afford to wed. That is part of the reason I decided to swear service to William. 'Twas my only hope of someday acquiring land and marrying."

"What of Brevrienne?"

"His father is a wealthy lord, but as a younger son, he could not hope to inherit his father's properties. He had to win his own." Fornay gave her a penetrating look. " 'Tis my duty to see that he keeps what he has won."

Edeva set her jaw. Fornay continued, "Now that he has land here in England, Brevrienne will be able to return to Normandy to seek a wife. By allying himself with a property-holder in Normandy, he can build a fine legacy for his children."

His words struck Edeva like a dagger to the gut, reminding her of Golde's sly taunts. Would Brevrienne bring a Norman wife to Oxbury? And what of *her*? Would she be discarded, like a worn garment which no longer serves its purpose?

Fornay must have guessed her turmoil, for he said, with a slight smile on his face, "Mayhaps you can remain his leman, for all he seems to lust for you."

FOURTEEN

"You see all these shops? The king collects rent from them. That's where the real wealth is, not in produce and barter goods, but taxes. Most of them pay in coin, or in goods which can later be resold. If you could expand your small hamlet into a real town, attract merchants and craftsmen, your sons would end up rich men some day."

Jobert nodded at Miles de Falaise's words as they walked down the crowded streets of Gloucester. In his mind he envisioned Oxbury in the future, the little village swelled to a walled town, with timber houses and shops, mayhaps even a small cathedral. And on the hill above, his castle of gleaming stonework, with a drawbridge, tower, and crenelated walls making it as formidable as it was beautiful.

He shook off the image. They had much work to do simply to hold onto the land his fantasy castle would be built upon. Tomorrow, they went out to fight the rebel Saxons.

"I envy you, Jobert," Miles said. "The lands William allotted to me are not near so rich. The manor itself was burned ere we arrived and since we took possession, we've been attacked twice."

"I wonder if the Saxons will ever admit defeat."

"These people have." Miles nodded toward the well-kept houses and shops.

"But they have goods to sell, services to offer. They earn their bread whether they are ruled by Saxon or Norman.

But, for a man to lose his lands means losing his livelihood, his very name. What are the dispossessed Saxons to do, starve quietly?"

"But William has not taken the lands of all of them. Only those who were sworn to King Harold's cause."

"In this part of England, that seems to be many. Whole families of landless men—uncles, brothers and sons of those who fought at Hastings, as well as the ceorls who served them."

"They cannot win." Miles shook his head. "William's forces are like a fist smashing through the heart of England. The Saxons must give way or be destroyed. Tomorrow, we go out and kill more of them."

Jobert nodded as the two of them went into a tavern. It was crowded with Norman knights called up for battle. A few Saxons could be seen among the mass of fighting men, barmaids pouring wine, and whores offering their services. But, except for the tavern keep, there were no Saxon men among the crowd.

Jobert and Miles sat down on a bench among the jostling customers and a plump wench with blue eyes and reddish curls came to fill their cups. Jobert took a swallow and made a face. "Jesu, what swill passes for wine these days! What I would not give for some fine red from Caen or Paris!"

" 'Tis still better than that piss Saxons drink."

"I could develop a taste for ale, if it is made properly. Oxbury has its own alemaster, and the man knows what he's about. Once I learned 'twas no profit in sending him to tend cattle when he should be about his brewing, the quality improved immensely."

"A brewmaster, eh? At my holding, there are few skilled workmen and no shops left in which they might ply their trade. And there is the matter of their cursed language. I cannot speak with them, nor they with me. How do you make your people understand what you want of them, Jobert? Do have someone among your troops who knows that English gibberish?"

Jobert thought of Edeva, a matter of contemplation he had tried to avoid. "There is a Saxon gentlewoman at Oxbury who learned Norman French from a servant," he told Miles. "She serves as my interpreter."

"A gentlewoman? Is she kin of the old thegn?"

Jobert nodded.

"Have you thought of wedding her? Or, is she a dried-up crone, too old to bear children?"

A wave of remembered heat went through Jobert. Edeva was as far from a crone as any woman could be. "Indeed, I've thought of wedding her. I've already petitioned William for the right."

"Good for you," Miles said. " 'Tis important to confirm your authority over your lands and a Saxon wife will do that. Which reminds me. You knew, didn't you, that Damaris de Valois went into a convent?"

Jobert took an expectant breath, anticipating the familiar throb of longing that the mention of Damaris always brought. To his surprise it didn't come. "I am pleased for her," he said. "She always said she wished to take holy vows."

"She finally convinced her sire that she wanted no man as husband. Valois took it hard. His only living child, and all his hopes of founding a dynasty, withering away in a holy house. He blames you, you know."

"He's a fool!"

"And a dangerous one. 'Tis fortunate you have King William's favor these days. I can well imagine Valois' quest for vengeance following you here to England. He cannot be pleased that you are now a landowner and a lord. He himself holds property in Hertfordshire. Near the other side of England, but not far enough away to keep him from causing you trouble. Valois has friends in high places, and methinks he will not hesitate to use them."

Jobert barely listened to Miles's words, his thoughts not on the vengeful father, but the maid. He could feel himself letting go of the memories, the dreams. Although he had

loved Damaris, time had reduced his affections to fondness. Now, there was no reason at all not to wed Edeva.

He thought of Iovin transferring the rolled parchment
bearing the Brevrienne seal to the saddlebag of a courier
bound for the coast and Normandy. How long before he
got his answer from William? Mayhaps by the time he returned to Oxbury, he would have received the king's permission to wed Edeva. It would make a fine homecoming
present, except for the one vague doubt gnawing at him.
What if she did not wish to marry with him?

"Jobert," Miles voice came to him through the haze of
his thoughts, "What say you that we find a cookshop and
fill our bellies? I've heard the mutton pies down the street
are excellent."

The autumn sun shone down upon them, turning the
three stone of mail and armor each knight wore into a
weltering prison. Jobert swiped at the sweat trickling down
his brow and thanked his Maker 'twas not high summer.

The huge destrier beneath him shifted restlessly. Hell-
fire was as impatient as he to engage the battle.

'Twould be like Hastings all over again. The Saxons
would form their shield wall, row upon row of ashwood
shields and jutting lances creating a near-impenetrable
barrier. Then, the Normans would charge, using the force
of a mounted attack to wear down the wall. Hour after
hour the battle would rage, until, like a wolf utilizing its
greater size and ferocity to rip apart a prickly hedgehog,
the shield wall would crumble, and it would be all over.

"What are they waiting for?" Miles rode up beside him,
struggling to control his own edgy mount. "All of the area
fiefholders have gathered. I see no point in delaying."

"We wait for the enemy." Jobert pointed to the rise
where the scouts had reported the Saxons were encamped.

A stillness enveloped the valley and surrounding hills,
despite the mass of soldiers arrayed there.

"Where are they?" Miles asked. "Do you think they have given up? Did the size of our host scare them off?"

With sudden comprehension, Jobert considered what fools the Saxons would have to be to allow such a large force to attack them, knowing that they had little hope of winning. He shook his head. "I have a feeling that the enemy has already dispersed."

Miles turned sideways to face him, his dark eyes barely visible through the slits of his helmet. "Should we ride ahead and tell Lord Berkeley of our thoughts?"

Jobert turned to look at the soldiers arrayed behind him. "He might be displeased if we break formation."

Miles nodded and went back to his own men.

They waited. As the time passed, the sunlight gradually faded. Jobert felt the need to relieve himself. His stomach growled. The battle fever piping through his body slowed and then went away.

"God's bloody bones," he swore, "this is tedious."

Rob drew up his mount. "Do we wait all day?"

"Berkeley has scouts. Sooner or later, they will return and tell us where the enemy is."

Rob exhaled a sigh.

At last, a messenger was seen riding up and down the lines. He reached Jobert and said, "The Saxon camp is deserted. It looks as if we've scared the bastards off."

"Our orders?"

"Berkeley says to go back to the town."

Jobert swore again, more crudely this time, then went to tell his men the news.

They stared at him. "I know it's a damned waste," he said, "but we can't fight an enemy who isn't there."

"What happens now?" Hamo asked. "Do we go home, back to Oxbury?"

"We are pledged to stay another fortnight. We'll probably have to go out in small parties and try to draw the raiders to fight that way."

Jobert suppressed a groan of frustration as they rode out of the valley. When he thought of what he could be accomplishing at his manor, it made him furious to be trapped here. He'd talked to the chief mason in Berkeley's train, and the man had agreed to come to Oxbury and draw up plans. Jobert wanted that much accomplished before spring.

And then there was Edeva. He did not wish to leave her so long. He'd grown used to working alongside her, talking with her daily about preparations for the winter, the servants, all the details of running the manor. It surprised him to realize that even more than he longed for her body, he missed her company.

For the thousandth time, he cursed himself for not going to see her before he and his men left to head north. He'd let Alan's doubts deter him, and at the time, it had seemed the prudent course. He was not yet sure of things between them. Even if Edeva did not plot against him, that did not mean she cared.

Foolishly, ridiculously, he longed for her regard. He wanted more than her acceptance of him as lord of Oxbury; he wanted her to desire him as a man and as a husband. If the king favored his request to wed Edeva, she would have little choice in the matter. *Even if she said she did not wish to wed with him.*

The thought cut into him like a knife. If that happened, what would he do? Force her to marry him?

Although it was his right to do so, he knew he'd get little satisfaction from such a marriage. He wanted Edeva to be pleased to wed him, to be eager to share his bed.

Which was the mistake he'd made. He should have bedded her again before he left. Seduced her into loving him. She was a passionate woman; if he could please her in bed, she might come to care for him for that reason alone.

"Jesu, it is quiet here. It makes me uneasy."

Jobert started as Hamo spoke. He should not get so caught up in his thoughts. What if the Saxons had doubled around and were planning to attack from the rear?

The skin on the back of his neck prickled as he heard a faint whistling noise. Before his mind could register it as the sound that an arrow makes when it leaves the bow, there was a searing pain in his shoulder. He stared, dumbfounded, at the fletched bolt piercing his mail shirt, and heard the gasps and exclamations of his men. Then the pain grabbed him like a giant claw and dragged him down.

The priest and Fornay were talking as Edeva entered the hall. She regarded the two men suspiciously. She did not trust either one.

"Father Reibald, Sir Alan," she greeted them. "I wondered if there had been any word from Lord Brevrienne."

"No word," Fornay answered.

"You expect none?"

"His term of service is half over. Why should he bother sending a messenger when we will see him within a fortnight."

"Of course." She forced a smile, trying to appear emptyheaded and helpless. Since Fornay did not approve of cleverness in a woman, she'd decided to pretend to be as guileless as Wulfget. "I hope he returns soon. I have questions I must ask him about the running of the manor."

Father Reibald regarded her with an oily smile. "Mayhaps it is something you can ask of me, child."

"Lord Brevrienne promised to decide how much seedcorn should be set aside for the next crop."

"Not a question for me." The priest turned to Fornay. "Have you an opinion?"

"Nay," the Norman knight responded. "Can it not wait until he returns?"

"I suppose it will have to." She turned her gaze toward an area by the fire which had been made private by the use of a large wooden screen. "How fares Wulfget? Is she eating?"

"I said she will eat and so she does."

"You are not bullying her, are you?"

Fornay puffed up in indignation. "I would not browbeat a gentle maid, especially one who has suffered as she has."

"My pardon." Edeva suppressed a smile. Odd to think that the hostile Norman had become nursemaid to frail Wulfget. Although she worried that the Saxon woman might suffer if Fornay proved fickle, a part of her rejoiced that the Norman captain had found something to divert his attention.

She crossed the hall toward the stairs. Still a fortnight to wait for Brevrienne. She had marked off the days he was gone on a tally stick by her bed, and every mark encouraged her. For a sennight after meeting with Beornwold, she had worried that the rebels would attack, but as time passed, she allowed herself to hope that her brothers had changed their minds.

Her sense of peace was shattered as a shout sounded at the door. "Sir Alan, come quickly! Lord Brevrienne's at the gate! He's been wounded!"

For a split second, Edeva froze. Then she gathered up her skirts and ran across the hall.

" 'Twas an ambush," Rob said as he, Fornay, and Osbert carried Brevrienne up the stairs, Edeva following behind. "We were supposed to meet the rebel forces north of Gloucester, but they did not show themselves. When Berkeley sounded the retreat, we left the valley the way we had come. The Saxons were waiting for us in the trees."

"Anyone else injured?" Fornay asked.

"That was the odd part. They must have been poor shots or quickly lost their nerve, for Jobert was the only one who was hit." Rob took a deep breath, grunting under the weight of his burden, then continued. "We stopped the bleeding as best we could, then took him into the town. A surgeon took out the bolt—he had to cut quite deep to get it out. Afterward, he said Jobert must not be moved. But Brevrienne, damn him, he insisted we bring him back here. He said if he were going to die, he would die on his own lands. Which he is like to do after this rough journey. The stitches broke open twice."

"Damned fool!" Fornay swore as they rounded the corner to enter the bedchamber.

"You know what a stubborn wretch he is. We could not gainsay him."

The three men carried their burden the last few feet and maneuvered him onto the bed. They stood there panting. Edeva pushed past them to examine Brevrienne.

The sight of his pale face was like an icy blade cutting through her. His long, powerful body sprawled limply. Edeva swallowed a sob and reached to feel his forehead. "He's fevered."

" 'Tis common after being wounded. That worries me much less than the loss of blood," Rob said.

"Where was he struck?"

Rob stepped forward and pulled back the cloak which had been wrapped around the wounded man. A large crimson stain spread over the upper portion of Brevrienne's tunic. Rob started to pull up the garment, then grimaced when he saw it was stuck to the wound. "You do it," he told Edeva. "You've a gentler touch than I."

Glancing at Brevrienne's waxen visage, Edeva doubted that he would feel anything. "Get me water," she said.

Rob brought over the ewer. Edeva dribbled water on the caked blood, loosening it, then eased the tunic up. She carefully lifted the blood-soaked bandage to reveal the wound beneath.

She could see the clean, but surprisingly large, incision the surgeon had made to excise the arrow. He had sewn up the opening afterward, but the stitches had broken open.

'Twas not a terrible sight; she'd seen much worse, as when Eadrer had cut off his foot with an axe. But the fact that it was Brevrienne who was injured made her feel sick. Once so vigorous and alive, he now lay before her as pale and still as a stone effigy.

"The healer," she said, "we must fetch the healer."

"What? Speak properly, woman!"

Fornay's sharp words broke her out of the stunned trance. She'd unconsciously spoken in Saxon.

"I said, 'we must get the healer'."

"You told me that she could not walk this far," Fornay accused.

"Then fetch her on a cart or a mule!"

Fornay turned to Rob. "There's an old witchwoman in the village. I know not if she has any skill."

"She does!" Edeva clenched her fists in aggravation. "Can you deny that Wulfget is better now?"

"That could be mere chance and sound reasoning. Anyone could see that Wulfget needed to eat properly or she would not heal."

She wanted to strike him, but remembering what she learned of the man, she made her voice meek. "I've never treated such a serious wound. I need the advice of someone more experienced if I am to aid him."

The men looked at each other. " 'Twas an old witchwoman who birthed me," Hamo said. "Else I would not have lived. I was too big and placed wrong in my mother's womb. The witchwoman turned me so I would come free. My mother even survived the birthing. That one, anyway. She perished with the next."

Rob shot Edeva a quick glance, then lowered his voice. "We have to trust her, Alan. I think it's what Jobert would want us to do. He sets great store by Lady Edeva's opinion."

Fornay made a sour face, then said, "Fetch the healer. She lives on the far east edge of the village in a pigsty of a dwelling. Take a cart and another man. She's no dainty thing if you have to lift her. I vow she weighs near as much as Brevrienne."

The two hurried off, obviously relieved to be doing something.

Edeva went to get a clean cloth. She dipped it in the ewer and began to bathe Brevrienne's face. Fornay stood where he was, watching her.

"Is there any wine?" she asked him.

"Yea. Jobert apparently bought several casks in Gloucester, and the men brought them back."

"You might fetch a skin of it. 'Tis useful for cleaning wounds and also as a way to give medicine."

Fornay didn't move.

Edeva straightened. "You'll have to trust me with him sometime!"

Fornay folded his arms over his chest and glared at her.

"Why is this different than before? I have been alone with him many times. I've slept beside him! If I wanted to murder him, why did I not do it then?"

"He was not wounded and helpless."

"You think I have no honor at all? 'Twould be the healthy man I would attack, not the injured one!"

"You're a Saxon." He gestured to the bed. "He lies there now because of an ambush by your people. They did not meet William's army like men, but cowardly attacked from the cover of the forest. Just as you and your kin tried when we first came to Oxbury."

"My people are desperate! They will use any method they can to win! Would you not do the same if you stood to lose everything?"

"I might. Which is why I do not leave you alone with him."

Edeva expelled a moan of exasperated fury. "I am not one of the rebels. I have resigned myself to Norman rule, at least to this man's." She nodded toward the bed. "I believe that it is the right thing to do for my people, the best way to protect them. And I have willingly bedded Brevrienne. I'm not such a Jezebel that I would now try to murder him!"

"Father Reibald says that women have no souls. In that matter, I believe we agree."

Edeva shook her head, anger fading to resignation. There was no point in arguing with this bull-headed fool. He would condemn her with his dying breath.

She drew up a stool beside the bed and reached to take Brevrienne's big hand in her own. His skin was warm; his fingers felt callused and strong. If she did not look at him, she could almost imagine that he was not badly wounded.

She closed her eyes, fighting tears. God help her, but Fornay was a lackwit to think she would harm Brevrienne.

In a short time, there was a clatter at the stairs. Fornay left his post and went to open the door.

Rob and Hamo rushed in. "She wouldn't come! We tried everything, even jabbing a sword in her belly. She merely laughed at us."

"Torture," Fornay hissed. "That's what Jobert would do."

"Nay!" Edeva jumped up. "She's old and helpless, for all her bulk. And if you kill her, we'll lose her knowledge forever! I'll go. I'll convince her. She probably didn't understand what you wanted."

Edeva hurried out the door and down the stairs. She would run all the way there if she had to.

At the gate, she rapidly explained her mission. The guard nodded and let her out.

She'd taken no mantle, and the cold air stung at her face and pierced her clothes. Halfway there, she remembered she'd brought no coin or valuables to pay the healer. She'd have to bargain with Helwenna and convince her that this was a matter of importance. This time 'twas not some frail villein's daughter who was ill, but the new lord. If Brevrienne did not live, it would go hard with all of them.

A few people stood outside of their huts as Edeva passed. " 'Tis the Norman lord," she told them. "He's been injured."

They watched her with stoic, patient eyes.

She was gasping for breath by the time she reached the healer's hut. Outside, she paused, feeling the sweat cool on her face, then went in.

"Helwenna, you must help me." She approached the old woman. "I have no coin to pay you . . . but you must aid me. The Norman lord has been badly wounded."

"So," Helwenna cackled, "that's what those soldiers

were making such a fuss about. Thought they were going to spit me like a roast goose." She laughed again. "No matter to me, I'd be grateful to be delivered from this woeful life."

Edeva bent nearer, trying not to gag at the odor. "I'm not going to threaten you, but you must help. When the Normans return, you have to go with them."

Helwenna shook her head. "I'll not leave here until I am carried to my byre."

Edeva knelt by the healer's pallet, her hands clenched into fists. "You have to. If the Norman dies, they will kill all of us, torch the village. Everyone will suffer. You cannot be so selfish as to let that happen!"

"Then they are evil men. Why should I work to keep one of them alive?"

"The Norman lord is not evil. If he lives, I think he will do well for Oxbury. He is just and strong. How many lords can that be said of?"

Helwenna's dark eyes gleamed. "You are fond of him? Why did you not say so?"

"Aye," Edeva said and took a shaky breath. "I am fond of him. I truly do not want him to die."

"I won't go with you, but I'll tell you what to do."

"I am no healer . . . I cannot . . ."

"Think you that these would be any use?" Helwenna held up her gnarled, swollen hands. "You must be my hands, Edeva. And my eyes. Tell me what the wound looks like. Where it is, how deep, everything."

"I would not have believed it, but it seems to be helping," Rob said.

Fornay moved nearer to the bed, then nodded grudgingly. "Still, he does not wake."

"Loss of blood, weakness . . . is that not right, Lady Edeva? But the wound looks better—that is something."

Edeva leaned over and stroked Brevrienne's brow, searching for fever. As odd as Helwenna's instructions had been, they seemed to have worked. The wound was closing up nicely, and Brevrienne's forehead felt cool.

"Who would have thought a poultice of moldy bread could heal?"

" 'Tis something in the blight, Helwenna said." Edeva stretched wearily. She'd scarce slept in the last day and a half. "It stops wounds from festering."

"My lady, you should rest," Rob said. "We'll keep watch and call you if he worsens or wakes."

She nodded and moved leadenly toward the door. For a moment or two, she'd lie down. If she did not, she'd be no good to anyone.

As if climbing out of a dark, empty pit, Jobert awoke. At first, he was aware of only the throbbing pain in his shoulder, then his other senses came to life. The smell of a brazier burning, the feel of warm, soft blankets against his naked skin. He opened his eyes. Dark shapes loomed over him. "Where am I?" he asked.

Rob's face came into view. "You're at Oxbury, my lord. You asked us to bring you here, and so we did."

Vaguely, Jobert remembered fevered, agonized dreams, the dread of dying. "Where is she? Where is Edeva?"

Alan leaned over him. "Rest now. Do not try to talk."

Jobert nodded feebly. The pain grew worse; the fire of it swallowed his thoughts.

"I'm going to give you some poppy and mandrake the surgeon gave us. 'Twill help you sleep."

Alan held a cup to his lips. Weary beyond reason, Jobert drank. He felt himself sliding down into the pit once more. "Edeva," he whispered.

FIFTEEN

"Should we not call Lady Edeva?" Rob asked.

Alan grunted. "He does not need *her* aid."

"I think you are wrong. I think he would recover more quickly if he knew she sat by his bedside. On the way here, when he was fevered, he asked for her."

"Brevrienne has always had poor judgment regarding women. First, it was Damaris. Even when her father forbid Jobert to see her, he could not stay away. Valois had Jobert thrown into a dungeon, very nearly cost him his life." He shook his head. "Now, he entangles himself with a scheming Saxon!"

"I cannot think ill of her. She has always done well by the manor. The people of Oxbury respect her. If Brevrienne wed with her, 'twould give his authority here more weight."

"She's a cunning slut. She has fooled all of you." Alan gave his companion a dark look. "I know she meets with the rebels. She has kin among them, mayhaps brothers or uncles. If a chance arises, she will aid them, have no doubt. She is no natural woman, even though she has traded her man's garb for kirtles, her weapons for a needle and thread. Mark my words, she waits until the time is right— then, like a viper, she will strike."

"She does not seem devious to me. Besides, if she were working with the rebels, why did they not attack while

Brevrienne was gone? 'Twould have been the logical time to make their move."

Alan smiled sourly. " 'Tis Brevrienne they want. Once he is dead, they believe we will all drift away and they can reclaim Oxbury."

"But I do not understand Lady Edeva's part in it. A dozen times, she could have killed him. Poisoned his food, cut his throat as he slept . . ."

"She is weak, like all women. Weak and afraid, though she does not show it. But someday the rebels will goad her to act. She will not have to do the deed, but simply betray him to his enemies."

Rob shook his head. "Your plot seems farfetched. Have you proof regarding Lady Edeva's plans?"

"I've seen her meet with the rebels."

"Have you told Jobert?"

"I've not had the chance to tell him of it yet."

"You're certain there could be no mistake?"

" 'Twas in the village. She'd convinced me to go there because of Wulfget, the woman who was burned in the kitchen fire. Wulfget was sore injured, 'tis true, but I doubt that was Edeva's motive. She insisted I escort her. While I was in the hut with the healer and Wulfget, she pursued her real purpose.

"I went looking for her and saw her meet a Saxon who came out of the forest. His beard was long, his clothes filthy. He did not look like a villager, but a warrior. They argued; he grabbed her arm and threatened her. She appeared guilty and nervous when she returned to the hut." He nodded slowly. " 'Twas one of the rebels, I'd swear it."

"But you said they argued. She may have refused to aid him."

"That time, mayhaps. But there will be other attempts. Eventually, she will do their bidding."

Rob sighed. "If what you say is true, then we should not leave her alone with Brevrienne until he heals enough to defend himself."

Alan glanced toward the prone form of his lord on the
bed. "Nay, we should not."

Edeva jerked awake. She'd been dreaming. A familiar
nightmare, where the manor was on fire and she could
not get her feet to move so she could run to get help nor
her mouth to scream out a warning.

She sat up, realizing she was on a cot in the women's
area of the hall. The panic gradually subsided, until she
remembered the other nightmare, the one that was real—
Brevrienne was wounded.

She jumped off the cot and hurried toward the stairs.

The upper bedchamber was dark, lit only by the glow
from the brazier beside the bed. Rob sat on a stool nearby.
"How fares he?" Edeva asked. "Did he wake?"

"For a few moments only."

She leaned over and felt Jobert's forehead, giving a sigh
of relief as she found his skin cool and dry. Reluctantly,
she drew her hand away. She wished she could touch him
more freely, but the knight beside the bed inhibited her.

She turned to Rob. "Leave us."

"My lady. Alan said that you should not be left alone
with him."

"Fornay be damned! If I wished to harm him, why have
I done all this?" She pointed to the bandage on Jobert's
shoulder.

Rob still hesitated. She rounded on him. "Go, I said! I
would be alone with him!"

"Spoken like a true hellcat."

Edeva gasped and faced the bed. "You're awake!"

"Barely." Jobert gave a heavy sigh. "I heard your voice
and knew that I was at Oxbury . . . at last." He looked at
Rob. "Do as she bids. That is an order."

For one second Rob paused, then he mumbled, "Milord," and went out.

"You should not have made them bring you here,"
Edeva chided. "You should have stayed in Gloucester and

let them tend you there. You nearly bled to death on the journey!"

"Don't scold me. I am too weak to endure the lash of your sharp tongue."

"I'm sorry." Tears stung her eyes. He was right. Always she acted the shrew. Why could she not be a proper woman, gentle and meek?

She moved closer to the bed and lowered her voice. "They said you were injured in an ambush. That there was no battle."

"The Saxons fled before our host. But some of them must have doubled back and hid among the trees. Our troop was one of the last to leave the field. I was fortunate. If the bolt had struck lower, or gone into my neck . . ." He paused.

She put a hand on his arm, sick with the thought of the gruesome death he had almost faced.

"Edeva, have you ever heard of your countrymen using the crossbow?"

She shook her head. "What manner of weapon is that?"

"A deadly one, capable of piercing armor. Even the finest mail is no defense against it, as I have learned."

Edeva suddenly realized the strangeness of Jobert's injury. He'd been in full armor, yet an arrow had gone right through his mailed shirt, imbedding deeply in his shoulder. She shook her head. "Nay, our men fight with swords, lances and axes, as well as the bow and arrow, but not the kind which could inflict the injury you have."

"The Saxons must be desperate. They know they cannot defeat us in fair battle, so they seek to kill us one by one. Still, it seems strange that they chose our band to shoot upon." He sighed softly. Edeva wondered what troubled him, why he wished to speak of the attack. She did not want him to tire himself.

"Rest now." She leaned over to smooth the covers. "Do you want me to bring you poppy and mandrake so you can sleep?"

"Nay, I wish you to lie beside me."

Her hands stilled on the bedding. The tenderness in his voice made her melt.

"I want to feel your warmth near me. When I lay in the tavern in Gloucester, I thought I would die. I dreamed that I was dead and cold already, even though they say I burned with fever."

A lump filled Edeva's throat. It made her ache to think of him suffering so.

She took off her shoes and started to get into bed with him. He said, "You'll be more comfortable if you take off your kirtle." His eyes shone in the light of brazier. Wistfully, he added, "I am not much use to you at this moment, but I would have you near anyway."

Edeva pulled her gunna over her head. Clad in her shift, she climbed over Jobert and settled herself beside him. He moved as if trying to turn toward her. "Lie still," she whispered.

She snuggled under the coverlet, then put her arms around his chest and rested her face against his good shoulder.

'Twas strange, but she felt safe for the first time in months. His chest rose and fell with the slow rhythm of his breathing, and his body felt cozy warm against hers. Closing her eyes, she could forget the hatred and violence whirling around them. There was naught but them, two creatures seeking comfort from each other.

There was a clatter at the door. Edeva jerked upright, wishing she had locked it. Fornay came striding in. He started to say something, then saw her in the bed. "Jesu, woman, have you no shame? Can you not wait for him to heal before you resume your whoring ways?"

Edeva climbed out of the bed, not caring that she wore only a shift. "He asked me to lie with him!" she spat. " 'Tis you whose thoughts are lewd!"

"You curl yourself around him like a snake coiling

around its prey." Fornay's lips twisted in scorn. "I vow I will be rid of you now, while I have a chance."

His dagger hissed from its scabbard. Edeva faced him defiantly, her body tense and ready. He would learn she knew a little of warfare; he would not find her easy to kill!

"God's balls, Alan, what madness has come over you!"

Alan turned to face the man on the bed. In that split second, Edeva charged. Head down, she butted her opponent hard in the belly. His sword clattered to the floor, and Fornay went down like a sack of grain. Edeva loomed over him, hands on her hips.

"Why do you not jump on him and scratch his eyes out while you have a chance?" Edeva turned as Jobert spoke. "Nay, I do not mean it," he said hastily. "I was merely jesting." He gave a short laugh, then moaned. "I fear I cannot properly appreciate the mirth of this situation, lest I tear open my wound."

Edeva, alarmed, rushed to the bed. "Lie back," she ordered.

"How can I remain still when the two of you are at each other's throats? I have problems enough without having to replace my captain and my chatelaine all at once."

"I'm sorry we woke you," Edeva said, "but 'twas he who started it." Embarrassment replaced her fury. Damn Fornay. He had goaded her into acting like a brawling squire!

"What's come over you, Alan?" Jobert asked the knight who was now getting to his feet. "Once you argued that I could not hang her because she was woman. Now you attempt to skewer her on your dagger."

"My lord, I . . ."

"He hates me," Edeva said. "He thinks I mean to betray you."

"She is in league with the rebels, I know it! Rid yourself of her now. If you do not want her killed, at least banish her from the palisade."

"And then who will order the servants and see to the household?" Jobert asked calmly. "I value your loyalty, Alan, but you do not speak Saxon. I have no wish to see things return to the disorder we endured when we first arrived here."

Edeva's heart sank. He did not care for her; he merely sought her aid in running Oxbury.

Fornay's lips drew together in a thin line, and his dark eyes glowed with barely restrained animosity. He leaned down to pick up his dagger and replace it in his belt. "If you need anything, milord, I will be outside the door."

Edeva watched Fornay stalk out, his dignity held stiff around him. She had her victory, but it seemed hollow. Once again, she'd acted like an uncouth virago. How would she ever convince Jobert to see her as a lady, a *wife*, if she did not learn to act like one?

With a shock, she realized that was what she wanted. She wanted the Norman to wed with her.

"Fornay is a stubborn one," Jobert mused. "When he gets a notion in his head, 'tis fair impossible to dislodge it. But I would not have him humbled, Edeva. He's my captain, and I need him to defend Oxbury. I won't have you castrating him while he sleeps nor poisoning him in the hall."

"I would not do that!"

"Nay, nor even making a fool of him, whether alone or in front of others."

Edeva bristled. Jobert was treating her as her brothers had, admonishing her to behave herself, as if she were but an unruly little girl. "Then, keep him away from me," she warned. "I allow no one to shame nor taunt me, either."

Jobert nodded, then closed his eyes and sighed.

Edeva felt her stomach twist with worry. What had she been thinking of—to distress a man so gravely injured? "Sleep." She stroked his cheek, roughed now by a sennight's worth of ruddy whiskers.

His breathing grew slow and deep. Edeva stared down at him, her body relaxing as his did. What was this hold that Jobert had over her, that the thought of him suffering filled her with dread? Once he had been her enemy, the monster of her nightmares; now she longed to please him, yearned to be near him, and dreamed that he might join with her in marriage.

'Twas madness. Her closest kin were locked in a battle to the death with this man, and she contemplated what it would be like to be his wife.

She closed her eyes. One afternoon of passion and she was his slave. Such bewitchment was not supposed to happen to women. The man was the one beguiled by lovemaking, ensorceled by his bedpartner's body. But she could not stop thinking about him. The sight of him, even pale and sickly, made her heart pound. His scent seemed the rarest of perfumes. The pleasure of being near him made her sigh with contentment.

She returned to her place beside him.

He woke from a dream where Saxons were everywhere, swords flashing, eyes shining with battle lust, eager to kill him. The familiar tension filled his body as he prepared to defend himself. Then the grinding pain in his shoulder reminded him of his true circumstances. Flat on his back in a bed, as helpless as a newborn puppy.

And the Saxon who lay near him meant him not ill but good. Fornay might doubt her, but Jobert could not. If Edeva had meant to harm him, she would have done so long ago—stabbed him in the back while he bathed that first time.

But even then, full of hate and visions of revenge, she failed to carry out the deed.

Nay, he would not mistrust her now. 'Twas not merely that he respected her sense of honor, that he believed she was not the sort for deceit and treachery, but also his dream that she might someday love him. She had cared for him so tenderly these last few days. Surely it meant that she had some feelings for him.

If only he were able to make love with her. But he was a useless, sickly wretch right now. Though his shaft grew hard at such thoughts, he could do nothing.

He stirred uncomfortably. Edeva immediately awoke. "What's wrong? Are you thirsty? In pain?"

She sat up in bed and leaned over him. The sight of her in the flimsy shift increased his arousal. "Get me one of the men," he said. "I need to make water."

"When you were delirious and weak, I tended you. It did not bother me."

"Well, I am awake now, and I would have one of the men!" His voice came out more brusque than he intended, but, God's balls, he did not need any reminder of her touching him!

She hurriedly climbed out of the bed, then slipped on her gunna and shoes and left. Jobert let out a deep sigh. If he concentrated on the pain in his shoulder rather than lustful thoughts, he might grow flaccid enough that he could make water.

Alan rushed in a few moments later. "What's wrong? Lady Edeva came and said you need me."

"Bring me the chamber pot."

When they had accomplished the thing, Jobert lay back, sweating from the pain.

"Would you like some poppy?"

"Mayhaps I would, but first, we will talk."

Alan's face grew guarded. "You know what I think of the woman."

"Yea, I know. But I am commander here, and 'tis my opinion that matters. She's not to be harassed or interfered with."

"Even if she is a Saxon spy?"

"Her loyalties do not concern me."

"You care not if she meets with the rebels and aids them in overthrowing you?"

"She would not."

"Hah! While you were away, she went to the village and there met with a Saxon warrior. What could they be planning except treachery?"

"Undoubtedly she has kin among the rebels. It means nothing."

"Nothing? How can you be so sure of her?"

"Because I am."

Alan's face set in bitter lines, then he went out.

Jobert shifted on the bed. Edeva had gone to the village and met a Saxon warrior. It meant nothing. He *was* sure of her. *Wasn't he?*

"You seem better."

He smiled at her. "That must mean that the one who nurses me is skilled."

Edeva felt herself flush with pleasure.

"In fact, I feel well enough that I would like to shave and bathe today."

"Should I call for Fornay?"

"Nay, I would have you tend me."

His voice was soft, teasing. Edeva felt the blood spread from her face to other parts of her body. She met his gaze. "Are you certain you trust me with a knife at your throat?"

His green eyes sparkled. " 'Twould be witless to murder a man whose life you saved. A practical woman like you can easily see that."

Practical. He thought her practical. 'Twas why he kept her around, so she could maintain his household. "I'll go order some hot water," she said.

On the way down the stairs, she tried to collect herself. Not a sennight ago, he had been near death. She should not be thinking base thoughts about a wounded man. 'Twas unseemly.

But the expression on his face had brought those ideas to mind. She could swear that he looked forward to having her touch his naked body as much as she anticipated it.

A pleasant kind of torment. To touch him and remember what they had shared, and yet know that they could do nothing more. How long would it take him to heal, before he was well enough to . . .

She *must not* entertain such thoughts. Her hands would

shake and she would indeed cut his throat as she shaved him!

She found some squires in the stables and bid them bring hot water for the lord's bath. Several of them asked whether he was mending well, and she reassured them that he was.

Still feeling nervous, she stopped in the hall to look in on Wulfget. The young woman appeared much better than Edeva could have hoped. There was color in her cheeks, and she was sitting up. "Where's Alan?" she asked as Edeva greeted her.

"He has many duties—I'm certain he is attending to them."

Some of the glow in Wulfget's cheeks faded at this news. Edeva decided that she should talk to Jobert about his captain and the village girl.

When she reached the bedchamber, Jobert was sitting up and trying to get out of bed. His face was ashen, and his limbs trembled with the effort. Edeva raced to him. "Nay, you must not rise! You'll hurt yourself!"

He allowed her to help him back into the bed, then lay there panting. "Jesu, I hate this! I cannot bear to be so helpless. Let me rest a moment and I will try again."

"And where will you go?" she asked caustically. "If, by some miracle, you do reach the bathing tub, you will have to remain there. I will never be able to get you back into bed by myself."

Jobert lifted his head, then lay back again, swearing.

"Stop it," she said. "I will bathe you where you lay. That is the best we can do."

White-faced, he nodded.

While she waited for the water to arrive, Edeva fussed with drying clothes and found something clean for Jobert to wear. She avoided looking at the bed, knowing that he was embarrassed by his weakness.

Finally, the hot water arrived. Edeva had them place the buckets by the bed, then shooed the squires out.

She rolled up her sleeves and dipped a cloth into the

hot water. Taking a deep breath, she approached the bed and started to pull back the covers, then paused. "I'll have someone fetch coals for the brazier. You'll grow chilled otherwise."

She ran down to the hall to find a servant to carry up glowing coals to fill the brazier. With this task was done, she once again took up the wet cloth.

"Should you not shave me first?" he asked.

She nodded, grateful for the reprieve. After wetting his whiskers with hot water and soap, she sharpened a blade on a whetstone. Praying her hands would not shake, she began to shave him.

She concentrated intently on her task, trying to remain unaffected by his nearness. 'Twas no different than sewing a straight seam, she told herself.

"Mayhaps I should have you cut my hair," he said, as she was finishing.

She paused, hands in midair. "Why?"

" 'Tis the Norman way."

"Which you have not followed so far," she pointed out.

A faint smile lit his features. "Do you like my hair worn long?"

"Yea, it makes you look more like a Saxon." She flushed. 'Twas likely not the best thing to say, but it was true. She had found it difficult to get used to the way Norman men shaved their faces and cut their hair above their ears.

"If it pleases you, I will keep it long," he said.

An ache of tenderness went through her to think he cared for her opinion.

She wiped the soap from his face and put the shaving things away. Then, when she could delay no longer, she uncovered his chest and dipped a cloth in a bucket of fresh water.

She drew the cloth along his neck, over his good shoulder and arm. He lay still, his eyes half-closed. She rinsed out the cloth and gingerly washed his underarm. He did not seem ticklish. It was she who quivered as she soaped the tawny hair there.

After rinsing what she had done so far, she started on his chest. His nipples puckered as she touched one of them, and Edeva felt her own nipples tighten in response.

As she had been the first time she bathed him, she found herself intently aware of every detail of his body: the way the hair on his chest was less red than that on his belly, the planes of his hard muscles visible beneath the skin, the corded strength of his neck.

The sight and feel of him made her feel hot and dizzy. She wanted to press her mouth to his skin, to taste him.

Instead, she rinsed the soap away and began on his other side. Washing around the wound took some care, distracting her from her provocative thoughts and reminding her that he was not yet mended. She was almost calm and collected as she helped him sit up so she could bathe his back.

Then it came time to do his lower body.

She spread a cloth over his chest so he wouldn't chill and pulled the covers lower. All her nonchalance vanished at the sight of his engorged shaft.

She froze as the vivid, shocking memories came rushing back. The feel of him inside her, stretching, filling and bringing her to ecstatic completion.

Swallowing, she leaned over the bucket of water and rinsed out the cloth. Surely her face was ablaze, her lewd reveries transparently obvious. What did he think of her? Did her embarrassment amuse him? She could not know unless she looked at his face, and she would not do that.

Somehow she got a grip on her nerves and returned to her task. With the blanket pulled farther down, she began to wash the less distressing parts, his legs and feet. She took her time, fighting for some relief to her turmoil. Mayhaps if he grew chilled, his erection would shrivel and she would not have to face it.

Silently, she cursed the brazier, which was now putting out substantial heat. He was not likely to get cold. For that matter, the water would warm him. The thought of him swelling and rising beneath her fingers disconcerted her even more.

"Do you wish me to turn over?" he asked.

Edeva let out the breath she had been holding, "Can you manage it?"

"If you aid me."

Helplessly, she glanced at his face, then downward. "What do you want me to do?"

"Lean close and support my shoulder."

She did as he bid, then stepped back. This view was only a little less titillating. Broad, well-muscled shoulders and taut, rounded buttocks formed an enticing picture of masculine pulchritude.

All at once, she gave up. Why fight the hunger his body aroused? Why not enjoy it? Certainly, he felt no discomfort. Her glimpse of his face confirmed that. She'd not seen a man undergoing a miserable ordeal. There was a hint of a smile on his lips, a distinctly lascivious look in his eyes. Whatever pain his shoulder gave him, he had forgotten it for now.

She rinsed the cloth and prepared to enjoy herself. This time, she allowed her hands to linger as she washed. She kneaded his shoulders, enjoying the feel of his firm muscles, ran her hand down the sleek curve of his lower spine and dared to cup one of his buttocks with her fingers.

He made a low sound and spread his thighs so she could glimpse his testicles hanging heavy between them.

Edeva removed her hand and stood back, wondering if she would swoon from the exquisite tension humming through her. Her insides felt liquid, her skin hot and tight. There was a piercing spasm at the center of her lower belly, and little points of sensation swirled outward from it. She wanted, oh, what she wanted—

"Edeva," his voice was a husky murmur, "mayhaps you should finish."

She rinsed the cloth and began to wash his buttocks. Her movements were slow, delicious, and thorough. After again dipping the cloth in the water, she gently soaped between his thighs. The thin cloth rasped against coarse hair, and Edeva let her fingers slip beneath the cloth, exploring the intriguing taut pouches, this essence of his virility.

She sensed Jobert held himself very still, as if he might explode if her fingers dallied too long. Then, with a groan, he turned sideways, balancing on his uninjured arm. "Do my front, Edeva," he said.

SIXTEEN

As soon as he had turned over, her eyes went to his shaft. Ruddy pink against the blaze of his pubic hair, it stood up bold and proud, a beacon of his desire. But was it desire for her, or could any woman stir it?

"Touch me. Please."

She reached out. His shaft also rose for Golde. Did his passion at this moment mean anything?

He groaned as her fingers hovered over him. "Edeva," he whispered. "My lusty she-cat, please touch me."

She rinsed out the cloth and washed his manhood. He was as hot as she remembered. And as hard.

She tried to be cold, disinterested. Not to fondle the velvety, arrow-like tip. Nor run her fingers lovingly down the smooth length of him. Or curl her fingers around the weight of the tight pouches hanging below.

But such willpower seemed beyond her. Though haunted by doubts, she could not help enjoying the moment. Skin against skin. Sensitive finger pads against keen flesh. She traced patterns along the heated column of his shaft, savoring the fit of him in her hand.

A droplet of moisture appeared at the quivering tip. Her instincts said to lick it. He was clean, smelling of soap, and her mouth had felt wet and yearning ever since they began this fascinating endeavor.

She leaned over and touched him with her tongue. He

gave a gasp and clutched the bedcovers in a deathgrip. "Dear God, you'll drive me to madness!

The desperation in his voice frightened her. She drew back. "Your wound! We should not be doing this!"

"Jesu, woman! Do you mean to kill me? If you do not finish now, I'm like to expire of frustration anyway."

Edeva gazed at him in amazement. "But how do we . . . that is . . . you cannot think to . . ."

"Do as you were doing. I will find release, of that I'm certain!"

She gaped.

"Never fear," he whispered, "I will satisfy you as well. I would not leave you to suffer aching loins, not after the delight I've experienced at your hands."

The warmth in his voice soothed her. If he did not love her, at least he cared for her feelings.

He sat halfway up on the bed, his green eyes dark with longing. "Take off your kirtle. I would see you naked."

She did as he bid, feeling half hot with embarrassment, half with desire. Her nipples were swollen, pulsing peaks. Between her thighs, she was so wet, she feared to find moisture dribbling down her legs.

His eyes swept over her, eager and hungry. "Straddle me."

Awkwardly, she climbed on the bed and did so. He leaned back, nostrils flared, lips parted. The pupils of his eyes were black pools. "Heaven forfend, but you're spectacular."

'Twas a heady thing, to display herself to this man. He did not make her feel too big, ungainly or unfeminine. His gaze upon her body was reverent.

"You have magnificent breasts," he said. "I would taste them . . . one delicious nipple at a time."

As if he willed it, she leaned over, offering herself. He took the gift, his mouth rough upon her succulent flesh. He swallowed her, drawing her deep between his lips, until the ache inside her erupted in a throaty moan. 'Twas unbearable. She wanted more. Leaning back, she arched her pelvis to meet his skillful fingers.

He thrust one finger inside her and used the others to rub her cleft, finding some magical spot. She braced her body and closed her eyes. Shivers of delight threaded through her flesh; spirals of fire exploded inside her.

As the peak passed, Edeva slowly became aware again. She was draped over Jobert, her body slick with sweat and the moisture of her climax. She looked down at him, fearing to see disgust writ on his features.

His eyes were wild; his features flushed and distorted. "Now, Edeva, you must return the favor." He took her hand and drew it down to his shaft.

He seemed as rigid as stone as she caressed him. "Faster," he whispered. "Yeah, my love, that is wonderful!"

In seconds, creamy wetness covered her fingers. Edeva stared at it, thinking of his wasted seed. She would have liked to have felt it gushing inside her.

But she feared to hurt his shoulder. And there would be other times. Wouldn't there?

She climbed off the bed and rinsed her hand in the wash water, then looked at him. His eyes were closed, his body relaxed. She could not help wondering if it mattered it was she who had brought him to release. Could any woman have satisfied him?

His eyes fluttered open. "Lie next to me," he whispered. "I would have you near."

She settled herself beside him. His lips brushed the side of her face. "Edeva," he murmured. "My lovely Saxon."

"A boy in the village, Leogyth, fell ill with a stomach ailment," Edeva said, looking up from her sewing. "Helwenna could do naught for him, and he died a day ago. They will have a pyre to burn his body. 'Tis one of the old ways. The church does not sanction it, but our people have always burned their dead."

She watched Jobert rock back on the stool. Although he

had improved greatly in the last few days, he still spent most of his time in the bedchamber, resting. She brought him news, detailing the events occurring in manor and village.

"I have decided to have Helwenna train someone else as healer." She smoothed the altar cloth she was embroidering. "She is old and will not last many more winters. I would hate for all her knowledge to be lost. I've decided on Eadelm. She is sturdy and quick-witted, and I think she might be good at it."

"Which one is she?"

"She works in the kitchen. A big brawny girl with a broad face and brown hair."

"Ah, the one none of my men wanted to bed."

" 'Tis a good thing, too. At least I have one kitchen helper who is not pregnant! Every day when I go to order the meal, I find myself assaulted by complaints and cries of misery. Half of them are ill in the morning—the other half, too tired to do their duties." Edeva's voice rose with aggravation. "I vow, by next summer, your knights will have turned my kitchen into a nursery!"

"Certainly you've had young female servants get with child before."

Edeva's hands stilled on the cloth, remembering when her mother discovered that Beornwold and Godric had been dallying with the kitchen help. Two of them came up pregnant not a sennight before King Harold and his train came to Oxbury, and her mother had counted it a disaster. She had had both of Edeva's brothers whipped, and the women had been given as wives to two of Leowine's villeins.

'Twas easy to find husbands for women carrying bastards of the lord's line; most sokemen were not adverse to having a cuckoo in the nest if they thought the sacrifice could earn them rewards in the future. Edeva feared it would be much more difficult to find enthusiastic spouses for women who carried babes from Normans.

"Husbands will have to be found for them," she said.

"And I imagine you will have to pay dearly to get decent men to take on women sullied by your knights. Most of the women do not even know which of your men is the father."

Jobert gave a grunt. "How much do you think it will take?"

"Mayhaps a cow or pig for each of them, plus increased grazing or fishing rights and other privileges."

"That seems rather dear. If your female servants keep getting pregnant, I'll be beggared in no time."

"Then mayhaps you should have spoken to your knights sooner!" Edeva said tartly. " 'Tis their pleasure you pay for!"

Jobert shook his head. "I could not keep soldiers in my garrison if I grew too strict about their rutting. 'Tis the way of fighting men. Most of them will never marry—they must find their release somewhere. Is it not better now that they know they must make certain that the woman is willing?"

Edeva felt a flush creeping up her neck. This talk of "rutting" and "release" reminded her vividly of what had occurred between her and Jobert four days before. The memory of her wanton behavior still embarrassed her.

"Even if the women are willing, there is still the problem of what to do when they get with child. 'Twould be better if your men confined their lust to one or two wenches. Then we would only have those to worry over."

"No man really likes to bed a wench who's had dozens of bedpartners before him," Jobert pointed out.

Edeva thought instantly of Golde. "The wench, Golde, is certainly well-used," she said, "yet men do not seem to tire of her."

"Oh, I do not think that is true. By now most of the knights realize that she only appears eager and willing when she wants something from them. If they go with her, 'tis because they have no better choice."

Edeva felt a wave of satisfaction. From the sound of it,

Golde had fallen from favor with Jobert. *At last, he has seen her for what she is.*

"I will agree to settle some property on the women," Jobert said. "Which ones are they?"

"Asa, Aldreda and Emma."

He grunted again. "They all look alike to me. Except Wulfget. She looks naught like anyone else."

Which is why Fornay favors her, Edeva thought. *Did Jobert also prefer delicate, fragile women?*

Once more, she grew discouraged. Both Fornay and Golde had warned her that Jobert intended to wed a Norman. *She could order his household for him for months, share his bed and still end up discarded when he took another woman to wife.*

Anger at the thought made her voice sharp as she said, "And what of Wulfget? Do you intend to see that Fornay does the proper thing and weds with her?"

"That is up to him. I do not decide whom my captains will marry. And I certainly would not order him to marry a Saxon if he did not want to."

His words stung, and Edeva feared that they held portent for her as well as Wulfget. "But he came to her when she was injured and helpless," she persisted. "If he abandons her now, 'twill break her heart!"

Jobert grew impatient. "If he has impregnated her, I will marry her off to some villein with the others. I am not responsible for every foolish, lovelorn maid at Oxbury!"

And what of this one? Edeva wanted to scream. *What of this foolish, lovelorn maid?*

"Tell me how the building progresses," Jobert said, clearly wishing to change the subject. "Alan said that they had begun to deepen the ditch. I suggested they move it out several feet, so there is more room for the stone curtain wall."

Edeva folded up her sewing and stood. "You can discuss your building plans with your captains. I have other things to attend to."

What ailed her? Jobert mused as Edeva left the room,

slamming the door behind her. *She* did not have to endure being bored and helpless, too weak to venture from the bedchamber!

With a curse, he rose from the stool. Although the wound healed well, the loss of blood had left him pathetically weak. Moving from the stool to the bed used up all his strength.

He took a few unsteady steps, then sank down on the bed, his legs trembling. The simple exertion made him thirsty, but the ewer of water lay on the table at the far side of the room. Too far away to make the effort worth it.

He would have to wait for Edeva to return. *If* she returned. She had been strangely distant since the day she bathed him. His shaft grew hard merely at the memory. The sight of her straddling him, bringing her lush, rose-tipped breasts to his mouth. Her beautiful, golden crotch spread wide so that he might pleasure her. And pleasure her, he had. Fondling her creamy opening until her breasts heaved, her hips trembled and she thrust her head back in a glorious vision of ecstasy, thick golden braids streaming behind her, full, tempting lips parted, her blue eyes half-closed.

He could scarce look at her without remembering that moment and wanting her with a great throbbing hunger that his miserable, wounded body could not fulfill. His weakness disgusted him, and because of that, he had vowed not to cajole her into lovemaking until he could do it properly. He wanted to join with her, fill her with his seed, possess her. And he wanted to do it every night, every day . . . forever.

The intensity of his feelings shocked him. What he had felt for Damaris was a mere twinge compared to this. A nagging toothache to a bone-deep wound.

When would his answer come from William? He'd sent the letter asking for permission to wed Edeva nearly a month ago. The king should have received the missive by now and sent a message back.

Alan would be appalled when he found out his plans, Jobert thought as he leaned back on the bed. The knight would think that his lord had lost his wits. But, in truth, was not wedding Edeva the perfect way to secure her loyalties? From what he knew of Edeva, she would never betray her husband, no matter what her other kinsmen might urge. Once she was his wife, she would be bound by law and honor to support him.

He wondered if she would resist the marriage. She was so proud, so headstrong. A woman like that might well fear the obligations of matrimony.

Of course, if she refused, he could coerce her. The law said a woman must wed willingly, but in truth, the bride's agreement was meaningless. For the right payment, Father Reibald would sign the documents asserting that Edeva had agreed to the marriage, even if she was brought to the altar bound and gagged.

But it would not come to that, Jobert decided. He had other means of overcoming her objections. Give him a day alone with her in this bedchamber and he vowed he could love her into submission! A smile touched his lips at the thought.

Unfortunately, he would have to be healthy and vigorous for such action. A far cry from his current condition. His smile vanished as he closed his eyes and gave in to the nagging fatigue.

He woke to the smell of smoke. Not the familiar scent of woodsmoke and charcoal, but the acrid odor of war, a conflagration of thatch and wood and burning flesh. He knew a moment of alarm, then he remembered the funeral pyre for the dead village child.

A primitive sort of rite, but it seemed that once the spirit had left the body, God should not care how the empty flesh was disposed of. Father Reibald was probably incensed by the custom, though. He would use the incident to point out the barbaric nature of the Saxons.

To Jobert, the English did not seem particularly crude, merely different. For all the warlike ways she exhibited in their first encounter, since then, Edeva had acted just like other women. If anything, her feminine skills were superior to most females he had known. Her needlework finer, her command of servants and gift for organization more impressive.

And the wealth and luxury articles of Oxbury also belied the image of brutishness and lack of culture which most Normans had of the English. He'd never slept in such a comfortable, well-appointed bedchamber. Even everyday, functional things at Oxbury were crafted with an eye toward beauty: the silver ewer and cups on the table, fashioned with ornate, curving handles and scrollwork around the lips; Edeva's carved ivory comb, decorated with horn inlay; the wooden chests in the corner, bound with embossed leather strips and secured with bronze fixtures.

As odd as it seemed, Jobert thought it might well turn out that the Saxons had as much to offer the Normans as the other way around. They were not savages to be killed or reduced to serfs. If a Norman treated fairly with them, they appeared willing to offer an honest day's work.

A pity about the village child. Some family mourned him. But children died frequently in any household. Even kings were not spared that sort of grief.

They were certainly sending off the unfortunate Saxon with a lot of fuss, Jobert decided. The odor of the smoke had not abated, but grown stronger. And was there not a lot of commotion and noise for a peasant funeral?

Jobert rose stiffly and went to the window and unfastened the shutter. A gust of cold, damp air assaulted his face. Squinting against the sudden brightness, he looked out across the valley to the village along the river. Not one, but a half dozen plumes of smoke rose from the group of dwellings.

He frowned as he stared out at the distant scene. Something was wrong. That was no funeral pyre, and the figures running between the burning buildings were not Saxon mourners, but his knights!

Jobert reacted in an instant. Ignoring his weakness, he left the bedchamber and groped his way down the stairs. The hall was almost deserted, but he found a serving wench polishing tableware by the main hearth. "What's happening?" he demanded. "What's going on in the village?"

She looked at him with wide, fearful eyes, but remained mute. Jobert quickly realized that she did not know what he was saying. He struggled to remember the Saxon words, then gave up and hobbled to the doorway.

He did not stop to question the handful of squires and servants in the yard, but hurried to the gate. "Guard!" he shouted. "What the hell is going on? Why are our men attacking the village?"

A helmed head peeked over the edge of the gatetower. "Brevrienne! My lord! Why are you out of bed?"

"I came to find out what is going on! Christ's balls! Will someone please tell me?"

The man started down the ladder. " 'Twas Fornay's order. He said that they should ride out. He said you were ill and not to be bothered."

"But why? Why?"

The guard reached him, panting in his heavy mail. "It all started with the fire. Lady Edeva went to the village—for a funeral, she said. The next thing we know, she comes running back here, screaming that people's homes are on fire. She demanded that some men go down and help the villagers put out the blaze."

The man shrugged. "I sent the men, I'll admit that. Fornay was nowhere to be found, and you know Lady Edeva. There is no arguing with her when she makes up her mind."

"But you said it was Fornay's order."

"That was later. After the Saxons attacked."

"They attacked?"

"Apparently so. I did not see it, but Hamo came back

here, yelling for reinforcements. Says two men are down, that it's an ambush. *Then,* Fornay shows up. He takes the rest of the men and charges down the hill. I would not be surprised if he torched the whole village himself. He was that angry. Shouting about 'the traitorous Saxon bitch' the whole time he armed himself.''

Jobert took a deep breath. He doubted he could stay on a horse; his legs already swayed beneath him. He would have to have Drogo enforce his will. "Go down to the village," he told the guard, "and tell Fornay that he is not to burn anything. Indeed, he is to help put out what fires he can. Also, tell him that he is to take what prisoners he sees fit, and bring them back here. Most of all, inform him that he is not to touch the woman, or he will face my wrath!''

Drogo gaped at him, wide-eyed. "I will do it, my lord, but who will watch the gate? If we were attacked now, the palisade would be completely unprotected."

"I will watch the gate. I may not be able to sit a horse or fight, but I can still shoot a bow well enough to hold off an attack for a short time."

Drogo nodded and ran to get his horse. Jobert opened the gate, and the knight galloped down the trackway. Bending over, Jobert vomited into the dirt, then regained his shaky legs and pushed the gate shut. With the quivering, agonized steps of an old man, he climbed the gate-tower and made his way to the edge of the walkway.

Drogo had reached the village. Jobert saw his mounted figure disappear into the billowing smoke. With a violent oath, he pounded his fist into the wall of the tower. "Damn Fornay! And damn her! What were they thinking of, either of them?''

He clutched the wall as another wave of nausea assaulted him. Part of his sickness came from fear. Had Alan been right and he, wrong? Had Edeva deliberately lured his men into an ambush? If she had, he would punish her. No matter her beauty, her womanliness, he would not be moved to pity. She would pay for the wasted lives of his men!

Why had she done it? Better that she had murdered him in his bath than inflict this treachery upon him. Like Eve in the Garden, she had tempted him, then brought about his ruin.

Bitterness choked his throat. If others suffered because he foolishly trusted a woman, he would never forgive himself.

He gritted his teeth and looked out at the smoke-filled valley. How could she treat his wound and nurse him for days, and then do this to him? It made no sense.

But mayhaps that was the key to it, he thought. Mayhaps there was no sinister plot behind the events unfolding before him. Edeva might well have gone to the village to comfort the dead child's family, and then, without her knowledge, her countrymen set the fires to draw his men into the trap.

Edeva need not have had any part in the ambush. 'Twould be her nature to run for aid if she thought her people were in trouble; it did not necessarily imply that she was in league with the rebels. In fact, the plan probably would not have gone so smoothly if Edeva had been part of it. Hers was an easy face to read; he would have sensed it if she were involved in some sort of intrigue.

All he had noticed during their conversation earlier was that she seemed slightly irritated with him. That happened often enough as to be meaningless.

Jobert felt some of the crippling tension leave him. Something serious had occurred; he might even have lost good men. But Edeva had not betrayed him.

He swayed on the watchtower, praying that his legs would hold him a while longer.

Relief surged through his body as he saw Drogo riding up the hill.

He started down the ladder. He was heading for the gate handle when he heard Drogo's shout. "It's over, my lord. We took two prisoners and scared off the rest."

Jobert pulled open the gate and waved the knight in. "Lady Edeva," he asked. "How fares she?"

"Fornay did not kill her, if that's what you mean, but there's other trouble. One of the prisoners is her brother. She near fainted when she saw him."

Jobert did not think to ask how Drogo had come by this information. He was too near fainting himself.

He waved Drogo up to the tower. "Keep watch. I'm going back to the hall."

His legs wobbled and shifted and waves of gray surrounded him as the shape of the hall loomed ahead. He stumbled through the doorway and collapsed on the nearest bench. He heard the servant girl's cry of alarm and her whispered exhortations. Then all went black.

SEVENTEEN

He regained consciousness a moment later and saw the maidservant bending over him, her face contorted with fear. "Bring me some ale or mead." He made the motion of drinking.

The woman ran off.

Jobert struggled to a sitting position as the servant returned with a cup of ale. He rapidly drank it down, then waved her away. The ale had helped fortify his feeble body, but any more would muddle his wits, and he desperately needed to think clearly when his captain and the others arrived.

Hearing a commotion in the yard, he got to his feet. Outside, Fornay was the first one he saw. The knight's face was set in grim, bitter lines. "Another ambush. Two men badly wounded. I doubt Nigel will regain the use of his arm, even if he lives. I told you she was a traitor."

"Where are the wounded men?"

"They're bringing them now. The bitch said to put them in the hall." He gave a snort of contempt. "If you trust them to *her* care, I vow you will regret it. They'll not live the night!"

"Do you forget that I am alive because of Lady Edeva's efforts?"

Alan shook his head, barely in control of his fury. "I know not why she aided you, what cunning plan she has.

I only know that she led our men into the Saxons' trap. For me, that is proof enough of her evil intent!"

"Where is she?"

"They are bringing her now, with the other prisoners."

Jobert looked toward the gate. His eyes alighted on two fair-haired men being jostled and pushed into the yard. Their arms were bound behind their backs and they both stared straight ahead with the desperate bravado of condemned prisoners.

The men were a study in contrasts, one old and grizzled, with silver threading his fair hair and skin weathered to a ruddy brown, the other, scarce more than a boy. A tall, gawky youth with striking blue eyes and finely modeled features, features which appeared sickeningly familiar to Jobert.

Edeva's brother. There was a curve to the brow, a fullness to the mouth which was unmistakable.

"I've ordered the men to build a gallows." Fornay spoke from behind him. "We'll hang them outside on the hill, in clear view of their cohorts. I do not think it would come amiss to torture them first. Make it clear how we deal with rebel Saxons."

"Nay." Jobert turned toward his captain. "We won't hang them, not yet."

Alan's face grew red and his eyes bulged out. "What do you mean? We cannot let this uprising go unpunished!"

"Have you considered that it might be wise to question them before we put them to death? I would be interested in knowing how many of their band remain and where they hide."

"You think they will betray their companions?" Alan regarded the prisoners thoughtfully. "Mayhaps you are right. With torture, they might well tell us something interesting. Especially the young one." His gaze jerked back to Jobert. "But *then* they must be hung. Justice demands it."

Jobert nodded, although something twisted inside him at the thought. *If he hung her brother, would Edeva ever forgive him?*

He forced his attention back to the present. "Put them in the *souterrain.*"

"And the woman?"

Jobert abruptly noticed Edeva. She stood behind the other prisoners with a knight on either side and her hands bound behind her. Her face was smeared with soot and dirt, her clothes filthy and bloodstained. Unlike the other prisoners, her head was bowed; she did not look at him.

He approached, then reached out and lifted her chin with his hand. She met his gaze, her expression a mingling of anger and despair. "Milord," she said clearly, "you should not be out of bed."

Relief swept through him. Whatever other turmoil her countenance reflected, he did not read guilt there. He released her and turned to Alan. "The woman will come with me."

Alan gave an outraged gasp. "I will not leave you alone with that treacherous bitch!"

"I'll deal with her." Jobert motioned for the men to untie Edeva.

"She must be a witch," Alan cried, "else you would see her perfidy! I tell you, I will not let you do this. I will not have you alone with her!"

Jobert took a step toward the hall, feeling the nausea and weakness strike again. The pain in his shoulder was near unbearable and his vision had begun to waver. "Find a man to aid me," he said. "Where is Rob?"

"He was one of the men wounded. They're bringing him on a litter."

Jobert turned. "How badly?"

"A dagger in the gut."

The grinding weariness bore down on him. *Not Rob. Dear God, not Rob.*

"Have Will aid me."

"My lord."

Jobert turned and vaguely saw the squire right behind him. "Support my arm. Nay, the other one." He closed his eyes, trying not to put his full weight on the much smaller youth.

There was a soft touch on his right arm. "You should not have left your bed," Edeva chided. "This will set your healing back for weeks."

They reached the bedchamber, and Jobert collapsed on the bed. The ringing in his ears and dizziness gradually went away, although the pain seemed worse.

He could hear Edeva moving around the chamber, speaking quietly with Will. She came to the bed and wiped the sweat from his face with a damp cloth. "Would you like some mandrake and poppy? 'Twill help you sleep."

He hesitated. They had much to talk about, but already he could not think clearly for the pain. He also dreaded where the conversation would lead them. The problem of her brother. The questions regarding her part in the ambush. "Yea, I would drink some," he said.

She went to the table and returned with a cup. He drank down the bitter mixture and waited for it to take affect.

Jobert heard Edeva sigh. He forced his eyes open, and saw her by the table, washing her face and hands.

"Is any of the blood yours?" Will asked.

"Nay. 'Tis from Rob."

Her voice was ragged with sorrow, and Jobert knew a sense of relief. If she had been part of the ambush plot, she would not be grieving for the injured men.

"How serious is his wound?" Will asked.

"I don't think the blade struck anything vital, but you must know gut wounds are dangerous. More often than not, they putrefy."

"Sweet heaven," Will whispered. "Is there naught you can do for him?"

"I have sent one of the women to the healer in the village to get her advice. Her suggestions aided your lord. Mayhaps she can tell us how to treat Rob."

Jobert heard rustling sounds as Edeva dried herself, then she said, "I have washed off the worst. Now, I'm going down to see to the wounded men. Lord Brevrienne should sleep. I'll be back before he wakes."

"My lady," Will protested, "Fornay said you must not leave here."

"Would you rather that I left your companions to die?"

In the vague, dreamlike state before sleep, Jobert sensed the squire's hesitation. Will, too, wondered if he could trust Edeva. Like Jobert, Will apparently decided he had no choice. "Go," he said. "I will keep watch over Brevrienne."

The wounded soldiers had been brought to a place near the fire, and the screen which the women used for privacy had been pulled up to shield the men from the commotion in the hall. Edeva went behind it and was surprised to see Wulfget leaning over Rob, wiping his face. She opened her mouth to order the woman back to her own pallet, then changed her mind. Wulfget had a gentle manner which might be useful. If she felt well enough to care for others, Edeva would not gainsay her.

The two women did not speak. Edeva went quickly to the other knight, the one called Niles. His arm had been slashed by a sword blow. Thinking that he went to fight a fire rather than into battle, he had not worn a mail shirt, but only a leather jerkin over his tunic. Above his elbow, a sword had sliced his arm down to the bone. Although his quick-thinking companions had gotten the bleeding stopped, the severed flesh now hung down limply. It would need to be painstakingly stitched back in place if the muscle were ever to function properly again.

The thought of sewing up his arm like a intricate embroidery project horrified Edeva, but she knew she had no choice. First, he must have something for the pain, or he would never hold still. She would need to fetch the sleeping drug from the bedchamber, as well as her needles and thread.

Bracing herself, she moved to Rob's pallet. He watched her as she examined him, but said nothing.

The wound had cut deep into the right side of the knight's belly. But it seemed clean, oozing clear blood when she pressed it, a sign that the entrails might have been missed. She let out her breath. There was a chance, aye, there was a chance.

She turned to Wulfget, still not meeting Rob's gaze. "Has Eadelm returned from the healer?"

"Nay, not yet," Wulfget answered.

Edeva stood away from Rob's pallet and repressed a sigh of frustration. The healer's hut had been one of the first set ablaze Edeva had discovered the fire and run to get men to carry the healer out. But the village men balked, saying they dare not touch Helwenna lest she put a curse on them. 'Twas Normans who finally dragged the old woman from the blazing hut.

Edeva did not think Helwenna had been injured, except her pride. But she was difficult under the best of circumstances; now she might refuse to do any healing work at all.

"I'm going upstairs to fetch some things," Edeva told Wulfget. "When I return, do you think you can help me?"

"With what, mistress?"

Edeva jerked her head toward Niles. "I will need someone to hold his arm while I stitch."

"I . . . I don't know if I am strong enough," Wulfget half whimpered.

"I will have a knight keep him still, but I will need other assistance. I must have someone who has a fine touch and who understands needlework."

"I . . . I will try."

"Good girl." Edeva nodded at Wulfget. Mayhaps she could mold the young woman into a useful servant despite her delicacy.

Edeva hurried upstairs and got the things she needed, then returned to the hall. After giving Niles a strong dose of the mandrake and poppy mixture, she washed her hands again, this time in near-searing water and the cleansing herbs Helwenna had told her about.

As she dried her hands, her fingers trembled. She had

restitched Jobert's wound, but 'twas a simple one, unlike to do more than scar a bit if she sewed it crooked. This time a man's whole future depended on her skill. If she failed, Niles might never wield a sword again.

A squire brought an oil lamp, and Edeva bent to her task.

The queasy thought that she sewed flesh rather than fabric soon left her and her hands steadied. Nothing mattered but lining up the fibers of the muscles and painstakingly stitching them in place.

Occasionally, Edeva glanced over to see how Wulfget fared. The girl went green-gilled early on, then, like Edeva, gradually calmed. Her pale, slender fingers gently smoothed the knight's forehead when she was not threading needles for Edeva or helping her tie off knots with the little silver scissors.

Edeva idly wondered if Wulfget might not be the one to teach healing skills to, rather than Eadelm. The fragile-looking young woman was proving to be much stronger than Edeva had thought. And there was clearly something in Wulfget's tender manner which anyone hurt or sick would find reassuring.

At last, Edeva motioned for Wulfget to bring the clean rags for bandages. "Why don't you bind it up?" she told the younger woman as she swiped at her own brow. "Wrap the arm securely but not too tight." She watched as Wulfget carefully followed her instructions.

Edeva's mood of accomplishment abruptly shattered as Fornay spoke from behind her. "Well done, lady. If I did not know better, I would think you actually had a care for whether Niles heals or not."

She sighed and turned to face the knight. "I mislike seeing anyone suffer."

"You were not always so gentle-natured," he taunted. "I remember a time when you wished to kill us all, when you would have scratched out our eyes if your hands had not been bound."

Edeva remembered, thinking how quickly the faceless,

hated enemy had changed into men whom she felt compassion for.

"Do you hope we will show the same pity toward the Saxon prisoners?" Fornay asked, "I would not count on it, Lady Edeva. Lord Brevrienne may have a tendre for *you,* but it does not extend to the rest of your kind. As soon as we have the information we seek of them, the Saxons will be put to death."

"Please do not torture them!" Edeva's stomach twisted into knots at the thought of Alnoth suffering. "If it's information you seek, let me speak to them. I will find out whatever you wish to know!"

"Not likely," Fornay answered, his dark eyes gleaming.

"But Alnoth's only a boy! He won't see fifteen years until after Yule!"

"He was man enough to set the fires which drew our men into your trap. Two men lie sore wounded because of his actions. Even if he were not a Saxon, he would be punished for that."

Edeva felt her heart grow heavy. There did not seem to be any way to save Alnoth. Unless she could convince Jobert to spare them. Jesu, she would do nearly anything to accomplish that. Vow to serve as his chatelaine forever . . . Spy upon her other brothers and betray them to the Normans . . .

Nay. As angry as she was with Godric and Beornwold for risking Alnoth's life and burning the village, she did not want them to die.

What could she offer Jobert to sway him to mercy?

"I would advise you not to do anything until Lord Brevrienne gives the order," she told Fornay, then started toward the stairs.

The Norman caught her arm. "Where do you go?"

"To see Brevrienne."

"Nay." Fornay's eyes gleamed. "You will not use your witch's wiles on him while he is weak and injured."

"Who will stop me?" Edeva challenged.

"I will." Fornay moved closer.

Edeva was tall for a woman, and Fornay short for a man. They stood almost face-to-face. "How?" she asked silkily

Fornay's grip tightened on her arm. "Do not try my patience, wench. I might decide to have you thrown into the *souterrain* with the others."

"Nay!" Wulfget gasped. "She is our lady. You cannot!"

Fornay looked at Wulfget as if she had sprouted two heads. Mayhaps if she had, he would have been less surprised. Edeva, too, was stunned. What had gotten into shy, meek Wulfget? *And where had she learned to speak Norman French?*

The young woman looked away and said in a muffled voice. "Do not do it, Alan. Please. 'Tis not right."

The Norman grew uneasy. "I was merely threatening," he said.

Edeva stepped past him. Behind, she heard Wulfget's soft voice. "Let her go, Alan."

Edeva wondered at the power Wulfget had over the Norman knight. It seemed Fornay would do whatever he could to please the young woman. Did *she* have any of that same sort of control over Jobert? If she begged him for Alnoth's life, would he heed her?

Edeva climbed the stairs, deep in thought. This would be the test of Jobert's feelings for her. If she could sway him to spare Alnoth, she would know he cared.

And if she could not?

She feared that if Jobert ordered Alnoth's death, a part of her would die.

Poor Alnoth! She thought of him down in the dark, cold cellar. Her little brother. She had cared for him since she was a toddling youngster and he, a wide-eyed, round-faced babe. At four years older, she had usually managed to make him do her will. But she had also mothered and comforted him, taking pleasure in his accomplishments as he grew. Now all her efforts would be wasted. His life ended before it had really begun.

A sob rose in Edeva's throat as she opened the door to

the bedchamber. There must be some way to convince Jobert to spare Alnoth. She had to try.

He woke at the sound of voices. Edeva's and a man's. Will, he thought, although he could not be certain. All of his recollection of the past day seemed hazy.

Something had happened. The fire in the village . . . an ambush . . . some men injured . . . Saxons captured.

The thoughts seemed far away, as if they were in someone else's mind. The sleeping potion. It eased his pain, but made him feel as if his head were stuffed with unspun wool.

He could not make out what Edeva and the man were saying.

Footsteps. The door opened and closed. Jobert forced his eyes open, wondering if they had left him.

Edeva stood on the other side of the chamber, washing. She had taken off her kirtle and pushed her shift down off her shoulders. Her back was bare and her braids fell forward, revealing her pale, slender neck. The sight made something inside him throb.

She pushed the shift down and began to wash her underarms and breasts. Jobert watched, entranced. Had ever a woman had such beautiful breasts? So full and opulent, yet firm to the touch, like some exquisite, ripe fruit. With round, smooth nipples the color of strawberries.

She dropped the washing cloth in the bowl of water and turned away from the table. Her breasts swayed enticingly with each movement.

Her actions were slow, almost dreamlike. He watched her undo her braids and smooth the rippling tresses with her fingers. Then she went to the chest in the corner and fetched her comb.

The comb slid sinuously through the wavy strands, then she brought it up again to repeat the journey. Curls of gold blanketed her breasts like a sheer, alluring garment.

He longed to sweep the soft locks away and reveal the perfection beneath.

At last, she put the comb aside and grasped some strands of hair as if she meant to plait it once more.

"Edeva." He forced the word from his dry throat.

She turned, and he saw her embarrassment as she realized he had been watching her. Instinctively, she tried to pull up her shift.

"Nay," he said. "I would not have you cover yourself. I vow the sight of you heals me with each glance." He smiled at her, trying to appear healthy and strong. At least one part of him was functional. His shaft strained against the blankets covering him, as hard and eager as ever. "Bring me a drink," he said. "My mouth is dry."

She went to do his bidding, and he admired the smooth grace of her movements. When she brought the cup to him, he reached out to take it, his eyes still fixed on her.

"I am pleased you seem so well and alert. I thought the drug would make you sleep through the night."

The drug. That was what made his thoughts swim, his vision almost dreamlike. He would not tell her that his wits were not yet aright. If he did, she might not be willing to do what he wished of her. She would see him as a sickly, injured man, not the randy stallion his lower body assured him he was.

He drank the water down. It seemed delicious, nectar from heaven. All his senses were keen and yet not quite normal. His thoughts still slipped away from him before he could fully think them.

"Take off your shift," he whispered. His words seemed slurred; he hoped she would not notice.

She hesitated. "Are you certain . . ."

"Yea, very certain. The sight of you . . ." He did not finish, knowing his hungry gaze told her the rest.

She undressed like a virgin, shy and uncertain. Jobert caught his breath, wondering if he could wait. She approached the bed, the gleaming gold triangle of her maiden's hair at the same level as his face. He forced his eyes upward, to the bounty of her breasts and then, her beguiling face.

He reached out and splayed his hand over one warm, silky peak. "Lean toward me," he whispered.

Slowly, smoothly, she did so. He took one nipple in his mouth and teased the nub with his tongue. With his hand, he caressed her other breast, matching the rhythm of his lips.

She liked it slightly rough, he recalled. Her body seemed to tense as he increased the pressure. He used his teeth with utmost delicacy, and was rewarded with a groan from her lips.

Suddenly, he wanted to kiss her. He released her breasts and reached up to draw her face down to his. Gentle, slow. Those full, petulant lips against his own. His tongue brushed across them, then sought the liquid warmth of her mouth. Exploring, mating with her tongue, then thrusting strongly, possessively between her lips.

She trembled, leaning over him, and he drew her onto the bed, rolling her across his body. "Jobert," she moaned, "you'll hurt your shoulder."

"Nay, I will let you do all the work."

She drew away, eyes wide. He knew she remembered the way they had pleasured each other when she bathed him. He shook his head and wordlessly pulled the covers back to reveal his bold erection. "I would be inside you this time."

She looked at his ruddy, engorged organ; then, again, she hesitated. "Jobert," she whispered, "do you care for me?"

He frowned, startled by her question. Never before had she asked anything like that of him. "Of course," he answered.

"And if I asked a boon of you, would you consider it?"

He reached up and drew her down, kissing her deeply. "What sort of boon?"

"Let the Saxon prisoners live, at least the younger one. Please, Jobert." She pulled away, her breasts jiggling before his fascinated eyes. His hunger for their joining made it difficult for him to think.

"Promise me," she whispered breathily. "If you will grant me this boon, I will do anything you ask. Anything," she repeated.

He nodded, his mind swimming with thoughts of the delights ahead of them. He had Edeva as a virgin and as a seductress, now he would experience her as his willing slave.

The only thing troubling him was where to begin. As much as he longed to drag out their foreplay, he knew his willpower would not last long. "I want to be inside you," he said.

She took a deep breath and looked at him, as if puzzling out the meaning of his request. Then she moved her body over his.

He watched her maneuver herself into position, her long, golden-skinned thighs splayed wide. Although he longed to touch, taste and explore the folds of her delicious womanhood, he forbore those splendors. This time, it would be she who guided him inside her silky opening. He would not aid her, only watch.

She grasped him with uncertain fingers, then brought her hips down.

Jobert closed his eyes as he slid into warm, slick paradise. He'd forgotten how tight she was, how exquisitely, torturously snug. For a moment, he wondered if she would be able to move, with him impaling her, penetrating deep. Then she gave a gasp and lifted her hips and thrust downward.

He gritted his teeth against the compulsion to climax instantly. Nay, he would not let this moment be the end of it. Somehow, he would last. Somehow, he would even manage to watch.

To distract himself, he concentrated on her pleasure, bringing his hand to the place where they were joined and stroking the swollen, distended opening which enveloped him. She shuddered at his caress, and he felt her grow even wetter.

His fingers moved faster, urging her on. She threw back her head and gave a helpless cry. He enjoyed an ecstatic vision of her release, reveling in the sight of her intent, lovely face, the dazzling beauty of her voluptuous body, primed now to the peak of sexual magnificence. He reached up and drew her head down, joining her mouth with his as he lunged upward with his hips.

Waves of vibration flowed over him as she reached the summit once more. His own control snapped and plunged him headlong into pulsing, violent rapture.

He came to himself again, still clutching her sweat-dewed body. Gently, he slipped out of her and pulled her down to rest her face against his chest. His fingers stroked her lush hair as he caught his breath. In the back of his muddled, hazy mind, he wondered how long it would be before he grew aroused again.

She had said she would do anything . . .

EIGHTEEN

Jobert sat up and clutched his head in his hands. Jesu, he felt wretched! As if he'd spent the night in some foul tavern where the wine had flowed as freely as water. His mouth tasted foul, and his body felt as if he'd been in a violent brawl, especially his shoulder, where a fierce pain stabbed to the bone.

He rose and went to rinse out his mouth and use the chamber pot, then started back to the bed, musing over his fanciful, erotic dreams. Not since he'd been a green squire had he experienced such heated, vivid fantasies. They seemed almost real . . .

Two feet from the bed, Jobert paused. Edeva sprawled across the other side, her long hair wildly arrayed over her naked, sleep-flushed body. Suddenly, he knew that those compelling, provocative images had not been dreams.

As if she sensed him watching her, Edeva stirred. She brushed the hair out of her face and raised her head. Her blue eyes met his nakedness. She looked him up and down, then went still. She, too, recalled the past night. She looked away.

Jobert watched her, puzzled. Though some of the things he remembered almost shocked him, he knew she had been willing. Why did she avert her eyes?

He moved closer, as if he meant to climb back in the bed. She took a sharp breath and slid back the blankets to reveal her breasts. But if her body presented an enticing picture, her expression appeared uneasy, almost distraught.

Worse yet, there was guilt in her eyes.

Jobert was mystified. Mayhaps it was natural for a modest woman to be a bit uncomfortable after a night of abandoned pleasure. But his instincts told him that this was something else.

Whatever troubled her, he was not up to dealing with it this morning. Not until he ate, at least.

He dressed, then looked toward the bed before leaving. She had lain down, but still looked troubled. He bent over to give her a quick kiss. She scarce acknowledged the brief touch of his lips.

When he reached the hall, he ordered the first servant he saw to bring him food. He sat down at one of the tables and exhaled a heavy sigh. His thoughts felt disordered, his body weak and fatigued.

"Jobert!" Alan hurried toward him. "I am relieved to see you up." He sat down on the bench across the trestle table. "I've come from the Saxon prisoners. I say it is hopeless. Even if we could get them to betray their fellow rebels, how would we understand them? The only people who speak enough Saxon to translate are the miller and Edeva, and we cannot trust either of them. I say we hang the wretches now and be done with it."

Jobert sighed as he recalled that he had to decide what to do with the Saxon prisoners.

Alan's expression grew harsh. "I know the woman will argue otherwise, but you cannot be swayed by her. The Saxons have cost us good men. Niles will mend, but his arm may not be the same. As for Rob, no one seems to know. The healer in the village said he should lie still and take only liquids, no real food. If he becomes fevered, there is a potion he is to take. Otherwise, we wait and see if the wound grows poisoned. Wulfget is watching him now." He jerked his head toward the screen in the corner of the hall.

Like blows to his aching head, worries assaulted Jobert. He used the excuse of eating to avoid commenting. Alan gave him more information about the conflict the previous day, then fell silent.

As he finished his food, Jobert looked up to see Edeva standing nearby. She'd braided her hair in the usual demure style and donned one of her simple work kirtles, but the image of her wanton nakedness lingered in his mind.

Seeing her, Alan's eyes narrowed, and he said, "What of it, Jobert? Do we hang the prisoners today? The gallows are almost finished."

"Nay! You cannot. You promised me, Jobert!"

Alan's mouth dropped open. "What did she do, completely sap your reason with her whoring ways?"

At his words, Edeva went crimson, and Jobert suddenly guessed the source of her guilt. Before they made love, she had asked that provocative, coaxing question, *"Do you care for me, Jobert?"*

A sense of uneasiness permeated his thoughts. Had Edeva bedded him simply because she wanted him to spare her brother? How much of her passion was pretense? Had she enjoyed any of it? If she would spread her thighs to save one brother, what might she do to save the rest of her kin?

Anger rose in him, swift and hard. She saw the change. Her eyes widened. "Please," she whispered.

Jobert pushed the remains of his food aside and rose. "Let us go see the prisoners, Edeva. You and I."

Anxiety clutched at Edeva's thoughts as she followed Jobert through the hall. He thought she had tricked him!

He might even believe Fornay's accusations. For all she knew, he was taking her to the *souterrain* to join the other prisoners.

Her heart pounded as she hurried to catch up with him. She glanced at his face, searching for some sign of sympathy or tenderness. His features seemed carved of stone, his mouth set grimly, his eyes staring straight ahead.

Her panic increased. Should she try to explain, tell him that she had pleasured him not simply because she hoped to win mercy for her brother, but because she longed for his touch?

Why should he believe her? To him, her actions must appear calculating. She could not forget how she asked him to show mercy to her brother, promising him "anything" if he agreed.

Anything. What a suggestive word, laden with possibilities. She had fulfilled her part of the agreement. The things she had done—she could scarce think of them without blushing to her toes.

Her thighs spread over his face, the intimate acts his tongue and lips had performed.

Or, the things she had done to him. *Near swallowing his shaft, tasting his seed and the flavor of herself upon him.*

His hands cupping her buttocks as he urged her on. His fingers flicking lightly against her cleft to make her scream, even while his own passion crested hot and wet deep inside her.

He awoke some madness within her. The more she experienced, the more she hungered for. She had been eager for every tantalizing secret he taught her.

But now, things between them were suddenly tainted with doubt and deception. Would he ever think of their wild, uninhibited lovemaking without believing she had manipulated him?

They reached the *souterrain* entrance and waited there while Jobert sent a squire back for a torch. Edeva began to pace.

"What is it, Edeva?" he asked. "Do you fear I will take back my promise?"

She met his cold, green gaze and the breath seemed to leave her body. "My lord, I . . ."

"Nay, do not speak of it. I would have my memories if nothing else."

He jerked around, as if he could not stand the sight of her. Edeva swallowed, wondering what he would do. He was a man of honor. His word given, even under deceptive circumstances, was still his word. He would not hang her brother, but there would be some other price paid—she felt certain of it.

The squire returned with the blazing torch. Jobert had the young man pull open the door for them. "After you, my lady," he said.

Edeva felt her way down the slippery stairs. Although the ground had not yet frozen, the cellar was numbingly cold. She thought of her brother, left there with no source of heat. Had they fed him? Brought water?

"This way," Jobert said, touching her shoulder, urging her down the right-hand passageway. He need not have given her direction; she recalled the way from when she had been imprisoned there.

But that was early autumn, before the stones seeped bone-chilling dampness. She had been so unholy angry then, so eager to kill the first man who approached, that she had scarce noticed the misery of her circumstances.

They entered the chamber and saw the prisoners, and a wave of relief washed through her. Although they were shackled, both Alnoth and old Withan seemed unharmed. The prisoners stood as they entered. Edeva sought to send a message of reassurance with her eyes. Then Jobert's big hand clamped around her body.

Withan remained impassive, but Alnoth's gaunt face twisted into a mask of hatred.

"Ask them how they fare, Edeva. If they have been well fed. If they are comfortable."

The words were taunting, but more distressing was what Jobert did. His hand came up to curve around the swell of her breast. Edeva saw Alnoth suck in his breath, and his expression grew murderous. *Does he mean to provoke Alnoth into attacking, and then kill him?*

"Speak to them," Jobert urged. "I trust you will repeat my words as I give them."

The word "trust" was laden with mockery. Edeva felt like an animal in a trap. She cleared her throat. "My lord asks if you have been fed."

"Aye," Withan answered. "We have been treated well enough."

"You are not too cold?"

The old man grinned crookedly. "A blanket would not come amiss, my lady."

"Oh, Withan, I am so sorry!" The words came out before she could stop them. The old man's bravery broke her heart.

Jobert gave her a shake. "I think you have said things I have not told you. Will you obey me, for once?" His hand kept higher, near fondling her breast. "Mayhaps you should tell them how you saved their lives. What you did to buy my largess."

The rancor in his voice cut into her. Edeva gave a kind of moan. Was this what her future held? She was not certain she would not rather die than face Jobert's cold contempt each day.

Alnoth stared at Jobert's hand, touching her familiarly. He took a step forward, and his eyes blazed with fury. "Has he hurt you, Edeva? Has he ravished you?"

She shook her head, realizing that she dare not let her brother see her distress. "Nay, nay, he has been just and reasonable. He has treated our people with respect and tolerance. He even allows me to order the manor as I see fit." Questions still lingered in Alnoth's eyes. She took a deep breath and added, "I share his bed, aye, but it is by choice, not coercion."

Alnoth's gaze grew horrified. Edeva feared that he might try to lunge at Jobert, despite his shackles. Withan anticipated her worries. "There now, boy." He took hold of Alnoth's arm. "You cannot expect a woman to do otherwise under the circumstances. If she is satisfied with her treatment, you will have to accept it."

"Is that true?" Alnoth asked, his voice cracking. "Is it true you are satisfied with him as your lord?"

Edeva nodded. So help her, it *was* true. Somehow her enemy had suborned her hatred and stolen her heart. *If only he would forgive her.*

"What do you tell him?" Jobert asked.

"I said that I shared your bed by choice. That you treated me well."

Jobert was silent for a moment, then he said, "If only I understood Saxon. If only I could be certain that you do not lie."

"You said once that my face showed everything," Edeva whispered. "Do you really think that I could have pretended all of what passed between us last night?"

She heard him take a deep breath. He remembered. He could not block out the magic of their joining.

His hand left her breast and moved to her waist. A possessive gesture, but not a humiliating one. "I won't hang them, Edeva, but neither can I let them go. Can you accept that?"

She nodded. "Mayhaps someday, if they swore to you, you could set them free."

"Mayhaps. But not now, not while Rob and Niles's lives hang in the balance. Do you think they can endure imprisonment? With some men 'tis more cruel than hanging."

"I will ask them." She took a deep breath. "Alnoth, Withan—my lord says that he cannot release you until things improve between his people and yours. Can you accept being prisoners, not knowing if you will ever be free?"

Withan smiled wanly. "My lady, you do not live to the age I am by acting foolishly. Of course I choose life over death. At least that way, there is hope. If he hangs us, that is the end."

"Alnoth?" Edeva prompted.

Alnoth moved restlessly, his shackles clanking. "How long, sister? How long are we to be kept here?"

"It depends on what the others do. If they continue to make trouble, to attack the Normans, Lord Brevrienne cannot risk letting you go."

"I would swear to him!" Alnoth cried suddenly, "Give him my oath not to fight him any longer!"

Edeva sighed. Once that might have been enough, but now . . . "I don't know, Alnoth. I imagine he will have to think on it, see how events unfold . . ." If she could regain Jobert's trust, there might be hope for her brother.

"In the meantime, are we to remain here?" Alnoth looked distraught. "Even sleeping in the forest was not so cold. And I hate the dark."

"Mayhap there is somewhere else . . ." Edeva faced Jobert for the first time since they left the hall. "My lord, I have another boon to ask of you. Will you consider moving the prisoners to somewhere less cold and confined?"

"Another boon, Edeva? And what will my generosity gain me this time? You have already promised me 'anything'. What else can you offer?"

She lowered her gaze. "Please, Jobert. I ask you this out of simple Christian charity. My brother is young and already thin and weakened. Withan is an old man. If you leave them here, they might well sicken and die."

Jobert set his jaw. Was he a fool? Edeva's plea moved him. If he showed mercy by not hanging these rebels, then mercy also demanded that he give them a chance at life. "If I can find a place which is secure and not too difficult to guard, yea, I will move them."

Edeva heaved a deep sigh. Even in the dim light, he could see tears of gratitude shimmer in her eyes. How could he condemn her for trying to save the people she loved? Would he not do the same in her circumstances?

Besides, it was her kind heart which had won his affection. That and her proud, tenacious spirit. If he thought about how he felt about her, it was frightening.

But he must not give in altogether. There were still many questions Edeva must answer. That she fought so valiantly for her brother's life made it reasonable to think that she might aid the rebels if she had other kin among them.

"Come, Edeva," he said. "I will send someone with food and blankets for them."

He took her arm and led her out the narrow passageway. As always, the dark, enclosed nature of the place made his flesh crawl and his thoughts fill with haunted memories.

He was glad to have Edeva near, to feel her warmth and strength as a remedy for his fears.

When they had climbed the stairs and were out in the open air, Edeva turned to look at him, her eyes yearning. He made his expression stern. "Go to the bedchamber and await me there."

The look of tremulous hope she gave him nearly made him weaken. She was so lovely, so beguiling. The sight of Alan approaching across the yard brought him to his senses. "Go, Edeva."

She hurried off, moving with that proud grace which he so admired.

Alan shot her a glance, his eyes narrowed. "Do you do as she bids? Do you spare her brother?"

"Yea, I do."

"Your pity is misplaced."

"I do not think so. What profit is there in hanging an old man and a boy?"

Alan exploded. "To show the others how we deal with rebellion! To make an example of them!"

"We have already done that. We hung the prisoners we took when we first arrived. If that did not deter the rebels, then nothing will."

"But what of the villagers? The Saxon servants? They will think you soft!"

"Nay, they will think me reasonable and compassionate. I would not have them hate me nor believe me to be a heartless monster."

"A commander must be powerful and ruthless, else he will lose all!"

"A commander, yea, that is true, but a lord's role is different. The war for England is over, Alan. Now we must make peace with her people. They are the ones who till the fields and reap the land's bounty. They are the ones who will make Oxbury prosper."

Alan shook his head. Jobert continued, "Can you not see how far we have progressed by gaining the Saxons' cooperation? The people have returned to the village, the servants do their duty instead of defying us. Have you considered that when the rebels attacked, the villagers did not aid them?

"They were busy putting out the fires, saving their homes."

"Exactly. The rebels, their own countrymen, became their enemies, and we, the invaders, were the ones who saved them. I believe there will come a time when the people of Oxbury will begin to work against the rebels. They will not want anything to bring down our wrath upon them—they may even alert us before an attack."

Alan rubbed at his face, suddenly looking weary. "There is sense in your words, but still, I am dissatisfied. I did not imagine when I decided to follow William that I would end up like this. I no longer feel like a warrior."

"If you wish to return to a life of war, I will release you from your obligation to me. I'm certain William would be happy to have another knight to fight for him, especially one who has no interest in owning land someday."

"I did not say that!"

"But 'tis what your words mean. To have land means to be a farmer and an administrator rather than a warrior."

"A lord must always fight for his land."

"In Normandy that was true, but one of William's goals for England was to keep Norman from fighting Norman. To that end, he has outlawed private war. I know the peace won't hold forever. There are always greedy men who want more. But for now, there seems to be enough land for everyone."

Alan was silent. Jobert wondered what his captain would decide. While he would hate to lose such a capable officer, there was no profit in having a man who desired war over peace command his household force.

"Mayhaps you should wed," Jobert suggested. "Having a wife might ease your restlessness. 'Tis clear you are fond of Wulfget."

"Wulfget! She is a Saxon!"

"Nonetheless . . . she seems to have gained your interest."

"She is . . ." Alan fumbled for words, "She pleases me, that is true."

"Have you bedded her?"

"Nay."

"Why not? She is only a Saxon." Jobert repressed a smile. He found it rather entertaining to turn Alan's words against him. The knight clearly felt much more for Wulfget than he was willing to admit.

"I fear to hurt her," Alan answered. "She is so delicate and slender."

"Hurt her?"

He nodded. "She is a virgin. You must know that the first time, the woman bleeds and it pains her."

Jobert raised his brows. He had not agonized greatly when he took Edeva's maidenhead. He had tried not to cause her more discomfort than necessary, but he had always anticipated that the pleasure he could give her would be much greater than the pain.

"Wulfget is like a rare, lovely flower," Alan said. "I cannot see her indulging in a crude, carnal act."

"Mayhaps she would like it."

Alan shook his head. "She is not like Lady Edeva. She is not earthy and strong."

Jobert considered Alan's description of Edeva. The fool had no idea how appealing "earthy and strong" could be. 'Twas a delight to bed a substantial, spirited woman he did not have to worry about crushing beneath him, to know his bedpartner was capable of matching him in vigor and enthusiasm. He did not think he would care to bed a timid thing like Wulfget.

He said, "If you do not have interest in Wulfget as a wife, mayhaps another man would. Edeva has urged me to find husbands for some of the other maidservants, lest we have a crop of bastards next summer. I feel I should marry off Wulfget as well, for the sake of propriety."

Alan's mouth dropped open. "How can you think of giving her to another man?"

"You have said you do not want her. And I certainly cannot have you wed a healthy young servant like Wulfget and then be squeamish about bedding her. There is no profit in it for me. If Oxbury is to grow and prosper, there must be babies born of every union where God wills it."

"Of course I would bed her if she were my wife!"

"For that matter, are you certain Wulfget is still a virgin? Plenty of other men have shown an interest in her. Mayhaps one less chivalrous than you has already planted his seed. If she is with child, I would obviously have to marry her off immediately."

"She is a virgin yet! I would swear my life on it!" Alan's face had grown bright red and his eyes were wild. Jobert could almost take pity on the hapless knight—if he did not think too much about the way Alan had always treated Edeva. Mayhaps he would tell her about this conversation, Jobert thought. She might know vindication of a sort to see her provoker suffer the tortures of the lovelorn.

But he got ahead of himself. He was supposed to maintain his suspicions of Edeva until she satisfactorily answered his questions about the raid. 'Twas going to be difficult to interrogate her with all this talk of "carnal acts" fresh in his mind.

Jobert excused himself from Alan, certain he had left the knight with enough to think about, then headed toward the hall. He went directly to the area where the wounded men were. There was no sign of Wulfget. Eadelm, the plain, brawny girl that Edeva had said she was training as a healer, watched over the men.

Jobert nodded to the maidservant, then went first to Niles's pallet. The wounded man sat up, "My lord."

Jobert waved him down.

"Nay, I will sit awhile. Indeed, I fear I will go mad merely lying here."

"You feel strong enough?"

"Yea, except for my arm. I don't know if it will ever work

right, but at least 'tis shaped like an arm again instead of a lump of mangled gristle. Your lady, I must commend her—she has amazing patience. They say it took her near two hours to sew me up, and all the while her hands stayed steady."

"She is a very skilled seamstress. Although, I vow, I would rather she practice her art on cloth rather than the flesh of my knights."

"I, also." Niles grinned back at him

Jobert felt unsettled. This was not going as planned. He'd gone to see the wounded men as a reminder of how disastrous the Saxon attack had been, not to hear Edeva's praises sung.

He gave Niles a few words of encouragement, then went to see Rob.

The knight greeted him with a cheerful expression. "You see, Jobert? I have found the perfect way to avoid work, to lie around all day with lovely ladies waiting upon me." Rob smiled warmly at Eadelm as he said this, and the young woman's homely face grew almost radiant. Leave it to Rob to be chivalrous, even on the sickbed!

" 'Tis pleased I am you enjoy lying on your lazy arse," Jobert said, mouth quirking, "but I vow it can't continue. There is much work to do. I cannot afford to have you shirk your duties much longer."

"I will do my best to heal, milord." Rob grinned back gamely.

"In truth, how do you feel? Is there anything I can get you?"

"Nay, I have everything a man could want, except the food leaves something to be desired." He made a face at Eadelm. "Always it is gruel, gruel and more gruel she brings me."

Eadelm approached the bed, looking distraught.

"Nay, nay, you've done nothing wrong," Rob reassured her. He turned to Jobert. "I know she's done her best for me. And at least I have not fevered. Lady Edeva says that is an excellent sign."

"It is," Jobert agreed. "If the wound were poisoned, you would have sickened ere this."

They were both silent, as if praying that his optimistic words were true. "Has the priest been to see you?" Jobert asked.

"Nay, not since he thought to give me last rites when I was first brought in."

Jobert frowned. What a useless bastard Father Reibald had turned out to be. He never seemed to be around when his services might be needed. What *did* the holy man do with his time?

He turned to Eadelm, wondering if she had learned any Norman French. He pointed to Rob. "Take care of him, keep him as comfortable as possible."

She nodded fervently.

"She understands a little," Rob said. "I have naught else to do with my time, so I've been teaching both Wulfget and Eadelm to speak our language."

"Wulfget also?"

"Yea, she had learned a bit already; but she was eager to learn more."

Jobert nodded thoughtfully. Rob would make a worthy rival for Alan. 'Twould be interesting to see how things played out. If nothing else, worry over Wulfget might distract Alan from his obsession with persecuting Edeva.

Did she deserve to be spared? he wondered as he climbed the stairs. What if she really were a spy and a traitor, and Fornay was the only one who discerned it?

The thought caused a chill along his spine. His feelings for Edeva might well blind him to her true nature. Heaven knew, he was besotted with her, and lovesick men were not known for being rational nor wise!

He paused in the stairwell. Should he keep his distance for a few days, then question her? By then, the intensity of his erotic memories would have ebbed, and he could deal with her more dispassionately.

But his desire for her was not likely to wane, and the cost of the ambush was fresh in his mind. If Rob and Niles

healed and all was well, 'twould be easy to forget the deadly
trap the Saxons had set . . . until the next time.

    Resolutely, he strode up the stairs.

NINETEEN

Edeva was sewing when he entered. She sat on a stool by the table, using a lamp for light. He breathed a sigh of relief to see that she remained dressed, her hair braided. If she had waited for him in a provocative pose, his suspicions would have only increased.

He sat down on the bed as his strength deserted him and his ailing body reminded him how pathetic he really was. Gathering his determination, he said, "Edeva, I must know what happened in the village."

She put her sewing aside. "I told you about Leogyth, the child who died?"

He nodded.

"Although the priest refused to come, they had a funeral anyway. The miller said a few words over the body and they lit the pyre. We stood around silently, showing our respect for the family's grief. Then, all at once, someone shouted that Helwenna's hut was on fire. I sent Baldric, one of the squires who accompanied me to the village, back to the gatehouse to ask for aid."

"Why did you take an escort?" Jobert asked. "Why not go alone? They are your people—why would you fear them?"

A bitter look crossed her face. "I sought protection not from the villagers, but from the opinion of your knights. I thought if I had Normans with me, they could report back that I had done nothing questionable nor sinister."

She took a deep breath and continued. "I could not get Helwenna to leave her hut, nor would any of the village men try to drag her out. She wanted to die there, but all I could think of was her knowledge perishing. When the first knights arrived, I asked them to carry her out, and they did. By then, several other huts were on fire. The villagers grabbed every bucket and tub they could carry to bring water from the river to put out the fires. I sent the knights off to help them and stayed with Helwenna.

"Soon, I heard one of the knights shout that the Saxons were attacking. I left Helwenna and went to see. Smoke was everywhere, but I could make out men fighting at the edge of the woods. I did not know what to do."

She shook her head. "I ran to help the villagers bring more water. When Fornay and the other men arrived, the attackers immediately disappeared into the woods, except for Alnoth and Withan, who were captured. Fornay grabbed me and accused me of plotting the whole incident. He called me a whore and a traitorous bitch."

Her face went rigid with anger, and Jobert felt his own body tighten. "Fornay gave me no chance to explain," she continued, "but ordered me bound like the other prisoners. I took satisfaction in the fact that his men did not want to tie my hands. He had to tell them twice." She raised her eyes to Jobert's. "I swear, I did naught but try to help the villagers. I was not part of the ambush. And I did not want Rob to be injured, nor anyone else. I had hoped for peace, that we could all work together . . ."

Jobert watched her, feeling her turmoil. She had been caught between two loyalties and had tried to do the best for her people. In the end, he believed that she had sided with him, with the Normans.

He rose from the bed and took a step toward her. "What are you sewing?"

" 'Tis an altar cloth. Father Reibald said I should make one, that it was my duty as the woman of the household."

"How near to finished are you?"

" 'Twill take a sennight or more to complete it."

"Then you will have to put it aside. I'm going to see King William. I could wear soldier's garb when I speak to him, but there will be courtiers aplenty, and I want to look like a real lord." He pointed to the coffer in the corner. "I want you to refashion one of those fine tunics for my court garb."

"Why do you make this journey?" she asked.

"I sent a message to William weeks ago and have not received an answer yet. Since I know that William is coming to London for the Yule season, I have decided to speak to him myself." He sat down on the bed and began to take off his boots. "And while you are at it, find some fine clothes for yourself, Edeva. I'm taking you with me."

She stared at him. "Why do you want *me* to go?"

Jobert regarded her thoughtfully. Dare he tell her that he had asked William's permission to wed with her? What if William refused?

"I wish your company on the journey." He tossed his boots aside and began to unfasten his crossgarters. Edeva still watched him. He knew she had many questions, but he was too tired to deal with them.

Once undressed, he climbed into bed and closed his eyes. He was weary beyond reason. If he was to be fit to travel, he would have to rest and gather his strength for the next few days.

He heard Edeva moving around the room, and he felt a throb of longing for her. 'Twould be easy to ask her to pleasure him as she had before. But, nay, he did not want it to always be like that. He would not bed her again until he could perform as a man should.

Edeva poked at the dying coals in the brazier, trying to decide whether to have someone fetch more from the hearth in the hall. But she did not want to go downstairs and find a squire. She told herself that she was not prone to taking a chill and there were plenty of blankets and furs on the bed. Besides, she was better off than her brother and Withan, down in that miserable, dank cellar.

Her heart twisted in her chest at the thought. Somehow she would have to convince Jobert to move the prisoners to a more comfortable place before they left to see William.

Jesu, would she ever fathom this man's mind? She could not imagine why Jobert was taking her to see the Norman king. Was it because he did not trust her at Oxbury without him? But why was *he* going? What was this message he had sent?

Mayhaps she should ask one of the knights. But Jobert Brevrienne was a very close-mouthed man, unlikely to share his plans with anyone. Except Fornay, and she would not ask that black-hearted wretch!

She blew out the candle and began to undress. When she had stripped down to her shift, she hesitated. Should she take it off and offer a clear invitation to the man in the bed?

But did he want her? She felt certain that he believed her innocent of plotting against him, but there might be other reasons he would not want to bed her—fatigue, pain, or that he had tired of her. If she slept naked beside him, she would feel a fool if he made no move to touch her. Leaving her shift on, Edeva climbed into bed.

"I'm going to see William," Jobert said.

Rob eased himself up on his pallet. Although he still appeared weak, he had not suffered the stinking sickness common to belly wounds. "Sweet heaven, I would like to go." He grimaced down at his body. "But obviously, I cannot."

"Even if you were whole, I would not ask you to accompany me. I need most of my knights here, in case there is another attack by the Saxons."

"You think they will try again? I would have thought that last failed ambush would have convinced them to give up."

"I'm not certain they will ever give up, until the last one is dead."

Rob nodded.

"I'm taking Edeva with me, which infuriates Alan. But I have my reasons. Indeed, she is part of the purpose for my journey."

"Which is?"

Jobert frowned and shifted his feet. "Near a month ago, I sent a message to William. I asked for the authority to rebuild the manor and palisade in stone. That was a mere formality—I know that William will not deny that request. I also asked for his permission to wed Edeva. In that matter, I am less certain. They say that Norman lords are taking Saxon heiresses to wife all over England, but I cannot do the same without William's blessing."

" 'Twould be good if you wed with her," Rob said. "Your hold on Oxbury will be legitimized. The Saxons hold her in high regard, and indeed, she would make a fine wife for any man."

Jobert nodded. "My plan is to gain William's approval, then have one of the bishops or priests at his camp marry us without delay. If all goes well, the journey should not take more than a fortnight."

"Godspeed to you then." Rob grinned and gave Jobert a merry salutation.

"There is something I need your aid in while I am gone."

"Ask it, my lord."

"I want you to keep Alan from mischief, either with the villagers or the Saxon prisoners. I have moved the prisoners to the granary, where it is warmer. I do not want to return and find that they have perished 'accidentally'."

"You think Alan would do that, knowing your orders are otherwise?"

"Mayhaps not, but I want to be certain."

"What can I do from the sickbed? Wulfget says I am healing well, but if Alan gets a notion to defy your orders, I'm in no condition to stop him."

"Ah, but you are. And Wulfget is the very means of it."
Rob quirked an eyebrow.

"If you were to pursue Wulfget, I think Alan would forget all about getting revenge on the Saxons."

"Oh, indeed, 'twould be my balls he'd want to slice off, rather than the Saxons'!"

"Yea, but he will not act upon his anger, since you are an injured man and his comrade. He has some notions of chivalry."

"So, all I have to do is set my cap for the fair Wulfget, is that the way of it?"

Jobert nodded.

" 'Twill not be such a hardship." Rob's gaze wandered to where Wulfget sat near the fire sewing.

"My thanks, Rob. I knew I could depend on you."

Jobert left the makeshift infirmary feeling pleased with himself. If only things went so smoothly once they reached William's camp.

" 'Tis not the most pleasant way to travel, is it?"

Jobert's remark stirred Edeva from her reverie as she considered how to answer him. The weather was cold, with intermittent rain and sleet, and she had already endured much discomfort as her thighs and buttocks adjusted to the travails of riding on horseback. But for all the drawbacks, there was something tantalizing about sitting between Jobert's muscular thighs, with his arms around her and his breath against her hair.

Since she'd never been on a horse before, Jobert had decided that she would ride *pillion* and change mounts frequently to keep the horses fresh. She wondered if he found riding close as enjoyable as she did. But, nay, his armor must be freezing and even with his long, marten-lined cloak spread around them, he had to endure the brunt of the weather.

She could lean back and dream, her head against his good shoulder and his big body shielding hers. He had to guide the horse and keep a wary lookout on the landscape around them. They traveled with an escort of six knights and three squires, but Edeva knew that Jobert feared to meet a larger force. She had asked him once if he expected trouble, and he replied that after the crossbow attack, he thought it wise to anticipate an attack at all times.

"Should we not stop soon?" she finally said. "I worry that you push yourself too hard, especially with your recent wound."

" 'Tis still a long way to London, and I want to meet with William before the rest of the Norman nobility arrives to ply him for favors."

For the thousandth time, Edeva wondered what boon Jobert wished to ask of the new English king. She wondered even more why he had brought her along. They would be staying the night at an abbey where men and women must sleep separately, so there would be no opportunity for them to make love, and although they conversed about various things regarding Oxbury as they rode, 'twas not likely that he had brought her along simply for company.

If anything, her presence was a burden. That she shared a mount with Jobert slowed their progress, and if they were attacked, having to defend her would be a liability.

Of course, if they gave her a sword, mayhaps they would find that she could defend herself!

She repressed a sigh. Her fighting days were over. Jobert had told her to dress like a lady for this journey, and she knew he expected her to act like one. 'Twas fine enough to dress in silks and samites, but she did not like feeling helpless, nor like a troublesome piece of baggage.

"Are you cold, Edeva?" Jobert asked, shifting his arm so the cloak better covered her.

"Nay."

"Tired?"

She shook her head. " 'Tis you I worry for, not myself."

He grunted intelligibly. Edeva fought another sigh. She had tried asking some of the squires if they knew the reason for this mission to London. None of them did. Either that, or their loyalty to their lord prevented them from telling her.

She would have to wait to discover Jobert's plans. "How many more days of traveling do we face?" she asked.

"If we keep at this pace and the weather holds, we should arrive the day after tomorrow."

Edeva resigned herself to watching the scenery and gave up her quest of unraveling the purpose of their journey.

For someone who had never been beyond the boundaries of Wiltshire, this journey was a revelation. They'd traveled through many kinds of landscape—hills frosted with silver, forests thick and nearly impenetrable, even with the leaves half gone, valleys crisscrossed by multicolored strips of farmland, dried hedgerows, and coppices. They'd seen rivers and streams, some iced over in the morning.

Foxes, deer, hares and squirrels they had sighted in abundance, but few people. Most of the villages they came upon appeared deserted, yet smoke rose from smokeholes and chickens could be found pecking in the middens along with pigs rooting for acorns at the edge of the woods. The Saxon inhabitants, observing a troop of Norman knights approach, had clearly fled.

The experience reminded Edeva that many of her countrymen had not resigned themselves to the Norman yoke. To their minds, she was traveling with the enemy. Furthermore, she traveled to a place where she doubted that a Saxon would be welcome at all. What would they think of her in London, with her light hair, her height and her unmistakably English features?

Was that why Jobert had ordered her to dress herself in finery? To use rich garments and jewelry as a means of distracting people from who she was, a member of a conquered race?

The idea made her angry. She hoped she would be able to hold her tongue if anyone spoke disparagingly of her countrymen. When she shifted on the horse, Jobert leaned near and whispered in her ear. "We'll stop soon. Malmsbury lies ahead."

"Thank you for your hospitality, Prior." Jobert handed the holy man a silver penny as they walked from the refectory. "The meal was excellent, and I trust the beds will be comfortable as well. We have stayed in several English abbeys, and found them to offer very pleasant accommodations."

The ruddy-faced monk gave him a small, sour smile. "If you wish to show your gratitude, mayhaps you would suggest to Duke William that he leave the bishopries of England to tend their own affairs."

"King William is a deeply religious man. I cannot imagine he would interfere with those doing noble Christian work."

The prior gave a most unreverent snort. "You are either an innocent or a fool if you believe that, my lord. Pope Alexander has always held that the English church has too much independence. In William he sees the opportunity to punish our presumption. Already, your liege has awarded half of the priory's farmlands to his battle companions and taken rights to the forest for his own use. When you pass this way next year, you may not find us so prosperous . . ." The man's eyes glinted, "Nor so peaceful."

Jobert nodded thoughtfully. Though sworn not to shed blood, a man like Prior Saewin could aid the Saxon cause in many other ways. "I will convey your thoughts to the king," he said. "But I must remind you that your duty as a 'shepherd of Christ' is to guide your flocks on the path of righteousness. If you encourage the local people to make war on us, they will end up suffering. King William is not a man to be denied. Right or no, he will do what he wills."

"I will think on your words, my lord. God speed you on your journey."

The prior left him, moving with a vigorous step which more suggested a fighting man than a monk. Jobert wondered how many men there were in England like Prior Saewin. If they all combined and pursued a course of rebellion, were there enough of them to throw off the Norman yoke? His instincts told him that there was much fighting yet ahead.

He made his way to the dormitory where visitors slept, then paused to gaze across the maze of buildings which separated him from the area where Edeva had been escorted soon after their arrival.

So close she was, so temptingly close. His body chafed at the enforced chastity. All day, he had ridden with her lush hips between his thighs, provoking his throbbing lust. When he reached London, he would have to find an inn with a private room and slake his raging desire, else he would not have the wit to argue his case before the king.

Surely the king would not deny him. 'Twould be no purpose to it. Why should not William want him to wed the woman who could give him complete control over Oxbury?

But something made him uneasy. Why hadn't the king responded to his letter?

He tried to shake off the mood as he entered the guest house and began to undress before the fire. Things had progressed smoothly so far. He had won a fine piece of property, and was well on his way to mastering it. If his dream of marrying Damaris would never be realized, that was because his dreams had changed. Edeva was the one he now wished to wed. Beautiful, bountiful, golden Edeva.

He gritted his teeth at the erotic image which filled his mind. Jesu! If they rose at dawn and rode like demons, could they be in London by the next night?

The bells of vespers sounded as Jobert lay down on his pallet. He might attempt it—if he could ever get to sleep, that is!

*   *   *

"Mother above! Have you ever seen so many people?" Edeva leaned forward on the palfrey to get a better look at the mass of knights, farmers, carts, and horses crowding the gateway into London.

" 'Tis not so large as Rouen," Jobert said. "But 'tis every bit as smelly and dirty."

Edeva wrinkled her nose, realizing he spoke true. London did stink like a midden heap. And the clamor, the chiming of church bells, the raucous shouts, the clatter of hooves and tread of feet, were near deafening.

"Why are they all going to London?" she asked. "Is it to see the Conqueror?"

Jobert spoke behind her, half-shouting to be heard above the din. "I fear so. I had hoped to be early, but God's toes, this is worse than the crowds in St. Valery before we sailed. We may be hard put to find a place for the night."

After they crossed the bridge, they were crowded into a small lane seething with horses and people on every side. When a man passed by carrying a newly butchered sheep's carcass over his shoulder, their already-nervous mount began to snort and prance. Edeva experienced a renewal of the panic she had first felt when she climbed on a horse's back. 'Twas such a long way to the ground!

She gave a gasp of dread and Jobert's arm tightened about her waist. "Steady now. If the mare senses your fear, she'll grow even more skittish."

Edeva tried to relax, but it was harder than ever. All the way from Reading they'd seen signs of the devastation the Normans had wrought after the Battle of Hastings. Although William's victorious army train had passed through more than a year before, the countryside still lay in ruin. There did not seem to be a hamlet or a farmstead left untouched.

The wanton waste reawakened Edeva's animosity. Now she was in London, seemingly surrounded by Norman knights on every side, and her anger was edged with fear. She recalled the horror and loathing she felt when she first beheld the enemy. Their cone-shaped helmets turning them into slit-eyed demons. The brutal glint of their heavy mail like the scales of a monstrous fish. The terror their huge warhorses inspired.

What had she been thinking of, to allow one of these bloodthirsty devils to steal her heart?

"Easy, girl." Jobert spoke soothing words to the horse, and Edeva tried to calm herself. Jobert was not a beast. She'd seen him behave kindly and generously; if there was harshness in him, 'twas tempered by reason. He did not cause suffering purposefully.

Besides, she had no choice but to trust him. She was in a frightening, hostile city, and she was a Saxon, one of the vanquished.

Around them, vendors called out their wares, offering eel pastries, skins of wine and ribs of beef. "The people of London appear to have accepted the Normans," Edeva said, a touch of bitterness in her voice. "One would never guess that only a little more than a year ago they rang the alarm bells warning of the enemy's landing."

"People in cities are different from those who make their living from the land," Jobert said. "Over the centuries most of them have been conquered and reconquered many times. They are used to changing masters."

"It seems so disloyal," Edeva grumbled.

"They see Norman coin as profitable as English, and they must sell their wares or starve."

Was she any better? Edeva wondered. She had made peace with the enemy. Did she capitulate to save her skin and keep her belly full?

Nay, she had done it because she felt it was her duty to her people, that she could not safeguard their well-being without yielding to the conquerors.

And she had done it because of Jobert. There was something about the proud, red-haired knight which moved her, touched some tender woman's place deep inside. A shudder went through her as she recalled how she had felt when he had been brought to Oxbury wounded and delirious, so intensely had she feared for him.

"I think there are some inns down this street," Jobert spoke close to her ear. "With luck, and plenty of your father's treasure hoard to grease palms, mayhaps we will find one where we can get a room."

A room, that was all it was. A single chamber with a hearth they could all bed down around. No privacy, no luxuries. And they had paid dearly for it, spending a handful of coin from the purse hidden beneath Jobert's tunic.

They unloaded their saddlebags and found stabling for the horses—almost as dear as the roof over their heads. Then Jobert decided to visit the taverns and seek news of the king.

Edeva looked miserable as he took his leave. "London at night is not a place for a lady," he told her. He fingered one of her golden braids, trying to make her smile. "Especially one who looks as you do."

She seemed very unhappy, and he could not blame her. The rented chamber was already rank with the smell of sweat, horse and damp wool. "When I go to see the king, you will go with me, I promise," he told her. "There might be ladies in attendance, and they will admire the fine needlework decorating your clothes and your fair hair." She looked doubtful. " 'Tis true. All Norman women wish for blond tresses. Mayhaps because so many of them have dusky skin and dark locks."

He leaned over and kissed her, despite the crowd of knights around them. "I will return as soon as I can."

Jobert had no interest in the strumpets and tavern girls glimpsed now and then among the horde of soldiers, but the two men he took as escort were not so particular. They reacted to the women like hounds scenting a bitch in heat. "God's teeth, would you get your mind off your cocks," Jobert grumbled as Hamo near-dragged him into a tavern called The Black Horse.

They were packed into the place like so many pikes in a barrel, but Hamo quickly found the object of his quest— a girl with dark hair, laughing black eyes and a face not yet careworn.

Hamo jerked his head, indicating his plans.

"Go on, then," Jobert said, "but meet me here before vespers."

Roald remained at his side, but looked so miserable that Jobert urged him off. "Find a wench, if you are so desperate, if you don't mind swimming in the seed of the half-dozen men before you."

Jobert took a seat at one of the scarred tables and struggled to find room to stretch out his long legs. He had always hated the crudeness and emptiness of bedding whores; now he would never have to do it again. He had Edeva—beautiful, sweet-smelling, passionate Edeva.

Not that it did him a bit of good under the present circumstances. By the Rood, how was he to endure it, with Edeva so tantalizingly near and yet so inaccessible? Mayhaps they could find a quiet copse of trees beyond the city proper. An outdoor tryst would be better than nothing. But the weather would have to clear, which it was not like to do. A soft drizzle had fallen all day, growing colder as night approached.

A barmaid finally brought him a jar of wine. Blowsy and with a face disfigured by knife wounds, she smiled at him seductively after he gave her the money. He shook his head and she sauntered off. He felt a stir of pity for the unfortunate woman, then realized that in this market, she would keep busy all night.

He took a swallow of wine and found it good, rich and full-bodied, not sour at all. Much better than anything they'd had at Oxbury. Jobert made a mental note to purchase several casks before they left London. They could strap them to one of the extra horses and take their time returning.

"Brevrienne, you ugly bastard, what are you doing in London?"

Jobert jerked around and spied a familiar countenance and a bushy head of hair brighter than his own. "Girard of Evreux, you puffed-up pig's bladder! Well met, well met."

Jobert stood, but soon realized he would be foolish to give up his seat, even for a moment. He waved the other knight over. "Come join me."

Although a sturdy fighting man, Girard was half a head shorter than Jobert and moved more easily through the cramped quarters. When he reached Jobert, he adjusted himself on the rickety bench, then took the jar of wine the serving wench had left and poured himself a cup.

"I'm in London to see William," Jobert said, "as it seems the rest of Normandy is. What do you here?"

"I came over with the king. I've been with him in Dieppe these past few weeks."

"The king is here?"

"Should be. My ship sailed before his, but the *Mora* was to put in before sunset."

"Jesu, and there are a million courtiers and knights waiting to speak to him," Jobert said in disgust. "I will be fortunate to get an audience before Christmas."

Girard took a gulp of wine, then regarded Jobert with steady hazel eyes. "What's your business? I thought he'd already awarded you some land. In Wiltshire, isn't it?"

Jobert nodded. "He enfeoffed me with a fine piece of property, and now I seek permission to build a castle there and to wed the Saxon heiress who comes with the place."

"You'd wed a Saxon?"

"You have not seen *my* Saxon," Jobert said, irritated with his friend. Why did so many Normans think that Saxon women were all rough-mannered, homely wenches?

"A beauty, is she? Still, you might take her for a concubine and have all the benefits. Why buy a cow when you can get free milk?" Girard winked.

"William has encouraged his men to claim the land by legal means. Marrying the old thegn's daughter will legitimize my right to the property and ease my acceptance with the local people.''

"The English have no say in who rules them," Girard scoffed. "If they do not accept your authority, intimidate them until they do."

How much he had changed, Jobert thought. Only a few months before, he had seen things much the way Girard did. Now he knew that conquest of a land was more complex than subduing the natives with brute force.

" 'Tis not that you wed a Saxon which surprises me," Girard said "but that you wed at all. I thought you'd given your heart to Damaris and were prepared to die celibate."

"Damaris was the fancy of a green boy. I believe my passion for her burned so long and so bright because she was forbidden to me."

"Well, she is forbidden to all men, now. She went into a convent this summer, St. Mary's in Caen."

"I had heard that. I am surprised Valois relented. I thought the greedy whoreson was determined she would make a rich match."

"He did not accept the situation graciously. Indeed, I heard that he went to William and accused you of ruining his daughter."

Jobert brought his cup down on the table with a thud. "That's a lie! Damaris and I did naught but kiss, and that only once!"

"Valois obviously thinks there was more to it."

"Why, that puling, cowardly . . ." Jobert took a deep breath and wondered if he could find an epithet foul enough to use against his enemy. "And what does the king think?" he asked quickly. "Does he believe Valois?"

"I'm hardly privy to royal opinion. You will have to ask him."

Jobert gave a long, drawn-out sigh. This was the ill news his instincts had warned him about. Valois was a powerful, wealthy Norman baron, and the king needed his loyalty. Even if he could convince William that Valois accused him unfairly, that did not mean the king would take his part.

"Jesu, Brevrienne, I am sorry if I've brought you bad tidings. At the time, I thought little of the story. I still cannot think that William would be so unreasonable as to blame a man for winning a maiden's heart." Girard preened. "Some of us cannot help being irresistible."

Jobert gave a choked laugh. "Irresistible, are you, you worm-faced lout! I'll wager here and now that you can't find a woman in all of London who will bed you unless you pay her."

Girard looked around the teeming tavern, where men outnumbered women nearly a score to one. "I'll admit the odds are a bit daunting, but there must be a lonely merchant's wife somewhere . . ." He turned back to Jobert. "I'll take up your challenge, Brevrienne. What do you offer if I succeed?"

Jobert tried to remember what treasures they had brought from Oxbury which might please Girard. "My woman is a seamstress of amazing skill. If you have any ceremonial garments, I could prevail upon her to embroider them with whatever design you wish—a device you could be known by."

"I've always fancied being known as the Red Cock of Evraux."

Jobert raised his brows. "I'm certain she can fashion an image of a proud, strutting cockerel. That *is* what you suggest, isn't it?"

Girard grinned broadly. "They are feisty, lusty creatures. 'Twill serve me well in both battle and . . ." his mouth curved lasciviously, "in other pursuits."

Jobert rolled his eyes at his friend's crudeness. "And what do you offer me if I win the wager?"

"An audience with the king as soon as he settles in at Westminster."

"You have that power? Jesu, you *have* risen high!"

"Nay, 'tis merely that William trusts his loyal soldiers to give him truer advice than the scheming noblemen who surround him."

"If you could do that, Girard, I would be most grateful.

I would have Edeva sew your device no matter which way the wager goes."

"Done!" Girard rose, gulping down the last bit of wine in his cup. "Now, if you will excuse me, I must be about the other business."

Jobert rose also. "We're staying at an inn near here called The Bishop's Mitre. Send me word there."

Girard disappeared among the crowd, and Jobert looked around for his men. Neither Hamo nor Miles was anywhere to be found, and Jobert decided to return to the inn without them. He would not begrudge them a night spent in the London brothels.

As he walked to the inn, a sense of unease crept over him, chilling him even more than the icy rain. *Valois had gone to the king and spread lies about him. His enemy had not forgotten him, but pursued him to England.*

Recent happenings took on a sinister cast. The crossbow bolt might have come from an assassin's bow rather than a Saxon one. His unanswered message to William could have been deliberately intercepted rather than lost or ignored

The hairs stood up on his nape and he glanced around the nearly empty street. Did Valois have someone watching him now, a cutthroat lurking in the shadows?

His hand went to his sword hilt and he walked more rapidly. Now it was even more important that he speak to William and defend himself against Valois' lies. If only Girard had the influence that he said he did.

With relief, he reached the inn and made his way to the room. Inside, his men slept sprawled in a sort of circle around the hearth. In the middle, nearest the fire's warmth, lay Edeva, wrapped in the fur cloak. Jobert stepped around the other bodies and went to her. The sight of her lovely face peeking out of the cloak's hood warmed him as much as the fire's heat.

For a time, he simply looked at her, admiring the enticing fullness of her lips, the curve of her smooth cheek, the way tendrils of her hair glinted pure gold in the fire-light.

Sweet heaven, she was beautiful! He wanted to possess her, to hold her and love her forever. He wanted to make her his wife, to fill her womb with his sons.

The intensity of his feelings made him breathless. Oxbury was his dream, but it would not fulfill him without Edeva. She was the thing he sought, the light he had prayed for when he was imprisoned in Valois' dungeon.

He took off his sword belt, then eased himself down beside her. She murmured in her sleep, until he pulled her against his chest and she settled there with a sigh.

TWENTY

The next morning, a bleary-eyed squire came to the inn and said, "Girard says to come to Westminster today, and the king will see you." When Jobert gaped at him, the youth gave a smug smile. "Oh, and Girard also says to tell you that you have lost the wager. He's merely doing this as a favor to an old friend."

"That clever wretch!" Jobert guffawed. He gave the squire a penny for his trouble, then went to tell Edeva.

She sat by the fire, eating one of the pasties Jobert had purchased to break their fast.

"The man was lying when he called this an *eel* pie. Why, 'tis naught but pastry!" She wiped a dribble of broth from her chin. "You should have let me purchase food. If the merchants knew they were dealing with a Saxon, they would not try their cheating tricks."

"Mayhaps I will let you bargain when we go to the market, but for now, there are other concerns. We go to see William today."

At his words, she gave him a stricken look. "I've scarce washed off the traveling dust." She glanced around the room where several of the knights still slept, sprawled on the floor, snoring. "How am I to get ready?"

"I'll get rid of them and have some hot water fetched for washing. Then, I will help you dress."

She gave him a doubtful look.

"Don't worry so." He approached her and took the pastie from her hand and had a bite. "Salty," he mumbled.

"You think the king will see you? You worried yesterday that he would be overwhelmed by those requesting favors."

"I met a friend last night who promised to smooth our way."

He heard her sigh and watched her twist the skirt of her kirtle in taut fingers. She was terrified. For all his own worries, he dare not aggravate her already potent fears. "What is the worst that can come to pass?" he soothed. "If William refuses to see me, then we will go back another day."

"But I am a Saxon, the enemy."

"There will be other Saxons there, and you speak Norman French, which will aid you in being accepted. Norman knights are taught to show respect to women, and William is no exception. He will not scorn you because of your blood."

But will he scorn me because I am your leman? Edeva found she could not voice the painful thought. She had not wanted to come to London, to meet the conqueror of her people. "Why cannot I wait here while you go?" she asked.

"Mayhaps I have a thought to show you off, wearing the exquisite garments sewn by your own fingers, decked in jewels which reflect the wealth of Oxbury."

Edeva sighed and went to the saddle packs piled in the corner and began to dig through them. With luck, her clothes would be utterly crushed and she could use that for an excuse not to go.

Jobert began to rouse the men, poking them with his boot. They got up, groaning and protesting. She heard Jobert tell two of them to fetch hot water from the inn-keeper.

By the time she'd found their banquet clothes, she and Jobert were the only ones left in the room. "You wash first," he told her. "I'll be back anon."

Buckets of steaming water had been pulled up near the fire, but Edeva still shivered as she stripped down to her shift and began to bathe between her breasts and under her arms. She had brought a handful of cleansing herbs to add to the bathing water, and their subtle, sweet aroma filled her senses, relaxing her.

When she was finished washing, she changed to a clean shift and pulled her gunna over that, hoping the dampness from her body would smooth some of the wrinkles from the rich crimson samite. She left the sleeves unlaced and sat down on the lone stool in the chamber and began to untangle her hair.

She'd kept it tightly braided while they traveled, and the plaits unraveled into masses of crimpy, wild waves she struggled to tame with her comb. As she was almost finished with the ordeal, Jobert returned. He came in the door and stopped, staring at her as if transfixed.

Edeva hurried to finish. She could feel her nipples tightening as he gazed at her.

He finally went to the fire and began to strip off his clothes. Edeva peeked a look at him, telling herself that she wanted to see how his wound was healing. Her eyes did not linger long on the red, raw scar, but quickly shifted to his bare chest, with its rippling muscularity and ruddy hair.

He leaned over and splashed water on his face and neck, then took a cloth and began to bathe the rest of his upper body.

Edeva looked away, trying to concentrate on her own task. Her whole being ached with an acute awareness of the man nearby. This was the first time they had been alone since leaving Oxbury, and she wanted him with a craving that near took her breath away.

But there was no bed, and they were supposed to be dressing for the audience with the king. She suppressed her lustful thoughts.

When next she looked, he had removed his hose and was washing his groin. Edeva, hands shaking, went to the other side of the room to fetch her stockings and shoes. She pulled up the silk stockings and secured them with jeweled garters, then slipped on soft scarlet calfskin slippers.

By the time she returned to the stool to replait her hair,

Jobert had put on clean hose and was cross-gartering them at his ankles. Edeva sighed in resignation. Of course he was not going to bed her now. They had other, more serious, business to attend to.

She divided her hair into two fat sections and began to wind the middle of one of them with crimson ribbon.

"You should have someone to help with your hair."

She looked up and saw Jobert standing over her, green eyes glowing.

"But I have no servant here, so I must do it myself," she said sharply.

"What of your laces?" His gaze traveled to where her gown hung loose under her arms. "Can I help you with those?"

"In a moment." She knew she was being short with him, but she resented how he tantalized her and then left her hanging.

She finished the other side of her hair, then stood, waiting for him to finish her laces. Instead of tightening them, his hand slipped through the sleeve and cupped one of her breasts. "Jobert," she chastised, "we cannot do this now. You'll muss my hair and ruin my gown."

He leaned over and kissed her deeply while his hand squeezed her breast. Edeva felt an exquisite shiver run down her body and strike lightning between her thighs. She gasped. "Oh, Jobert," she groaned.

She felt his other hand carefully easing up her skirts. "I cannot endure it, either," he whispered as he kissed her neck. "I see you, looking so beautiful, so magnificent. And I think that you are mine . . . almost."

His hand found bare skin. Edeva arched her back, longing for him to . . . She smothered a moan of satisfaction as his fingers slid between her thighs, sampling the creamy wetness there. "My gown," she whispered in one last helpless attempt to bring them both back to their senses.

His questing fingers found what they sought. He slipped one inside her, while the others stroked silky circles against her cleft.

In seconds, she surrendered. She did not care if he tore her clothes from her in pieces, if she had to go see William in rags. She wanted . . . oh, how she wanted . . .

She gave a cry as she felt him lifting her, one hand still between her thighs, the other under her arm. He carried her over to the table and gently put her down. After adjusting her skirts, he kissed her again, long and hard. Then he began to undo his hose.

His shaft sprang out, huge and ready. Edeva gave a whimper of longing. He reached under her again, cradling her buttocks with his fingers as he pulled her to the very edge of the table. "I don't want you to get splinters in your bottom," he said. "You'll have to guide me."

She took hold of his hot, smooth shaft and placed it against her feminine opening, then spread her thighs as wide as possible. The pressure of him made her wetter and more aroused than ever. He thrust forward sharply, and his shaft slid inside her.

Edeva took a deep breath, almost mindless with the sensation. So deep he was, stretching her inner sheath to the limit. His fingers dug into her hips, easing her body around his. "Touch yourself," he whispered. "Open for me, Edeva, lest I should die of delight."

Shamelessly, she obeyed. She could feel herself stretched around his rigid manhood, and with tentative fingers she sought the sweet spot he had revealed to her. The touch of her own hand made her dissolve into rippling madness.

The pressure eased, and she could feel Jobert begin to move, using his hips to thrust into her. Short, rapid strokes which made them both bounce against the table. Through a haze of spiraling pleasure, she heard him cry out, "Edeva, my love, Edeva . . ."

She grabbed his shoulders, hanging on for dear life as they both neared the precipice. One final, pulsing thrust flung them both over the edge.

They rested, faces pressed together, bodies still joined. Jobert kissed her cheek. "Jesu, I waited so long for this.

'Twas hell these last few days, holding you, seeing you, and not being able to love you."

"I did not know you wanted me."

Jobert gave an incredulous laugh. "Wanted? Oh, if you only knew. I have been in an agony of wanting."

Jobert released her. Edeva stood and smoothed her skirts. Moisture from both of them trickled down her legs. She went over to the wash water and used a cloth to wipe herself. "Jobert, before we go to William, please tell me what your business with him is. It makes me uneasy not to understand the purpose of this trip."

Jobert began rearranging his clothes. When he did not answer, Edeva grew irritated. "Tell me, Jobert. I deserve that much."

He found the richly embroidered tunic she had taken out of the pack and shrugged it over his shoulders. " 'Tis complicated, Edeva. Mayhaps we should wait to discuss this until after I have seen William."

"Nay, we will settle this now! If you won't talk to me, I will refuse to go with you! I will walk back to Oxbury alone if I have to."

He looked at her, worry writ clearly on his features. "You have that right, although I would send some of my men with you for protection."

His words sent a blow to her stomach. "What do you mean—'I have that right'?"

"If William denies me permission to wed you, I have no claim on you, Edeva."

The ground seemed to shift beneath her feet. "You mean to ask William if you can wed me?"

He nodded. "I thought 'twould be a simple thing, a mere formality. You are the heiress of Oxbury—it makes perfect sense for me to wed you and claim by law what is already mine by the king's decree. But now I fear that I have fallen out of favor with William and will lose everything."

"Why? What have you done?"

Jobert shook his head, looking more distressed than ever. "There is a Norman lord who wants to see me destroyed. I have had news that he has gone to William and accused me of dishonoring his daughter." A muscle twitched in his jaw. "He implies that I took her maidenhead and ruined her for marriage."

Edeva stared in shock. To think of Jobert dishonoring a young woman seemed preposterous. Why, he had not even ravished *her*, but waited until she came to his bed willingly. "Why does he hate you?" she asked. "Is it the result of a conflict between your families, or have you done something to earn his animosity?"

"I had a *tendre* for his daughter, 'tis true. I even stole a kiss from her years ago, but 'twas no more than that. If Damaris chose to become a bride of Christ, 'tis not because of me."

"You loved her?" Her voice came out in a breathy whisper.

"I thought I did. I carried a lock of her hair close to my heart for nigh on five years. I kept my hair long because she once said she liked it that way." His eyes met hers. " 'Twas but a silly fancy, a boy's infatuation."

Edeva nodded, wondering if she believed him. *Five years.* "And because of this . . . 'infatuation,' her father bears you a bitter grudge?"

Jobert paced across the room and back. "That is the way of it. He discovered that one kiss, and he would not listen to reason. He threw me into an oubliette, told me that I would rot there. Mayhaps I would be there still—or my bones would—if my father had not petitioned Duke William for my freedom."

"What is an oubliette?" Though she asked the question, Edeva already knew it was someplace dark and dank and confined. That was why Jobert had rescued her and why he had moved Alnoth and Withan to the stables. He could not bear to think of anyone suffering as he had.

"An underground prison." His green eyes stared straight at her, stricken by ugly memories.

"How long were you imprisoned?"

He paced back to the other end of the room, rigid with

tension. "A month, mayhaps longer. The whole time I was there, I thought of her, of Damaris. How good she smelled. How lovely and sweet she was. She kept me alive."

The blade twisted deeper in Edeva's belly. He denied loving this Damaris, but 'twas clear he had. *Did he still?*

Edeva could imagine her. Delicate and dainty, with perfect white skin which had never known the heat of the sun nor the travails of work. The Flemish seamstress, Hawise, had told her about the ladies of the Norman courts, of their pampered way of life.

She looked down at her own hands. The summer gold had begun to fade from her skin, but calluses from driving a needle through heavy fabric marked her thumb and forefinger.

He traversed the room once more. "When I got out, I vowed I would never again be at another man's mercy. I might die in battle, but I would not swear to any except Lord William." He raised his gaze to hers. "When I fought at Hastings, I fought for my freedom. For land of my own, and the power to choose my own destiny."

"And William gave you that. He gave you Oxbury."

"But now I fear to lose it." Jobert moved closer to her. "I also fear to lose you. If he will not allow me to wed you, what will I do? Keep you as my concubine?"

Aye, she longed to answer, *better that I be your whore than nothing at all.*

His fingers came up to brush the corner of her mouth, then he sighed and turned away. "I meant for you to dazzle them with your beauty, your elegant garments. Now, I wonder if I will not make some other man covet you . . . and Oxbury as well. If the king should believe Valois . . ."

"I will not go," she said. "I will stay here while you plead your case."

"Nay. I want you with me."

"But you said . . ."

He approached once more and took her face in his hands. "Possession of a piece of land can aid a man in keeping it. It might also be so with a woman, at least with a man like William." He brought one hand down to press against her waist. "If your belly were already swollen with my babe, I know he would give you to me. He abhors the thought of any child being born outside of wedlock and suffering as he did."

"I have hopes," Edeva whispered.

"We shall have to try harder." He leaned over to kiss her neck. "By the saints, when I see you like this, I want to . . ." He whispered some foreign word in her ear, making her blush.

"Jobert." She pulled away, shaking with reawakened desire. "If you start that, 'twill be terce ere we even set out!"

He nodded. "Mayhaps I should call in the innkeeper's wife to do your laces."

"You do not trust yourself?" she teased.

"Nay, not when they are so close to your delicious breasts." His gaze roamed downward, and Edeva felt her nipples grow hard. How could this be, that she ached for him so soon after their wild joining?

"Have you ever done that before?" She nodded toward the table.

"Nay, never." His smile was breathtaking. "With most other women, I would fear to hurt them."

"But not with me?"

"Nay, I know you can take every inch of me. Is that not how the English measure it?"

She blushed again, even more furiously. "Jobert, call the innkeeper's wife, lest we never get ready!"

"Nay, I will do it. If I concentrate on what is ahead of us, my mood will grow sober and my hands steady."

Edeva stood still while he laced up the sides of her gown, then pulled them tight so that her breasts pushed up against the square neckline. "Is this the Norman fashion?" she asked.

"I know not," he said. "But I would have us use every weapon we possess to gain William's favor."

"He is a lecher?"

"Not at all. Indeed, he is said to be the most faithful of

men, never straying from his wife's bed, even when separated from her for months. But," he leaned to straighten one of the tight sleeves, "William does have eyes in his head. And your beauty might sway his opinion toward our request." He stepped back. "Now for the jewels."

He brought the leather bag from the pack and helped Edeva put on the necklace made up of three pieces of gold-work decorated with dozens of garnets and the matching wristband around her arm. "There is a ring also," he said.

"Enough," she laughed. "I already feel like a maypole hung with ribbons at Beltane. If there are more baubles, mayhaps you should wear them."

"Impertinent wench." He slapped her on the behind. She wiggled her hips provocatively, and he grabbed her and kissed her hard. "Now," he said, releasing her, "we must go."

It took them near the whole morning to reach Westminster. They left the city, with its narrow lanes and crowds of people, and came into open green space. After passing scattered farmsteads, many still abandoned and unrepaired from William's army's last visit, they reached a small village. The rain had stopped, and a hazy fog drifted in and out. They did not sight the abbey built by Edward the Confessor until they were almost at the gates.

They were waved in without question, and once inside, Edeva could see why Westminster was not more closely guarded. The place crawled with knights, looking more like an army camp than a holy house. Edeva's unease returned. She did not see any other women, nor Saxons, and she could not help wondering if Jobert had been wrong to bring her.

In the courtyard, Jobert slid from behind her and came around to the front of the horse. "I'm going to see if Girard's word is good, if they will let us in," he told her.

Before she could think to respond, he had admonished

Hamo and Roald to look after her, then disappeared into one of the buildings.

The horse snorted and pawed the ground, and Edeva went rigid. What if her mount decided to run away with her on its back? She leaned forward and said something soothing. Amazingly, the beast quieted, and Edeva turned her mind to other worries.

Her thoughts whirled around in circles. Jobert wanted to marry her, he seemed to care for her . . . but he had loved a Norman woman, might love her still . . . William might not let them wed anyway, he could strip Jobert of Oxbury and give it to another man . . . *she* might be given to another man . . . but she would kill anyone who tried to touch her. She would not accept another man as her husband . . . she would not . . .

Her dread grew. She was back at Oxbury before the Normans arrived, determined to kill them all, determined to return her life to the way it had been before her father went to fight at Stambridge and everything changed, everything went horribly awry . . .

"Jesu, lady, are you well?"

She looked over to see Hamo staring at her. "You're white as bleached linen, lady. What's wrong? Are you ill?"

Edeva nodded. Her stomach churned. She felt light-headed and dizzy.

Hamo dismounted rapidly and grabbed her by the waist, pulling her off the horse. She stood trembling against him. "I'll fetch one of the monks," Hamo said.

"Nay, I'll be well in a moment." She took a deep breath, trying to breathe deeply and evenly. She must get over this panic. Jobert depended on her.

"You're certain you can stand?"

She nodded. "When Jobert returns, don't tell him of this," she said.

Hamo regarded her thoughtfully, then gave his assent.

Jobert arrived in a few moments. "He'll see us," he told her. "I don't know what sorcery Girard worked, but we are to have an audience with the king of England."

Jobert took her arm and they went into the largest of the buildings. Inside, the anteroom was crowded with richly dressed Normans. They whispered to each other as she and Jobert passed through. She caught the word "Saxon" and tensed. Jobert rubbed her arm soothingly. At another doorway, they paused and waited.

The whispering grew louder. ". . . Jesu, look at those tits . . . do you suppose her quim is gold, too . . ." Edeva felt Jobert's tension, saw his hand go to his blade. But he did nothing. Obviously, he dare not challenge anyone in this setting.

After an interminable time, while Edeva tried not to listen to the hushed words and guffaws, a squire came out. He nodded at Jobert, but when Edeva started forward, the youth shook his head. Jobert gave her a desperate look. Edeva forced herself to indicate that he should go on without her.

She waited, standing stiffly, holding her head high.

" 'Tis a Saxon queen."

"Yea, and I would like to 'conquer' her."

The jeers echoed mockingly in Edeva's ears. But she noted that the men kept their voices low. They did not want their crude banter reported to the king.

She raised her chin a notch higher and fingered the extravagant gold and garnet necklace. Let them make jest. She was proud of who she was. *Daughter of Leowine, a loyal thegn to King Harold, and a descendant of Alfred, the greatest English king of all.*

"Did you see her jewels? Why, she carries a fortune around her neck!"

"And an even richer gold prize between her thighs!"

Sniggering laughter surrounded her. Edeva forbade herself to blush. There was a sort of awe in the way they spoke, an obvious admiration. They did not think her overlarge and unfeminine, an undesirable, clumsy wench. Sweet Mary, it was all too clear that they found her attractive!

She saw now why Jobert had brought her. He was proud of her and wanted to show her off.

The thought made her feel weak and liquid inside. Jobert wanted her to be his wife. He had come to the king to ask for *her*.

Suddenly, her fears vanished. If Jobert had loved another, she would make him forget her. She would make certain she filled his heart so completely, there would be room for no other.

Jobert appeared at the doorway and nodded to her. For a moment, she considered how impressive he looked. The rich green tunic draped over his tall frame, accenting the rich hue of his hair and his proud features. She moved to take his arm.

King William was a massive man, like a broad oak tree with formidable arms and a noble, stern-faced countenance. He watched impassively as Edeva and Jobert approached, although she did see his gaze drop to examine the heavy necklace and then, more briefly, her breasts.

Jobert knelt low and pulled Edeva down with him. When William raised Jobert, she stood also, facing the king's keen, dark eyes.

"So, this is the heiress."

"Yea, my lord. She is daughter to Leowine, who held Oxbury from King Edward."

"And you wish to wed with her?"

"Yea, the people of the manor hold her in regard. 'Twould assure my control over them and secure the area."

The king turned and walked to the other side of the small room. "But I hear there have been troubles at Oxbury. Ambushes, fires set." He met Jobert's gaze. " 'Twould seem you do not have the place secure after all."

"There are rebels in the woods, a handful only."

"Yet they have caused you much trouble. I have even today a report that they have burned the manor house at Oxbury and caused serious damage."

Edeva heard Jobert suck in his breath. "Where did you learn such news? When we left Oxbury three days ago, all was well."

The king frowned. "I don't remember the man's name, but he said the priest had sent him."

"I did not think they would attack again, or I would not have left the manor," Jobert said.

"It seems you were overconfident, that there is work left to do before Oxbury is firmly under Norman control."

Jobert said nothing.

The king went to a table where a clerk sat with rolls of parchment piled around him. William fingered one of the manuscripts, but did not look at it. "There has been a charge against you, Brevrienne. Do you know of it?"

"Yea, my lord, and I can answer."

William held up his hand, forestalling Jobert's next words. "Naught can be changed anyway, so there is little purpose to discussing the matter. What concerns me more are the difficulties you have had at Oxbury." William's gaze rested on Jobert, and Edeva felt a chill to her core. " 'Tis not so large a fief. If I am to secure England, I must depend on others to enact my will."

His glance shifted to Edeva, then back to Jobert. "Mayhaps your fondness for the woman has made you soft toward the English. Mayhaps you have not dealt harshly enough with them. If they dared to attack as soon as you rode away, they obviously have not tasted the full weight of Norman authority. See that when you return, they are made properly aware of what it means to defy their new king."

"Of course, my lord." Jobert cleared his throat and added, "With your permission to erect a stone curtain wall and reinforce the property against attack, 'twill be clear to them that their cause is hopeless."

"Build your fortress, and the sooner the better. I will send a mason to aid you in the planning of it." William nodded to the clerk, who wrote something down on the parchment in front of him.

"And my other request?" Jobert asked.

William's gaze flicked to Edeva, taking in her appearance from head to toe. He approached and her heart began to race.

He reached out a massive, scarred hand and touched the banding on her sleeve. " 'Tis exquisite work." He met her eyes. "Flemish?"

Edeva licked her dry lips. Her voice came out in a breathy whisper. "In a way. The woman who taught me the skill was from Flanders."

"You sewed this?"

"Yea, my lord."

William turned to Jobert. "Do you know what my Matilda would do if she saw this workmanship? She would insist that I bring your woman to Rouen and marry her to one of my household knights. Such skill is rare and much coveted. And the fact that she speaks Norman French makes her even more desirable."

Edeva saw Jobert's hands clench. He said, "But what of Lady Edeva's wishes? Is Queen Matilda so hardhearted she would doom another woman to a life of loneliness away from her people and . . ." he hesitated, his eyes meeting Edeva's, ". . . the man she loves?"

"Love?" William's brows—reddish streaked with gray—rose sharply. "I would have thought you would have abandoned such nonsense. It near cost you your life once already."

Jobert's gaze remained bold. " 'Tis said that your marriage to Matilda is a love match. Would you not say that her affection has aided your cause many times?"

William gave a bark of laughter, so sudden that Edeva jumped. "I recall now that it is directness and persistence which makes you such a valiant knight, Brevrienne. Yea, Matilda's affection has aided we. There are even times when I wonder if I could have gone on without her."

He looked again at Edeva. "And nay, Matilda is not a hardhearted mistress. She would not keep your Saxon like a bird in a gilded cage, pining away for her homeland." He faced Jobert. "I will consider your request further. For now, go back to Oxbury and do your duty."

TWENTY-ONE

It could have been much worse, Jobert told himself as they rode out of the abbey. William had not refused him altogether, nor sent Edeva to his wife's court.

Jesu! He had considered that some lord more powerful than he would see Edeva and think to steal his prize—he had not imagined that Edeva's sewing skill would arouse the queen's interest!

He glanced down at Edeva's sleeve, peeking out from the marten fur. 'Twas exquisite, in truth. With needle and thread, she could create flowers and birds whose beauty rivaled the real.

He tightened his arm around her waist. For now, she was his. He would not let her go.

As soon as they reached the inn, Jobert ordered his men to prepare to return home. "Trouble at Oxbury," he told them. "We'll set off as soon as possible."

Leaving them to fetch the rest of the horses and pack, Jobert started out for The Black Horse. His prayers were answered when he found Girard hunched at a back table, dosing what looked to be a miserable hangover with a platter of chops, a loaf of bread and a bowl of steaming pottage.

"God's teeth, man, you look wretched!" Jobert greeted him.

Girard looked up with one eye blackened shut. "Ah, but she was worth it," he said around his swollen lips. "If only her bastard husband had not come home early." He shrugged. "At least he had no dagger on him. Besides, I won the wager. Cleave told you, didn't he?"

"Yea, he told me." Jobert sat down. "He also told me that you had worked your magic and gained me an audience with William. My thanks, Girard. I am indebted to you."

"Indeed, you are. I will not forget you owe me a boon, beyond the one promised." Girard tried to grin, but it turned into a grimace of pain. "Did William grant your request?"

"Nay. It seems there has been trouble at Oxbury, and William thinks I have been too soft in my dealings with the Saxons." Jobert pounded the table with his fist, making the wooden platter leap upward. "Bloody Christ! I don't see how they dared attack. I thought their numbers were dwindling, that they were growing discouraged."

"A last desperate effort?"

Jobert shook his head. "I don't think so. I fear that someone is helping them, someone who wishes me to fail."

"Valois?"

Jobert sat back. "I didn't think his quest for vengeance would follow me all the way to England. But he wants to see me ruined, and he is obviously paying someone to spy upon me, aid my enemies and mayhaps even try to murder me."

"I do not think he would resort to that."

"Oh, no? I was struck by a crossbow bolt while riding through the woods on duty for the king in Gloucestershire."

"Mmmmm," Girard mumbled, taking a bite of bread.

"I put it off as part of a failed ambush, but no other man was wounded, and the Saxon woman tells me that her people do not use the weapon."

"Mmmmm," Girard said again. He dipped another piece of bread in the pottage and stuffed it in his mouth. He gained strength and vigor before Jobert's eyes. The fool would probably plan another liaison with his lover this very night.

"I did not think much of any of this until you told me about Valois going to the king," Jobert said. "Then I realized that he had determined to destroy me by any possible means."

"You'd best watch your back, my friend. Valois has formidable resources."

Jobert nodded grimly and stood. "I have to return to Oxbury, to see what is left of my demesne. I mentioned to Edeva about the device for your pennant. If our paths do not cross again by chance, come to Oxbury and collect it. You will always be welcome there, Girard."

Girard rose and the two men shook hands.

"I'm sorry, Jobert, I did not think my brothers would attack again. I thought that if you showed mercy to Alnoth, they would consider making peace with you."

" 'Tis not your fault, Edeva." Jobert settled her on the horse as they mounted to begin the journey home. "You could not know what the rebels would do."

Nor could she know that the rebels might be aided by some outside enemy, Jobert thought. This was the first time they had spoken of the situation at Oxbury, and he had decided not to tell Edeva of his fears. She already seemed so distraught.

"My brothers are such fools. Don't they realize they cannot win?"

"Mayhaps they find the idea of life under a Norman lord unbearable and they intend to fight to the very death."

Edeva sighed heavily, and he wished he could ease her. But, better she face the truth of what the future held for her kin now, rather than discovering it the day he was forced to hang them.

"What could they be thinking of, to burn the manor house? I wonder if anyone was hurt. If the fire reached the upper bedchamber. All my cloth, my mother's things . . ."

"Hush now. You cannot do anything until we get there, so 'tis no profit in worrying."

She nodded, sighing again. Jobert decided he must find some way to distract her.

When they stopped to water the horses in a half-frozen stream, he took her arm and began to lead her into the woods.

"Where are we going?" she asked.

He turned so he faced her and gazed into her crystalline blue eyes. "I'm going to divert you from your troubles."

"How?"

He smiled at her. "How do you think?"

She flushed and he sensed her breathing quicken. He guided her deeper into the underbrush. She said, "You'll find no tables here, my lord. Not to mention a bed."

"I am a resourceful man," he assured her.

When they reached a thicket of hawthorne bushes, Jobert stopped. He looked around, seeking a tree fit for his purpose. He found one and drew Edeva toward it. Before they had even reached the spot, his hands were under her cloak, tracing the shape of her breasts. "I wish you had worn a kirtle with laces," he said.

"I only have two gowns fashioned like that, and neither is appropriate for traveling."

"A pity," he whispered, kissing her neck. Finding no way to reach bare skin from this direction, he began to pull up her skirts.

"Your hands are cold," she murmured.

"Not for long."

He felt her shudder as his fingers found their goal. "I want to strip you naked and look at you, Edeva. To see you spread out beneath me, golden and rosy. A feast for my eyes. And a banquet for my hungry mouth." He nuzzled her neck, then brought his mouth to her ear and traced the dainty lobe. Nibbling tenderly, he licked the whorl of her ear and finally stuck his tongue deep into the silky recess there.

Edeva gasped and her body buckled against his. Honeyed warmth covered his fingers, and his own body felt close to bursting. He released her to grab a handful of her skirts and drag her toward the tree. He pressed her up against it, kissing her roughly. She clutched at his tunic. "Jobert, oh, Jobert."

"Ah, my love, I'll give you what you want."

He freed his shaft and raised her skirts once more. Lifting her, he fitted himself against her slippery opening. She squirmed, trying to ease his way. When he found his mark, she gave a harsh cry. He braced her against the tree and drove into her.

Pulsing, shattering waves washed over him as he climaxed.

When he had released her and they both leaned panting against the tree, she said, "How many other ways are there we have not tried?"

He chuckled and brushed his fingers across her glowing cheek. "What? Bored already, are you, wench?"

"Nay, only curious."

"Well, there are others, but we will have to wait to reach Oxbury to try them."

"How many?"

He shook his head. "I have not pursued the matter."

"But you knew of all these ways," she persisted.

Incredibly, he felt his shaft stirring. Nay, he would not take her again, even if she provoked him. "We'll explore together." He brought his face to hers, kissing her sweet mouth, then grazing her plump lower lip with his teeth. "Come, we must go back. My men will wonder what we were up to."

"Jobert." she resisted as he took her arm. "I cannot ride like this. I'm sticky and wet everywhere."

"I had not thought to bring a cloth." He looked down and spied a patch of snow in the deep shadows beneath the tree. Bending over, he grabbed a handful. He held it out. "Lift your skirts."

Her passion-warmed cheeks grew even rosier, but she did as he bid. He caught a glimpse of golden paradise as he washed her.

"Better?"

She nodded, shivering. "At least I am clean now." She straightened her skirts, then he took her hand and pulled her after him.

"The snow gave me an idea," she said, as he settled her on the horse.

"What?"

"Shhh, 'tis a secret. I'll share it with you when we reach Oxbury."

He had succeeded in his goal, Jobert thought as they rode north. Edeva appeared completely distracted from her earlier turmoil. And he—Jesu, he was still half-hard! When Edeva was near he felt like the randiest bull, capable of performing until he dropped from exhaustion.

He reminded himself to keep his wits about him as they rode through another secluded glen. With Edeva he might be able to fulfill all his fantasies, but only if he stayed alive.

"Mother of God, how could they?" A sense of horror struck Edeva as she stared across the valley and saw the ugly marks of fire blackening the side of the manor house.

"At least it still stands. They must have sounded the alarm almost immediately. And there . . ." Jobert pointed, "it looks as if they fired the palisade wall."

The sick feeling in Edeva's gut deepened. Her brothers had tried to burn down Oxbury with no regard for who might be hurt.

"I did not realize they were so desperate," she said. "I did not imagine they would do anything like this."

"Desperate, they are that," Jobert said grimly. " 'Twas a bold plan. We are fortunate to find more than a smoking ruin. My men must have acted quickly."

"Or *my* servants and workers."

Jobert nodded. "It took all of them to fight a blaze like that one. Which is why I plan to rebuild the hall and the curtain wall in stone, to reduce the effectiveness of fire as a means of attack."

"I wonder if anyone was hurt. Poor Rob and Niles—they have barely recovered from the last attack."

Jobert spurred the horse, and they rode at a fast clip through the valley. The rest of the knights followed close behind. As they neared the gate, Jobert gestured that his men should proceed cautiously.

"You think we might be attacked?" Edeva asked.

"We cannot be too careful."

But it was one of Jobert's men who greeted them at the gates. "My lord, 'tis pleased I am to see you are safe," the guard bellowed down to them. "We've had such troubles here. But, God willing, they are over now. The rebels have been captured!"

With those words, Edeva's foreboding turned to full-blown anxiety. If the rebels had been captured, they would be hung. She could not argue for mercy this time.

"Let us in," Jobert ordered, "and tell us what has happened."

They were inside the gate in seconds, and listening to the guard give a rapid account of the last few days: "The attack came on the very eve of your leaving for London. We would all have burned in our beds if it were up to the worthless bastards at the gate, but one of the kitchen wenches saw the flames and raised the alarm.

"We all ran for buckets, tubs, anything we could carry water in. Even then, we would never have succeeded in putting out the fire if it had not been for the hand of the Almighty. When it began to sleet, that gave us the edge to get the blaze under control. But no sooner had they got the one fire out than there was another at the backside of the palisade behind the granary."

"Did you see them?" Edeva demanded. "Did you see the attackers?"

The guard shook his head. "I think they shot burning arrows into the palisade wall while we were distracted."

"But how did they set the hall ablaze?" Jobert asked. "That is too far to shoot a flaming arrow."

"No one knows," the guard answered. "One of them must have gotten inside and done the deed under our very noses."

"And the men set to guard the gate?" Jobert's voice was tight with anger.

"Drunk. They did not know anything was amiss until the alarm was raised."

"Was anyone hurt?" Edeva asked.

The guard shook his head. "A few burned hands and singed beards, but nothing like the kitchen fire."

Jobert dismounted. As he helped Edeva down, she saw that his face was white with rage. "And the rebels?" he addressed the guard, "Did you say they were captured?"

"Yea, although that was afterward. The priest suggested that he speak to the prisoners in the granary. When he returned, he told us to saddle our horses, and he would lead us to the rebels. And, by the Rood, he did. Surprised them during a meal, and we had them surrounded before they could flee. One of them grabbed a knife and was cut down. We took the other seven prisoner."

Seven! Was that all that was left of her brothers' forces? And what of the man who was killed? Had it been Godric or Beornwold, engaging in one last foolish, defiant act?

Although she knew it was witless after all the terrible things they had done, Edeva paled at the thought of her brothers being hung.

"Where are they?" Jobert asked.

"In the *souterrain*, my lord. I did not think you would give a care for their comfort."

The other guards and the knights who traveled to London had gathered round. "What are you going to do, Brevrienne?" Hamo asked. "Hang them at first light?"

Jobert did not answer, but his jaw worked and his eyes

were like shards of green glass. He said, "I want the men who were on duty the night of the fire brought to me."

Payne and Osbert nodded, looking grim. As they turned to head toward the hall, Jobert added, "And the woman named Golde. Last time my guards overindulged, she was the cause of it."

Edeva waited tensely. She wanted to ask Jobert how he meant to deal with her brothers, but she feared what his answer would be. She also feared he would hang Alnoth and Withan along with the others.

"My lord?" She moved close to Jobert and spoke softly. "Alnoth and Withan aided your men. I pray you don't forget that. Please consider what you once said, that if they would swear to you . . ."

"Do you think I would trust men who turned on their own? You misunderstand the thing, woman. I have no interest in the oaths of *traitors.*"

Jobert turned on his heel and stalked off. Edeva stared after him. The warm glow of their passion seemed to have turned to ice. The man who had teased and enticed her in London, who had begged the king to be allowed to wed her, was now a stranger.

Heart heavy, she walked toward the hall, wondering what other losses she would discover.

The wind blew raw, threatening to tear off Edeva's head-wrap. She shivered even in her heavy woolen mantle, and her sympathy was aroused even more for the two knights, stripped to their hose and tied to a pole, stoically awaiting the lash of the whip.

Her feelings regarding Golde's punishment were more complicated. Jobert had not ordered the woman stripped, but unless the brawny man chosen to do the flogging administered only the lightest of strokes, Edeva knew that the serving woman's woolen gunna would soon be shredded and her bare skin exposed.

Mayhaps the man would succumb to her beauty and give

her only a perfunctory whipping. Edeva was surprised to find that a part of her hoped that he would go easy with Golde. She might be a sneaky, untrustworthy bitch, but a public flogging was humiliating enough, without also scarring the woman permanently.

The man raised the hazel switch over the first man's shoulders. Edeva turned away before the blow fell; she began to walk toward the granary. Her eyes filled with tears as she walked, and not all of it because of the bitterly cold wind. Her insides ached, twisting with anxiety.

She could not blame Jobert for his anger. Oxbury could have been destroyed. The hall was badly smoke-damaged, and the bedding and wall hangings in the upper bedchamber ruined. The clothes and other valuables in the chests remained safe, but only by a near miracle. If not for Edwina's quick-wittedness, lives would have been lost and they might well be facing famine before spring. Oxbury had survived a near catastrophe, a catastrophe her brothers were responsible for.

They must be punished, she knew that. And yet . . . yet . . .

Could she ever feel the same way about Jobert, knowing that he had ordered her brothers' deaths?

And what of Alnoth and Withan? It seemed unfair that they should have to pay for something they had no part in, especially when they had helped the Normans by revealing the rebels' hiding place.

Which one of them had divulged the location of the camp in the forest? She would like to think it had been Withan, and that she could go to Jobert and claim that Alnoth had no part in the betrayal. But in her heart, she knew that was unlikely. Alnoth was young, vulnerable and frightened. He must have been the one who told the priest where to find the others.

Edeva stopped walking suddenly. Father Reibald did not speak Saxon, so how had he spoken to the prisoners? Had he taken someone else with him?

Edeva again started toward the granary.

The man guarding the place frowned at her when she asked to see the prisoners. "My lady, you know I should get the lord's permission."

"Of a certes," she said, "but he is busy seeing to the disciplining of his men. Would you bother him now and risk his wrath coming down on yourself?"

The man hesitated, then moved to unbar the door. "I will let you see them, but for a moment only."

"Thank you, Baldric." Edeva bestowed a warm smile on the man. He held the door open and she went in.

In the light from the doorway, she could make out her brother and Withan, sitting in the straw. Their hands were tied, but they wore no shackles, and she could see that they had blankets for warmth and bundles of hay to rest on.

"Alnoth." Edeva approached her brother, resisting the impulse to hug him. "How fare you?"

He stood to greet her. "Well enough. We have been treated tolerably since your last visit."

"Why did you betray the others, then? Did you hope to save your own skins?" Edeva winced as words came out more sharply than she intended.

Alnoth blinked at her. "Betray the others? What do you mean?"

"Did not a priest come to see you and ask you where the rebel camp was?"

"A priest came, aye, but the woman with him told us he meant to bless us. We thought certain that we were to be executed after that, but nothing happened."

"The woman?"

"Aye, I do not know her name, but she is one of the serving women."

"Golde." Withan spoke up. " 'Twas the one called Golde."

Edeva took a deep breath as pieces suddenly fell into place. Golde, the treacherous bitch, had betrayed her Saxon lover as well as her Norman ones. Mayhaps she was getting what she deserved, after all. "Did you speak of the rebels with anyone?"

Both Alnoth and Withan shook their heads.

Edeva's hope returned. She might still be able to sway Jobert to spare them.

Alnoth moved nearer. "What's happened, Edeva? Several days ago, we heard shouting, a loud commotion, and smelled smoke. Did Beornwold and Godric attack? Have they been captured?"

Edeva nodded.

"Will Brevrienne hang them?"

Again, Edeva nodded. Her insides ached.

"What of me?" Alnoth demanded. "I said I would swear to him!"

"I don't know, Alnoth," she said gently. "He is very angry."

"But you can convince him, I know it," Alnoth's voice cracked with anxiety. "He desires you, Edeva. You can use his lust to convince him to let us live!"

"I will try, Alnoth. I will do my best."

Alnoth straightened, as if suddenly realizing how craven and weak he sounded. "If he does not change his mind, I promise I won't shame you. I will face death bravely."

"I know you will." Edeva embraced him, the lump in her throat near choking her.

She heard the guard behind her clear his throat. She released Alnoth and bid him farewell.

Walking back toward the yard, she struggled to sort out her troubling emotions. She understood why Jobert must order her brothers' deaths. But that did not change the bitterness which welled up inside her when she contemplated the execution of her kin. *Could they ever overcome this?*

Once, Jobert had been her enemy, the demon of her nightmares. Despite that, she had come to desire him, to care for him, and finally, to love him.

Now, it seemed she must lose that, the promise of their

loveplay and teasing banter turning to ashes before the brutal realities of war.

When she reached the yard, the floggings were almost finished. The men were being untied, and Edeva guessed that Jobert would have them taken to the hall and their wounds treated.

Golde was still bound, the lash falling across her slender back. Edeva heard the crude calls of the men each time a blow landed. "Strip her! Let us see her tits!"

She grimaced, wondering how anyone could find a beating arousing. It sickened her to see the crimson streaks etching Golde's milky skin, even knowing what the woman had done.

She had betrayed one of her lovers, and now he would hang.

Edeva turned away. She could not stand to watch. Golde's suffering would not make any difference.

"Enough!" Behind her, Jobert called out to the man doing the whipping. "Set her free."

She heard some of the men grumbling among themselves. "He scarcely broke the skin . . . give her to me, I'll punish her!" Harsh laughter sounded.

Edeva turned around. A man was helping Golde walk, but she did not look cowed or humiliated. Indeed, her face still wore that smug expression which Edeva despised. As she walked past the jeering men, Golde straightened, and her hips swayed with a characteristically seductive movement.

Edeva decided that she would have to think on a better punishment for Golde than flogging. Mayhaps something tedious and disgusting, something which kept her away from the men.

But her plight had moved Jobert to pity. If he spared Golde, he might also consider giving Alnoth another chance. Especially if he knew that Alnoth had not been the one to give away the rebels' camp.

Edeva started toward Jobert. He met her gaze coldly.

"My lord, if I could speak with you."

"Not now, Edeva," he gritted out. "I have things to see to." He jerked around and walked away.

Edeva's heart sank. She started back to the hall, contemplating the future. When Jobert reported to the king that he had hung the rebels and regained control of Oxbury, William might well give him permission to wed her.

Did she want to wed a man responsible for destroying what family she had remaining? Could they go on with that between them, and somehow rebuild the trust, the tender intimacy and playfulness?

The hall was in chaos. Old wall hangings had been nailed up over the burned wall, and the household activities moved to another area. Weavers crowded in one corner, the infirmary in the other. Edeva spied Wulfget and went over to her. "How fare Rob and Niles?" she asked.

"Niles has been up and about for days. And Rob, even he sometimes goes into the yard for some fresh air."

Edeva wrinkled her nose. The place did reek of fire. "I am pleased they have healed so well," she told Wulfget. "And I thank you for your part in it."

Wulfget blushed. " 'Twas not unpleasant. I have learned much Norman French, and Rob knows a few Saxon words."

Edeva regarded the young woman carefully. "And what of Sir Alan?"

Consternation creased Wulfget's pale brow. "He still comes to talk to me in the evenings. But he is always so angry. He frightens me."

"And Rob is gentle and quiet?"

Wulfget nodded.

Edeva excused herself from the young woman and went to check on the weavers. As she crossed the hall, she wondered which knight Wulfget favored. If it were her, she knew she would much prefer Rob's boyish charm over Fornay's scowling manner.

Nay, that was not true. Only one man could hold *her* heart.

Or break it beyond repair.

* * *

"Where do you go?"

Jobert kept walking toward the gate. He had no desire to speak to Alan, to have him demand to know when the hangings would take place.

Fornay rushed up beside him. "Have you ordered the carpenter to build a scaffolding?"

"I need to be alone for a time. I am leaving the palisade."

"Let me accompany you. Although we've captured the rebels, you cannot be certain of the loyalties of the villagers. A lone man makes an easy target."

Alan's words sent a shiver down Jobert's spine. He did not fear the villagers, but he might be in danger from another enemy. "I'll wear my helmet and hauberk, but I go alone."

"Let me arm you."

Jobert grunted assent and changed direction, heading for the stables where his armor had been stored after the trip to London. He would ride. Being mounted would give him another advantage over an assassin.

Alan walked beside him but said nothing more. Jobert guessed that his captain realized he could only press so far.

When silence grew uncomfortable, Jobert said, "How are things between you and Wulfget?"

Alan swore. "You suggested I take her to bed—Jesu, how am I to do that, in a crowded hall with that puffed-up toad of a knight Rob looking on?"

"Have you ever asked her to walk with you in the yard?"

"She never seems interested. She is uneasy around me now, and it is all that preening bastard's fault! They have been learning each other's languages, and you know what they speak? Poetry!" Alan made a disgusted noise.

They reached the stables and went to the anteroom where the armor was hung. Jobert took down his heavy hauberk and had Alan hold it while he put his gambeson on underneath. "So, are you giving up, then?"

"Of course not. She is the only woman at Oxbury I desire. I know it makes me sound foolish, but there is something about the way she smiles . . ." He shook his head. "God's blood, look at me, I sound as henwitted as Rob."

Jobert's mouth quirked with amusement at seeing gruff, grouchy Alan so smitten. "Rob will be well soon and no longer so much in Wulfget's company. You can resume your suit. Now that Wulfget knows some Norman French it will be easier to speak to her."

"But what should I do if I get her alone?" Alan asked helplessly. "What should I say?"

"What do you *want* to do?"

"I long to kiss her, to hold her in my arms, but what woman will be captivated by that?"

A woman who truly cares for you, Jobert thought. *A woman who loves you for yourself and not fancy words or deeds.*

They spoke no more of women as Alan helped him put on his mail and helmet. A squire saddled his horse and Jobert rode the beast through the yard and out the gate. A gust of bitter wind struck the exposed part of his face as Jobert urged the horse into a trot down the hill toward the shelter of the valley below.

TWENTY-TWO

The gray sky sulked above him, threatening rain. Jobert shivered in his armor and wished he had worn an extra tunic underneath. Foolish, to ride out decked like a soldier for battle. The valley was peaceful enough.

Smoke rose from the village huts, and outside one of them, a woman shook out a cloth, the russet-colored fabric billowing in the breeze. She nodded to him as he rode by, and the child clutching at her skirts raised his chubby hand and pointed at Jobert, eyes wide with curiosity.

Jobert thought how much things had changed since he came to Oxbury. Once the sight of him in his battle attire would have struck terror in the hearts of the villagers. The woman would either have dragged the boy inside the hut or fled to the woods.

Now the people of Oxbury accepted and depended on him. If a crisis arose, someone would come running to the palisade, begging for help. They had learned that he was a fair master, that he cared for their welfare and valued their labor.

Jobert knew that many lords weren't like him. They were cruel and harsh, squeezing all they could from their workers without thought for their well-being. But he could not see the profit in it. If a man starved and abused his people, they would grow weak and sick and less useful. Their children would die of hunger or illness. In a few years, there would be a lack of laborers to tend the lands.

Besides, he misliked causing suffering. Being a younger son who was passed over for nearly everything, he could more easily imagine what it was like to be poor and powerless. And, after spending weeks in the horror of Valois' prison, where the only face he saw was that of his gaoler—a frail, bent old man who showed him kindness—he could not look at anyone, even the lowliest serf, and not see a man rather than a brute to be used and discarded.

But his soft heart threatened his ambitions. King William thought him weak, unable to hold Oxbury. Somehow, he must prove him wrong. And the most obvious way was to execute every one of the rebels.

Jobert grimaced as he imagined three men bearing Edeva's blue eyes and proud features dying by his decree. He thought of her tender gaze growing hard with bitterness. A shudder went through him. Though he might get to keep his lands and his heiress, at what a price. Was Oxbury worth enduring a cold woman in his bed the rest of his life?

Jesu, better to send Edeva to Matilda and wed some other woman! But how could he do that? Edeva *was* Oxbury. Having her golden beauty at his side was part of his dream. He needed her, not merely to be his chatelaine, his advocate with her people, but in his heart, in his bed, loving him, desiring him, sharing her life with him.

But somehow he must prove to William that he had defeated the rebels and gained complete control of Oxbury. That the last vestiges of insurrection had been wiped out. Meanwhile, Valois worked against him, seeking to convince the king that he was unfit to be a lord.

Jobert reached the river and looked out at the water, as dark and cold-looking as the overcast sky. The chill seeping through his armor seemed to settle in his heart. Was there no way out, no way to keep from losing everything he cared about? To survive, must he become a man like Valois, ruthless and cruel, acquiring land and power at any price?

Nay, he would not do that. His very soul rebelled at the thought. Men like that were not truly strong. Deep down they were fearful and helpless, terrified they could not control their fates.

And, in the end, they could not. Valois' wife had borne him no sons, and his daughter refused to be a pawn in his ambitious plans. Valois' power would die with him.

Jobert knew he wanted more than what his enemy sought. He wanted a life of accomplishment and honor, rather than one of conquest and greed.

His thoughts again returned to the Saxon prisoners. There must be some balance to the thing, some course of action between the brutality of execution and the risk of mercy. What would William do? he wondered.

Then, like a thunderclap, it hit him. He did not have to decide the prisoners' fate—he could take them to the king for judgment! William's decision might be cruel. If he did not hang the rebels, he was likely to order them maimed. But it would be William's decision, not his.

He took a deep breath. Like Christ in the garden, he had asked that the bitter cup be passed from him, and God had been merciful.

Dusk was falling as he rode back to the palisade in the dense, heavy twilight which made a man know that winter had the land in its fierce grip and might never let go. But Jobert felt almost jubilant, for summer awaited him in the palisade. Edeva's warmth and loveliness were not lost to him after all.

Edeva was nearly asleep when the door opened. Fatigued by the past hours of cleaning the smoky bedchamber and finding fresh bedding, she had decided not to wait up for Jobert. Though this might be the time to discuss her brothers' fate, she had no strength for it.

She had already decided she would not beg nor bargain. Why demean what they shared? Jobert had no choice that she could see. If he made the decision to hang Beornwold and Godric, she would have to live with it. Mayhaps over time, the grief would pass and she could forget.

Alnoth's death would be more difficult to endure. In some ways, he still seemed a boy. As the youngest, he had been sheltered from many of the challenges and responsibilities of life. If he had followed his brothers in a hopeless cause, 'twas not completely his fault. Edeva had hope that Jobert might see that.

She heard him undressing, then the creak of the ropes supporting the bed as he climbed in beside her. He pulled her close and kissed her neck. Although surprised by his show of affection, Edeva wriggled nearer. Why should they not have one night together before the anguish of his decision came between them?

He kissed her on the mouth with slow tenderness. Edeva responded helplessly. How could anything break the bond between them?

His body fit with hers as if they had been made for each other. The scent of him, the texture of his skin, the smooth firmness of his muscles—everything sublime, magic. She ran her hands along his back, stroking, reveling in his masculinity and strength.

When he entered her, it felt perfect, as if they made two halves of a whole. His rhythm was slow, his thrusts deep, searching. She clutched at his shoulders, then reached down to caress his powerful buttocks, feeling them contract each time he pushed into her, penetrating her wet, eager opening.

They moved in rhythm together, a sinuous dance. Jobert brought his mouth to hers. They were joined, melded. Breath to breath, breast to breast, sex to sex.

The tension built as their heated bodies strained, seeking release. The wild creature they made together writhed and keened its pleasure. Transformed, they burst into flame.

The sense of joining remained even as their breathing slowed and they collapsed into sweaty disarray. Jobert stroked her face, whispering love words. Edeva felt tears sting her eyes. How could she let anything shatter this sweet closeness? She wanted the rest of the world to go away, so there need never be anything but them and the wonder that they shared.

"Edeva, Edeva, how I love you."

His soft, whispered words touched the core of her heart. She drew a shaky breath. He settled her against his body, enfolding her in his strength. "I've decided what to do."

She tensed, dreading this moment of reckoning.

"I'm taking the prisoners to William. He will decide their fate. I will argue for mercy, and tell William that if your brothers swear to me, I would accept them in my *mensie.*"

Relief made her unable to speak. She could accept the king's decree. At least then she would not have to hate her lover.

"I cannot say what William will do. He has been sore tried by the rebels, but, in the past, he has been known to accept the oaths of Saxons."

"When do we leave?"

"Nay, you cannot go this time. If William's judgment be harsh, I don't want you there."

A pang of worry went through her at the thought of being separated from Jobert. "I will wait at the inn," she said. "I vow to accept whatever happens."

"I need you here."

"Why?"

"I must take a strong force with me to guard the prisoners. I want you to remain here and support my claim to Oxbury."

"What do you mean?" she asked. "Besides my brothers, who would claim it?"

"If rumors of the king's concerns have reached other ears . . ." He sighed. "There are always greedy men who seek to profit from another man's troubles."

"You trust me to guard your interests while you are gone?"

His fingers stroked her hair. "You are my fierce warrior woman. Who better to protect our children's heritage?" His hand moved down to lovingly touch her breasts, then rest against her belly. She knew he was thinking of his seed inside her, of the promise of a new life which might be growing in her womb.

Tears threatened again. He wanted her to bear his child. She longed for the same thing, more intensely than she had ever wished for anything.

"I don't feel strong and fierce," she said. "When I think of something happening to you, I . . ."

"Shhhhh, shhhhh . . ." He pressed his fingers to her lips. "I did not survive Hastings and a dozen other battles through carelessness. I will guard my back every moment I am away," When she sighed, he added, "I have the greatest incentive to stay alive that a man ever had." He pulled her close, so she could feel his shaft rising against her leg. "Do you think I would risk losing what we share?"

Her nipples hardened as he fondled her breast "Let me love you again," he whispered. "I leave on the morrow, and I would have more delightful memories to take with me."

"Pure stupidity," Alan said when Jobert told him of his plans. "Why don't you hang them and be done with it?"

Jobert pushed the remainder of the cheese and bread aside and took a swallow of cider. "If they swear to me and William, I gain warriors to defend Oxbury."

"You'd trust those Saxon wretches? How can you think they will cease scheming against you!"

"I have my doubts about Edeva's older brothers, 'tis true. But the younger boy and the other men—what have they to gain by continuing to fight me? They know if they break their oath, they will die. And they had no better future before I came. The younger son would have eventually had to leave and fight for his own place in another household. 'Tis clear his older brothers would not have allowed him any authority here. And the old thegn's household guard, what's left of them, would have sworn to another lord at some time. Why not me?"

"Because you're a Norman, you fool! They hate you for your foreign blood."

"But my sons will be only half Norman, which will make it easier for them."

"Sons!" Alan looked startled. "Have you hopes of that?"

"Jesu, of course I have hopes!"

Alan stared morosely at his food. "I wish I could say the same. The few times I have been alone with Wulfget, nothing has come of it."

"I cannot advise you any more than I have, except to say that when the moment is right, you will know it. Mayhaps you should talk to Edeva about Wulfget."

"Edeva!"

"Yea, she is a woman and she knows a bit of Wulfget's mind. I vow she would help you if you asked her."

"I would sooner ask Hamo, that crude, fornicating lout!"

" 'Twas only a suggestion. You might think on it over the next few days while I am gone."

"I don't go to London with you?"

"Nay. Although I have asked Edeva to look after my interests in Oxbury, she does not know much of real warfare. She will need a strong captain by her side."

"By her side!" Alan sputtered. "I will not share my command with a woman! Especially a Saxon one!"

"Peace, man. I do not ask you to share your command. But the truth is, you need *her*. If there is an armed threat, only she can mobilize the villagers and servants to fight. My mission has its dangers, and I can leave only part of our force to guard Oxbury. Without Edeva's people, I fear you cannot hold it."

"But, why should they fight their own . . ." Alan's words trailed off and his eyes widened. "You do not fear rebels, do you?"

Jobert nodded. "I pray I am wrong, but my instincts tell me that there are other dangers threatening Oxbury. Indeed, I fear there is someone inside the palisade working against me. How else was the king informed of the last raid on the manor ere I even knew of it?"

Alan looked around the hall uneasily, then leaned closer to Jobert. "Do you think one of our men is in the pay of Valois?"

" 'Tis possible. Or, it could be one of the Saxons. If Valois were going to plot against me, whom better to choose as his allies than men who already hate me?"

"Which is exactly the reason they must hang!"

"I would like to find out the truth before they go to the gallows. If I bring them before William, one of them may reveal something regarding Valois. My plan serves another purpose than simply sparing me from hanging my future wife's brothers, I hope to prove to the king that Valois is a malicious, corrupt man who cannot be trusted. Only then can I be certain that William will take my part."

"And if the spy is one of your own men?"

"Then sooner or later he will act, and we, both of us, must be ready."

"And if the woman is the spy?" Alan asked, his voice tinged with bitterness.

Jobert rose impatiently. "I trust Edeva with my life, and I advise you to do the same."

Edeva turned away from the gate, unable to watch her brothers being led off to face William. She had sought to speak to both Godric and Beornwold before they left. Beornwold had spat at her and shouted that she was a whore who shamed their father's memory. Godric had merely looked at her with a weary, hopeless expression.

The experience made a hard knot in her stomach and dulled her warm satisfaction from the night before. The sight of Fornay glaring at her as she made her way to the hall did not soothe her mood, either. Clearly, he still mistrusted her.

She walked past him, wondering how they would ever be able to cooperate if there was a real threat to the manor.

As Edeva neared the hall, the priest called to her. She met his shrewd gaze, and he motioned that she should follow him to the chapel.

"A pity," he said once they were inside. "You know, of course, that your brothers will be hung . . ." He sighed dramatically. ". . . . Or something worse."

"What could be worse than death?"

The priest's air of melancholy grew more pronounced. "My lady, no matter what Brevrienne has told you, King William is not a man known for lenience. If he does not hang your brothers, he will maim them. Do you not think that they would prefer death to life without their tongues or hands?"

His words made Edeva's stomach roil. "Why do you tell me this when there is naught I can do?"

He patted her arm. "Only God can aid them, my child. But there are other ways to see that justice is done."

Edeva, wary, said nothing.

"I do not think it is God's will that Brevrienne hold Oxbury. He is merely a younger son of a lord of modest means. No more than a common knight. King William raises these men to power, but he forgets that they are not born to rule."

The priest steepled his hands, looking thoughtful. "I believe King William will eventually see the error of his ways and appoint someone else to hold Oxbury. 'Twill be a man more deserving than Brevrienne, someone worthy of wedding the daughter of an important Saxon lord."

"Why do you tell me this?" Edeva asked again.

"There may come a time when your aid will be required by the new lord. I wanted you to know that I do not think it proper that you have to share the bed of a man like Brevrienne. You had no choice but to submit to his crude ravishing, but if you act wisely you can better your circumstances."

Edeva stared at the priest. She had always sensed he did not like her, nor any of the Saxons; now he spoke as if he wished to help them. She longed to confront him with his hypocrisy, but instinct held her back. Better to learn more of his plans.

"Brevrienne is a strong commander," she said. "How can you think that he will allow another man to usurp his property?"

The priest's features twisted into a macabre smile. "Brevrienne has gone to London. By the time he returns, 'twill be too late. Oxbury will already be lost."

Edeva swallowed her shudder of fear and tried to appear cool and calculating. "Do you know the man who comes to seize control?"

The priest grew uneasy. "I cannot say more," he said hastily. "I risk much to warn you."

"I am surprised that you do so," Edeva could not help saying. "I would not think you would want to aid any Saxon."

"When I first arrived in England, I shared the prejudices of most Normans. But over time I have come to admire your people. The wealth and luxury goods you possess make it clear that you are not the barbarians I once believed. And you, my lady . . ." the priest drew near and Edeva stayed her ground only by sheer force of will, "your beauty is exceptional. I would not see it wasted on one such as Brevrienne."

Edeva smiled stiffly. The cunning cleric sought to flatter her into betraying Jobert. She had no doubt that if she did so, Father Reibald would immediately argue for the new lord to have her executed as a traitor.

"I will think on what you have said."

She started to leave. "Don't forget your brothers," the priest called after her.

Outside the chapel, Edeva paused, shuddering with mingled dread and rage. The priest's chilling hints filled her with fear, while his obvious manipulation infuriated her. He meant to use her to destroy Jobert. Did he truly think she was that disloyal?

She took deep breaths to calm herself and tried to think. It was obvious that Oxbury was in danger. Jobert had suspected as much, which was why he left her behind. Somehow she must prepare for the upcoming conflict.

Edeva knew little about defending a fortress. Oxbury had never been besieged in her lifetime, and her brothers had not sought to defend the palisade from within, but rather to ambush the Normans before they reached it.

But an ambush would not work in these circumstances. There were not enough of them to even try such a strategy.

With dismay, Edeva thought of the burned place in the palisade wall. The rebels had done much damage to the fortress defenses, only to be captured and defeated anyway. Now Oxbury lay vulnerable to attack from other enemies.

The wall would have to be repaired, and quickly, and Edeva was certain there were other precautions that must be taken. She would have to speak to Fornay. She wondered if she should tell him of the priest's words?

Nay, Fornay would either not believe her, or imagine she had some sinister motive for warning of an attack. His distrust of her was so great that if she suggested some plan of defensive action, he might very well decide to do the very opposite. But surely he could not argue against repairing the wall. That was only reasonable.

She went looking for Jobert's captain and finally found him in the gatehouse. "Sir Alan, if I might speak with you."

He regarded her coldly, then followed her down the ladder to the yard. Edeva decided they should seek some privacy. Having seen the priest leave the chapel, she now led the Norman that way.

"Where are you going?" he demanded. "What do you have to say to me?"

"Before he left, Lord Brevrienne suggested that Oxbury might be attacked. If we are in danger, I think it prudent that we plan for it. Jobert also hinted that he did not trust all who dwell here."

Fornay nodded grudgingly and followed her into the chapel. There in the flickering candlelight, Edeva chose her words with care. "I know little of defending a demesne and must rely on your expertise in these matters. It seems to me that the palisade wall must be repaired. What else must we do to prepare for attack?"

Fornay regarded her skeptically and said, "We will need archers to man the walls. Are there any among your people who have the skill?"

"Of course. Many of the villagers and sokemen hunt game with bow and arrow."

The Norman's mouth twitched. "Can these men be relied upon to follow the orders of a Norman?"

Edeva squared her shoulders. "If *I* asked them to help defend the palisade, they would do so."

Fornay scrutinized her again; then his tone became matter-of-fact. "We will need a good supply of arrows for the archers. Set your people to making them. We have food and water aplenty and should be able to endure a long siege. The chief worry is of fire. We must have vats and buckets of water ready. Also rags and raw wool to wet down and smother the flames."

"In this weather, water left out will freeze."

Fornay nodded. "We'll have to store it somewhere, mayhaps in the blacksmith shop and the hall, wherever there is a hearth to keep it from freezing."

"What else?"

"If we are attacked, there may not be time to send a messenger to the village. How will we alert your people to come to the defense of the palisade?"

Edeva frowned. Although Oxbury was situated so it was easy to sight an enemy entering the valley, it would still take time to get the archers inside the palisade and into position on the walls.

She looked up at the nave. "There is a bell in the upper part of the chapel. It has not been used since my mother died, but I'm certain it still works. We could ring it when we wanted the men to gather."

Fornay's gaze followed hers. "I'll have a squire climb up and search for the rope."

TWENTY-THREE

"Poor bastards." Giles nodded toward the Saxon prisoners crowded into the wain.

"I vow it is warmer where they sit among the blankets and hay than it is out here in the wind," Hamo growled in response.

"I would rather suffer the rawness of the wind than be a Saxon facing King William."

Hamo gave a grunt of assent and reached up to take his pack down from his saddle. "Still, I do not relish trying to sleep in full armor. Jesu—are such precautions really necessary?"

"Yea, they are necessary." The two knights turned as Jobert strode up. "Bands of rebels still roam England, and with our cargo, we make a most enticing target. Would you rather sleep sound and wake up with a war axe in your back?"

At Jobert's words, Hamo shrugged and went off to the fire. Giles remained to unload his horse. "Do you think William will hang the Saxons?" he asked.

Jobert glanced at the prisoners in the wain. Would William think him weak if he argued for mercy for the youngest of Edeva's brothers? "I don't know what William will do," he answered. "Much will depend upon whether he's had trouble with the English recently, if he sees them as a serious threat."

And on whether he believes Valois' lies, Jobert added to himself.

He looked around warily at the copse where they had decided to camp for the night. The tall pines and firs which appeared sheltering by day had acquired a menacing aspect as the light faded. Jobert repressed a shiver, thinking of what dangers might be waiting for them in the shadows.

He approached the wain where the Saxons huddled together, their hands bound in front of them and linked together with stout ropes. There was room to sit in the cart, but not lie down, and Jobert briefly considered allowing them to bed down on the ground as the Normans would. Some inner sense warned him not to.

His squire came up and asked where Jobert wanted his tent set up.

"I'll sleep out in the open so I can take first watch at guarding the prisoners," he answered.

After a visit to the cookfire for a welcome hunk of hot venison and a few swallows from a skin of wine, Jobert did just that, arranging his bedroll a few paces from the wain. He told himself that he need not worry about falling asleep, that the ground was too hard, especially with the sharp rings of his mail digging into him.

The next thing he knew, someone was shouting. He shook himself from dull, heavy unconsciousness and started to sit up. The feel of cold iron against his throat froze him in place.

There was more shouting from the wain. Although he could not understand much of it, he did recognize the Saxon word for "kill." His predicament grew clear. Somehow the prisoners had cut their bonds and one of them held a knife to his throat.

His heart thudded so loud he seemed to hear it above the moan of the wind in the trees.

His attacker spoke to him, whispering some vile epithet. Jobert inched his hand down toward the misericord he wore at his ankle. The blade at his throat sliced into skin, releasing a trickle of warm blood.

"Brevrienne! To Brevrienne!" There was a commotion across the camp. Jobert used the moment of distraction to jerk away and roll sideways. By the time the Saxon caught up with him, he was on his feet.

He could see the glint of the knife in the light from the fire as he faced his attacker. The man swore and threw the knife, narrowly missing Jobert's face.

The Saxon turned and darted toward the woods. He screamed as Jobert's misericord caught him in the back.

Jobert grabbed his sword and took off after him. A dozen paces into the trees, he stumbled over the fleeing Saxon, facedown in the wet leaves.

The man was still alive, breathing in choking rasps. Jobert grabbed his tunic and rolled him over. The Saxon made rattling sounds in his throat. Jobert struggled to think of the Saxon words to ask who had been helping the rebels. The words would not come.

"Is he dead?" Jobert's squire, Will, spoke from behind him.

"Not yet."

The man's breathing grew more labored, then stopped. Jobert stood. "Where are the other men? Why did they not come to my aid?"

"They must have been drugged. Only now are the knights rousing."

Drugged. Someone had provided weapons for the prisoners and drugged the wine. Jobert's sense of foreboding increased, and he led the way back to camp with cautious steps.

"Brevrienne, thank God!" Hamo stumbled toward them as they reached the copse. "We thought the Saxons had you."

Jobert started to answer, then saw Alnoth and Withan in the wain. "What the devil?" he whispered.

Giles and the other knights came up with a torch. "What's happened? Where are the other prisoners?"

"Gone," Jobert said, "except for the one who tried to kill me. He's dead."

They all stared at the two Saxons in the cart. Alnoth's young face blazed with proud defiance. Withan watched them with a weary expression.

Jobert approached the wain. "Why . . . not . . . run?" he asked haltingly in Saxon. He gestured toward the woods.

Alnoth answered rapidly, baffling them all. Withan spoke in a slow, careful voice. "Swear to you . . . Brevrienne." Alnoth nodded.

Jobert drew a deep breath. Edeva's brother and the old man had honored their vow to serve him. They had not escaped with the others, and it had been Alnoth's shouting which had alerted him to the attack.

"Thank you," Jobert said in Saxon. "I . . . accept . . . your oath."

But would William honor the loyalty of a Saxon? The thought troubled Jobert. He might well argue for mercy for the remaining prisoners, only to have the king order them hanged.

Yet, he had to try. Edeva's brother had saved his life. He must try to do likewise.

He rubbed his forehead as a throbbing headache began. "Fetch the wine," he told Hamo.

The knight returned with a wineskin. Jobert pretended to drink the contents, then acted as if he were falling asleep. He held out the skin. "Who?" he asked in Saxon. When they didn't answer, he gestured as if pouring something into the skin.

The two men shook their heads, clearly puzzled. Jobert started to walk away, but Withan called out, "Golde . . . Godric . . . lovers." When Jobert looked at him, Withan nodded meaningfully.

Jobert's jaw went rigid. The serving wench had obviously helped plan the escape attempt. But had she done it all on her own, or did she have an accomplice? The plot seemed far too complex for a lone woman.

Jobert threw the skin to the ground. "Pack up and saddle your mounts," he told his men.

"Now? 'Tis hours til morning," Ramo protested.

"Do you want to stay here and risk the other Saxons coming back and murdering us in our sleep?"

"I could stay up and watch," Will offered.

Jobert shook his head. "I'd not risk it. I'll not leave one man to face seven cunning Saxons."

"Six," Will reminded him.

Jobert grunted and went to retrieve his pack.

When all was ready, they mounted and proceeded cautiously through the dark forest. The strain of trying to see the pathway ahead helped Jobert stay alert, but his head still felt fuzzy and his stomach pitched. He'd only had a few swallows of wine; he pitied the men who had indulged in more.

Every time a branch swayed or there was other movement in the gloom around him, his muscles twitched. He had been far too close to death this night—he could still feel the crust of dried blood on his neck and his instincts thrummed with warning. There had been a spy at Oxbury; there might be a spy with him still.

He recalled the expressions on the faces of his men as they gathered around while he questioned the remaining prisoners. They had all appeared groggy and addleminded, except Will, and he, like Jobert, had only had a few sips of wine.

The moon peeped out from behind the clouds, abruptly lighting the ghostly bare branches and bushes around them. For the dozenth time, the hair on the back of Jobert's neck prickled with warning.

But nothing happened.

"My lady!" Osbert rushed up, looking alarmed. "I think you should come to the gatetower. There are knights in the valley."

Edeva gathered up her skirts and ran headlong across the yard. *Knights.* Although the guard did not say it, she knew what he feared. If they were attacked by a strong force, they had no hope of holding out.

But why should they be attacked? What was it that Jobert anticipated? Why had he warned them to prepare to defend the manor?

By the time she reached the tower, Edeva was breathless and gasping. The sight which met her eyes forced the rest of the air from her lungs. A whole army spilled along the river trail, a force of Norman knights at least as large as the one Jobert commanded. And they with barely twenty trained soldiers and a half-repaired hole in the palisade walls.

"Sweet Mary," she whispered. She turned to Osbert. "Do you recognize the leader's banner? Are they allies of Brevrienne?"

"Nay, I've never seen that device before. At least I think not."

Osbert squinted, staring down at the black banner with some sort of gold figure adorning it. "A *fleur de lis,* I think it is called, but I cannot remember which Norman lord carries it."

"Would Alan know?"

Osbert shrugged.

"Get him," Edeva ordered. "Before I would treat with these men, I would know their connection, if any, to my lord Brevrienne."

Osbert hurried down the ladder. Edeva continued to examine the approaching force. They did not look as if they meant to attack. They had not drawn their weapons and only a few wore their helmets. But they proceeded toward the palisade with a purposeful air which chilled her blood.

"Payne." She called down to the knight at the bottom of the ladder. "Run and get one of the stable boys to climb the chapel tower and ring the bell."

The man ran to do as she bid.

Edeva turned to look down at the valley again. Her heart raced; her hands felt clammy with perspiration. Unless

Alan could identify these men as otherwise, she must assume that they were enemies of Jobert. She must not let them inside the gates. Although the timber walls afforded little protection, it was better than nothing.

The bell in the chapel tower began to ring and the yard filled with people as women, children, and workmen assembled in the open area near the manor house. Edeva knew she should speak with them, reassure them somehow, but she had not yet decided what to say.

She saw Alan come tearing across the yard, his mail shirt hanging crooked and his helmet in his hand. "What's going on?" he shouted up to her.

She motioned that he should climb the ladder and see for himself. He did so, still yelling, "Osbert said that we were about to be attacked. Who is it? What army does he speak of?"

When he reached the tower, panting, Edeva said nothing but merely waited for him to look out and spy the approaching force.

He stared hard. "I don't know the device, but 'tis a Norman one."

"Can you think of what their business with us might be?"

Fornay shook his head.

"We must decide what to do, whether to let them into the palisade."

"Why would we not let them in?" Fornay asked.

"Did Jobert not warn us that we might be attacked?"

"But it looks as if these men come in peace."

"It might be a trap. They may mean to lull us into thinking they mean no harm, then, when we allow them into the palisade, turn on us and attack."

Fornay's eyes narrowed. "So, it is your judgment that we do not let them in?"

"Yea," Edeva answered, "at least until we know their purpose and whether they mean us ill."

Fornay gave her a cold, suspicious glance, then smiled

bitterly. "That is enough for me." He started toward the ladder.

"No!" Edeva grasped his arm. "Don't do this! Don't let them in merely to spite me, I beg you!"

Fornay turned. "We really have no choice. If we refuse these men hospitality, and they go to William and complain of it, 'twill go bad for Brevrienne. Nay," he shook his head, "we cannot risk it. I will order the men to open the gate."

He turned and started down the ladder. Edeva stared after him. Every instinct warned her not to let the band of knights inside the walls. But what could she do? She was merely a woman, and Fornay was officially in charge of Oxbury's defense.

A plan flashed through her mind, and in another second, her body followed through with it.

There was a pottery jug on the walkway. Edeva picked it up and hurried toward the ladder. As Fornay neared the bottom, she threw the jug, hitting him in the head. He crumpled and slid the few feet to the ground. The helmet in his hand went spinning, landing some distance from his prone body.

Edeva hurried down the ladder and knelt by the knight. He groaned and mumbled something, reaching for his temple. She breathed a sigh of relief. She had not meant to kill him, merely disable him for a time.

"Jesu, what happened to Sir Alan?"

Edeva flinched as Osbert came up behind her. "He fell," she said flatly. "I think he hit his head. We must get him into bed."

"Now?"

"Yea, 'tis dangerous for him to be up with a head injury."

"But what about the soldiers in the valley? Mayhaps if we splashed him with water, he would come to." She could hear the doubt in Osbert's voice. She thought frantically as Fornay began to groan. Leaning over the injured man's body so she blocked Osbert's view, she put her hand over Fornay's mouth.

"Heed me, soldier," she said to Osbert, making her

voice sharp. "I am a healer and I know what I am about. If we do not get this man to a bed, he could die!"

Osbert responded immediately to her imperative tone. "Of course, my lady. Stand aside and I will carry him."

Edeva straightened, praying that Alan would stay unconscious for a little while longer.

The burly Osbert picked Alan up and hoisted him over his shoulder. "God's feet, I wish he did not have mail on," Osbert grumbled. "It adds near two stone to his weight."

"Hurry," Edeva implored.

She helped clear a way through the yard, explaining to the crowd that Sir Alan had fallen from the ladder. Several of the Saxons stared at her in puzzlement, and she guessed some of them must have seen her deliberately cause the fall. Fortunately, the Norman knights and squires had been too busy arming themselves to have observed the happenings on the tower. No one stopped them as they headed toward the manor hall.

Once inside, Fornay began to mumble and groan again. "Take him to the upper bedchamber," Edeva ordered. As Osbert moved past the trestle tables, she grabbed one of the torches from a wall bracket and held it near the wounded man's face as he hung over Osbert's broad back. Fornay's incoherent ramblings quickly turned to coughing.

She followed Osbert up the stairs in that fashion, ostensibly lighting the way. By the time they reached the bedchamber, poor Fornay was all but choking to death.

"Jesu, what's wrong with him?" Osbert asked after he lay his convulsing burden on the bed.

Edeva tsked sadly. "I've seen it before. The bump on his head has made it hard for him to breathe. Quickly now," she motioned toward the doorway. "Fetch me some wine from the kitchen. 'Twill aid him."

"But lady, there is wine here." Osbert pointed to the ewer on the table.

"Nay, we must have fresh wine. Hurry! If we do not bring him round soon, he may never recover his wits."

Osbert started toward the door, then hesitated. "But what of the soldiers in the valley?"

"I'll deal with them, anon." Edeva waved him urgently toward the door. "I swear, as soon as I have Sir Alan safe, I'll go to the gate and speak to them."

Osbert's brow furrowed, but he finally departed. Edeva ran to the chests in the corner and dug out a badly smoked bedlinen. After tearing the fabric into strips with her teeth, she quickly bound Fornay's wrists together and tied his feet to the bedposts.

He stopped coughing and began to moan again.

Edeva rushed to get the container of poppy juice and mandrake and mix it with the wine. She returned to the bed and sloshed the mixture into the knight's mouth, forcing him to drink. He choked a few times, then swallowed.

When she thought he'd had enough, she took the cup away. There was a commotion on the stairs. Edeva hurriedly arranged the bedcovers over the knight's bound body. By the time Osbert reached the doorway, she was calmly leaning over the bed, her hand on Fornay's forehead as if feeling for a fever.

"He sleeps now," she announced. "I think he will be well as soon as he wakes."

"But what of the wine?"

Edeva shrugged. "I thought to use the other, to see if it worked."

"But you said we must wake him, lest his wits slip away."

Edeva straightened and left the bed. "He did rouse briefly. Enough so that I believe he will recover completely." She moved toward the door. "But now I must tend to the business at the gate."

Osbert looked doubtfully at the still form in the bed. "Should I stay with him?"

Edeva put her hand on the big knight's shoulder, urging him from the room. "There is no purpose to it, and I require your help below. If these knights attack, we will need every man to help defend the palisade."

Osbert shot one last forlorn look at his unconscious captain, then preceded Edeva out the door.

Edeva was halfway to the gate before she realized that she could not appear on the tower and speak to the army below. Normans, and indeed, most men, did not consider warfare or politics matters for a woman's concern. In Jobert's absence, Fornay was the obvious person to act as Oxbury's representative. Since she had incapacitated him, she must find someone else, someone she could trust.

The sight of Rob coming out of the stables filled her with relief. "Sir Rob," she called, "I have need of you."

He walked stiffly toward her. "I don't know how much use I'll be. I'm still weak as a babe. I had not realized how far I had to go until I put on my mail. I vow, it takes near all my strength merely to walk around."

"I don't need you to fight, yet," Edeva assured him. "Simply stand on the gatetower and look and sound like a strong warrior. Someone must speak to the leader of these men and find out their business here."

"That is Alan's duty," Rob protested. "He is Jobert's first captain."

"Fornay fell off the gatetower ladder and is indisposed." Rob's jaw dropped. "When did this happen?"

"Not long ago." Edeva took Rob's mailed arm and tried to propel him toward the gate. "I put him in the upper bedchamber. He should be well in a few hours."

Rob set his feet. "Jesu, are you certain? Should you not go see to him?"

"The matter of the men at the gate seems more pressing. I'll tell you what to say."

Having been under the care of a woman for the past weeks, Rob was used to receiving orders from them, and he finally submitted to Edeva's urgings.

When they reached the gatehouse ladder, Osbert was in a state. "The archers are in position as you asked, milady. But it still feels strange to me. Why should we not let these men in? Why should we prepare for attack? They are Normans, like us."

Rob gave her a look. "Yea, that is right, lady. Why should we expect that these men mean us ill?"

Edeva thought she would explode with frustration. "Before he left, Lord Brevrienne warned that there might be a threat to Oxbury. We must guard his interests."

"But surely he thought the threat would come from Saxons," Rob said.

"Are you so certain Brevrienne does not have other enemies?" she demanded. "From what I heard of it, before your people came to harass the English, they fought bitterly among themselves in Normandy for many years. How can you assume that such warlike men have suddenly become peace-loving?"

"But William outlawed fighting among his nobles," Osbert said, quoting the king's decree like a child reciting by rote. "He said that if any of them fought against each other here in England, he would withdraw the lands awarded to them."

Gritting her teeth, Edeva forbore to point out that, human nature being what it was, simply outlawing an activity seldom eradicated it. Instead, she said, "Mayhaps you are right and these men mean us no harm. But 'tis only prudent to be certain before we open the gates."

Both men agreed to this, and Rob slowly climbed the ladder, Edeva a step after him. When they reached the tower, she situated herself behind the low wall near an arrow notch, where she could not be seen, but from where she could advise Rob on what to say.

"Identify yourselves, and state your business with the manor of Oxbury," Rob called out to the leader of the force.

"My name is Ralph of Bourges, and I come on behalf of Lord William, king of England and duke of Normandy."

"The king!" Rob turned to speak to Edeva. "Of course we must let them in."

"Nay, nay," she hissed. "Ask him if he has any emblem or document identifying him as the king's man."

Rob did so. Edeva could hear the arrogance in the man's

voice as he responded. "Of course I have documents identifying me. But they are packed away on one of the sumpter ponies. If you will let us in, I will have a man get them out and show you."

"Tell him we will see the documents first," Edeva said. Rob regarded her with dismay. 'Twas clear he was not used to arguing with men who gave him orders. "Tell him," she insisted.

"My lord," Rob began, "there have been troubles here, and we must be cautious. If it so please you, we would see the document ere we open the gates."

"Nay, it does not please me!" the man shouted. "I was told this manor was firmly under the control of one of the king's men, but it appears that Norman authority has yet to be established. William will be most displeased to learn of this. Indeed, he may well rescind the grant of this property after such a display of defiance! Tell me, sir knight, what will Lord Brevrienne do when he returns and finds that through your foolishness, he has lost Oxbury?"

Rob shot Edeva a stricken look, and from the ladder, she heard Osbert call out, "Good God, lady, we must let them in!"

Edeva drew a deep breath. Bourges' threats and his refusal to show his credentials convinced her that he was up to some trickery. But how could she persuade Rob and Osbert? Somehow, she must contrive it so Bourges revealed he was not truly acting on the king's behalf.

"Tell him that we will meet him halfway," Edeva said. "That you will send a man out to discuss this matter face-to-face." When Rob looked skeptical, she added, "Certainly, that is not an unreasonable request. If the man has nothing to hide, why would he refuse?"

Rob thought on this, then turned back to the ramparts. "Although I'm certain you speak the truth, Bourges," he called down, "I must follow the orders given to me by Lord Brevrienne. To break the stalemate, I will come out to you."

"As you will," Bourges' voice was harsh with contempt. Edeva saw Rob's jaw tighten.

"You are right, lady," he said. "Something is not right here. This mans rudeness alarms me. I cannot think that the king would employ one such as him on a peaceful mission."

"You're going out to meet him?" Edeva asked.

"Yea, 'tis the only way. If he fails to produce a missive from the king, we will know Bourges plays us false."

"But I fear for you. You are barely recovered from your wound, and now you go to meet a man who may be a deadly enemy." Edeva's insides twisted with anxiety. She was fond of Rob; if anything happened to him, she would be wracked with remorse.

" 'Tis time I quit my sickbed and acted as a soldier, lady."

Edeva nodded, reminding herself that the man was a knight, trained to face death on a daily basis. Yet, as Rob climbed down the ladder and motioned for the guards to open the gate enough to let him pass, she wondered how she would ever explain to Jobert if the sweet-faced young knight were hurt or killed.

She moved closer to the edge of the tower so she could see over it to watch the scene below. Foreboding afflicted her as she beheld the mass of armed men crowded together on the trackway. With their mail gleaming like fish scales and the points of their lances sticking up like prickly spikes, the Norman force reminded her of some hideous creature about to ravage Oxbury.

She told herself that she had once viewed Jobert and his men the same way, but the choking dread would not leave her.

Rob walked out to meet the leader of the force. His sword was sheathed, to show he went in peace. As he approached Bourges, the knight climbed from his mount and strode to meet him.

Edeva could not hear what they said to each other. She held her breath, praying that Rob would be careful, not the easygoing soldier who had once guarded her so carelessly.

Bourges gestured that Rob should follow him back to the rear of the train where the packhorses waited, stamping their feet in the cold. Edeva knew a momentary sense of relief. Mayhap the man did have a missive from the king after all. They might have worried for naught.

When they were halfway down the line of soldiers, Bourges suddenly shouted, "Seize him." The two nearest knights wheeled their horses, pinning Rob between them. Within seconds, the rest of the army began to move into battle formation.

They were going to be attacked! Edeva felt as if her legs would give out beneath her, and she fought the urge to grab helplessly for the edge of the rampart. Without Alan or Rob to give orders, she was in charge of the palisade's defense. *Mother of God, she knew nothing about this sort of warfare!*

She dashed down the ladder, hoping that Osbert had some idea of what to do. By the time she reached the bottom, she had come upon a plan of her own. "Barricade the gate!" she yelled. "And give the order for the archers to prepare to fire!"

Like the good soldier he was, Osbert immediately echoed her orders in his booming voice. Then he turned back to her. "What's happened?"

"They have Rob, and it appears that they mean to charge the gate."

He regarded her only a second before cramming his helmet on his head and drawing his sword. "The treacherous bastards!" he thundered. "By God, we'll gut them all!"

"Brevrienne, Brevrienne!" he bellowed, starting a chant which echoed through the palisade. Edeva watched in amazement as the Saxons gathered in the yard joined in.

Then an arrow landed a few paces from the hall, and Edeva remembered the danger. "Get the children into the chapel!" she screamed. "The rest of you, pull out the water barrels and be ready to put out fires!"

The Oxbury archers shot hail after hail of arrows, trying to prevent the Norman force from getting near enough to attack the palisade directly. The invaders returned fire, loosing arrows dipped in pitch and set ablaze.

At first the enemy's fiery arrows fell harmlessly to the

ground, then one landed on the thatch of the stables and the battle was on.

Within moments, it seemed that everywhere Edeva looked, there was a fire. She joined the rabble of shouting servants and took her place in one of the lines of people passing buckets of water from the cisterns to the fire.

Time passed in a blur. Edeva's eyes burned from the smoke, her throat felt raw. How long could they keep this up? she wondered. Even if they kept the palisade from burning down, there were other threats. Bourges and his force could easily use a battering ram to break down the gate. Once inside, what would they do?

There was pause in the action as the fire line shifted to meet a new threat. Edeva stopped for breath and reached down to feel for the dagger strapped to her ankle. She would not die easily, of that they could be certain! She would fight for her life, and that of the life beginning inside her.

She'd known that morning, when she vomited for the third day in a row, that she was carrying Jobert's child. The awareness filled her with awe and joy—and now that all their lives were threatened, with a fierce will to survive.

The blaze threatening the tannery was close to the water supply, and Edeva took the opportunity to leave the fire line and seek out Osbert. Mayhaps he would know what to do, how to defend the palisade from the next assault.

When she reached the gate, a begrimed soldier met her. "They're leaving," he told her exultantly.

"All of them?" she asked.

"Yea, the whole force."

Edeva climbed the ladder to see for herself.

Indeed, the enemy appeared to be in retreat. But unlike the young knight, she did not believe it reason to celebrate. Men like that did not ride away simply because their first attack was thwarted.

TWENTY-FOUR

"Christ's bones!" Hamo exclaimed. "This is hopeless! I doubt that the king himself could find a room in London this night."

Jobert nodded grimly. Since arriving in the city, they'd found it even more crowded than last time. "We might as well return to the others and tell them we must camp outside the city walls."

"At least now we do not have to worry about what to do with the Saxon prisoners while we wait for an audience with the king," Will said cheerfully.

The rest of them glared at the squire. After the harrowing night just passed, none of them relished sleeping on the frozen ground.

"With luck, I will get in to see William quickly," Jobert said. "In fact, I will go to Westminster now and see if I might have a word with the king ere he has his evening meal."

"Who goes with you and who returns to join the others?" Hamo asked.

Jobert regarded his men thoughtfully. He misliked splitting up his forces further. If there were a spy among them, this was likely when the man would act. "Hamo, Giles, Fulk—you will come with me. The rest of you, go back and join the others waiting with the wain."

"Must we keep the prisoners fettered?" Will asked.

"They have already proven they respect their oath to you, and they would be more comfortable if they were freed."

"With their obvious Saxon blood, it is for their own protection that we maintain the appearance that they are prisoners. If they were allowed to roam free, some passing Norman might think to make sport of them."

Will looked downcast, and Jobert suspected that the squire had formed some sort of friendship with young Alnoth. The two of them were of an age, and ignoring the contrast between the Saxon's fair hair and Will's dark curls, of similar build and appearance.

Jobert and his escort wearily mounted their horses once more and set off for Westminster.

The abbey was also more crowded than last time they visited. Jobert knew a sinking feeling as he observed the noisy throng stationed at the entrance to the building where the king resided. Without Girard's influence, they might wait days for an audience.

Fortunately, Jobert recognized the knight stationed at the door. "Well met, Warrene of Toscny," he greeted him. "I see you've risen high. The king's personal guard, are you now?"

"Brevrienne! Yea, I am sworn to William's service, and 'tis not a bad sort of duty. The food is better than average, the women plump and accommodating." The knight winked merrily.

"And some power comes with the duty, I'll wager. No doubt you have your say in who gets in to see the king."

"Ah, I see now. You mean to use your good will with me to get an audience."

" 'Tis not a frivolous matter. William charged me a fortnight ago to subdue the rebel Saxons in the area of my fief. I can report to him that I have done that. Of a certes, he will be pleased to learn that at least my portion of Wiltshire is securely in Norman hands."

"He will at that. There is rumor of trouble in the southwest. Though he keeps court here until Easter, when spring comes, the king marches into battle once again."

Warrene scowled. "What ails these English, that they cannot see when they are beaten? The Londoners submitted easily enough—why do so many others resist?"

"The Londoners grow rich off of William's troops, but for the other Saxons who have lost their lands and livelihoods, Norman conquest is a disaster. Even if they surrender and submit to the lord who now holds their property, the best they can expect is to serve in his army. Wealthy noblemen have been reduced to landless knights, and they do not take kindly to their diminished station. Would you?"

"Most likely not. Norman gain is Saxon loss, in truth. I had not thought of it from their side."

"Most Normans have not," Jobert agreed. "I'm not certain I would have either if I was not smitten with a Saxon woman. She taught me that her people can be valuable allies."

Warrene grinned. "Is that how you secured your property then, with kisses and fond love words?"

Jobert smiled back. " 'Tis not so useless a method as you might think. Though men wield the power of the sword, I vow women are the cleverer ones. They find more subtle ways to enforce their will. Can any argue that Queen Matilda could not have the best of the king if she so wished it?"

"Blessed Jesu, such thinking gives me the shivers! If I get you in to see William, will you cease such morbid philosophizing?"

"I'll not speak another word on it," Jobert assured him.

The anteroom to the king's private chamber was filled to bursting. Knights, merchants, clerics—men of every ilk waited to argue their causes and request favors. Jobert took his place among them and considered what he would say. He wished that the rest of the Saxon prisoners had not escaped. Although he expected no further trouble from them, he was not certain how William would see the matter. Mayhaps he could discreetly delete that detail from his report.

When the clerk called his name, he went in. The king was seated at a table, eating while he perused the pile of parchment set before him. A clerk sat to his right, pointing out some detail on a document.

Jobert waited while the king finished his business. At last, William looked up, and mouth full from the capon leg he was gnawing on, nodded to him.

"Your highness." Jobert bowed low.

"Do you bring me good news or ill?" William asked.

"Good, my lord. The rebels harassing Oxbury have been captured. Among them are a boy and an old man whom I have brought to you for judgment. Since these two aided me in the capture of the others, I forebore to hang them. In fact, with your permission, I would like to accept their oaths and offer them a place in my mensie."

William's deep-set eyes narrowed. "You are willing to trust men who once rose up against you?"

"You have been known to do such a thing, my lord."

"And mayhaps I have been overhasty at times."

Jobert hesitated. How far dare he go in arguing for Alnoth and Withan's lives? "My lord, the men in question saved my life. I think I owe them something for that."

"And how did they save your life?"

Jobert ignored his doubts and plunged ahead. "I thought to bring the rest of the rebels to you for judgment. There was an escape attempt on the way here, and I woke to find one of the prisoners with a knife at my throat. Had the Saxon youth not distracted the man so I could get away, I would not have lived to bring this matter before you."

William rose from his high-backed chair. "What happened to the man who tried to kill you?"

"Dead, my lord."

"Were there others who also sought to escape?"

"Yea, my lord."

"And where might they be?"

Inwardly wincing, Jobert answered, "I know not, although I expect no further trouble from them. The man who was killed was the leader of the rebels. Without him, I vow they will not harass Oxbury further."

William began to pace. "But they might well join some rebel forces elsewhere. I cannot say I am pleased with this news, Brevrienne. I charged you with subduing the rebels. All you have done is run them off your demesne. I ask you, why should I honor any of your requests, when I cannot depend on you to carry out your duty?"

I am caught in a trap, Jobert thought miserably. By trying to save Alnoth and Withan, he had lost further ground with William.

The king turned his back and approached the pile of work on the table, as if signaling Jobert's dismissal.

"There is one other thing, my lord." Jobert drew a deep breath before continuing on. He might be risking everything, but it was his only hope. "I don't believe that all the troubles at Oxbury have been caused by Saxons. I believe that someone else has been aiding the rebels and causing me difficulties."

William cocked his head. "And have you any idea who this 'someone' might be?"

"Robert de Valois, my lord. You know that he hates me, that he blames me for his daughter's decision to enter a convent. I think he has set men to spy on me and paid them to inflict damage in whatever way they can."

"What proof do you have?"

"Strange things, my lord. A few weeks ago, the rebels' attacks suddenly became more daring, their awareness of the palisade's weaknesses much more acute. Someone had to be helping them."

"What else?"

"I was injured while in Gloucestershire in the attempt to suppress the rebels there—shot in the shoulder by a crossbow bolt. No one else around me was hurt, and from what I can learn of it, the crossbow is not a Saxon weapon. I believe now that the bowman's intent was to kill me."

"Now you talk murder, a very serious charge."

"Yea, my lord. But you well know that Valois hates me enough to plot my death."

William paused and drummed his fingers on the table, then looked at Jobert. "I will not say I do not believe you. My instinct tells me that Valois is capable of such ruthlessness. But your proof is slim, indeed, near nonexistent. And . . ." he arched a brow meaningfully, "Valois is a powerful force in Normandy. With the arduous task ahead of me here in England, I cannot afford to offend my allies there."

"So, what do you advise, my lord? That I go back to Oxbury and wait for the next attempt on my life, the next threat to my property?"

"You must do what you see fit, Brevrienne. I have lived all my life with the shadow of the assassin's blade hovering over me. All I can advise you is to surround yourself with men who have more to benefit from your remaining alive than from your death. In the end, your fate is in the hands of God, anyway."

Jobert could not be angered by William's casual attitude. In truth, the king had survived numerous challenges to his power, beginning in his boyhood when he woke in a bloodsoaked bed and found that his trusted seneschal and protector had been murdered next to him while he slept.

The king sat down at the table, and Jobert realized his audience was nearly at an end. "And what of the Saxon prisoners?" he asked. "What is your judgment for them?"

"It appears you need all the loyal soldiers you can find, Brevrienne. If you desire to accept their vow of allegiance, you may do so."

"And the matter of my marriage to Oxbury's heiress?"

William did not look up. "I have not yet decided."

"What think you, lady?" Osbert came up beside Edeva on the gatetower, and his steady gaze met hers.

"I think they will try again."

He nodded. "The archers struck a few, but 'tis scarce

more than a burr in a bear's paw to an army such as that. It puzzles me that they are so easily turned away." Below the helmet, his mouth twisted into a frown. " 'Tis almost as if they meant to harass us, but not overtake the palisade."

"I know. Something is not right here. What is their plan?"

"To learn that, we must consider why they came here to begin with. If we had opened the gate to them, as Bourges requested, what would they have done?"

Edeva shrugged. "Seized control of the manor and murdered all inside?"

"And when Brevrienne returned?"

"I suppose they would kill him as well."

"But their actions would eventually be reported to the king and Bourges would end up an outlaw. William will not tolerate private war among his barons. Bourges can conquer Oxbury, but he cannot claim it, not without writ from the king. And if he had that, why bother doing battle at all?"

" 'Tis a puzzle."

"Yea, and we must decipher it."

Edeva sighed. She did not feel up to solving riddles at this moment.

Beornflaed called to her from the bottom of the ladder. "My lady, is it safe for the children to leave the chapel? They are hungry and fussy," the cook added apologetically. "If the danger is past, 'twould seem better to let them leave for now, in case they must seek shelter there again later."

"Yea, feed them and let them have their rest. Where is the priest, by the by? Did he not stay with you?"

"I have not seen Father Reibald," Beornflaed answered. "In fact, I believe he has left the palisade. Before the enemy soldiers even arrived, I saw him by the postern gate."

The priest was missing, having conveniently disappeared before the palisade was attacked. Edeva thought it odd. But then, Father Reibald was a strange man. The way he pretended to admire her, even though he did not. His suggestions that Jobert was unfit to control Oxbury, that King William would send another man to take his place . . .

Edeva stared blindly across the yard. *Father Reibald had warned that another Norman would come to claim Oxbury. What if Bourges were that man?*

"Lady, what do we do next?" Osbert prompted.

She turned to him. "If we could find the priest, we might find the answers we seek."

"How is he entangled in this?"

"I know not. But he was seen leaving the palisade ere Bourges and his men even arrived."

Osbert gave her a puzzled look. Edeva decided she did not have time to explain her suspicions. If Father Reibald were a spy, 'twas unlikely he would return to the palisade until the invaders had triumphed.

"Send your swiftest man down to the village," she told Osbert. "Have him offer the women and children there sanctuary inside the palisade. I fear what Bourges and his men will do if they return."

Osbert nodded and left.

Edeva remained on the tower, thinking furiously. What if she sent a man to London to find Jobert and alert him to what was happening? She gazed up at the overcast sky. A storm was coming. If it snowed, 'twould be near impossible for a lone knight to get to London in time. Should she risk it?

Below, she heard the creak of the gate opening. A knight on horseback—probably Payne—started down the muddy trackway toward the village. Edeva fought the urge to call him back and send him to London instead. She must see to the safety of the villagers first, then she could decide what her next action would be.

The gate clanged shut, and Edeva climbed down the ladder. She paused to speak to a dozen different people in the yard, reassuring them, answering questions. The turmoil inside her deepened. Everyone depended on her and looked to her to make sound decisions regarding the safety of Oxbury. She wanted to scream that she didn't know a thing about defending a fortress. She wanted to run away.

Going to the chapel seemed the next best thing.

She went inside and closed the door behind her, breathing a sigh of relief. At least it was quiet and private here. The candles glowed soft and mellow. The place smelled of incense and beeswax.

She walked to the rail, her footsteps echoing on the stone floor. Kneeling, she made a silent petition for strength and courage. Some of the anxiety seemed to leave her. She bowed her head again, this time praying for the souls of her mother and father. Her brothers. And Jobert.

A lump formed in her throat. What if she didn't live to see him again, to look into his beautiful green eyes, to kiss his wide, grinning mouth?

Nay, she could not think like that. He had asked her to keep Oxbury safe, and somehow she would manage it.

She stood. A shout from the yard made her hasten to the chapel door.

Outside, she blinked at the sudden whiteness. Flakes of snow were falling, drifting down with a quiet, deadly grace. The sky was a thick, opaque gray.

She ran toward the gate. The villagers filed in, clutching bundles of their possessions, carrying crying babies and wide-eyed, frightened children. Edeva tried to reassure them. "You'll be safer here," she said. "We have twenty knights to defend us. Lord Brevrienne said the palisade could withstand a siege if necessary."

Her words did not ease their apprehension. She wondered a little at their continued anxiety, until Osbert came up beside her and said, "We've found the priest. Lying at the side of the trackway with an arrow in his back."

Hot anger rose in Edeva. "Fools! To kill a man of God, even if he was a worthless, scheming wretch. I vow King William will not forgive this!"

"My lady." Osbert's voice was mournful. " 'Twas a Saxon arrow we found in his back."

Edeva knew that her mouth was hanging open in a very

unladylike fashion, but she simply could not believe what she was hearing. The people of Oxbury would not have done such a thing. 'Twas unthinkable of such simple, stolid folk.

She started to make her thoughts known to Osbert. The words froze in her throat as she beheld Alan of Fornay walking toward her across the yard. On the side of his face shone a livid purple bruise. He limped slightly and fat flakes of snow gleamed in his dark hair.

"You're not coming back with us?" Hamo asked as Jobert and his escort left Westminster.

Jobert shook his head. "I'm going into the city. There is someone I must speak with."

"God's blood, I don't like this," Hamo grumbled. "You want us to leave you on your own in a place crawling with Saxons."

"The Londoners are not such fools as to attack a well-armed Norman knight."

"I hope you are right, but if you are not back by dawn, where shall I fetch you?"

"I'm going back to a tavern near the inn we stayed at. The Black Horse, it is called."

"Yea, I remember." Hamo grinned. "Give my greetings to the curly-haired wench."

"You think she will remember you?" Jobert gibed.

Hamo stuck his chest out. "Of course she'll remember me. How many men has she had who are hung like a stallion?"

Jobert shook his head at Hamo's conceit and turned his horse down the roadway toward the city. His errand was probably a foolish one. There was really no reason to suppose that Girard would be at the same tavern he had frequented a fortnight ago.

But the conversation with the king had left Jobert unsettled. He needed to find proof that Valois was behind his difficulties at Oxbury. Otherwise, William would continue to think him weak and incompetent. His claim to the manor, and to Edeva, would not be resolved.

It was almost twilight and the traffic on the roadway had begun to thin. Jobert saw only a few knights and some farmers with their empty wains heading back to their steadings after selling their produce to merchants in the city.

When he reached the city itself, the streets were more crowded, but not as bad as during the day. He could take in the sights without being constantly distracted by the bustling stream of humanity jostling him and making his horse shy.

Here and there among the clutter of wooden houses, he spied fantastic archways, ancient pillars and other elaborate stonework, made almost invisible now by years of soot and dirt, but still impressive if a man looked closely and imagined the effort and creativity it took to fashion them. So many centuries ago the Romans had built these wonders, their engineering brilliance surviving all who came after. Mayhaps that was why the Londoners accepted their new conquerors so easily, Jobert mused. They expected to prosper under the Normans as they had under all the other invaders.

King William was in the process of leaving his own mark on London, with a tower built close to the river on the east edge of the city. Constructed first in wood, it would eventually be rebuilt in stone, and would form the first line of defense in maintaining Norman control of the Thames. Jobert could not help wondering if William's tower would last half as long as the Roman structures had.

The streets grew narrower, and he was forced to leave his horse at a stable and proceed on foot. It seemed farther to The Black Horse than he remembered.

Once he arrived at the tavern, he futilely searched the crowd for Girard's bright mane. Should he wait? Might not his friend appear here later, after one of his amorous assignations?

He purchased a pot of greasy soup and a skin of wine, then drank the soup standing up as there was no place to sit. Finding a place where he could lean against one of the inn's dirty, smoke-stained walls, he settled in to watch, taking occasional sips of his wine.

Hours passed, and no one paid him much mind. Despite the usual awareness people had of him because of his size, it appeared he had been there long enough that the drunken louts surrounding him had forgotten his presence.

He finally stretched to loosen up his stiff joints and went out to relieve himself. The night seemed even darker. Jobert wondered if he would be able to find his way back to the stables without a lantern. But he had no way of obtaining one, and he was weary of his mission.

He fell in step behind a group of raucous knights who had a squire carrying a torch for them. They progressed some ways in the direction Jobert needed to go, laughing and singing, stopping now and then for one of them to piss or be sick. At last he had to quit them and turn south.

His footsteps sounded loud on the hardpacked street. He was alone and around him the city slept, although the endless sound of church bells echoed in the night, calling the office of matins. The icy air penetrated his cloak and hauberk and settled numbingly against his skin.

Weariness and cold dulled his senses, and when he caught a glimpse of a movement behind him, he reacted sluggishly. By the time he turned, the assailant's dagger had caught the side of his neck. Jobert jerked out his sword, but the man disappeared into the shadows.

Jobert stood there, breathing hard, afraid to move. Someone meant to sneak up on him and cut his throat from behind, and they had almost succeeded. Instinct told him to run, but reason overruled it. Mayhaps he could lure the man into trying again. If he could capture the assassin and make him confess who hired him, he would have proof to take to the king.

He began to walk again, thinking what a deadly game of cat and mouse he played. The man with the dagger, he could handle, but what if there were a crossbow directed at his back?

Nay, 'twas too dark for an archer to aim and shoot accurately, he told himself, hoping it were true.

Every muscle was rigid, although he tried to walk casually, feigning unawareness. He swung his arms easily at his sides, though his fingers itched to draw his sword and face his attacker.

Two streets he passed. Three, and still nothing. He began to think that the man had given up. He passed an open alleyway and the hair on the back of his neck prickled.

The attack came from above, the man landing on him hard, knocking the wind out of him, then grabbing his hair and pulling up his head to reach his throat. Jobert rolled sideways, but the bastard hung on, clinging to his shoulders, yet keeping his body away from Jobert's crushing weight. It was like having some sort of pincer bug stuck on him. Though he flayed and rolled, he could not dislodge his assailant.

He reached back to grasp the attacker's face and the man bit him. Sudden rage swelled through Jobert. He lurched to his feet and crashed backward against a wall. The man gave a grunt of pain and let go. Jobert grabbed for him, but captured naught but thin air as the nimble devil danced away.

Jobert, hampered by his heavy armor, went after him.

They were in an alleyway, as dark and evil-smelling as sin. Jobert pursued by instinct, seeing nothing. His labored breathing echoed harsh in his ears as he paused to listen. A sense of despair enveloped him. If the man escaped, then all his wretched struggle would be for naught.

A ways ahead, there was a clatter, the sound of something falling. Jobert waited, reluctant to go further until he could get his bearings. The yowl of a cat rewarded his patience. Nay, the man had not gone that way. He was nearby, hiding.

Jobert jabbed the darkness with his sword, then swept

the weapon in a wide arc around him. He took another step and repeated the motion, reaching as low as he thought the man could crouch, slicing the air with the deadly blade.

His sword struck something solid, hard. Not a man, a cask or something else made of wood. He poked the sword behind it and was rewarded with the feel of the blade cutting into something soft and yielding. The man shrieked and upended the barrel as he tried to get past him. Once more, Jobert swung his sword. It hit its target with a wicked sound, cutting into flesh, crunching into bone. There was a sickening thud of a body hitting the ground.

Jobert was there in a second. He knelt down and lifted the man's head, praying he wasn't dead already. "Who sent you?" he demanded. "Who?"

The man made a gurgling sound. Jobert shook him. "Tell me, you bastard."

He coughed and sputtered, then mumbled something in Saxon. Realization dawned and Jobert switched to the English tongue to repeat his question.

"Valois," the man finally groaned.

Exultation swept through Jobert, but it was short-lived. Would the king believe him? He needed to take this man to William and have him speak the name to the king.

There was no hope of that. He could feel the life seeping from the Saxon even as he held him. The man would not live a breath beyond the alleyway even if Jobert managed to carry him that far.

He laid the man down and reached for the dagger at his waist. Before he had time to perform the act of mercy, the Saxon gave a shuddering moan and went still.

Jobert leaned back on his heels and pondered what to do. Should he take the assassin's ruined body to the king? He grimaced at the thought of arriving at Westminster carrying a bloody corpse. Nay, he had no stomach for such an errand. Already, he was exhausted and half-frozen. 'Twould be all he could do merely to make his way back to the king on his own.

Stiffly, he rose. He made the sign of the cross over the dead man's body, then turned and left the alleyway. Surely someone would find the corpse and carry it to the church for burial. It made him a little uneasy to leave without really even knowing what the man he had killed had looked like, but there was no help for it. He must keep moving.

He finally reached the stables, and after rousing the sleeping ostler and then soothing the man's bad temper with silver, set off for Westminster.

TWENTY-FIVE

"What have you done?"

Edeva flinched as Fornay bore down on her, eyes flashing. The news about the priest rattled her. She did not feel so certain of her decisions as she had been a few moments before. *What if Bourges went to the king and told him that the villagers of Oxbury had killed a Norman priest?*

Osbert rushed toward Fornay. "Sir Alan, thank God. We could use your assistance. I fear those bastards are going to take another run at us. What can we do? We're near out of arrows already and the walls won't hold if they get any siege engines up here."

"We're under attack?" It was Fornay's turn to frown.

"Yea, sir," Osbert said. "The Lady Edeva was right about Bourges. Not a fellow to be trusted. They've taken Rob prisoner, and there's no telling what they mean to do."

"Rob—a prisoner?"

"Yea, sir. Are you certain you feel all right? You look damned pale."

"Who is Bourges?"

"The leader of the men who have Rob." Osbert pointed to the palisade walls. "There's a whole troop of knights in the valley. Remember, that's why you and Lady Edeva were up on the gatetower. You do recall that part, don't you, before you fell off the ladder and hit your head?"

Alan's jaw tightened when Osbert mentioned him falling off the ladder, and Edeva thought he would tell him the truth. He did not, merely saying to Osbert, "How many are there?"

"Oh, two score at least, plus squires and servants. They could put us down easy, which is why their retreat is so puzzling."

"They've retreated?"

Osbert nodded. "For now, but I vow they will be back, and this time with proper siege engines. These old walls will crumble like twigs," he added gloomily.

"I don't understand any of this," Alan said. "Did these men say what they wanted, or simply attack?"

"Bourges claimed to have a message from the king," Osbert said. "But he would not produce it. And when Rob went out to speak with them, they took him prisoner."

Alan shook his head, as if trying to clear it. Edeva did not doubt that it still ached after the blow she had landed.

"What do we do, sir?" Osbert asked again, obviously made anxious by his captain's silence. "Somehow we have to defend this place. If Brevrienne returns to find Oxbury destroyed or in the clutches of another Norman lord, there'll be hell to pay!"

"Send the squires and village youth out to gather up the loosed arrows," Alan said. "And if you fear a siege, have all the oil stores put in pots over the fire and heated until it boils. We'll dump it on their heads if they get too close to the walls."

Osbert, looking much relieved, started off to do his bidding. A few paces away, he turned. "What about the priest, sir?"

"The priest?" Alan asked blankly.

"What should we do with his body?"

"Jesu, how did the priest die?"

"No one knows. The men found him outside the palisade with an arrow in his back. A grim way to go. I'd not wish it on any man, even a sour-faced, stingy cleric like Father Reibald."

Alan shot Edeva a suspicious look. "Have you examined the arrow which killed him?"

"Of course. Plain ashwood, fletched with goose feathers."

"A Saxon arrow."

"In truth, sir, but that does not mean a Saxon shot it." Osbert gestured toward the gate. "With all the arrows launched by both sides in the last skirmish, there were likely some which were reused. 'Twould have been as easy for the enemy to have shot him in error as for our own archers. That fool priest had no business wandering around outside the palisade during a battle!"

Alan shook his head again. "Have his body put in the *souterrain*," he ordered Osbert. " 'Tis cold enough the corpse will not putrefy. We'll wait until Brevrienne returns before burying him."

Osbert ran off to carry out the orders. Edeva stood where she was, waiting for Fornay to confront her. "So, you were right," he finally said. "There is treachery afoot."

Edeva breathed a sigh of relief. He accepted their predicament. Though he might despise her for what she had done, he would not sacrifice Oxbury's safety to punish her.

"You think this man Bourges means to seize control of Oxbury?" she asked.

"I know not. Indeed, I can fathom none of it," he answered flatly.

"Mayhaps this is the danger Brevrienne feared, the reason he spoke to us about working together to defend the manor."

"I wish he had told us more." His gaze met Edeva's. "Have you thought of sending a message to London?"

She glanced up at the leaden sky. "If it snows, a messenger would not be able to get through."

"If it snows, that will delay Brevrienne's return." Fornay turned away from her, his hands clenched into fists.

"We'll simply have to carry on as best we can without him," Edeva said. "I was thinking of sending the women and children to hide in the woods. That way they would be safe if the palisade were overrun."

"But if there is a siege, they would be caught outside in the weather."

Edeva nodded. There was no good solution, at least until they knew the intentions of the enemy. Would they be satisfied to claim the manor, or did they mean harm to the people of Oxbury?

"The priest warned me of this," she said. "He came to me soon after Brevrienne left and suggested that Jobert would not be able to hold Oxbury, that another Norman would come and claim it. He implied I could make a better match with the new lord."

"God's toes!" Fornay exclaimed. "Why did you not tell me this sooner?"

"I did not think you would believe me. Besides, the priest was always saying strange things, and I knew he disliked Brevrienne. I thought his musings naught but wishful thinking."

"But mayhaps he knew that Bourges would come. Mayhaps he was even part of the plot."

"Then, why did they kill him?"

"It could have been the Saxons," the knight argued. "Or simply an accident. As Osbert said, 'twas senseless for him to be outside the walls."

"Unless he was meeting Bourges."

Alan nodded. "It seems likely the priest was part of this, but I still do not see the logic behind the plan. Bourges may seize Oxbury, but he will have no legal right to it. What man would risk King William's wrath for a demesne no richer than this one?"

They stared at each other, both troubled by their inability to reason out the purpose behind the enemy's actions.

"What do we do now?" Edeva asked.

"We prepare for their attack."

She nodded, feeling utterly helpless. After a moment, she started to walk away.

"Lady!" Alan said sharply.

She jerked around.

"You have a mighty arm for a wench, but your knots are

a disgrace. It took me only a moment to wriggle free."
There was a slight quirk to his mouth as he spoke.

"What of the drug? I gave you enough poppy juice to
make you sleep til sunrise."

"Luckily, I puked it up. Again, you miscalculated, lady."

He was actually grinning at her. Edeva stared at him in
astonishment, then smiled back. "I must say, I would not
have risked hitting you if I were not certain that you were
such a hard-headed, stubborn lout that you could survive
it."

"Yea, I am that, lady. Mayhaps at times, I am too stubborn. I don't always listen to reason."

Could he actually be apologizing? Edeva could scarce
believe it. She approached him and reached out to examine the livid bruise on his temple. "Tincture of woodsage
and wine would bring down the swelling."

"I have not time for it," he said, pulling away. "If you
would help, then think of a way to fortify the walls ere we
are attacked again."

William frowned as Jobert entered the spartan bedchamber. The king sat on a stool with his legs stretched out as
a servant unfastened his crossgarters. Without his armor,
wearing a plain linen tunic and with his eyes smudged with
weariness, he looked like an ordinary man rather than the
formidable Conqueror.

"Brevrienne, what is it this time?" he demanded sharply.

Jobert moved into the lamplight so the vivid stain on
his mantle was plainly visible. "I come to you wearing the
blood of my would-be assassin. Before he died, the man
spoke a name to me, the name of the lord who hired him—
Valois."

The king's brows lifted, but his eyes betrayed nothing.
Jobert waited. A dozen heartbeats passed before the king
motioned the servant to leave.

When they were alone, the king rose, a slight jerk in his
movements revealing the stiffness in his legs from which

all old soldiers suffered. "You have his name from the lips of a dying man," he said, then grunted. " 'Tis not enough."

"My lord—" Jobert began angrily.

William raised his hand to hold back his words of protest. "I did not say I did not believe you. I am convinced that Valois does plot against you." He reached to pick up a chess piece from the game set up on a nearby table and fidgeted with the piece, turning it over in his fingers. "You must see my predicament, Brevrienne. I may be king of England and duke of Normandy, but my power still depends on the good will and support of other men. God may have granted me success, but He daily tests my worthiness."

Jobert took a deep breath. "You won't accuse him?"

"Not publicly. I will send a carefully worded letter reminding him that the lord of Oxbury has my favor, and if he comes to harm I will have the matter investigated."

"But your highness, the man has tried thrice to murder me!"

"And, through the grace of God, you have survived."

"Worse yet," Jobert continued heatedly, "his reason for hating me is a false one. 'Tis not my fault that his daughter chose the Church rather than a wealthy husband! Why should I be the victim of his greed and bitterness when I am innocent of any wrongdoing? Why should his treachery and evil go unpunished?"

The king carefully set the chess piece down. "I did not say he would go unpunished. He has broken faith with me. I warned all my barons that I would not allow them to pursue their grievances against each other in England. But as the Lord in his wisdom says in the scriptures, 'for every thing there is a season'. This is not the time for Valois to pay his debt."

Jobert was silent. The king's decision frustrated him, but he could see there was no point in arguing further.

When he looked up, the king watched him, an amused expression on his face. "Mayhaps giving my permission

for you to wed the Oxbury heiress will help ease your disappointment. Consider what I have done for you already,
Brevrienne. I have raised you from a landless knight to a
baron, and from what I hear of it, Oxbury is a wealthy
demesne with the potential to be even wealthier. You
should be rejoicing in your good fortune, rather than cursing me."

Jobert nodded. In truth, William was giving him much
more than he had once hoped for, not only land and a
title, but also the woman he loved. Possessing Edeva was
worth much more to him than gaining revenge against
Valois. He was a fool if he did not accept that.

He bowed low. "Never would I curse you, sire. You have
indeed made me a fortunate man. I will repay you with a
lifetime of loyalty, and should Edeva bear a son, I vow to
name him 'William' after the most generous and valiant
of men."

The king approached and raised him. "Hurry back to
Oxbury then, and wed your heiress, lest she bear another
'William the Bastard'."

The two men laughed, then Jobert quickly departed, but
not before inviting the king to visit Oxbury when he had
an opportunity to pass that way.

Outside the Westminster compound, Jobert paused to
look up at the sky. A heavy mass of clouds still concealed
the stars, and that and the cold, damp air suggested that
a snowstorm was on the way.

He urged his horse into a trot. Now that things were
settled with William, he was anxious to get back to Oxbury.
Though he was already weary beyond measure, he had
made up his mind to rouse his men as soon as he reached
camp and set off for home before the weather closed the
roadways.

Edeva sat up on the hard bench and stretched her stiff
muscles. She had insisted that Joan, who was near to her
time, and several of the other village women with very

small children use the upper chamber while she bedded down in the hall.

She smoothed the wrinkles from her gunna and tucked a stray lock of hair into her braid, thinking of all the work ahead of her. Though she was grateful for their battle expertise, neither Alan nor Osbert had an inkling of what must be done to maintain a fort full of people. Merely baking enough bread to feed everyone required hours of labor. And there were other foodstores to prepare, water for drinking and washing, clean rags for swaddling babies . . .

Briskly, she shook out the mantle she had used as a blanket and put it on, then made her way from behind the screen to the main portion of the hall. Most of the adults were awake, although a few soldiers who had had guard duty the night before still snored. She directed some of the women to tend the fire and the others to cut up the remaining loaves of bread and feed the children.

A shower of icy pellets struck her face as she opened the door of the hall. This was no soft, gentle snowfall but a vicious, treacherous mixture of sleet and freezing rain.

Edeva pulled her hood farther over her face and hurried to the kitchen shed.

As she entered, the heat from the ovens instantly melted the ice on her mantle and face. She nodded to Beornflaed. "I see you have the bread started. Make some bean and bacon pottage as well 'Twill help warm everyone as well as stretching the food supply."

"You think we are in for a siege?" the cook asked.

Edeva hesitated before responding. Although she hardly thought it possible that they could hold out for more than a few days, she dared not share her fears with the servants and the villagers. "I'm not privy to Sir Alan's battle strategies, but it seems to me only wise to ration our food supplies."

The cook nodded vigorously. "Pottage it is. I'll send the spit boys for a few baskets of beans and a flitch of bacon.

You should eat yourself, lady," the woman added. "You look as pale as a wraith."

Edeva sank down on a stool by the bread oven as the familiar queasiness struck again. Despite her churning stomach and woozy head, she knew a sharp sense of satisfaction. 'Twas almost certain she was pregnant.

The cook approached Edeva with a steaming jar. "Whist now, drink this down. 'Twill strengthen your blood and hearten the babe."

Edeva met her gaze. "What makes you think there is a babe?"

Beornflaed rolled her eyes. "I saw your mother through six pregnancies, not to mention all the sluttish kitchen wenches I've had to endure, puking out their guts a few weeks after your brothers—and now these damned Normans—had their way with them. I know the look of a woman who's breeding, and you have it."

Edeva took a sip of the hot broth and then another. As her stomach settled, she released a long sigh.

" 'Tis a good thing, my lady," Beornflaed said. "Between you and Lord Brevrienne, you will make a son as can hold Oxbury against any man. You are both brave and strong, lusty and proud. 'Tis a fine match and it bodes well for all of us."

Edeva felt a sudden stab of anxiety. If only she could be as certain of the future as Beornflaed. All she could think of was Jobert returning to find Oxbury burned and ruined. Worse yet, what if he never returned at all? What if she never had a chance to tell him about the babe?

"Drink it all," the cook ordered sternly. "You won't get better unless you learn to eat and drink soon after rising."

Edeva obeyed, then got to her feet. She would not dwell on her worries, not when there was so much to do.

She left the kitchen shed and started toward the well, intending to see if the men had drawn enough water that the women could do some washing. The sudden clanging of the chapel bell made her change direction.

By the time she reached the gate, she saw that Osbert

and Alan were already up on the tower, conferring. She rushed up the ladder, shouting, "What's happening? Have they brought siege engines?"

Osbert shook his head as she arrived on the tower. "Nay, they look as if they mean to negotiate."

Edeva went to the tower wall and gazed down at the trackway. It did appear that the enemy came under truce; their weapons were not drawn. "What if it is a trick?" she said.

"It does not hurt to hear what they have to say," Alan responded. "Mayhaps there has been a mistake—mayhaps they did not mean to attack us yesterday."

Edeva and Osbert exchanged a skeptical glance. They both knew there had been no mistake.

Alan climbed up on the battlement so the approaching army could see him. "Halt and state your intentions," he called out.

Edeva saw Bourges signal his men to stop, then he rode forward alone.

"Who are you?" Bourges asked as he saw Alan.

"I am Alan of Fornay, first captain of Lord Brevrienne's mensie."

"Sir Alan," Bourges spoke ingratiatingly. "We are pleased to treat with you. I fear our actions yesterday were misconstrued. We come today in the hope that we can settle things peaceably."

"What do you want?" Alan asked.

"We have a message from the king. If you will allow us entrance into the palisade, we will share it with you."

Alan gave a snort of contempt. "I am no more a fool than Sir Rob. I will see the king's seal ere I order the gates opened."

"That is not possible," Bourges said smoothly. "But mayhaps we can find agreement on another matter. We hold hostage one of your knights. We are prepared to exchange him for the Lady Edeva."

"What the devil?" Alan whispered under his breath.

"What business do you have with Lady Edeva?" he shouted.

"The king himself has asked that she be brought to him. He is prepared to recognize some of her father's, Earl Leowine's, claims to property in several other shires. The king will not grant these claims unless he first speaks to the lady herself."

Alan shot Edeva a puzzled glance. "Know you anything of this?"

She shook her head. " 'Tis true that my father held charters for other lands, but I thought all that was forfeit, as was Oxbury itself."

"But is it possible that Bourges' assertion is true?" Alan demanded.

"I know not."

"Enough of this damned foolishness!" Osbert sputtered. "We cannot exchange the lady for Rob, no matter what skein of lies this man spins. I'm astonished that you would even consider the matter, sir!"

"Let us not be hasty," Edeva said. "I can see merit to the exchange. With Rob returned, you would have one more knight to defend Oxbury. And I cannot imagine that Bourges would hurt me."

"I do not like it." Alan fidgeted with the pommel of his sword, his face as stormy as the winter sky. "I think Bourges means to use you to lure Brevrienne into an ambush."

"I am willing to take that risk," Edeva said. "At least it draws them away from Oxbury. You've said yourself that we cannot defeat such a force under these circumstances. Would it not be better to placate them and save the manor?"

"You would go with them willingly?" Alan asked.

Edeva nodded. "From what I've learned of Norman men, I do not think that they would abuse me. And I would do near anything to save Oxbury from destruction."

Alan eyed her carefully, as if considering the matter, while Osbert looked on, clearly distraught.

Edeva tried to quell her own fears. She thought of the

baby growing in her womb. What if Bourges raped her and made her lose the child? Or, what if he used her to lure Jobert into a trap?

The risks were great, but somehow they seemed less real than the prospect of seeing Oxbury burned to the ground. With the men he took to London and the knights in the fort, Jobert's army was near evenly matched with Bourges', and Edeva had no doubt that her lover was the superior warrior and battle commander.

"I will go," she said again.

Alan gave her another look, then said, "So be it."

Edeva took a deep breath and shifted her body to maintain her precarious position on the white palfrey. She felt foolish and helpless, like a prize filly decked out for a summer fair. But from what she knew about Normans, it seemed wisest to appear in the guise of a refined and elegant lady, so that Bourges would not dare mistreat her.

To that end, she had bathed and washed her hair, then changed into her gown of bronze sarcanet, covered with the rich, fur-lined mantle. She had forbore to wear any jewels, fearing that Bourges would steal them, but she had insisted that a fine horse be prepared for her so she might ride to meet the invaders looking like a queen.

A queen about to fall facedown in the snow, she thought grimly as she approached the waiting army. If it had been more than a few hundred paces, she would never have attempted it. Having never ridden a horse alone before, she was finding it much more difficult than she imagined.

The mare balked and pranced, and the tighter Edeva gripped the reins, the more unsteady the horse's gait became.

With relief, Edeva saw that this part of her trial was almost over. Bourges rode toward her, leading a horse carrying Rob. The sleet had coated the men's clothing and helmets with a frosty film, so the whole Norman army looked like phantoms.

She pulled the reins and the mare came to a jerky halt. Bourges stopped beside her and gave her a stiff bow. "My lady."

He released the lead of Rob's horse and reached out to grab the palfrey's bridle. As he led her past Rob, the young knight met her gaze with a miserable expression. "Fare thee well, my lady," he murmured.

Bourges took the reins from her and guided her horse into the troop of Norman knights. Sudden dread clawed at Edeva's chest. These were the faceless, monstrous demons of her nightmares. The ghostly white of their attire made them seem even more chilling and ominous.

They rode through the valley and along the riverbank. The men spoke little, except a few low mutterings which she couldn't decipher. The palfrey trotted along easily, responding to the authoritative strength of the man holding the reins.

Edeva wondered if they meant to leave immediately for London. She thought them fools if they did. Despite her fur-lined mantle and warm gloves, she was already half frozen through. The men in their armor must be even more miserable.

They passed a stand of tall beeches, glazed silver with ice, then moved into a clearing where a dozen leather tents were set up. Edeva felt a surge of relief. They would camp here, waiting for the storm to pass. By then, Jobert would be on his way from London.

The men began to dismount. One of the knights helped her off her horse, then took her arm and guided her into the largest of the tents. There was a lit brazier by the tent opening and by its light, she could see that the inside of the shelter was furnished with two stools, several chests and a fur-covered bedplace.

She had barely taken a seat on one of the stools when Bourges pushed his way into the tent. Another man ducked in after him.

She saw that her captor was not tall; in fact, she likely

would have overtopped him if she were standing, but he was wide-bodied and powerfully built.

He removed his helmet, revealing brown hair which thinned on his crown and a weathered, red-brown face. Rubbing his hands together before the brazier, he stared at Edeva.

After a moment, he motioned at her mantle, indicating that she should remove it.

Heart racing, Edeva did so.

Bourges' gaze roamed over her face and neck, then her body.

"Not my taste exactly." The other man spoke from behind Bourges. "Too big and sturdy, like a peasant. But her tits appear to be spectacular. Let's have a better look at them."

At his words, Edeva pulled out the dagger she had hidden in her sleeve. The blade glittered in the torchlight.

"Christ's balls!" the man in the shadows chortled, "I do think you've got more woman here than you bargained for."

"Shut up, Henry!" Bourges growled. "This business is tricky enough without the wench squawking to the king that's she's been ill-used."

The other man moved into the light. "You're going to wed with her, Bourges. Why shouldn't you inspect your property?"

"Jesu, will you get your brains out of your chausses?" Bourges said. "I've difficulties enough without your stupidity. Even if Brevrienne *is* dead, even if I can claim the Saxons attacked us and Brevrienne's knights did nothing, I still have to convince the king that I have a right to Oxbury. To do that, I need the woman's cooperation."

"Cooperation? That's easily enough gained from a wench. Give me a night with her, and I vow I'll have her begging the king to let her wed you."

"Never!" Edeva cried, unable to remain silent any longer. "You can kill me now, for I will never agree to wed you!"

The two men stared at her. "Quite a fiery little bitch, isn't she?" said the man named Henry.

"Shut up," said Bourges. "She obviously knows more Norman French than we anticipated."

The dagger cast sparkles of light on the ceiling of the tent as Edeva shifted it from one hand to the other. Her voice came out in a hiss of fury. "I've heard every word, and I know you've murdered Jobert. And now, I'm going to kill you."

"Jesu," breathed Henry, "I think she means it."

Bourges gave a weary sigh. "I told Valois that this was madness. Jesu, I don't even want Oxbury—not enough to endure this sort of trouble. I have land enough in Normandy."

"But you hold that of Valois," Henry argued. "And if you refused to do his bidding, you well know what will happen."

Bourges sighed again. "Lady," he said, "I did not kill Brevrienne, and, in truth, I mean you no harm."

"If you did not kill him, who did?"

"Valois sent an assassin to murder him in London."

Jobert was dead. Edeva's hand went limp on the dagger. She felt numb, utterly empty.

"I mean you no disrespect, Lady Edeva," Bourges said, "but you are the heiress of Oxbury, and to claim it, I must wed with you."

TWENTY-SIX

"All looks peaceful," Jobert said, gazing across the snow-covered valley toward the palisade on the hill.

" 'Twould appear you near killed yourself for no reason," Hamo grumbled. "I told you another day would not matter. You have a whole lifetime to be with your ladylove."

"I feared that Oxbury might in danger," Jobert said. "I had to get here and see for myself." He swayed on his mount as the numbing fatigue caught up with him. "Jesu, I swear I could sleep for a week."

"Let's get on with it then." Hamo urged his mount forward and Jobert and the others followed.

The ride from London had been hell. They'd lost their way twice, then had to stop and build a fire near midday lest some of the men lose fingers or toes to the cold.

A few hours earlier, the snow had ceased and they'd suddenly found themselves riding through a silent, almost magical winter world. Ice covered the curve of every branch and dried leaf and transformed the scenery into a lacy white tracery. Then the sun came out, and their eyes were dazzled by the light from a trillion sparkling ice crystals.

The beauty of the landscape had helped keep them going, despite their fatigue and cold. Now they were almost home and the effort to guide their horses along the slippery, slushy trackway took all their strength. Jobert found himself shivering from head to toe as his muscles protested this final test of endurance. What he would not do for a hot bath, then have Edeva massage his sore muscles and crawl into a warm, clean bed with him . . .

He jerked himself upright as the lulling images relaxed him so much he slipped sideways in the saddle. God's toes, he'd better concentrate on what he was doing or he'd end up in a snowdrift!

He forced himself to focus on the peaceful landscape around them. Odd how wrong his instincts had been. He'd felt almost certain that Valois would send someone to seize control of Oxbury. His death alone would not be enough to satisfy his enemy. A greedy man like Valois would also seek to take control of his property.

But, obviously, nothing had happened. The palisade walls remained intact, although there seemed to be another burned place along the east end by the gate. Jobert squinted, trying to see better.

A helmeted head appeared at the top of the gatetower. There was a shout; the guard had spotted them. Only a few more steps and they would be home.

The gate opened and they rode in. The yard seemed strangely quiet. Jobert had expected a more exultant welcome. And where was Edeva?

Alan stood stone-faced, but one look at Rob, and Jobert immediately knew something was wrong.

"What is it?" he demanded, sliding from his horse. "Where's Edeva?"

The two knights exchanged a glance, then Rob said, "Bourges took her to the king. At least, that is what he said he was doing. In truth, I fear for her."

Jobert's insides seemed to turn to ice, but the anger spilling out of him was hot and furious. "How could you let anyone take her? I charged you both with protecting her, yet I return and find no signs of a battle, and her gone, and you know not where!" He could barely contain himself from the urge to grab one or both of the men and throttle them to death.

"She went willingly," Alan said in his tight-lipped manner. "She offered to go." His mouth curled. "Mayhaps she was lured away by Bourges' promise that the king meant to award her property elsewhere in England. Or, mayhaps she has planned this all along."

Jobert stared at Alan, slowly realizing what he was saying. As his mind screamed in protest, he turned to Rob. "Think you that Lady Edeva . . . that she . . ." he could scarce get the words out, ". . . that she betrayed me?"

Rob shot Alan a glance, then shook his head. "I think she went with Bourges in order to save Oxbury."

"Save Oxbury? From what?"

Alan started to speak, but Rob interrupted him. "Nay, let him hear it from the beginning." He turned to Jobert. " 'Twas not as if Bourges rode up to the fort and Edeva ran off with him. Indeed, she was the one who urged us not to let the envoy in. She insisted that they meant us no good. And they did act in bad faith. They took me hostage when I went out to speak with them.

"They treated me well enough, but I sensed that they were plotting something. Besides, they did attack the palisade with burning arrows. 'Twas not a full-blown attack, and they soon retreated, but 'twas clearly an act of aggression. Then, they brought me back the next day with the proposal to exchange me for Lady Edeva.

"I thought it utter madness to let her go, but I think she felt that she would be safer than I was, and that by going with them, she would draw their attention away from Oxbury. I know she assumed that you would return shortly and be able to set things right."

"Huh," Alan said. "If you ask me, she was all too eager to go once she heard she was heiress to other property."

Jobert took a deep breath, trying to expel his anger and fear so he could think clearly. "Who is Bourges?" he asked. "And what is this about Edeva's having other lands?"

"Bourges is the leader of a troop of well-armed Norman knights," Rob said. "In truth, we know no more than that. He came here demanding admittance into the fort, claiming he had a message from the king. Edeva insisted that he furnish proof of his mission. Bourges refused, then took me hostage. The next day, they returned to the palisade. This time Bourges said he had come to fetch Edeva, that she was heiress to other property in England, but that William would not recognize her claim unless she came to him in person."

"Based on that, you gave him Edeva!" Jobert felt his outrage building once again. "He showed you no writ, no proof of who he was, and yet you let him take her!"

"But she wanted to go," Alan said. "She is not your wife yet, lord, else I would not have allowed it."

"But I told you to guard her! I meant that you should protect both Oxbury *and* Edeva!" Jobert turned and took a few stumbling steps. He was bone-weary and trembling with cold, and that did not help him make sense of this disaster. "How long have they been gone?" he demanded. "Did they ride toward London?"

"They took her back to their camp at the end of the valley," Rob said. "I had one of the village boys follow and watch. He came back to say that they seemed to be settling in for the night. But the next morning, when he went again to spy on them, he found that they had broken camp before daybreak. Their tracks led not toward London, but to Winchester."

Jobert struck his fist into his palm. "How could you? You let them take my woman, my wife-to-be!" He whirled on Alan. "The king gave me his consent to wed Edeva! If you had not let her go, we would be in the chapel at this moment saying our marriage vows before Father Reibald!"

Rob cleared his throat. "I'm sorrowed to say that Father Reibald is dead, although we are not certain how or why. He died of an arrow in the back. It appeared to come from a Saxon bow, but even that is not clear. Edeva thought that the priest was somehow connected with Bourges, and that they might have killed him for some reason."

The spy. Jobert's sense of frustration increased. He had suspected all along that Valois had planted a spy at Oxbury. Who better than a priest, a man who could come and go as he pleased?

As he had thought, Valois' scheme was much more complex than simply murdering him. And the villain had now entangled Edeva in his sinister plans!

"Have water heated for a bath for me, and some warm food prepared," he said. "As soon as I have refreshed myself, we will set out."

Hamo, who had been listening to the exchange, stepped forward. "If you have a care for Lord Brevrienne," he advised the other men, "you'll make him take a day of rest before he rides. He is already so tired he can scarce keep his seat on a horse."

"He's right," Rob said. "Why not let Alan and me pursue Bourges while you get your strength back?"

Jobert shook his head. "I cannot rest until I have Edeva safe. Tie me to my horse if you must, but I *will* go after her."

Bourges had half a day's head start, but the weather would have slowed them down, and with their baggage carts and servants, the army troop could not travel as quickly as a handful of men. Jobert had considered taking a larger force himself, in case he was forced into combat in order to rescue Edeva. But he had decided that 'twas more important to catch up with the enemy quickly. He hoped that once Bourges knew he was being pursued, the knight would abandon whatever plans he had regarding Edeva.

That is, if they had truly taken Edeva hostage. As Alan kept insisting, there was always the possibility Edeva had gone along willingly.

Unthinkable, Jobert told himself. The woman he knew would not desert him for another man. Even if Edeva had discovered that she was a greater heiress than supposed, he could not imagine that she would turn against him.

They trailed the army all the way to Winchester, but when they arrived in the town there was no sign of Bourges and his men. Jobert and the others stopped at an inn to rest their horses and to eat some hot food, while Rob made inquiries at the farmhouses near the roadway.

Soon after they delved into the leek soup and fresh bread the innkeeper offered, Rob came bursting in. "They have been here and have gone on to the priory. It seems they stopped and watered their horses at one of the farmer's wells. While they were there, they inquired as to where they could find a priest, and the farmer advised them to seek out the holy men of Wherwall Abbey.

"A priest!" Hamo exclaimed. "What need do they have of a priest?"

Frightening thoughts went through Jobert's mind. *Edeva was hurt and her captors sought a man learned in the healing arts, as many priests were.* Rob's explanation horrified him even more: "They said they needed a priest so that the Norman lord could wed the lady traveling with them."

Jobert put down his chunk of bread. He shook his head, willing himself to believe his own words, "She would not wed any other man unless they threatened her. And if she was coerced, the marriage will not be valid."

The men were silent. Hamo rose and said, "If they passed by here only recently, 'tis possible the ceremony has yet to take place. You know how tedious holy men are. I doubt that they could perform a wedding without praying over the matter for hours beforehand."

Jobert got to his feet. "Let us go. The priory is only a mile or two from here."

The porter at the priory gate refused to admit them at first, grumbling about "hordes of soldiers disrupting a place of peace and refuge." He finally agreed to allow Jobert and Rob to enter, as long as they left their weapons behind.

Jobert felt naked and vulnerable without his sword as they followed the brown-clad brother to the chapel. If there were trouble, how would he fight? He had made up his mind to claim Edeva even if she appeared unwilling. He'd made her love him once, he could do so again. If only he could have time alone with her. Time to remind her of what was between them.

He heard the sound of monks chanting prayers as he

approached the Saxon-styled chapel. His body grew tight. What if he were too late? What if Edeva was already bound by vows to another?

Rob opened the arched door and they went in. Candles lit the high-beamed building with wavering light. Rows of monks stood praying along the length of the nave. At the far end of the long, narrow building, near the altar, stood a knight and a lady.

Jobert waited motionless as his eyes made out details in the dim light. Then he recognized the rich bronze of the woman's gown and the glint of golden braids beneath her veil. He strode forward. "Stop, priest," he called out. "This woman cannot wed this man. Lord William, king of England and duke of Normandy, has given her to me!"

The knight and the woman turned. The monks paused in their singing. For a long moment, the church was silent. Then Edeva picked up her skirts and dashed toward Jobert. "You're alive! Thank God!" She threw herself into his arms, near knocking him down.

"Oh, Edeva, my love," he murmured into her hair as he found his balance. " 'Tis true, the king has agreed to let me wed you. Let us do it now, before something else comes between us."

She pulled away, her eyes wide. "Bourges," she whispered.

Jobert held her close to his body as the knight at the altar moved toward him. Although Jobert had no weapon, he had no intention of relinquishing Edeva. Not while there was a breath in his body.

"Brevrienne?" The man stopped a few paces away and surveyed Jobert carefully.

"Yea, I am Brevrienne."

The man nodded. He glanced briefly at the priest behind him, then said, "As God as my witness, I never meant you harm. Valois forced me into this thing. He made it seem a simple matter. That you would meet with an accident in London and all I had to do was claim your demesne." He paused, and when he continued, his voice sounded desperate, "He is my liegelord—how could I refuse him?"

"Did it not trouble your conscience at all that he meant to murder me?" Jobert said coldly.

"He said he had good cause. That you had ruined his daughter and then abandoned her."

"And for that I should have my throat cut in some filthy London alley and my property stolen?"

Bourges gestured helplessly. "He is not the first father to seek such brutal vengeance."

"Valois is not some doting parent who seeks redress for his daughter's shame. Let me tell you the facts, Bourges. My relationship with Damaris de Valois was chaste and innocent. She chose to enter a nunnery because she believed it to be her true calling, not because she was shamed. If I am guilty of anything, it is for exposing Valois for the greedy, scheming wretch he is. His anger stems not out of concern for his daughter but from having his plans for a profitable marriage alliance come to naught!"

Bourges digested this a moment, then ran a hand over his balding pate, looking near as weary as Jobert felt. "I beg your pardon, Brevrienne. I knew none of this."

"Of course, he knew nothing!" Another man stepped from near the altar and spoke in a harsh, mocking voice. "The fool was merely a pawn of my lord Valois."

He addressed Bourges. "You did not really think that Sir Robert would let you keep the Saxon heiress? Hah! You were to be eliminated after Valois had convinced the king that no Saxon, and especially a female one, could be trusted. Valois intended to claim the lands himself and put the wench in a nunnery." The man's dark, narrow eyes raked Edeva. "Of course, myself, I think that would be a waste of luscious English quim. I'd much rather see her set up as a harlot in London."

Jobert felt Edeva tense in his arms, and he guessed this man was the one he must fear. But how could he protect her, weaponless as he was?

Abruptly, Edeva began to swoon, and Jobert turned all

his attention to her. "Let me fall," she whispered as he leaned near.

She crumpled to the ground. Jobert immediately called for someone to get water, then knelt beside her. She pressed a dagger into his hand. "Be careful," she whispered.

Jobert picked her up and started to carry her toward the door. Halfway there, he felt a weapon prick into his back. "I'll take the woman, Brevrienne."

Jobert turned slowly and faced the dark-eyed man, who held a wicked-looking sword pointed at Jobert's unprotected throat. "There will be no wedding today," the man said. With his free hand, he gestured that Jobert release Edeva.

Jobert slowly set Edeva on her feet, keeping his hand holding the knife hidden behind her skirts.

"You cannot do this!" The priest spoke for the first time, his voice shaking with outrage. "This is a holy place, and I claim sanctuary for all gathered here. If you take the woman by force, you will live your life cursed and condemned!"

The dark-eyed man laughed. "Think you that I am not already cursed and condemned? I *have* no soul, you stupid priest. Now," he added to Jobert, "give the woman to me."

Edeva took a step toward the man. Jobert's fingers itched to use the knife, but he held back. He must take this man by surprise, or his chance of failure was too great.

"You killed the priest," Bourges spoke suddenly, as if the realization had just come to him. " 'Twas not the Saxons after all, it was *you*."

The man turned toward Bourges, a sinister smile on his face. "Of course. I took pleasure in ending Father Reibald's miserable exi . . ."

The last word ended in a scream as Jobert's dagger sank deep into the man's neck. He made another gruesome noise, then collapsed. Edeva backed away from his twitching body and Jobert heaved a huge sigh of relief.

"Appalling!" the priest cried, striding toward them. "Simply appalling. The man might have been a villain, but

you need not have murdered him in our church! I doubt
that *your* immortal soul can survive this horrible sin!"

"I will take my chances with the Almighty," Jobert said.
He groped his way to the church's smooth, whitewashed
wall and leaned against it. "I have found God to be more
merciful than men with sharp blades at my throat."

Edeva came to him and wrapped her arms around him.
"Oh, Jobert," she whispered. "Do not anger the priest.
He has yet to perform our wedding."

It took some coercion from both Jobert and Bourges,
as well as some outright begging from Edeva, but the prior
finally agreed to conduct the ceremony.

"At least *I* am properly attired," Edeva said as she took
her place beside Jobert at the altar.

"For all my grimy, travel-stained clothes, I have had a
bath this day," Jobert retorted.

"A bath," Edeva said and looked at him, eyes luminous.
"I believe that is the first thing I wish to do when we arrive
at Oxbury."

"Share a bath with me?"

"Yea, that is exactly it. A long, leisurely, very hot bath."

Jobert heaved a shuddering sigh. " 'Twould be paradise."

The prior cleared his throat. "This is a sacred rite I am
about to perform. You should strive to cleanse your mind
of all base and sinful thoughts ere I begin"

"Mmmmm," Edeva whispered, " 'tis not your mind I
wish to cleanse, milord."

"Hush," Jobert whispered back. "We are in disgrace
enough without your lewd thoughts."

Edeva giggled. The priest cleared his throat again,
frowning more severely.

When the ceremony was over, Jobert and Edeva shared
one brief kiss, then parted, she to go to the guest quarters
for women visitors, he, the one for men.

Jobert sat down to a plain meal in the refectory where
Hamo tried to console him regarding his celibate wedding
night. "It's not as if you haven't sampled the woman's

charms already," the knight said. "Tired as you are, you might even have trouble performing."

"I would not have trouble 'performing' with Edeva unless I were unconscious or dead," Jobert asserted. "For that matter, one time when I was out of my head with fever from my shoulder wound, we actually . . ." He paused, realizing that every man at the table regarded him with amused curiosity.

Jesu, what had come over him—he'd grown as loose-tongued as Edeva.

He cleared his throat. "The soup's tolerable. At least it is warm. Although I prefer Beornflaed's choice of seasonings."

Hamo guffawed and the other men suppressed chuckles. The light mood vanished as the door opened and Bourges entered. He looked around uneasily. "I do not know if I am welcome here, but I would offer an explanation of my actions if you would hear one."

Jobert gestured with a crust of bread that the knight should seat himself.

The older man took a place at the table and drank deeply from a cup of wine before speaking. He said, "They say there is no greater fool than an old fool, and I am one. I knew Valois to be treacherous and corrupt, yet I listened to him."

"Tell us of his plan," Jobert said. "I would know how the pieces fit."

Bourges nodded. "I've told you the story he gave me regarding your treachery with his daughter. He said that you would meet with your death while in London, and I was to go to Oxbury and take over the manor, then wed the Saxon heiress in order to seal my claim."

Bourges heaved a sigh. "But there were problems from the beginning. Your men would not give in without a fight, and there were more of them than expected. I realized that if we engaged in battle with other Normans, we would be in violation of the king's orders. I had to think of a way to get the woman to come with us without bloodshed.

"But Henry—may God assoil him—kept pushing me to attack. He told me that the Saxons had killed the priest and that was sufficient excuse to storm the palisade. Although I did not know for certain that Henry was a spy for Valois, my instincts told me not to trust him. Instead, I remembered that Valois had said that the Saxon woman was heir to other property besides Oxbury, and I decided to use that as a means to convince her to come with me."

"You mean there is some truth to that?" Jobert asked.

"I believe so. Although I do not know how Valois knew of it."

"And was the promise of wealth the means you used to convince Lady Edeva to wed with you?" Alan spoke the question. The other men looked around uneasily, as if unwilling to meet Jobert's gaze.

"Nay," Bourges answered, " 'twas the fact that she thought Lord Brevrienne was dead. She agreed to wed me if I would use her wealth to gain revenge against Valois. In truth, I half suspected that Valois would find me inconvenient, and that I might have to choose between my own life and loyalty to my liegelord. I agreed to her bargain."

Jobert felt a self-satisfied smile spread across his face. "So, you see, Alan, a woman can be as loyal and trustworthy as a man."

"My apologies, sir," Alan said. "Mayhaps it is my own circumstances which make me doubt all women."

"What circumstances are those?" Bourges asked.

Hamo clapped Alan on the back. "Fornay has a *tendre* for a certain Saxon wench, but she flirts and dallies with every man but him. Daily, Alan must swallow the bitter gall of jealousy as fair Wulfget bestows her smiles elsewhere."

"Wulfget!" Rob exclaimed. "I did not know you still fancied her. You always appear so sour-faced and grim whenever you are in her company!"

"Why should I not seem grim? The woman is a fickle, heartless creature who finds pleasure in torturing me!"

"Wulfget—heartless?" Rob got to his feet. "I'll not hear

you disparage her name so cruelly. She is the kindest, the most patient of maidens."

"As you should know, after all these weeks of shamelessly exaggerating your wounds so she would fuss over you."

"A belly wound is a grave thing. I might have died!"

"I wish you had, you bastard! If you were gone, Wulfget might finally notice *me!*"

Jobert stood. "Sweet Jesu, you are like two dogs fighting over a juicy bone! If the wench is causing this much trouble between the two of you, I vow neither one of you shall have her. Indeed, I'm of a mind to marry her off to some man outside of Oxbury. How would you like that, you half-witted fools!"

The two knights immediately looked contrite. "I did not mean to provoke you, Alan," Rob said. "In truth, although I am fond of Wulfget, I had not thought of marrying with her. If you wish to win Wulfget's favor, I'll not oppose your suit. But, be advised—the way to woo a woman is not to mope and curse around her, but rather to be lighthearted and pleasant when in her company."

"I try, but when I see her with you, the pretty words I have thought of turn to vinegar in my mouth."

"Have you spoken to Edeva about the matter yet?" Jobert asked. "I think she would help, if you asked her."

"How can I beg a boon of Edeva after all the awful things I have said about her?" Alan asked.

"Edeva is ever generous-hearted. She knows you did not mean them," Jobert answered, smiling.

They all sat down and began to eat again. Jobert spooned the warm soup into his mouth, then took a mouthful of bread. The next thing he knew, someone was shaking him. "Wake up, Brevrienne. You'll sleep better lying down, even on a hard monk's pallet."

He was vaguely aware of being half-carried out the doorway and through the snowy yard to the guest house. Then he sank down on the straw-filled pallet and knew no more.

TWENTY-SEVEN

In the morning, Jobert thanked the prior, then went to the abbey gate where his men waited with Edeva. Jobert gave her a quick kiss, then drew away. 'Twould be torture enough to ride pillion for their long journey; he did not need to stoke his lust any higher!

He helped her onto the horse, then climbed up behind her. As they left the priory and started down the frost-covered road, he heard her heave a sigh. "Are you weary, love?" he asked.

"Nay, merely relieved. These last few days have been so trying. You cannot know what it was like to think you were dead."

He leaned close to murmur in her ear. "Yea, I can. The thought of losing you filled me with a dread so great I could scarce go on."

She reached back to caress his cheek. "But now all our foes are vanquished. No one will take Oxbury from you as long as William lives."

His jaw tightened. "Myself, I will not be satisfied until Valois is punished. He was behind all of this. If not for his treacherous plotting, so many would not have suffered."

"But my brothers played a part—they kept the conflict alive."

"In truth, I think they might have given up long ago if Father Reibald had not been giving them encouragement and supplies."

"You think the priest used them to damage your claim to Oxbury?"

"Yea, I do. I think he convinced them to attack the palisade when we were in London."

"And then the priest—and Golde—betrayed them."

Jobert nodded. "Father Reibald wanted the rebels to be captured so I would hang them and further alienate you."

"But it did not work."

"Nay. And then he changed his plan to helping the prisoners to escape so they could kill me on the journey to London."

"What?" Edeva turned on the horse, her eyes wide. "I did not know of this. Hamo told me after the wedding ceremony that Alnoth was safe and that Beornwold, Godric and the others had escaped. I did not know any of them tried to kill you."

"That is mostly true. Alnoth is safe and Godric and his companions did flee. But Beornwold . . ." Jobert took a deep breath, wondering if he could say the words. If he told Edeva that he had killed her brother, would the tender warmth between them vanish?

"Beornwold tried to cut my throat. I have no doubt that it was at the urging of Father Reibald."

Edeva said nothing.

"I was able to twist out of his grasp before he did the deed, but I could not let him get away. I . . . I drew my own dagger and killed him."

Edeva faced forward again, and the silence stretched between them. Jobert felt his throat swell with anguish. He could not argue that it was self-defense. Beornwold had been fleeing when Jobert cut him down. 'Twas pure instinct which made him throw that dagger.

Edeva spoke softly, "If I must choose, 'twould be your life I would preserve. Beornwold might be my brother, but he does not hold my heart as you do."

Jobert released the breath he had been holding and squeezed Edeva tightly to his chest with his free arm.

She was silent for a while, then she said, "Father Reibald

has paid the price for his treachery, but what of Golde? She betrayed Godric and the rest of her countrymen. Though she may have been your lover once, surely you can see that she must be punished for her part in the plot."

Jobert started. "My lover! Whatever gave you such a foolish notion."

Edeva spoke tartly. "I saw you together one morning soon after you arrived at Oxbury. And *she* told me that you shared her bed. In fact, she taunted me with the information!"

He could not help chuckling. "Ah, my faithless Edeva, always believing the worst. I told you that I found women like Golde unappealing. 'Tis very clear she lets men bed her not because she enjoys lovemaking, but to gain power over them. Besides, why would I pursue a harlot like her when I could have a beautiful virgin like you?"

"You could not *have* me, then. We'd made a bargain that you could not touch me if you wanted my aid in running Oxbury."

"A bargain which you chose to ignore."

He felt her stiffen and wondered if he'd offended her. Despite Edeva's wild abandon in the bedchamber, she was still embarrassed when teased about her passion. "My love," he leaned forward to nuzzle her silky hair, "I am very glad you decided to alter the terms of our arrangement. If you had continued to be cool and distant, I don't know what I would have done. I was near out of my mind with desire for you."

"I've always wondered why you did not take me by force. There are many men who would have disregarded an agreement made with a Saxon—and a woman."

"I was not brought up that way, Edeva. I was taught to honor my agreements and to treat women with respect."

"Even vicious hellcats like me?"

He laughed and leaned to kiss her cheek. " 'Tis your fire which makes you such a passionate, exciting bedpartner. I would not trade that for a whole court of boring Norman maidens."

"Truly?" she whispered.

"Truly."

He cuddled her close, enjoying the simple pleasure of having her near. *His wife. His lover.* Nay, best not to think such thoughts in the present circumstances.

"Jobert," she interrupted his suddenly lustful musings, "what are you going to do about Golde?"

"Mayhap I should have her whipped, but properly this time."

"But if the flogging hurts her too badly, she might not be able to do her weaving work. I can scarce afford to lose a skilled servant."

Jobert laughed. "Always the practical one, aren't you, Edeva? Tell me, do you seek retribution against the woman or not?"

"I want her to pay, but I don't think that is the means. Golde's weakness is her pride. She thinks no man can resist her. Nothing would humiliate her more than for her to lose her looks so she had no power over men."

"But deliberately disfiguring her seems too cruel and barbaric."

"Yea, it does. But there must be something . . . I have it!" Edeva turned in the saddle, her eyes bright. "We'll send her to live in the village, where she'll not have an opportunity to seduce the knights!"

"That hardly seems like sufficient punishment after what she's done."

"But that is not all of it. We'll send her to live with Helwenna!"

"In that pigsty of a hut?"

"Helwenna needs someone to look after her, and she's not likely to be swayed by Golde's wiles. 'Twill be a loathesome, miserable existence for the wench."

"What if she runs away?"

"Where will she go? Once the villagers know of her

treachery, they'll not shelter her, and she's not such a fool
as to try to survive alone in the forest."

It seemed an odd discipline, Jobert thought, but for a
woman it might work. At least it saved him the unpleas-
antness of having Golde whipped.

"And once we have done that, will that satisfy your taste
for vengeance?"

She gave him a haughty look. "Do you imply that I am
vindictive?"

"Nay, merely highly concerned with justice, as all your
people are. The English appear to have a very strong sense
of right and wrong."

"And the Normans do not?"

Jobert shook his head ruefully. "Among the Normans I
know, too often 'might makes right'."

"Is that why the king has refused to deal with Robert
de Valois?"

It was Jobert's turn to sigh. "He says that this is not the
time. In truth, I cannot blame him. For all he has accomplished in England, William needs his Norman allies if he
is to finish his work here."

"You mean his work of oppressing Saxons?"

Jobert could not help grinning. Edeva would never let
him forget they had once been bitter foes. "Peace, wench.
You are married to a Norman now, and you must stop
thinking of us as the enemy. Someday you will carry a child
of mine in your belly. You'd best learn to speak more kindly
of your son's heritage."

"How do you know I will give birth to a boy?"

"You must. How else will I honor my pledge to name
one of my children after the king? 'Twould be odd to have
a daughter named William."

"Mmmph. We shall see about what we will name our
children, be they boys or girls. If King William does not
do right by you, I don't think he deserves such an honor!"

"William will do right by me, though it may take him
twenty years. Whatever he is, the king is a man of his word."

That seemed to satisfy Edeva, and Jobert felt himself

relax. He enjoyed sparring with his wife, but he'd not want to do it all the way to Oxbury!

Alan rode up beside them, but said nothing. Jobert watched him out of the corner of his eye. When Alan cleared his throat, Jobert forced his own mouth shut. There was still a matter between his captain and his lady, and he'd not intervene.

"Lady Edeva . . . I must ask your pardon."

Edeva suppressed a smile as Fornay spoke. She knew Alan had been working up to this for the past half-mile of riding beside them. Should she make him worry over her answer? Nay, that seemed too cruel. "You have it, Sir Alan," she answered.

He shot her a wary look. "I have made many mistakes."

"Have not we all?"

"But mine are . . . serious ones. I have treated you ill, worse than I have any man."

"That may be, but you have asked my pardon and I have given it. There is naught more to say."

"But there is! I would ask a boon of you."

Edeva felt her mouth quirking. She could easily guess what Alan's "boon" might be.

"I have a . . . fondness for a certain maid, but I fear she does not know it. I would ask your advice in the matter."

Edeva considered. If she wished to repay Fornay for all the trouble he had caused her, he had given her the perfect means. Nay, she could not wish him ill in his quest. The obvious desperation in his voice touched her heart. "Very well, Fornay. My advice is to tell the woman how you feel."

"That is all?"

"She cannot read your mind. If you do not tell her, how will she know?"

"But I thought . . . that is . . . I cannot . . ."

"Alan of Fornay, are you a coward?"

She saw his face flush and wondered if she had provoked

him into despising her once more. "I thought better of you," she added, "than that you should fear a dainty maid like Wulfget."

"I do not fear her!" he bellowed.

"Then speak with her. Prove your mettle, sir knight. If you do not take this risk, then you do not deserve to have her."

She heard him draw in his breath. "I'm afraid of what she will say."

He was weakened, vulnerable, the perfect moment to land the crippling blow. But she would not. Alan of Fornay was not a bad man. He had persecuted her out of loyalty to Jobert, and his own misguided sense of how a woman should behave. She said softly, "If it aids you at all, then know that I think she will favor your suit."

"Truly?" Alan's face lit up like an eager squire's. "You believe she might care for me?"

" 'Tis only a woman's silly fancy, of course. The sort of thing that a sensible *man* like you might well discount—"

"I yield, Lady Edeva," Alan broke in. "I submit to your counsel. I have found you to be right many times over."

"Of course you have, Fornay," Jobert said wryly. "Leowine of Oxbury raised no foolish daughters. Sons, mayhaps, but not daughters."

Edeva felt a pang of tenderness well up inside her. How fortunate she was to have been "conquered" by this Norman. She would thank blessed Jesu every day for her beloved Jobert.

If only she could show him how she felt, how much she desired him . . . but mayhaps she could . . . "Jobert," she said, "I am feeling rather faint. It must be the turmoil I endured yesterday. Could we stop for a time?"

He immediately pulled their mount to a halt. "What is it? How can I aid you?"

She turned around to whisper in his ear. A spark gleamed in his green eyes.

He motioned for his troops to halt, then dismounted and helped her down. She leaned heavily against him, pretending to be ill. "Fornay," he told the knight, "you and the rest of the men go on ahead."

"Milord? What of you and the lady?"

"We will resume the journey as soon as Edeva feels better. Milady requires a moment of privacy. I will stand guard for her."

"Of course." Alan motioned to the other men to follow him. The troop set off at a sedate pace.

Edeva started to giggle as soon as they were out of earshot. "Will we be able to catch up with them?"

Jobert gave her a dazzling grin. "That, Lady Edeva, depends upon how quick we are at our endeavor." He moved nearer. Edeva felt her breath catch as she gazed into his lust-filled eyes.

Hours later, Edeva walked around the bedchamber, lighting candles. She wanted everything to be perfect for their first night home at Oxbury. The wooden tub was filled to the brim with steaming, herb-scented water. The small table held goblets of wine and some honey cinnamon cakes she had coaxed Beornflaed into making. Candles illuminated the bright wall hangings and cast a soft glow over the rest of the room's furnishings, and the two braziers near the tub helped make up for the draft of winter wind blowing through the burned place in the wall.

Satisfied, Edeva sat down on the bed and began to undo her braids. Her hands trembled with anticipation. Soon, Jobert would be there and they would enjoy hours of blissful lovemaking. It seemed like a dream that she was married to him—married to the proud Norman knight she had once considered her deadliest enemy. Now, he was as dear to her as her own life.

She thought back to the terrible hours when she believed him dead. The only thing that had kept her going then was the thought that she must bear his child and avenge his death. To accomplish those solemn duties, she had been willing to do almost anything, even bind herself in marriage to a man she scarcely trusted.

But to find that Jobert was alive and safe—the memory of the relief and happiness she had felt near took her breath away. He was her heart, her soul . . .

As if her thoughts had summoned him, the door opened and Jobert strode in. He looked at her, smiling his wide, bewitching grin. "Ah, my Saxon maiden," he said.

"Not maiden, wife," she corrected him.

"A wife I have not even properly bedded yet."

"That is, not *in* a proper bed," she murmured.

At the shared memory of their recent woodland tryst, the mood in the room turned intensely erotic. Jobert gestured to the steaming tub. "Mayhaps bathing could wait."

" 'Twould be a shame to waste such lovely hot water."

He nodded. "In truth, it would." He began to remove his clothes. Edeva's breathing quickened as he pulled off his tunic and exposed his broad, muscular chest and beautiful shoulders. Her mouth went dry as he lowered his chausses and revealed his engorged, ruddy shaft. The memory of the first time she saw him naked flooded her mind. Even then, she had desired this man, this proud, formidable warrior.

Jobert grinned at her, then leaned down to unlace his crossgarters so he could take off his hose. "Now you," he said when he was fully unclothed.

Edeva gathered up her skirts and pulled the loose gown over her head. She'd worn nothing underneath.

"Blessed Jesu," Jobert breathed. He approached her, then reached out to caress her breasts. "I'd forgotten how exquisite you are."

"More beautiful than the women in London?" she teased. "Fairer than the Norman ladies in Caen?"

His answer was a kiss, long and deep. Then he drew away, his eyes glowing like emeralds. "Get into the tub," he rasped, "lest we waste the water."

"You mean to bathe me?"

"Among other things."

Edeva climbed into the tub, feeling the steaming water heat her already blazing skin. " 'Tis almost too hot," she murmured, "but it feels good." Jobert leaned over her and began to rub soap on her neck, then her shoulders and arms. His strong, callused fingers felt wonderful against her sensitive flesh. Her nipples thrust out, throbbing, aching. She thought of them filled with milk, for his babe.

She had not told him yet. The few private moments between them since the wedding had been taken up with kisses and caresses. She meant to give him the news after their lovemaking—that he was to be a father by the end of next summer.

His hands dipped lower, to lather her breasts. Edeva leaned back and breathed deeply, feeling the hard ache of desire fill her. She did not know how long she could wait. Already she was near mindless with arousal and she had not even touched him yet.

"Stand up."

Her legs felt unsteady beneath her as she stood in the tub. He knelt on the drying clothes on the floor and began to soap her lower body. He lathered her abdomen, dipped his fingers near her crotch, but not quite touching, then moved his hand in smooth strokes down her buttocks and legs.

At last, his provoking fingers traced the line of her inner thigh, up, up . . .

She parted her legs, helpless to deny the longing to have him explore the throbbing, tender core of her. Lavishly, he soaped her maiden's hair, yet he did not part the folds of her swollen womanhood and offer her the soothing release she longed for.

Her whole body was afire as he stood up beside her, his eyes raking her body. "I'll rinse you now."

She suppressed a groan.

The much cooler water from the rinsing buckets poured over her, easing the worst of her sexual tension. Edeva took a deep breath, reminding herself that she was the one who had suggested the hot bathwater not be wasted.

She stepped out of the tub and into the warm drying cloth Jobert held. He held her close a moment and kissed her. Wet and hungry, their mouths mated. Tongues probing, licking, lips nibbling and melding.

He released her and took a deep breath. "Mayhaps I could wait to bathe."

"Nay, nay, 'twould be a waste." The urgency of her passion had slackened, and now she was determined that he would suffer the torture he had inflicted on her. "Get in the tub," she ordered, "ere the water cools too much."

He did so, and Edeva began her own tantalizing ministrations.

Soaping those broad shoulders, deliciously hard and smooth beneath her fingers. The sleek planes of his chest, with the soap making whorls in the coarse, reddish hair, under his arms and down their long, battle-scarred length. Then, exploring his belly, tracing the arrow of hair to within inches of his rigid shaft, which thrust upward in the eddies of soapy water.

Then, she abandoned that tantalizing endeavor and turned her attention to his broad back. Massaging, rubbing, oh, so slowly smoothing the soap over his warm, firm skin.

She heard him half-groan, then his hand came up and grabbed hers. "Have pity, Edeva."

He stood and turned toward her. "Touch me," he whispered. "You know where."

He released her and she reached for another handful of soap from the wooden bowl. Kneeling, she started at his knees and moved upward. She soaped the front of his long thighs, pretending to be intent on her business and ignoring his prodigious erection. Then she moved her fingers upward, gliding them to the back of his thighs and the lower curve of his buttocks. "Turn around," she whispered, "I think I missed a spot on your back."

"Cruel wench," he murmured. "Cruel, cruel."

But he turned so she could do his backside. Edeva stood, and from behind him, brought her sudsy fingers around to enclose his shaft. She soaped him there with gentle, teasing strokes. He grew harder as she fondled him. When she cupped his testicles in her hand, he expelled a moan. "Rinse me, woman! I've had enough of your hellish torment!"

Giggling, Edeva drenched him with water from the buckets.

They stared at each other, water everywhere, beading on Jobert's rosy skin and glinting in the firelight. The yearning inside Edeva swelled and deepened. Now they would be joined. His hard shaft filling her womanhood, soothing the ache and yet provoking her to even greater longing. Longing for that moment of completion when their bodies moved as one and they left the earthly realm for a more magical, splendid one.

"Lay on the bed," he said.

The linen bedclothes felt cool and smooth against her damp skin. The sweet and wild scent of lavender and mint from the herbs she scattered among the covers rose to her nostrils. Jobert climbed on the bed and leaned over her. Edeva spread her thighs and smiled up at him.

"You think I will ease your misery?" he said. "Nay, I have other plans. A beautiful banquet you make, and I will feast." His mouth came down on her trembling, still-damp skin as he kissed her neck and shoulders. Edeva arched her body, begging. Only slowly did he lick the swell of her breast and then bring his lips to suck one turgid nipple. She shuddered, helplessly caught in the net of sexual energy he wove around her. Her body writhed and she moaned and gasped.

He tasted the other aching point, drawing it into his mouth until she cried out.

"Your breasts seem fuller," he said after a few moments of exquisite suckling. "Your nipples a deeper pink."

" 'Tis you," she whispered. "You have made me a

shameless wanton and my body reveals my never-ending lust."

"You are my wife now." He fingered her breasts with a tender caress. "There is naught of shame in anything I do to you. And"—he smiled—"I can do *anything* I wish."

"Ohhh," she pleaded. "Please do it, do it now!"

"Patience, wench. We have all night."

Edeva closed her eyes and clutched frantically at the bedclothes as his bedeviling mouth moved lower. She felt his hot breath on her belly, her woman's mound. Flushed with embarrassment, she spread her thighs wider, beseeching him for mercy.

He blew on her, sending little curls of fire deep into her womb. Then his mouth descended.

She felt his hands kneading her bottom as his mouth urged her on. His tongue pacified the worst of her quivering need, then his lips moved upward, exploring the kernel of exquisite pleasure hidden at the top of her cleft.

Mindless waves of sensation washed over her, punctuated by sparks of gleaming delight. The ripples went on and on, carrying her higher and higher . . .

She awoke from her dream of ecstasy to find her body heavy and sated, her thighs slick with the juices of her passion and Jobert smiling down at her.

"You are beautiful in your release," he said. "And to think that I could make you do that over and over . . ." He brought his hand to her still-throbbing womanhood. She shuddered, on the verge of beginning the wild journey yet again.

"What of you?" she said through dry lips. "How do you bear the waiting?"

"I am readying you for me. I am so big and hard now, I fear to tear you asunder if I do not ease my way."

He stroked her slippery folds. "Yea, now I think you can take me."

"All of you," she purred, "every beautiful inch."

"Inch," he said. "Such a delicious Saxon word."

He filled her deep. Stroking slowly, then with long, extravagant thrusts. Edeva found her peak . . . once . . . twice . . .

Then she let him turn her over and enter from behind, the pressure of him inside her so intense, she near fainted. But he played with her breasts and then her cleft as he pressed his shaft deep against her womb. Edeva's body adjusted, the spirals of near unbearable pleasure spreading through her body and stretching her inner flesh to accommodate his hot length.

Rhythmically he moved, as they galloped madly to the stars . . .

"Satisfied?" Edeva asked as they lay side by side, savoring the musky afterglow of their love.

"For now." He pushed a sweaty tendril of hair away from her face. "There are other things I would like to try."

"Such as?" She raised herself to look down on him, admiring his chiseled features and vivid, catlike eyes, the long, beautiful length of his body.

"We've yet to taste the wine. I rather fancy trying it a new way." He gazed pointedly at her body. "*Licking* it up instead of drinking it."

A shudder of renewed heat shimmered down her body and her nipples grew hard. Would they ever get any sleep this night?

Jobert got up slowly and stretched. Edeva watched him go to the chests in the corner of the room, wondering what he was about.

He returned after a moment with a piece of cloth in his hand. Pausing by the bed, he unfolded the cloth. "I have a present for you. I bought it in Gloucester. You have so many jewels already, I was at a loss as to what to give you. But the gold in this piece reminded me of the wonderful embroidery you fashion." He held out a filigree brooch set with pearls, the delicate lines of it like the lacy petals of a flower.

" 'Tis beautiful," Edeva breathed, taking it in her hand. "I will cherish it forever."

"A poor piece compared to the treasure store your father left you, but this is yours alone."

She raised her gaze shyly to his. "I have not had time to purchase or sew anything special for you, but I do have a gift. I carry it close to my heart, where it will be safe." She placed her hand on her stomach.

"Yea, your body is the most splendid gift any man could receive."

She shook her head. "Not my body, but the precious thing it carries."

He gazed at her, puzzled, then his eyes widened. "Do you mean . . . ?"

She nodded, beaming at him. "You noted that my form was changed—'tis your babe that changes it. Fortunately for you, you missed the mornings when I was crouched over the chamber pot, cursing you and your lust for doing this to me. Now, you have only to endure my body growing huge and ungainly."

He leaned over and took her face in his hands. "You will always be beautiful to me, my sweet, my beloved Edeva."

EPILOGUE

"They're here," Payne shouted down from the gate-tower. "The king's banner has been sighted at the other end of the valley."

Edeva drew a deep breath, then started toward the manor house. A dozen worries beset her. *Would there be enough food for everyone? Would there be room for the royal assemblage to sleep comfortably? Enough fodder for their horses?*

Jobert came up beside her, dressed in the green tunic she had made for him the previous winter. The front of it was embroidered with his new device—a golden lion *couchant*. She thought the graceful yet powerful image suited him perfectly.

"Jesu, did William have to pick the hottest day of summer?" he complained. "I am near roasting."

"I keep thinking we have forgotten something."

"All will be well." He leaned down to kiss her. "You've been worrying over the details for a fortnight. Run and change now. I'm going out to greet the royal party, and I don't wish to return and find my wife in her work kirtle."

Edeva nodded and continued toward the manor house. It had been rebuilt in stone the previous summer and now housed two upper chambers above the main hall. The finest one had been readied for the king. Edeva headed for the other one and stripped off her soiled gown. She put on a clean shift and over it, a deep blue kirtle embroidered with silver.

She wrapped her braids with blue ribbons to match her
gown, then placed a thin blue veil over her hair and fastened it with a gold and pearl circlet. She started out the
door, then remembered her shoes. She quickly replaced
her plain tan footwear with slippers of butter-colored
leather. She feared they would get muddy when she went
down to the grassy area near the river where the trestle
tables had been set up, but she did not want to spoil the
elegance of the rest of her attire. After all, 'twas not everyday the King of England came to visit!

The hall seemed oddly empty as she hurried through.
Most of the servants would be in the kitchen shed putting
the finishing touches on the feast to come. Two whole
steers had been roasted in a firepit by the river. The rest
of the meal—trout and eels boiled in butter, the baskets
of fresh bread, the custards and cheeses made from the
fresh milk of summer, the last of the fall's apples baked
with honey and cinnamon—would be prepared at the
manor and carried down to the eating area.

As Edeva left the hall, Wulfget came rushing up. "I'm
sorry, my lady. I turned my back only for a moment, and
he got into the tarts."

Edeva stared with dismay at the fair-haired toddler
Wulfget held. His chubby face and hands were smeared
with crimson whortleberry juice. "Oh, William, what am
I going to do with you?"

"Mama," the child said and reached out for her, smiling
broadly.

"Give him to me," Eadelm offered. "I've not yet
changed my clothes. I'll get him washed up in time to
meet his namesake."

Wulfget handed the boy to the other woman, who carried the squirming toddler off to the cisterns.

Edeva felt a piercing tenderness as William waved merrily over Eadelm's shoulder. Hard to imagine that he would
be two years in another month. She'd almost stopped nurs-
ing him, what with the bounty of cow's milk available in

the summer, and she had hopes she would be expecting again soon. Mayhaps a girl this time.

"How are you feeling?" she asked Wulfget as the young woman pressed a hand to her lower back.

"Tired, as always, and hot. But Eadelm promises that the babe has dropped and will come soon."

Both of them looked at Wulfget's rounded belly. "Are you afraid?" Edeva asked, remembering her own anxiety as her time neared.

"Nay, but Alan is terrified." Wulfget laughed. "He is so serious, worrying over everything."

"He dotes on you. I'm so pleased that the two of you finally wed."

Wulfget rolled her eyes. "I thought the fool would never ask."

Edeva nodded, feeling a surge of satisfaction. Jobert had given Alan a small property further down the river, and he and Wulfget lived at the manor house there, coming to Oxbury only for occasional visits. Although she and Alan still sometimes clashed, the truth was, Edeva liked the stubborn knight and was pleased he had found happiness with gentle Wulfget.

There was the sound of horse hooves thundering across the new wooden bridge over the ditch. Edeva started toward the gate. She decided not to run, but to wait to greet them like a dignified chatelaine.

The royal party entered and Edeva saw Jobert riding beside the king. The two men dismounted and strode toward her. Edeva sank into a deep curtsy.

The king came and raised her. His face was coated with dust and he looked older and more weary than she remembered. "Lady Edeva, you are as beautiful as ever," he said. "I see that you still find time to do embroidery." He gestured to the elaborate design on her gown. "My Matilda still covets your skill . . . but we will speak of that later."

With that enigmatic remark, the king turned away and began to converse with Jobert about the improvements made at Oxbury. Not only had the hall been rebuilt in stone, but the wooden palisade was replaced with a stone curtain wall and the ditch around it deepened. The bridge across it could be raised in case of attack.

"The defenses look excellent," William was saying. "I wish I had more castles like this one and strong lords like you protecting my interests in other parts of the country. The southeast has been troublesome for two years now, and recently I've heard word of rebellion in Northumbria. What's your secret, Brevrienne? The Saxons here appear to have accepted you as their overlord. How did you subdue them so effectively?"

Jobert grinned, looking at Edeva. "I did not subdue them, they subdued me." His attention returned to the king. "In truth, I tried to convince them that they had more to gain from cooperating with me than fighting me. I am proud to say that I have in my mensie a half-dozen Saxon warriors who have sworn to me and now defend Oxbury in my name. Edeva's youngest brother is one of them. A likely youth, I think he will win his spurs someday and swear fealty to you, sire."

Jobert caught Edeva's eye. They had recently discussed the idea of having the king knight Alnoth. They had both agreed that it was too soon, but that when the time came in the future, Jobert would take Alnoth to William and ask him to bestow the honor.

"This is all very well done, Brevrienne," the king said. "But at this moment, it is your wife's services I require. I would like to change from my traveling clothes ere we eat."

"Of course, Your Highness," Edeva said. "Let me escort you to the guest chamber. I have had water heated if you would like to bathe."

"That sounds excellent," the king said. "I would dearly like to wash off some of the good English soil covering me."

As they passed through the hall, Edeva motioned to the stable boys tending the fire that they should carry the kettles of hot water up the stairs for the king's bath. "I would be happy to bathe you, sire," she told the king as they climbed the narrow stairs.

"Nay, that will not be necessary," William said over his shoulder. "I will have my squire tend me. Although I know it is the custom for the lady of the household to fulfill the duty, I would not arouse my lady wife's jealousy by risking that she might someday learn that I had been alone with a woman as beauteous as yourself."

William turned and winked at her, and Edeva suppressed a giggle. She had not expected the king to be so teasingly familiar. Pious and loyal to his marriage vows he might be, but the king was still a man!

Edeva sat in her place beside Jobert at the head table set up under the beech trees and reflected that the weather had favored them. The sun shone brilliantly in a cloudless blue sky, and the knights, freemen and their women sitting at the tables out in the open would not get rained on. Nor would the villagers seated on the ground have to run to get their livestock in before a storm struck.

Everyone living in Oxbury and the surrounding hamlets had come for the feast, from the newest babies, cuddled at their mother's breasts and passed around to be admired, to elders who could no longer walk and who had to be transported there in wheelbarrows or carts. Even old Helwenna had come. She sat propped against an old oak tree, complaining to everyone who would listen. Occasionally, Golde would go to tend the old woman, leaving behind her own one-year-old son, sitting on his proud papa's lap.

Not long after Edeva had ordered Golde to go live with Helwenna, Hamo had come to Jobert and asked to wed the serving woman. He vowed that he could control Golde—that once she was his wife, she would not pursue other men nor plot mischief. His authoritative attitude appeared to be exactly what Golde needed, for she no longer behaved in a cunning, manipulative manner but instead had become a quiet, almost demure matron.

Or, it could be that a few weeks with Helwenna had taught Golde to appreciate her relatively comfortable existence as a respected knight's wife. At any rate, Hamo and Golde seemed happy together, and they both delighted in "little Hamo."

Edeva stifled a yawn. Birds twittered in the trees and bees hummed as they collected nectar from the buttercups, daisies and pink campion carpeting the ground around the banquet area. The lazy mood and fine red wine from Paris were making her sleepy. She barely followed Jobert's conversation with the king until the name Valois came up.

"This time Robert was too reckless," the king was saying. "When he dared to take advantage of my absence in Normandy to seize one of his neighbor's castles, I had to punish him. I stripped him of Valachele and Mordeaux. He complained bitterly, of course, but I will not tolerate defiance of my orders."

"What of his property in England?" Jobert asked.

"I have allowed him to keep the two minor fiefs in Hertfordshire, but I doubt he will ever see them. He has little use for England. No doubt he maintains the property only for the sake of his grandson."

"His grandson?" Jobert exclaimed. "I thought Damaris was in a convent!"

The king grew grim. "It seems she was with child when she entered St. Mary's Priory. The boy was born soon after." William frowned. "I thought you knew. I thought that was the reason that Valois tried to kill you, because he blamed you for his daughter's disgrace."

"Upon my word, sire, I am not the father! Damaris and I shared no more than a kiss, and that years ago!"

"So you have said, and I always believed you. But some man sired a child off her."

Jobert looked at Edeva, and she read the confusion in his face. Was it possible that his sweet Damaris was not so innocent after all?

"But enough of this," the king said, changing the subject. "I have a bargain to make you, or rather, to make with your wife."

Edeva and Jobert both regarded the king warily.

"I have had my ministers review the lands seized from Saxon eorles who supported Harold," the king said. "They came upon the name of Leowine as a property owner in Berkshire and Buckinghamshire as well as Wiltshire. I thought those other lands were forfeit because he fought me at Hastings. I have since discovered that Leowine died at Stambridge. Under those circumstances, I can afford to be lenient. I intend to allow those properties to remain under the control of Leowine's descendants."

Edeva felt her flesh tingle. The king was offering back her inheritance. But she knew him well enough to guess he did not do things out of simple benevolence. *What did he want?*

"Of course," William added as he took another leisurely swallow of wine, "I would expect certain services to be rendered to me in return."

The unease built inside Edeva as the king's eyes focused on the embroidery on the sleeve of Jobert's tunic. "Your needlework is extraordinary, Lady Edeva. I have remarked on it several times, and I know my queen would think the same." He raised his gaze to hers. "I would very much like you to join Matilda in Rouen and teach her ladies a little of your skill."

"Rouen?" Edeva's voice came out in a cracked whisper.

" 'Tis not so far away as all that. And I would not expect you to be separated from your family. Jobert could come with you, and the child as well."

"For how long?" Jobert asked. From his impassive expression, Edeva could read nothing.

"A few months. Mayhaps if you liked it, you could return again another time."

Edeva slowly expelled the breath she had been holding. In exchange for a few months in Rouen, she would become one of the few Saxon landowners left in England, and likely the only female one. 'Twas a bargain Indeed.

Jobert's broad smile showed his own relief. He raised his goblet. "A toast, Your Highness, to the fair Edeva and her nimble fingers."

The king smiled and raised his cup to clink with Jobert's.

"Mayhaps I should not ask you to do things like this for me now that you have found such favor with the king," Jobert teased as Edeva knelt to unfasten his crossgarters as they prepared for bed. "Surely your hands are too valuable to risk them on such humble tasks."

"You speak nonsense, milord. The most important duty of a Norman wife is to please her husband."

"And you do please me. More than I can ever tell you." He drew her up for a kiss and they lingered long, sampling the sweetness of their growing passion.

Jobert slipped his hands under her arms and began to undo her laces. "Mayhap we can conceive another child ere we leave for Rouen."

"Mmmmm, we can try, milord," Edeva answered. "We can try very hard."